The Gift Bag Chronicles

Also by Hilary de Vries

So 5 Minutes Ago

The Gift Bag
Chronicles

a novel

Hilary de Vries

VILLARD NEW YORK

A Villard Books Trade Paperback Original

Copyright © 2005 by Hilary de Vries

Published in the United States by Villard Books, an imprint of
The Random House Publishing Group, a division
of Random House, Inc., New York.

VILLARD and "V" CIRCLED Design are registered trademarks
of Random House, Inc.

LIBRARY OF CONGRESS CATALOGING-IN-PUBLICATION DATA

De Vries, Hilary.
The gift bag chronicles: a novel / Hilary de Vries.
p. cm.
ISBN 1-4000-6349-3
1. Hollywood (Los Angeles, Calif.)—Fiction.   2. Special events—
Planning—Fiction.   3. Caterers and catering—Fiction.   4. Divorced
women—Fiction.   5. Parties—Fiction.   I. Title
PS3604.E89G54 2005
813'.6—dc22   2005042057

Printed in the United States of America

www.villard.com

2 4 6 8 9 7 5 3

Book design by Susan Turner

Well, time is on my side, yes it is.

—*The Rolling Stones*

The New Rules

Because, the thing is, they keep changing. You get them down—and, frankly, they weren't all that easy to figure out in the first place. Like getting your hair blown out before hitting the red carpet is a no-brainer, but who would know you're supposed to lie about your yoga obsession? Or that you should never, ever expect celebrities to be your friends. Even if you are on their payroll. After several years in the trenches as a Hollywood publicist, I finally get a handle on the place and then it goes and changes.

Or maybe it's me who changed, because living here is a lot like that old Woody Allen joke about relationships being like a shark—if you're not constantly moving forward, you die. In the interest of living at least into my forties, I present the new rules for staying alive in Hollywood:

1. *If celebrities don't walk your red carpet, you don't exist.*

2. *If you don't make Page Six, you don't exist.*

3. *Too many photographers will ruin a party.*

4. *Too many fashion stylists will kill a party.*

5. *When in doubt, find another sponsor.*

6. *When in trouble, hire a wrangler.*

7. *Because there's never enough time.*

8. *And there never will be.*

9. *To get ten celebrities to show up, invite four hundred.*

10. *And send a car.*

11. *A-list is best, but B-listers will work harder.*

12. *The gift bag totally matters.*

13. *A paper bag full of Benjamins matters more.*

14. *The List matters most of all.*

15. *Live feed beats B-roll.*

16. *Electronic beats print.*

17. *Always, always shadow the client.*

18. *Never give them an inch.*

19. *Never give them a reason.*

20. *Never leave them alone.*

21. *Tip sheet, tip sheet, tip sheet.*

22. *Rope line, rope line, rope line.*

23. *Headsets, headsets, headsets.*

24. *Publicity is the only job where you can do it perfectly and still fail.*

25. *In Hollywood, you only fail upward.*

The Gift Bag Chronicles

1

Two Steps Forward . . .

"Honey, are you up? There's a call for you."

There's a call for me. I'm sorry, but is there one morning when I don't wake up with that pulse-jumping late-before-you-start feeling? Like I've forgotten something and by the time I remember it, it will be too late. I mean, could I have one day when I don't wake up wanting someone else's life? Someone who gets a lot more sleep than I do.

"Honey, are you awake?"

I fish my arm out from under the covers and try to focus on my watch. The latest must-have designer model, but I still can barely read the dial because God knows a watch isn't about time anymore but about making a *statement*. Like, I have the time. I squint at the dial. 5:30, I barely make out. That would be A.M. judging by all the light pouring in through the blue toile curtains lining the windows of what used to be my old bedroom before Amy talked Helen into letting her redo it as the guest room. I don't know which was more insulting, my kid sister wanting to erase all traces of me, or my mother letting her.

"Alex? Are you up?"

At 5:30 A.M.? I don't think so, except now I'm realizing that must be L.A. time, because in all the screwing around last night with the delayed flight out of LAX, which meant another delay in O'Hare before I finally landed in Philly at God knows what hour, I forgot to change my watch. So that means it's really— I try to do the math and give up. Too fucking early.

"Honey?"

"Mom," I say, or rather croak. "Can you just take a message?"

"Oh, you are up."

The bedroom door cracks open, and twenty years flies out the window. Amazing how that happens every time I come home. Instead of Alex Davidson, president of one of Hollywood's oldest publicity agencies—DWP-ED/PR; that's me, the second D— divorced but with a serious boyfriend who's about to meet my parents for the first time, I'm Alex Bradford, high school honors student with my kilts in the closet, an egg on the boil downstairs, and Mom at my bedroom door.

Mom. Even at this hour, she's perfect. Or rather, error-free. Silvery-blond hair neatly coiffed, crisp white shirt, slim trousers, flats. Imperturbable. Mary Tyler Moore would play her in the movie.

"I'm glad you're up, because there's a Jennifer Schwartzman or Schwarzkopf on the line."

"Yeah, I'm up," I say, struggling to sit up, rubbing my eyes and pushing my hair from my face. When I come to, Helen's handing me the receiver.

"She called me on your line?" I have a cell phone, an assistant with a cell phone, and an office back in L.A. with twenty-five different extensions, but Jennifer Schwartzbaum tracks me down at my *parents'*?

Helen shrugs. "She's already called three times."

"That's what she does, Mom," I say, reaching for the phone. "She calls me three times, ten times, when once would do."

Helen smiles one of her unreadable smiles and turns for the door. "I'll leave you to your call."

"Jennifer," I say, flopping back in bed.

"Alex, thank God I reached you."

I don't even bother asking. Her tone of voice is one decibel short of a 911 call, but given the cotton candy world swaddling Jennifer Schwartzbaum, a former exotic dancer and now bride-to-be of Jeffrey Hawker, the much-married, much-divorced star of the long-running drama *Taskmaster*; her problems, such as they are, tend to top out at "Collagen or Restylane?"

"What's up?" I say, stifling a yawn.

"Okay, so I was going over the print media list, and I see *InStyle* is the only magazine confirmed."

"Well, that's because—" I manage to get out before she cuts me off.

"Okay, but then the prototypes came in."

"Prototypes?" I say, racking my brain.

Jennifer sighs. "The *gift bags!*" she says so loudly I have to hold the phone away from my ear. "I mean, the Stila lip glosses are fine and the new Oliver Peoples sunglasses are fabulous and I totally love the new BCBG fragrance. But we have a serious problem with the garters."

"The garters?" I say, flaking for a moment. Oh, right, the *garters*. The traditional wedding favor, along with the cake slices wrapped for all eternity. Now that gift bags—or goody bags, if you live in New York—are de rigueur at *every* event, public and private, it had taken me a minute to remember this was an actual wedding, not a movie premiere or a charity gala.

"Yes, the garters," Jennifer snaps.

Okay! Still, how much can go wrong with a strip of elastic a half inch wide covered in ribbon? "Too big?" I say, sitting up in bed, trying to concentrate now. I hear her sigh, like I'm a complete dunderhead. "Too small?" I say, trying again, realizing I'm sounding like Goldilocks.

"The ribbon finish!" she hisses. "It's matte not sateen!"

I collapse back onto the bed. God knows, the gift bag matters. At some events, it's the only thing that matters. That and the WireImage photos. I should know. I'm a Hollywood event publicist. Known in some greedier circles as the Keeper of the Gift Bag. Like I'm a character in *The Lord of the Rings*, with a mysterious and enviable power to conjure swag from the air and bestow it on the deserving, perfumed, partygoing masses. Still, explaining the nuances of matte versus sateen, not to mention *InStyle*'s bullying event coverage at 5:30 A.M. or whatever time it is, is going to take a lot more energy than this wizard has at the moment. At least before coffee. I sigh and punch the damage control button in my brain.

"Jennifer, that is a disappointment, but one, it can be fixed. Two, Steven is on top of the media coverage, and three, the gift bag is really something to bring up with him. He's the one handling the corporate outreach to, ah, our sponsors, as well as production of the garters."

I may be the agency's newest partner, president and account director for event planning or whatever title we've dreamed up for this jolly new service we at DWP-ED/PR now provide, but Steven, my former assistant and law school student for all of a semester until he realized how dull it was to actually sit in a law library, is the actual account executive. Aka the heavy lifter. The one who takes Jennifer's calls. Or depending on his mood, palms them off onto his assistant. And then there's Oscar. Our ace in the hole. A refugee from Colin Cowie's office with a bouncer's physique and Martha Stewart's organizational skills (preindictment), Oscar — aka Oscar Parties — is the hottest event producer in a town that does not lack for hot event producers.

In fact, event production is the latest Hollywood career du jour. First it was personal trainers. Then publicists. Then stylists. Now it's event producers. Even by Hollywood's normally lax standards for self-reinvention, the bar is inordinately low. Anyone who ever threw themselves a birthday party where people weren't too drunk to remember it the next day has hung out a shingle. Club promoters. Maître d's. Interior decorators. Bored housewives. Heiresses. They've all joined Hollywood's newest growth industry.

And why not? God knows, it's not every town where someone just hands you a check for half a million to throw a party. And hands it to you *every year*. Because if there's any rule of thumb these days, it's this: stars come and go, movies come and go, series come and go, but the parties — the endless roundelay of premieres, benefits, awards shows, product launches, weddings, and bar mitzvahs — go on and on. An endless trail of gift bags yearning to be filled. Which means every publicity agency in town has opened an event planning division to cash in on the trend. Which is why, as the agency's head event publicist, I'm on the phone with Jennifer Schwartzbaum, listening to her ream me out about garter ribbons at God knows what time it is.

"Alex," Jennifer purrs, changing tactics. "I know Steven is on it, but I don't like it when I can't reach you."

I close my eyes. I'm out of the office for not even twenty-four hours, her wedding's not for another three weeks, and already she's hunting me down? No wonder no one wants to handle actors. All that hand-holding, 24/7. And that doesn't even include the members of their posses, which in Jeffrey's case are in the high double digits. Starting with Jennifer (who has her own posse) and ending up with his AA sponsor. Or maybe it's the other way around.

"Jennifer," I say, trying not to sigh audibly. "You have our office number, you have my cell number. You have Steven's cell. You even have Oscar's office number as well as his cell. I don't *have* another number to give you."

"Well, obviously there was one or I wouldn't be talking to you now."

Actually, how the hell did she get this number? Steven would never have given it to her. "Actually, how did you get this number?" I say.

"Your assistant gave it to me when I told her you weren't answering your cell phone."

Figures. Caitlin. Or *Kaitlyn,* or however she spells her name to distinguish herself from the other million Caitlin/Kaitlyns who've descended on L.A. in the past year, one of whom took up residence just outside my office. I'll deal with her later. Right now I have to get Jennifer and her gift bag issues down from the ceiling and off the phone.

"Jennifer, it's Labor Day weekend, and actually, what time *is* it out there?" I say, trying to focus on my watch again.

"I know it's early, but I had to talk to you."

"We are talking."

"In person."

"Jennifer." I sigh. "I'm in a suburb outside of Philadelphia, and I will be here for at least three more days. Either you can talk to me now or we can meet when I get back to L.A."

"I'm putting the garters in FedEx," she says, and I can tell by her tone she's accomplished her mission. Made her problem officially my problem. "Call me when you get them."

"Fine," I say, my only thought to end this conversation and start the day — ostensibly one of my only days off — over again. Maybe even catch another hour of sleep.

"Honey."

I look up. Helen, at the door with a tray carrying, if I'm not mistaken, a boiled egg.

"Well, I certainly hope you can take some time while you're here to relax."

"Mom," I say, taking another hit of coffee, "I'm totally relaxed."

I've made it as far as the kitchen. Not dressed and my hair in a ponytail, mascara smudged under my eyes, but I'm here, sitting at the old pine table in my old plaid flannel robe drinking coffee from one of our old Royal Doulton mugs while Helen tidies up the already surgically clean counters.

"Well, you know what I mean," she says, leaning against the counter and crossing her arms and eyeing me like she used to, like I'm pretending to be sick to get out of going to school. "It just seems that ever since you got that big promotion of yours, all you do is work. I mean, how can it be that you spend half your time in New York—"

"Mom, I don't spend half my time in New York," I say, flopping back in the chair. "I just go there more frequently now on business."

"I only meant that we're less than two hours away, and somehow we've never met Charles."

She has me there. Charles Evers, my former boss and now copresident at the agency—the E of DWP-ED/PR—and more important, my boyfriend, lives in Manhattan and where I technically live when I'm in town from L.A. Somehow, and I'm still not sure how this happened, but he—we—have never crossed paths with my parents until this weekend.

I mean, how long has it been—three years, plus or minus—that Charles and I have been together, although frankly, how does one carbon-date these things anymore? First time you sleep together? First time you go out? First time you start talking to each other regularly on the phone, telling each other things that you realize you are not telling anyone else?

It gets even trickier when you work together. As Charles and I technically did. Still do. I mean, when I started at DWP's New York offices God knows how many years ago, Charles was the agency's most senior publicist, just one notch below the three founders. More to the point, he was the agency's only good-looking heterosexual male under the age of sixty. Given how gay and female the publicity world is, he didn't even have to be good-looking to get noticed. Just a Brooks Brothers shirt, rep tie, and his slightly mussed, slightly graying hair would have done it.

Not that I really noticed. Not back then, when I was a newly divorced, newly minted junior publicist running around like a maniac just trying to learn the job. It wasn't until I made the leap out to L.A., got promoted to senior publicist, and the whole agency became ensnared in a very brief, very nasty little takeover coup with a rival agency, which caused Charles and me, together with our boss, Suzanne Davis, the original D of DWP-ED/PR, to band together and fight off the interloper, that I realized he was such a stand-up guy. And he liked me. There's always that Sally Field moment when you realize, no matter what your feelings are, nothing's going to happen until the guy decides he really likes you. Or at least is into you enough to ask you out. More than once.

So despite the fact that Charles still lives in N.Y.C. and I still live in L.A., we're an item. Or as much of an item as you can be when you're 2,800 miles apart. Which is most of the time, frankly. I mean, back when we started officially going out, I thought we'd be living together by now. Somewhere, somehow, we'd have a place together. Of course, back when I was at Brown, I thought I'd be married and have two kids by the time I was twenty-six. Still, I thought Charles and I were at least headed in that direction. But somehow it's never been the right time. Or the right place. Or the right *something*. So now we spend most of our time on the phone, in e-mail, or via Charles's favorite mode of expression, his Black-Berry. Am I the only girl in the modern world who's fallen asleep staring at I♥U on her BlackBerry, rather than having the sender in bed next to her? Cyber-love. Who knew?

Still, a decent boyfriend is a decent boyfriend, and Charles is, if nothing else, decent. He might also be developing a serious workaholic attitude of late, with maybe a little control freak thrown in for good measure. But hey, plenty of women marry guys like that and wind up living happily ever after. At least it looks that way. In any event, I am not going to spend the first weekend I've managed to get Charles out to meet my parents—because if I'm honest about it, I would have brought him out here months, even a year ago, if he had made the time—dwelling on that.

"I know, Mom, and I'm sorry about that," I say, debating whether I should have another cup of coffee or just quit while I'm ahead and hit the shower. I'm just deciding to head upstairs when I hear a car in the drive. I check my watch—now showing just past 10:00 A.M. Philly time—and pray it's Jack back from the course or errands or wherever he goes in the mornings and not Amy dropping by with Bevan. Bevan, my year-and-a-half-old nephew. Or as he was known in cattier circles, the prize-winning heifer.

"She's raising him like she's going to enter him in the Pennsylvania state fair," Steven had said, staring at the photos I'd downloaded showing Amy holding a beefy blond toddler with, amazingly, a blue ribbon tied to his tufted hair.

"I know he's milk-fed, but she's actually raising him to enter Episcopal Academy, where Barkley went, followed by Swarthmore, where they both went."

"I think she's the one who wants the prize," Steven said.

"Well, that's true," I say. "Mother of the Year."

"And you, all but barren."

But then, as my best friend, Steven gets to say things like that.

The kitchen door swings open. Jack, thank God. "Hey, gals," he says, pushing in with all his blustery paternal energy, the testosterone ballast that has kept our family on more or less even keel all these years. "Alex, how'd you sleep?" he says, pausing first to kiss Helen on the cheek and then coming over to give me a kiss on my head.

"Fine, Dad," I say, smiling up at him.

"She had an early call," Helen says, arching her eyebrows slightly. "I was just saying, I hope she can stop working while she's here, since we don't get to see her all that often."

"Well then, what do you say we get this weekend under way this morning and shoot a quick nine and grab some lunch at the club?" Jack says, doing what he alone seems able to do, thread the impossibly narrow needle between Helen's shifting moods and the reality the rest of us live in.

"You two go ahead," Helen says, pushing off from the counter. "I have too much to do before everyone gets here. Besides, Amy's coming over to drop Bevan off this afternoon while she runs some errands."

"Oh, you've got to see him, Alex," Jack says, reaching in the refrigerator and emerging with a brown bottle of pills. Or maybe it's vitamins. I can't tell from where I'm sitting.

"I saw him at Easter, remember?" I say, watching Jack. I've never seen him take vitamins. Well, other than a gin and tonic. And pills in our family had been largely limited to aspirin taken only in emergencies. Nothing in a brown bottle that needed to be refrigerated.

"Oh, that doesn't count, they change so fast at this age," Helen says, filling a glass from the tap and handing it to him.

I watch my father knock out two pills or whatever they are and down them. I'm about to ask what he's taking when I think better of it. At least while Helen's in the room. Besides, it's going to be a long weekend, and I'll have time to get the scoop from Amy. The one good thing about her living back out in the suburbs again. Better intelligence about our parents.

"Well, Mom, if you're sure you don't need me for a few hours," I say, pouring one more hit of coffee.

"I need you to keep your father company," she says, which strikes me as not something she would normally say. "By the way, when *is* Charles arriving?"

"He's going to call," I say, heading up the stairs, cup in hand, wondering suddenly if I have anything suitable to wear on the course. If I brought anything other than flip-flops and mules, and if my clubs are still in the basement. It's been so long since I've done anything that didn't involve work, I've completely lost track of that part of my wardrobe. I mean, when was the last time I actually wore a bathing suit? On a beach? "He's going into the office for a few hours and then catch a three o'clock train," I add. "Four at the latest."

"Well, just so long as I know he'll be here for dinner."

"He'll be here for dinner," I call down. "Hey, Dad, are my clubs and shoes still in the basement?"

"No, your mother had a garage sale and we got rid of the clubs, but I think your shoes are still there."

I stop in my tracks. I haven't played in years, but my clubs had been a birthday present from Jack during my freshman year in college. Just a set of irons and two drivers in a little plaid bag, but during my summers home he and I had played nine holes every weekend and I'd actually gotten pretty good.

"You got rid of my clubs?"

"Honey, when was the last time you played?" Helen says. "You can borrow Amy's."

"You threw out my clubs but you kept Amy's?"

"She plays more often than you do," Jack says.

"She never plays."

Helen sighs. "Well, not now that she's had the baby."

"We'll get you a set of ladies' graphite at the club. Better than what you had," Jack says.

"That's not the point," I say, realizing that between my redecorated room and now the missing clubs, there's almost nothing in the house that belongs to me anymore. "I can't believe you just threw out my clubs. Without even asking. What if I wanted them in L.A.?"

"You play in L.A.?" Jack says.

"Honey, I'm not going to stand here on Labor Day weekend

and argue about a set of old golf clubs," Helen says. "Time moves on. Whether you want it to or not."

I've been here what, six hours, four of which I've been asleep, and already Helen and I have resumed our old battle positions. It's like my own version of *Groundhog Day*, where I'm reliving the past over and over again.

"You're right, Mom," I say, turning back upstairs. "They're just old clubs. Not worth arguing about."

"Are they on your case yet? Have you had some quality time with the heifer? Have you launched the watch yet?"

I'm back upstairs, door closed, cell in hand, Steven on the line. I used to hide all my reading from Mom. Now, I'm hiding all my work. "Yes, no, and no, although the weekend is only just starting, so I could still send out a distress signal from my wrist," I say, heading for the bed, phone in one hand, coffee in the other. Steven had gotten us the latest Hollywood must-have watches last Christmas — stainless steel monsters with built-in transmitters that call rescuers in emergencies. Like terrorist attacks or hijackings. Or the Barneys sale. Ever since he'd accidentally summoned the coast guard during a charter cocktail cruise off Maui, he'd insisted I wear mine whenever I traveled.

"I knew they'd come in handy," he says.

"Yeah, but other than Helen, I don't see a lot of disasters waiting to happen in Bryn Mawr."

"Well, it only takes one and Helen will do."

"Hey, I'm the only one allowed to make cracks about my parents," I say. "Besides, I have nine holes with Jack in my future, so things are looking up. By the way, did Jennifer reach you? She's having a fit about the gift bag and the media confirmations."

"Yes, she's messengering the garters to me even though I told her I had the same samples, which were, not so coincidentally, *exactly* what she'd approved."

"Why do we even go through the whole client approval process if they just forget what they've approved?"

"What, and take all the fun out of changing their minds *and* blaming us for it? She doesn't remember what she approved. None of them do. I swear all the memos we send them — media contacts, corporate sponsors, gift bag participants, the materials board — they're just toys to shove in the baby's hand. Like a rattle or a mobile. 'Look at all the pretty colors, Jennifer.'"

I laugh so hard I spill my coffee on the bedspread. Oh, *shit*. A nice black stain on the toile Amy picked to match the curtains. Oh well, that's what she gets for tossing out my stuff. "Yeah, but she's still not supposed to call *me* about it," I say, trying to wipe up the spill with the hem of my robe. "I mean, what's the point of this elaborate hierarchy if she just jumps the chain of command?"

Steven sighs. "That *is* the point. Otherwise how would we know she's really upset?"

"Okay, okay," I say, bored now with the Kabuki dance of Hollywood power plays. Not that it really mattered. The entire town was infected with celebrityitis. The divalike behavior that had once been the province of only A-listers had become the industry's default mechanism all the way down the food chain. And not just the B- and C-listers, but any star's entire entourage, their *posses*, just come armed with way too much attitude. Now, if you are Charlize's stylist or Jennifer Lopez's hairdresser or the DJ Leonardo DiCaprio hired to reorganize his CD collection, you expect, *demand*, to be treated like a star. Which means handling the Jennifer Schwartzbaums of the world is now no different than handling the Jennifer Anistons.

"Okay, let's just deal with this when I get back on Tuesday," I say. "I mean, we are trying to have personal lives."

"Speaking of that, is Chuck there yet? Has Helen met her future son-in-law?"

"*Charles* will be here by dinner, and as you well know, he is not her future son-in-law, although God knows you're probably right about Helen thinking that. I'm still trying to figure out exactly where Charles and I are right now, and she's probably thinking we're picking out rings. God knows, she's already giving me shit about working too much."

"And the baby you forgot to have?"

"I'm sure that's coming, but so far Bevan's distracting her."

"See, I knew the heifer would come in handy."

"Yeah, well, he's due here this afternoon. Right now, I have to go play golf."

"Well, break a leg or whatever they say," Steven says. "If you need me, I'll be at the beach all weekend."

I hang up and am just debating about whether to call Caitlin and yell at her for giving out my parents' number — there's a reason everyone at the office calls her Princess behind her back — when my cell burbles. "Lara's Theme" from *Doctor Zhivago*. Charles.

"Hey, big guy, I was just going to call you," I say.

"Alex" comes crackling down the line. It may be Charles's phone, but it is definitely not Charles. Taryn, Charles's assistant, and with what sounds like midtown roaring in the background.

"Taryn?" I say, shouting over the noise. I've gotten messages from her before, but never on his cell phone.

"Alex," she shouts back. "Charles wanted me to call you and say he's catching the —" The rest of her sentence is drowned out by static and traffic noise.

"What?" I say. "Where's Charles?"

More static and then Taryn's voice. "— okay, so he'll call you from the station before —"

This is pointless. But unfortunately typical of how he's been lately. Going in a million directions at once and where I feel like

I'm another one of the items on his to-do list. I don't even bother saying I'll call back but click off and dial the office. The service picks up. Shit. Everyone's already gone. I try Charles's apartment and get the machine. I don't want to talk to Taryn again, but I redial his cell. Voice mail. I'm about to leave a message and move on to Caitlin and the Mount Everest of messages I know she'll have for me, holiday or no holiday — God knows, we're already in the thick of the annual Sundance–People's Choice–Golden Globe–Oscar party–planning cycle that starts every July and won't finish until the last envelope is opened in February — when there's a knock at the door.

"Yeah," I say, sounding more irritated than I mean to, the phone still pressed to my ear.

"Honey, I found these downstairs." I turn. Jack, holding my old golf shoes.

I look at him. My dad. Or he was once. Now, I see a gray-haired man in a cardigan sweater holding out a pair of scuffed golf shoes like a peace offering.

"Hey," I say, clicking off without leaving a message. "Let's go play golf."

"You look happy. Didn't you shoot well?"

Amy. Without breaking stride from spooning what looks like green slime — excuse me, *organic* green slime — into her son's mouth.

Jack and I are just back from the course, clattering into the kitchen in that noisy, flushed way you get after nine holes and lunch at the club with the rest of the silver-haired retirees. My tee shots stank — I shot so badly, I quit keeping score after the fifth hole — but the Bryn Mawr Country Club never fails to leave me with a God's-in-his-heaven-all's-right-with-the-world feeling. A feeling that lasted until I spied Amy's Volvo SUV—preppy piety on steroids—parked in the drive. She and I have never been close. We're sisters, but it's like we were from two different gene pools. Or generations. Now that we are officially the Career Divorcée and Stay-at-Home Mom, well, anyone can do that math.

"Actually, we both shot *great*," I say, ignoring Amy to plant a kiss on Bevan's slightly sweaty head, my hands on his tiny shoulders.

"Careful, Alex, he's eating, and watch out for that watch," Amy says, wiping Bevan's mouth. "That could hurt him."

Gee, really? I'm about to say something equally stupid back— *Yeah, I was really hoping to bean my nephew with my Dick Tracy two-way wrist TV*—when Helen bustles in with her purse and suede jacket.

"Oh, good, you two are back," she says. "Amy and I were just trying to decide how to get these errands done, but now we can go and leave Bevan here with you."

"Consider yourself saved," Jack says, bending down to kiss Bevan, and I wonder, briefly, given all the affection they get as kids, why men turn out to be so difficult in adult relationships.

"What errands?" I say, heading for the refrigerator in search of the bottled water I know Helen won't have. "I hope you're not going to a lot of trouble just because Charles and I are here, because we don't—"

"We're not," Helen says. "I just have to pick up some things for the party."

Party? I haven't heard that word for two years without knowing it's only a euphemism for months of mind-numbing, grinding work followed by hours of harried hand-holding, troubleshooting, nose-wiping, all of it frantically masquerading as "fun." Now, on one of my only weekends off, there's a party I'm expected to attend?

"Okay, stop right there," I say, backing out of the refrigerator. "*What* party?"

"The cocktail party we're throwing tomorrow night," Helen says, rummaging in her handbag for her keys.

"Aw, Mom, why are you doing that?" All my hard-won equanimity after nine holes and lunch with a nice glass of pinot grigio is totally out the window.

"Honey, it's just a Labor Day get-together," she says, looking up in that pained way she gets when someone, usually me, isn't going along with her plans. "Some of the neighbors and our friends from the club. We thought it would be nice since you're hardly ever home and what with Charles coming in and all."

Oh, God. I should have guessed she'd pull a stunt like this. Ever since I upended my life, divorced my stockbroker husband, Josh, and bolted from Manhattan and my job in publishing for life in L.A. as a Hollywood publicist, I'd been suspect in her eyes. Even if half my clients wound up on the covers of the magazines my mother leafed through at the checkout stand, I'd still given up a perfectly respectable life, emphasis on the *respectable*, to run away to Hollywood with the rest of the misfits, dropouts, and other assorted weirdos. Now that I was returning to the fold with a guy in tow, Helen was wasting no time in trumpeting the news. Just when I'm starting to seriously wonder where Charles and I are actually going, Helen's probably hoping we're going to announce our engagement or something.

"Well, I only meant that my time here was so limited it seems a shame to spend it talking to the Schmidts from next door," I say, futilely trying another tactic.

"It's not just the Schmidts. The Atwaters are coming. And the McIlleneys. They're all looking forward to seeing you."

The Atwaters and the McIlleneys. And I had thought getting through the weekend with Charles and my parents was going to take all my concentration. Now I have Charles, my parents, and half of Bryn Mawr to deal with.

"Look, you two go shop, and Alex and I'll babysit," Jack says, stepping once more into the breach.

"Yeah, Dad and I'll stay with Bevan," I say, still annoyed about Helen's impending party, but brightening at the idea of an Amy-free afternoon. I check my watch. Just about 2:30. If I'm lucky, by the time they get back, Charles will be here and I'll have my buffer in place. Speaking of that, I need to check my messages and find out what train he's catching.

"Well, he's going down for his nap, so there's really nothing to do," Amy says, spooning the last of the slime.

"Well, if that's the case, I can man the fort myself if all you gals want to go," Jack says.

"No!" I say a little too quickly. "I mean, I'm a little tired from golf, and after the flight last night, I wouldn't mind cleaning up before I go pick up Charles."

"Doesn't jet lag work the other way? I mean, if you're flying west to east," Amy says, unstrapping Bevan and lifting him out of the high chair. "I thought you'd be waking up right about now."

I shoot her a look, but, typically, her face is unreadable.

"Well, Jack, if you're sure you'll be okay on your own, we could get more done if we all went," Helen says, still rattling around in her handbag for her keys.

"More done?" I say, eyeing her. "Where are you planning on going?"

"Alex," she says, looking up with a mixture of surprise and fatigue. "Even with Maria coming over tomorrow to help with the hors d'oeuvres, there's still all the shopping to do. And I thought you might have some ideas about the favors we could hand out."

"You're doing *a gift bag*? At a cocktail party?" I can't believe this.

"Not a *bag*. Just a little something. Give it some thought," she says, pulling her keys from her purse. "I gather you're the expert at these things."

"Mom," I say, sighing. "You don't need to do this."

"I know I don't *need* to do it, honey," she says. "We want to do it. We want our friends to meet Charles and see you after all these years."

"It's your coming home party," Amy says, her tone equally unreadable, as she heads for the stairs with Bevan. "I think it will be fun."

My definition of *fun* has topped out with golf with Jack and lunch with wine. From here on out, whatever transpires this weekend falls under the heading of family obligations and nothing else. God knows, I wish it was otherwise. I mean, there are families where they actually get along. Maybe if I'd stayed in New York, it would have been different. Or if I'd stayed married to Josh. We might even have a kid by now, a little Josh Jr. running around in a yarmulke. Like that would warm the cockles of Helen's WASPy heart.

Or maybe I'm just fooling myself. Maybe time ends up fracturing the tightest of families. Maybe we never even had a chance.

"Okay, I'll go," I say, opting for the high road and praying it's worth it. "I just want to be back in time to pick up Charles."

2

. . . One Step Back

As it turns out, I don't have to be back to pick up Charles because Charles never catches the train out of New York. A meeting that ran late and what with the rush-hour crowds at Penn Station, Saturday noon is now his ETA. So much for my buffer. So much for my boyfriend.

"I'm sorry, I told Taryn to give you the message," he says when we finally connect while I'm standing in the produce aisle helping Helen pick tomatoes for the tart she's having Maria make.

"Yeah, I got it," I say as brightly as I can, given that Helen and Amy are within earshot and there's no way I'm letting on how disappointed I am, not to say still a little pissed about him having Taryn call me from his cell. I mean, we are both agency presidents, both superbusy, but I would never have Caitlin call him for me.

"Tell Charles I say hi and we can't wait to meet him," Helen says, sidling by me, her hands full of apples, her suede jacket catching on my suede jacket.

"Mom says hi," I say dutifully.

"Is it terrible? Can you handle it until I'm there?" he says in that joking, intimate way he has that always makes me forget I'm mad at him.

"Yes and yesss," I say, dropping my voice and then adding more loudly, "Charles says hi too."

"Oh, you are the dutiful daughter," he says. "It's why we love you."

"Oh, that's the reason?" I say, turning away from Helen and into a bin of oranges for some privacy. I'm just about to remind him of a few other reasons why he loves me when I hear my other line click. "Oh, hang on a second," I say, not totally annoyed that I have to put him on hold. "Hello?"

"Can I give you your messages now?"

Caitlin/Kaitlyn/Princess.

"Umm, not really," I say, staring at the bin of oranges. "I'm going to have to call you back."

"Well, it's just that the office is closing and I'm about to leave."

"Well, are you leaving this minute?"

"They're locking the office and I don't have a key."

"You can always get *out*," I say and realize how pointless this is. First Jennifer, then Helen and Charles, and now Caitlin. I mean, if I have such an important job, why do I always wind up accommodating everyone else? "Okay, hang on," I say, clicking back to Charles.

"Hey, it's Caitlin with my messages, so let me call you back when I get home."

"Fine," he says. "If you don't reach me later, I'll be on the ten-thirty train tomorrow morning."

I hang up and click over to Caitlin. "Okay, just give me the important ones," I say, reaching into my bag for a pen and something to write on, given that my BlackBerry is back at the house along with my laptop. I root around in my bag and come up with a deposit slip from my checkbook.

"Uh, okay, shoot," I say, shoving the phone against my ear and propping my purse on the oranges to make someplace to write. There's the usual long list. "Look, just give me the ones that matter," I say, tearing out another slip as Caitlin drones on. My ear is starting to ache, and I don't have enough hands to juggle the phone, the pen, my purse. I try to wiggle everything more securely onto the oranges.

"They all seem important," Caitlin says, sounding hurt.

"Look, just put the rest in an e-mail, and I'll get them when I log on."

"That's going to take a while."

"Well, not that long, since we've already gone through most of them."

Silence.

I can either be the boss from hell or just forget about my job for seventy-two hours, which might actually do us all some good.

"Look, is there anything that needs doing by Tuesday?" I say, trying for some middle ground. "I'm not in until the afternoon."

I hear her sigh and shuffle through the list. "Just this one," she says finally.

"What is it?"

"A meeting Jennifer Schwartzbaum has scheduled with you at ten A.M. She says you know about it."

I close my eyes. "Steven can cover that," I say, trying to keep my voice even.

"Well," she says, pausing, and I hear her fumbling with more slips. "I think he's out of the office all morning at a walk-through."

"Alex, we're at the checkout stand."

I look up. Amy. I nod and hold up my hand. "Look, call Steven and see if he can move the walk-through back and babysit Jennifer. If he can't, then call Jennifer back and reschedule the meeting."

I hear her sigh.

"Look, I'm sorry," I say before I realize what I'm doing, that

I'm *apologizing* to my assistant. My assistant, who has just gotten out of doing exactly what I asked her to do. Not only have I not yelled at her for giving Jennifer my parents' number but now I'm actually apologizing for asking her to do her job.

"Okay," Caitlin says sulkily. "But if I can't reach her, I'm just going to leave a message."

"Fine," I say, rushing to end the call before she realizes what a complete failure I am as a boss. As any kind of authority figure. "Now go. Make the calls and I'll see you Tuesday."

She hangs up without saying goodbye. God, why had I hired her? Some niece, or a cousin, or some niece of a cousin of Suzanne's. Well, never again, I don't care what they say about the favor bank.

"Do you always work on your days off?" Amy says, eyeing me as I'm trying to shove everything back into my bag.

"Actually, I do," I say, giving everything a final shove and stepping away from the bin of oranges. At least there's a moment — a moment that means it could, *technically*, not be my fault — before they all give way, tumbling to the floor like a flood of tennis balls.

"In fact," I say brightly, striding past Amy, "it's actually amazing how much work you can get done in a grocery store."

Amy splits with Bevan right when we get home. He was fussy after his nap, and she wasn't much better after our hours of shopping. Between the grocery store, the florist, the card shop to get the actual gift bags, the cleaner's, and wherever else Helen insisted we had to go — God, does every party have to be a production? — we were all a little worse for wear. I still have no idea what I'm going to come up with for the gift bags — miniature vodka bottles and, given the season, an ear of corn? — and I have even less of an idea what time zone my circadian rhythms are in, but wherever they are, they could kill for a nap. Or a drink.

"We'll see you tomorrow," Helen says, kissing Bevan goodbye. Jack's already in the kitchen uncorking a bottle of wine. "You must be ready to drop," he says, handing me a glass.

"According to Amy, I should just be hitting my stride," I say, checking my watch. 6:30 EST. 3:30 PST. Normally, I'd be on my third latte with hours of work left to do. And maybe a yoga class if my third eye was still open. "But when in Rome," I say, hoisting the glass in a toast.

At least dinner tonight should be gimme. Just the three of us. Followed by the first real night's sleep I've had in months. The lull before the storm of the rest of the weekend. And it is pretty much as I expected. Chitchat about the lawn, the new weed killer Jack is having the lawn service use, their trip to Bermuda back in May, the fact that my rental house needs a paint job and how much my landlady is willing, or rather not willing, to spend on hiring painters. Just the usual nonconfrontational but semi-intimate stuff any grown child turns to when spending hours with her parents. I'm actually starting to relax when Helen breaks the news. That she and Jack have bought a place on Cape Cod where they plan to spend the summers after Jack retires next spring.

"You're kidding," I say, startled that (1) my parents are thinking about retirement already and (2) it involves leaving Philly. One trip to Florida when Amy and I were still in high school was as much travel away from the Quaker State as they could take. And then there was their disastrous trip to L.A. to visit me three years ago, when all it did was rain. They're such homebodies, I'd always envisioned them in their golden years hanging out in Bryn Mawr being older, more palatable versions of themselves. Like Siamese cats that finally stopped screaming because they just didn't have the energy anymore.

"Well, they've got a great little course on the property," Jack says. "Plus a center with a gym and a concierge, and the food's not bad either, although nothing like the club here, of course."

Center? Food? Concierge? A little alarm bell goes off in the back of my mind. "Wait, is this some kind of sheltered living thing?" I say. A vacation house is one thing, but a senior center, or whatever they call them, is a totally a different story.

"Honey, it's a *planned* community," Helen says, annoyed that I've glommed on to the worst possible characterization of their plan.

"You mean like a condo except with houses?" I say, still not sure I'm getting the picture. Not sure if I'm supposed to be getting the picture.

"Well, most of them are duplexes," Jack says, spearing another stalk of broccoli from the platter.

"Duplexes?" If there's one place I couldn't see Helen, it's in a duplex, sharing a wall — or anything — with neighbors.

"Obviously, ours isn't a duplex," Helen says. "No, it's a gated community. With more services. The Brookses — you remember them from the club — bought in there last year and loved it."

"We spent a week there with them last August," Jack says, reaching for the soy butter or whatever Helen has them eating now. "Got in a lot of golf. Plus your mother liked the weather."

"We *both* liked the weather," Helen says, eyeing him. "You said so every time you came off the course without looking like you were about to pass out from the heat."

Great. Not only are my parents throwing cocktail parties in my honor without asking me but now they are sailing off into the sunset without consulting me. Their oldest child, a fully functioning adult who has demonstrated an ability — a highly paid ability — to be consulted on many subjects. Senior publishing executives seek my counsel about their event planning needs. Marketing executives at international luxury brands — Gucci! Fendi! Target! — consult me on how best to infiltrate Hollywood. Celebrities, okay, mostly B-listers but still stars, retain me to plot their media campaigns. But my parents still have me on a need-to-know basis only.

"Aren't you a little young to be rushing into all this?" I say, trotting out my best corporate mode. "I mean, Dad, I know you're retiring, but you're not sixty-five yet, and Mom, you aren't —"

"Honey, we are not 'rushing' into anything," Helen says, cutting me off. "This is something your father and I have talked about doing for a while now. This is a lot of house to take care of, in case you hadn't noticed," she adds, gazing around the dining room, which is large — okay, very large. "And at some point we may not even need it anymore," she adds, straightening the silverware on her plate. "Or maybe we'll work something out with Amy and Barkley as their family grows. It just seemed like the right step at the right time."

Oh, now I get the picture. Or at least a big piece of it. They could so easily leave, because Amy, who obviously has been consulted, is the heir apparent of the family manse. No wonder she'd been so eager to turn my bedroom into the guest room. No wonder Helen had had that garage sale.

"Well, it sounds like you've really thought it through," I say as chiperly as I can, because I'm not about to let them know how I really feel. Not when I'm not sure how I feel. About any of it. My parents leaving Philly. Planning for their retirement. Getting older, which means I'm getting older, which is technically impossible since I haven't even started yet.

Well, okay, I've *started*, and actually more than that, but still, it's not like I planned it this way. It all just kind of happened and I'm going along with it. For now. Like I'm in a holding pattern, circling forever up here, waiting to land, waiting for a gate — my gate — to open up. When I can find the time to figure it out for real.

Meanwhile, it's all there on my to-do list. The list that always has about five thousand things on it, no matter how much I get done, how much I accomplish. It's like *Sisyphus: The Hollywood Years*. Good job? Check. Boyfriend? Check. For the time being.

Career? Well, that's still a question, but technically any job you have for more than five years counts as a career, so yes, check. House? Rental and needs that paint job, but check. But then there are the issues I thought I'd rolled to the top of the hill. Marriage? I'll get back to you. Kids? Yeah, right. I mean, I'm still working out "Ashtanga or Iyengar?" "Caf or half-caf?" "Atkins or Zone?" Meanwhile, my parents have everything all planned out. Years in advance.

"Great," I say again, raising my glass. "Sounds like a plan."

"We knew you'd see it our way," Helen says, smiling in the candlelight. "Once we explained it to you."

Two hours before the cocktail party on Saturday night, I'm upstairs in my former bedroom sitting in the lotus position. Okay, half lotus, because nobody except yoga freaks can do the full lotus. Travel noise machine on; the "Woodland Brook" setting, even though it always makes me want to pee. I'm trying to envision myself back in my house in L.A. I'm just seeing myself in my own living room — far from my parents, far from Jack hitting balls in the backyard with Charles, from this party I can already hear the beginnings of downstairs, and really far from my last-minute, oh-so-rustic gift bags of first-crop-of-the-season organic Heritage apples and a wedge of artisanal goat cheese from the local farmers' market tucked in a small brown paper bag tied up with a red-and-white-checked ribbon — when my cell rings. Shit. Without uncrossing my legs, I kind of hop-drag myself over to my bag and pull out the phone. Steven.

"I can't talk now because I'm doing yoga."

"You only do yoga when you're trying to calm down."

"You're supposed to do yoga to calm down. Otherwise why would anyone do it?"

"My point exactly. Actually, why aren't you having sex with Chuck to calm down?"

"Because Charles is out hitting balls in the backyard with Jack. Because Helen put him in the other guest room. Because, because, because," I say, slumping against the bed. "Any other questions?"

It's true. Ever since Jennifer's call at God knows what hour yesterday, the whole weekend has been a blur. Or maybe I'm just a blur — an overworked, jet-lagged blur — and everything else is totally clear. Jack and Helen seem very clear, and God knows, Amy is never anything but clear. And don't even get me started on Jennifer's and Caitlin's capacity for clarity. Even Charles seems annoyingly clear. Maybe I need to reconsider that macrobiotic diet. Or bring this up with my yoga teacher. Like it's that simple. "No dairy, no sugar, stand on your head." "Oh, now I get it!"

By the time I picked up Charles at the station Saturday morning, my jet-lagged blur had coalesced around suburban America circa 1950. The train doors opening, the passengers pouring out into the long-shadowed late-summer sun. I was even driving Jack's old Volvo. For a second, I had a vision of what my life would have been like if I'd stayed in Philly. If I'd never gone to New York. Or L.A. It looked something like Julianne Moore in a twinset and a long-suffering smile.

"Hey," Charles said, sliding in next to me with that slightly unreadable grin of his. "You in a Volvo," he said. "Thought I'd never see the day."

I wondered briefly if that was some kind of dig, if he really would prefer me in a twinset, barefoot and pregnant.

"So you like the whole Cheever country thing?" I said, leaning across the seat for a kiss. A really fast kiss, because here in my dutiful Julianne Moore mode I'm starting to chatter away mindlessly about my parents, Amy, the weekend, so that he can't get a word in. Maybe it's nerves. The fact that, after all this time, Charles is finally meeting my parents. Or maybe it's because we're actually together so infrequently that I'm talking really really fast to get everything in. Before he leaves again.

"Hey," he said, reaching across the seat to finger my hair. "It'll be fine. I've met parents before. I was married once, remember?"

"Yeah, well, so was I, but it turns out my parents have outlasted any relationship I've ever had."

He looked at me quizzically.

"Don't look at me like that," I said, shaking my hair free of his fingers. "You'll see."

Turns out, he didn't see. Or actually he did. Charles and my parents saw each other across Jack's freshly weeded and mown lawn and fell completely and totally in love. I mean, Charles Evers of Chevy Chase and Georgetown U. and the salt-and-pepper hair, blue blazer, and khakis was made, just *made* for lunch in Bryn Mawr with Jack and Helen Bradford, iced tea and cold chicken on blue willow plates. Merchant-Ivory could have filmed it.

"Charles is marvelous," Helen said when she and I were back in the kitchen, stacking the lunch plates and getting out the lemon icebox cookies for dessert.

"Yes, he is," I said from deep in my fog, where I was no longer Julianne Moore but Emma Thompson in an Empire waist gown and a chignon. A Jane Austen spinster with a BlackBerry and one last shot at true love.

"I had no idea such normal people worked in Hollywood," Helen said, never lifting her eyes from the cookies she was painstakingly arranging on the blue and white china plate.

I was tempted to ask her what she meant by *normal*. But even in my Emma Thompson fog, I knew exactly what she meant. That she's amazed, *stunned* to find in the moneygrubbing, back-stabbing, synagogue-worshiping tribe that is Hollywood in her mind, there's a college-educated, Emily Post, paper-trained WASP. Like the prize at the bottom of the Cracker Jack box. If anybody still eats Cracker Jacks. And what's even more amazing: he's with *me*. "Well, Charles handles a lot of our corporate clients, if that's what you mean," I said, treading carefully, because suddenly I was no longer the Emma Thompson lonely spinster but a slutty Britney Spears wannabe stuck in a Woody Allen fantasy sequence with my Rittenhouse Square lunch-at-the-club mother. A fantasy sequence with subtitles.

"Oh? Is that something you could get into, too?" Helen said casually.

Oh, does that mean you could stop thinking only of yourself and your silly career, leave that Sodom and Gomorrah you call Los Angeles, and move back with the righteous and live on Park Avenue like we always expected you would?

"Well, all the agency *presidents*," I said, hitting the word hard, "have sort of specialized, and my specialty is event planning."

Oh, for God's sake, I'm a boss and probably make more money than Dad did at my age, so get off my back about moving back east.

"So, does that mean you could change specialties and move back to New York?"

If you think you can outargue me, you are sorely mistaken.

"Only if I really wanted to."

I knew you were hocking me about New York!

Suddenly, I'm not Julianne, or Emma, or Britney, but a thirty-six-year-old president of a major Hollywood publicity firm who knows all there is to know about getting celebrities to walk the red carpet. I can land covers of *Vogue, GQ,* and *Entertainment Weekly* for a single star for the same movie. I can fly across three time zones and still run a meeting. I can drive a stick shift, run a party for seven hundred, do the eagle, the pigeon, and a full back bend, and tell me that doesn't do wonders for a girl's social life.

"Yes, I could move back, but I don't want to," I said, suddenly dispensing with any need for subtitles. "I like it right where I am."

"I see," Helen said, picking up the plate and heading toward the door. "It's just that's what you said when you were still married to Josh. And look what happened there."

Now I'm upstairs twisting myself into a pretzel trying to calm down before half of Bryn Mawr descends, cocktails in hand, on my parents' living room. Or I was until Steven called.

"Wait, after all that, your mother put your boyfriend of three years down the hall in the other guest room?" he says, laughing. "How very *Meet the Parents.*"

"Yes, very," I say, anxious to change the subject. "How's life at the beach?"

"Life's a beach," he says, yawning. "I'm so bored I'm thinking of setting off the watch again just to see the coast guard turn up and impress the other boys."

"Isn't there some kind of limit on the number of times you can pull that fire alarm without them confiscating it?"

"No," he says, yawning again. "You just keep paying the fine. Best three grand I ever spent was watching them chopper out to the boat in Hawaii and call my name on the bullhorn."

"And to think you never got enough attention as a child. By the way, did Caitlin ask you if you could run the Tuesday meeting with Jennifer?"

"Umm, yeah," he says airily.

"What'd you say?"

"I said, 'What Tuesday meeting with Jennifer?' "

"Oh, come on, you have to."

"*Have* to?" he says in his fake arch voice. "I know you still out-rank me, but you're not technically my boss. We're *colleagues.* Besides, I can't. Even if I wanted to. Which I don't. The walk-through on the *TV Guide* Emmy party has been scheduled for Tuesday morning for weeks. Half the masthead's flying out for it. Plus, we're going over their gift bag, which is actually more of a minefield. So far we've only got a copy of the magazine, snore;

Altoids, like that's anything special; some new energy bar; a T-shirt; and a miniature of Absolut's new 'Wonder' vodka, which is just their old vodka but in a new bottle. I mean, it's all so predictable and low-rent I can hardly stand it."

"Half the masthead is coming out?" I say, ignoring the gift bag problem for the time being. You can always get some CD or DVD from somewhere at the last minute, and besides, MAC is very close to signing on as a sponsor, and they can always be counted on to throw in some new lip gloss or eye shadow to sex up the bag. "Who has that kind of money in publishing anymore?"

"*InStyle, Vanity Fair, Entertainment Weekly* — you want me to go on? — although God knows our big magazine client, C, doesn't but still manages to expect the world for it."

C magazine. Don't get me started. Our big status client. *My* big status client, which given their anorexic editorial budget and neurotic insecurity vis-à-vis *Vogue, Harper's Bazaar, Entertainment Weekly, InStyle,* and *The New York Times* Style section means they're really just a big pain in the ass. I don't know if it's because they're a fashion magazine or because their L.A. office is just a revolving door for yet another set of know-it-all New Yorkers who are clueless about L.A. — most recently one Patrice Fielding, who is, even more annoyingly, one of those leggy, snaggle-toothed know-it-all Londoners — but there's always a problem with C and their events. This one's too big. That one's too small. This one didn't get the right A-list. That one got too many B-listers. This one had too many fashion stylists, like that would really be a problem, given that the party C threw was for Louis Vuitton. Frankly, if we lost the account, my life would be a hell of a lot easier. Still, they're one of our oldest clients, and Charles has a long history with the magazine, especially the fusty old editor, Andrew McFeeney, so my little fantasy of them dumping DWP-ED will never happen. Not in my lifetime.

"Okay, never mind," I say, trying to keep the conversation to the topic at hand. "I get it, you're busy. I'll get Caitlin to reschedule Jennifer for Wednesday. But you're handling it. I have no intention of seeing Jennifer Schwartzbaum until the walkthrough for her wedding."

"What, and miss all the hysterics with her gift bag?"

I hear a click on the line. God, who now? "Hang on," I say, clicking over. "Yes?"

"Hey, babe, how's it shakin'?"

Oscar. Our event producer. Or as I like to think of him, the big brother I never had, even if he looks like Mr. Clean. A straight Mr. Clean, which is its own miracle. Except of course for his penchant for being a serial dater of twentysomething actresses. Or wannabe actresses. Well, you can't have everything in Hollywood.

"Thank God it's you," I say. "Everything's shaking, and given that I'm not in earthquake territory, that's not a good thing."

"Come on," he says loudly over what I take to be a Dodgers game in the background, baseball being Oscar's other fetish. After the twentysomething actresses. "You're doing a good deed for your parents whether you think so or not. Relax."

"I don't think so."

"Trust me, I'm right on this. I'm also right about those fucking gift bag garter ribbons."

"Oh, please, don't talk to me about Jennifer's gift bag. I can't take it. Besides, it's not your problem."

"I just called to say I heard she's a pain in the ass and I'll deal with that when I see her at our meeting on Tuesday."

"I love you. Did I ever tell you that?"

"Yes, but keep telling me that. I respond well to affection. Unlike the rest of Hollywood. When are you coming back?"

"Monday. No, Tuesday," I say.

"Okay, good. Call me and I'll see you at the production meeting on Thursday."

I click back over to Steven. "Yes, I'm still here," he says in his fake hissy fit voice.

"Sorry, it was Oscar. Saying he would take care of Jennifer on Tuesday."

"God, I love him. It's one of the great tragedies of my life that he's not gay."

"Why is everything about sex with you?"

"Because everything *is* about sex."

"You only think that because you're still young. Or pretending to be. You'll see. Life isn't about sex. It's about getting enough sleep." I hear a knock at the door. "Hang on," I say, covering the phone. "Yes?" I yell out, banking on Helen.

Charles sticks his head in. "So this is where you live," he says, eyeing my yoga mat and the travel noise machine.

"Well, it was once," I say, lunging for the noise machine. Or as much of a lunge as I can muster given my legs are still in pretzel mode.

"Don't get up. I just dropped by to tell you your dad has a hell of a swing."

"Yeah, he does," I say, smiling up at him. I'm just about to launch into how Jack and I used to play golf together and that frankly my own swing isn't that bad, or at least it wasn't once, and maybe the three of us could actually shoot a round together, when I hear squawks coming from the phone. "What?" I say to Steven.

"Put Chuck on. I need to ask him about the pitch meeting next week for the Fred Segal Sundance gig," Steven says.

I look up at Charles and point at the phone. He shakes his head. "Umm, actually he's out," I say. "Can I take a message?"

"Very cute," Steven says. "Okay, I'm going. I just have one piece of advice."

"What?"

"If the two of you don't start fucking under your parents' roof, you'll never know the meaning of freedom."

"Thank you, Dr. King, for those inspiring words," I say, smiling up at Charles as I slowly untangle my legs.

⏰

"Honey, are you up?"

I have no idea how much time has passed or even what time it is.

"Honey, are you awake?"

I fish my arm out from under the covers and attempt to focus on my watch. 5:30. That would be P.M. judging by all the shadows falling in the room.

"Honey?"

"Who's at the door?" Charles says sleepily, rolling away from me and reaching for his BlackBerry on the bedside table.

"Alex?" The door cracks open.

Oh, *shit*.

"Mom! Mom, we're up. I mean, I'm up. I'm up. I just dozed off, but I'm getting up. I'll be right down. Can you just wait—"

The door flies open, and that twenty-years-out-the-window thing happens again.

"Oh," Helen says. "I didn't realize you were entertaining."

⏰

"So, you really like living out there in Cal-i-forn-I-e?" he says, pronouncing it like in the theme song of *The Beverly Hillbillies*.

You mean like "swimming pools, movie stars, and movin' to Beverlee"? No, I can't say that. Not to Mr. McIlleney, who's on his second martini and wearing red corduroy pants with little embroidered blue whales on them. Besides, he's no different from 99.9 percent of the people Helen's gathered in the living room and on the sunporch for this cocktail party. California's been a member of the union since 1850, and why I know this I can't even say, except the entire population of Bryn Mawr, or at least this cross-section of it, seems to act like it's the joke tie hanging around the neck of the body politic.

"Oh gosh, yes," I say, smiling into his bleary eyes. "I mean, I've been out there for what, five years now, and after all those Philadelphia winters, well, you can really get used to L.A." I sound like I'm reciting the Chamber of Commerce handbook. Circa 1950. But then, I've had a martini or two myself.

"Oh, well, sure the weather's good," Mr. McIlleney says. "But don't you find —"

"Of course, they don't broadcast the Eagles games often enough, so yes, there's definitely a drawback or two."

Mr. McIlleney blinks a couple of times. Like he's trying to focus. Oh, got it. Sports. "Oh, well, yeah, and what a tragedy that was last year when their offense was so explosive," he says, shaking his head, happy to be back on terra firma.

"Yeah, Terrell Owens?" I say, arching my eyebrows. "Amazing."

"Did you see that Atlanta game?" he says, clapping a hand to my shoulder. "Of course you didn't. Well, let me tell you, that was a game to see."

God, I'm getting good at this. Cutting them off before they get to whatever fill-in-the-blank objection and/or question they have about my having bolted the East Coast for Los Angeles. All of which are variations on (1) what's the matter with Hollywood these days, but then that's what you'd expect from a bunch of sex-crazed liberals, and (2) do I know any movie stars? *Real* movie stars. But then I've been doing this for the past two hours. I've had a chance to hone my technique.

"Roger, now don't go pestering Alexandra about sports teams. She's got better things to do than listen to you go on about the Eagles."

I turn. Mrs. McIlleney, looking like a carbon copy of Helen in her version of the Mary Tyler Moore outfit from her *Dick Van Dyke Show* days — slim, pegged trousers, gold bracelet, flats, and perfect hairdo.

"Hey, Mrs. McIlleney," I say, reaching out to give her a hug.

"Mary, please," she says, sliding her arm around my shoulder. "So good to have you back home again. I know your mom is thrilled, even if you're only here for a few days."

"Well, I'm embarrassed at how long it's been. I mean, seeing you all I realize . . . Well, anyway, it's just great to be home."

They both beam at me. "And your boyfriend?" she says, raising her eyebrows at me like I've just won the lottery. "I was just talking to him in the kitchen, and what a lovely young man. And so bright. I understand you both work at the same firm."

"Yes, he is very —" I start.

"Yeah, but is he an Eagles fan?" Mr. McIlleney says, clapping me on the shoulder again.

"Oh, Roger."

"No, but ask him about the Yankees and you're good for an hour," I say, realizing I'm quickly running out of sports talk. That my knowledge of the Yankees tops out at "Steinbrenner bad, Joe Torre good." Even if I spent almost ten years in Manhattan after I got out of Brown, five years in L.A. on the Hollywood publicity treadmill and I can no longer recite the pinstripes' lineup. I can name all the last five covers of *Vanity Fair*, *Vogue*, *InStyle*, and *Entertainment Weekly*, and list the release dates for all the studio films between now and Christmas, but I can't name a single Yankees player.

"Hey, there you are. I wondered where you'd gone."

I turn as Charles slides in next to me and plants a kiss on my cheek. "Hey," I say, flashing him a huge smile. He looks even more fetching than I remember him at the start of this evening in his blue button-down shirt, navy blazer, and his green eyes with the crinkles around them, especially when he laughs. Or maybe that has more to do with all the martinis and the fact that Mrs. McIlleney is smiling at him very, very intently. I'd been so dreading this party, and now here I am, belle of the ball and with Prince Charming on my arm to boot. "Charles, Mrs. McIlleney — I mean *Mary* — was just saying how much she enjoyed meeting you," I say, grabbing his arm.

"Yes, I had the pleasure a few minutes ago," he says, thrusting out his hand to Roger. "Excuse me, I don't think we've actually met. You must be Mary's husband. Alex's told me a lot about you."

"Roger, please," he says, grasping his hand. "Alex was just telling me you're a big Yankees fan."

Charles doesn't even shoot me a look. Which one might expect, given his interest in sports is even less deep than mine and pretty much tops out at alumni tailgating parties at Yale home games. "Only if they're winning, and only if we're not talking about Steinbrenner," he says. "But hey, after last season's massacre by the Red Sox, I'd rather be an Eagles fan. Talk about a season. Wasn't that Atlanta game something?"

It's like he's speaking in tongues. Or maybe all publicists are blessed with silver tongues and souls of brass. Or is it balls of brass?

"Oh, you boys and your sports," Mrs. McIlleney says, shaking her head and shooting me that commiserating women-who-love-men-who-love-sports look.

"Well, what are you going to do?" I say, smiling at her — at them — so hard my face hurts. Or it would hurt if I could feel it. But two hours of cocktails with the world's smoothest boyfriend, at least when it comes to meeting my parents and their friends — well, a girl could die happy. Or at least put all her worries and frets about whatever it was I was worrying and fretting about on ice. On ice and with another splash of vodka, thank you very much. It's been so long since I've been to a party where I wasn't working, I've forgotten you can actually enjoy yourself. Eat. Drink. Talk to people without one eye on the room and the other on your watch.

Mr. McIlleney says something more. About the Eagles, I think. Or maybe he's talking to Charles about bird-watching now. Hard to tell because another hand claps to my shoulder, accompanied by another version of "Oh my gosh, is that little Alex?" I turn. The Harrisons, or maybe the Schmidts, in matching crew-neck sweaters, beaming at me over their wineglasses.

"Oh, I was hoping to see both of you here," I say, leaning in for another round of hugs.

I am spun off, pulled away from Charles and his new best friends, the McIlleneys, by the Harrisons — and it was the Harrisons — who are succeeded, some minutes later, by the Atwaters. After that come the Schmidts and more couples whose names I don't recall or perhaps I never knew, given that it's been, yes, much too long since I've been home and obviously Helen and Jack have made new friends whom I've never encountered until now.

It goes on like this for another hour or so, getting passed from couple to couple until I feel like I'm in one of those elaborately choreographed dance sequences in a *Masterpiece Theatre* episode or a Merchant-Ivory movie. I'm waltzed around by various partners, up and down Helen's prized Oriental, the votive candles blazing away on the mantel, Jack's Cy Coleman on the stereo. "Well, it was great meeting you," I say, prying myself out of my latest conversational cluster — Chartman I think their name was, moved in down the street a year or so ago — and turn for the relative refuge of the kitchen. A seventh-inning stretch, to get some water or see if Helen and Maria need any help, or God forbid, run into my real date, who seems to have disappeared into the crowd.

I'm just heading down the hall, wondering if Charles is out back giving golf tips to Jack and his buddies, when Amy comes around the corner, carrying a platter of stuffed mushrooms.

"Hey, nice party," I say.

"*Yeah.* I mean, I don't know what you were so worked up about," she says, shoving the platter at me and turning to the hall mirror to reclip her hair. "Mom always does a nice cocktail hour. So yes, the party's great, and by the way, everyone totally loves Charles."

"Yeah, they do, don't they?" I say, smiling. Even Amy can't irritate me now.

She turns back and eyes me over the mushrooms, which are giving off a tidal wave of garlic. "So how long have you guys been together now? Three years?"

"Yeah, about that. Why?" I say, feeling my eyes start to water from the garlic.

"No reason," she says with a shrug. "I was just remembering that Barkley and I were engaged after we'd been going out for a year."

Oh, here we are. The so-are-you-guys-going-to-get-married third degree, which I knew, just knew, someone was going to give me before the weekend was over.

"Really, I hadn't remembered that," I say, trying to wipe my eyes while still holding the tray. "Well, it's different with us. Charles and I both really love our jobs, and so it's complicated by . . ." I let my voice trail off. Over Amy's shoulder I catch sight of Charles at the center of a knot of people, all of whom are looking at him like he's running for office and they can't wait to hand him their vote.

For a second, it hits me that he's working the room. That he's working Helen's cocktail party like he works every event, when he turns and catches my eye. We stand there, staring at each other through the crowd for a minute, when suddenly he cocks his head and, just for an instant, crosses his eyes. I burst out laughing, partly from surprise but mostly from relief. It's the first time I've seen Charles be, well, be himself again. The guy I fell for three years ago in L.A., during one of all our agency meetings in the midst of our takeover by BIG-PR, when it seemed like he and I were the only people in the room, in the world, with a sense of humor. Who didn't take it all so seriously. Who knew the difference between their lives and their jobs. And knew which mattered more. I'd almost forgotten about that guy. Until now.

"What's so funny?" Amy says.

I turn to her. "Sorry, what?"

"What are you laughing at? You were saying it's complicated."

"Oh, right. Yeah, well, it *is* complicated. Or it was," I say, shoving the platter of mushrooms back into her hands. "Or actually, it's not. We're working it out."

"Girls, what are you doing just standing here?" Helen sails by, bracelets rattling, barely pausing. "Amy, you're supposed to be taking those mushrooms out to everyone, and then I think Barkley could use some help with Bevan, and Alex, do you want to help me get the gift bags out? I think people are going to start to leave soon."

"Absolutely, Mom," I say.

Amy sighs and calls after her. "Where did you see them? I left them in the den watching the Phillies game."

"That's where I saw them," Helen says over her shoulder as she pushes through the kitchen door.

I turn to follow her when I hear Amy hiss in my ear. "Well, all I'm saying is I wouldn't wait too long. Charles is great, and you're an idiot if you don't see that. And see that others see it too."

"Well, girls, don't you look a pair."

We look up. Mrs. Schmidt heading our way. "Is Helen in the kitchen? I thought I'd see if she needed any help."

Amy and I both nod. "Yes, I'm sure she'd love that," I say, shooting her a smile. "Tell her I'm coming right in."

She floats off in a cloud of perfume, and I turn back to Amy. "Thanks for the advice."

"It's not just me," she says, nodding at the living room, where Charles is still holding court. "Look at the evidence. He's cute, got a great job, everyone loves him, and he doesn't even like sports, and I say that as the wife of a man who would die perfectly happy as long as some game was on."

I look at her. It's like she's toting up a scorecard. "You think that's why I'm with Charles? Because he's good-looking, has great people skills, and hates baseball?"

She studies me like I'm crazy. "Well, it doesn't hurt that he's a partner in your agency."

"*I'm* a partner in the agency."

"Okay," she says, her voice rising. "So you're both partners. It's what I'm saying. You're perfect for each other. I don't know what you're waiting for."

"Who's perfect for who and why are you two still standing here?"

We turn. Helen shouldering her way past the kitchen door, her arms filled with the brown bags of apples. I have to say, tied up with their red-and-white-checked ribbons, they look totally adorable.

I reach for the bags. "Here, let me help you."

Amy shakes her head impatiently. "I was just saying I thought Alex and Charles were really good together. And that I didn't understand—"

"Well, only if Mrs. McIlleney doesn't get him first," Helen says, eyeing me over the bags.

"*Mom!*"

"Alex, I'm kidding. Although there was the one summer when Mary . . . Well, never mind. The point is, Charles is lovely," she says, piling the rest of the bags into my arms. "Now, let's put these on the dining room table, because we don't want anyone to leave without their party favor. Something to remember this night."

I look at the bags and back at her. Helen's face is unreadable. I can't tell if she's kidding, or teasing me, or siding with me over Amy—and that would be a first. Or maybe it's like with Charles a minute ago. It's the first time I've seen Helen in a long time when she wasn't annoyed, or tired, or disappointed. "You're right, Mom," I say, turning for the dining room with the bags. "We don't want anyone to forget their gift bag."

3

And Then There's Just Marking Time

Somewhere over Palm Springs, the pilot clicks on the way they do, sounding like Robert Mitchum or Dan Rather, with their all-American drawls—right out of Tulsa or Dallas, football games and barbecues and Purple Hearts won in the war. Like they've just flown through hell and back, but damn if they aren't bringin' us down for a sweet landing and maybe a nice steak dinner after. It makes you happy just to be alive. Wedged in seat 5B, I pull the blanket around me, craving only more sleep, more of the pilot's lullaby: "Folks, we sure do thank you for flying with us today."

No, thank *you*. I burrow deeper into my business-class seat, upgrades being one of the only consolations for the freneticism of my life. Thank *you*, for my cocoon in the sky, this hammock between here and there, between then and next. Like the bubble in a level, I'm perfectly balanced in the air.

"Ma'am, you'll have to bring your seat back up. We're about to land."

So much for my cocoon. I pull the blanket from my head and gaze sleepily around the cabin. Light is pouring in, and everyone is moving in that restless, get-me-out-of-here way, snapping closed briefcases and laptops, jamming magazines and newspapers into the seat back pockets. Like they can't wait to spring free of this steel canister. Get back to their real lives.

Fools.

I lean into the aisle and check the line to the bathroom. At least three people. Shit. I check my watch. Almost 5:00 P.M. Or it was. I pull out the stem and rewind it, unspooling the hours, hurtling backward. 2:00 P.M. A whole day in front of me. Again. I run my hands through my hair and attempt my first executive decision of the day: do I join the potty line or wait to pull myself together after we land? I reach between my feet for my bag, pull it into my lap, fishing around for my lip gloss and BlackBerry. With one hand I smooth the Sahara of my lips, and with the other I click on for my e-mails.

"Ma'am, please turn off all PDA devices; we're about to land."

"I'm not turning it *on* on," I say futilely as she hustles up the aisle, collecting glasses, napkins, trash as if her life depended on it. Oh, screw it. I toss the blanket aside and scramble to my feet. I can never think clearly when I have to pee.

"Hey, Alex, how was your weekend?" Tracy the receptionist says when I finally call the office. I'm standing on the lower level of the United terminal at LAX waiting for the car. Technically, I'm outside, but given the concrete overpass above me and all the traffic and exhaust down here, I might as well be in another of Dante's circles of hell. The one he happened to miss by about seven hundred years.

"My weekend? Fabulous," I shout over the roar of traffic, because honestly, given how much I had been dreading the whole

Meet the Parents weekend, it had turned out great. Better than great. Not only was it fine being home again and Jack and Helen had totally hit it off with Charles — even the cocktail party was fun, and my gift bags of Heritage apples were as much a hit with the suburban crowd as my boyfriend — but Charles and I were back to normal. After weeks, months, of feeling like we had been drifting apart, pulled away by our jobs and living in two different cities, it finally seemed like we were back to where we were when we first started going out.

Still, I'm hardly going to share all that with our receptionist. Not that my relationship with Charles is a secret. But I'm just not crazy about having the nuances of it broadcast all over the office. That's the downside of a workplace romance. Everybody knows way too much about your life. Your sex life. And it's even worse if, despite your best efforts, it all goes horribly wrong, and then what are you left with? Sympathetic glances and whispers from co-workers, and worse, their assistants, who still have to work with both of you. Alex Davidson: Chief Spinster in Charge. Or something to that effect.

Never mind that Suzanne was one of those brave eternally single women who plowed into their fifties with their unmarried heads held high. Symphony subscriptions. Book clubs. Pilates. A *full* life. Compared to her, I'm pathetic. Still, God knows, given the right job, *my* job, for instance, work could — would — eat you alive. Before you know it, you're in your forties, still single, still exhausted, and wondering how you missed the turnoff back there in your thirties: MARRIAGE, NEXT EXIT. It had taken me years since my divorce to find a guy normal enough, *willing* enough, to go the boyfriend-girlfriend route. Besides, after this past weekend, I'm even more convinced that the only thing wrong with us is the fact that we don't spend enough time together. Still, the lower level of LAX at rush hour is hardly the spot to ponder one's place in the cosmos.

"So is Caitlin there?" I yell over the traffic, trying to move things along.

"She's not back from lunch yet. Do you want me to put you through to her voice mail?"

"No, just tell her to call me on my cell when she gets back." I'm tempted to add "unless, of course, I beat her back to the office," which is always a possibility, given Caitlin's deeply appreciative attitude toward lunch and time away from the office in general. What is with that generation? Even worse than the baby boomers and their sense of entitlement. At least they were willing to work for the BMW and the Sub-Zero. "Is Steven there?" I add.

"I think he's still at the walk-through with the magazine," Tracy says. "Do you want his assistant?"

Not really. "Sure, put Aaron on."

I get up to speed, or as much as I can take in, given the jet-lagged-dehydrated-carbon-dioxide-fume fog that is my brain at the moment.

"You can also try him on his cell," Aaron says.

"That's okay," I holler. "I can barely hear you. I'll just see him when I get to the office."

I click off and scan the line of traffic for the car. All the exhaust is giving me a headache. What was the car number again? BLS1049. 1059? Well, they usually have your name on a card in the window. I pull out my BlackBerry and start to scroll down the list of e-mails. Jennifer. Oscar. Steven. *E.T.* Two publicists from another agency. A million from Caitlin. Jennifer again. Mom. The Absolut vodka rep. One of Oscar's minions. The Evian account guy. Charles. Finally. Charles. I click open his.

Good wknd, but bad news in real world. Call ASAP!

Bad news? I've been out of commission for only what, five hours? How much bad could have happened? Aaron and Tracy didn't say anything. Either it's so bad, Charles is keeping it from the rest of the staff or, more likely, nothing's actually wrong but there's a chance it could be, so he's doing a preventative worst-case scenario.

That is another thing I've learned about him during the past three years. Back when I was a publicist in L.A. and he was a rank above me in the New York office, he just seemed in control and like he had a plan. Okay, so his plan had a million different contingencies, but it was a plan. Now that we're together, and more important, both agency partners, I see how differently we actually work. How I just plow ahead, putting the big picture in motion, dealing with stuff as it comes up — because, let's face it, women who are any good at their jobs, I mean, really good — not those needy, angry, bossy women who manage up the food chain while creating endless chaos for everyone below them — no, the good women are closers, maniacs for organization, for finishing things and *moving on.*

Men, I don't know, must be genetic or testosterone or whatever, but they just can't close anything. Something is always unfinished, some unresolved problem somewhere, and if there's not, God knows they will *make* one. And if they're total shits and in a position to do so, they will make someone else deal with it. Ideally, a woman.

Charles isn't that bad. He just likes to sweat every detail. And sweat it several times over. And then, after everyone is exhausted running the different options, he swoops in and resolves everything. Judging by what I've heard from some of the junior publicists in the New York office, it can be annoying, but really, if you think about it, he's just being conscientious and looking out for everyone's well-being. Still, I'm happy that as DWP-ED's grown larger, we've also grown more balkanized. That I have my own little event planning division to run the way I want to run it without interference.

I stand there for a minute rereading his e-mail, debating whether to call him, get the so-called bad news over with. Given the roar of traffic and my mushrooming headache, I think better of it and drop the BlackBerry into my bag. Time enough for that when I'm in the car. Smoked windows. Air-conditioning. Maybe get the driver to tune in to 88.1. A little jazz to soften the inevitable reentry.

* * *

"Think of it this way," Steven says. "Time out of the office, even if spent with your parents, is better than no time out of the office."

"You know, it actually turned out fine. Better than fine. I mean, Charles was brilliant," I say, downing the iced latte Steven has brought me. Actually, it was his latte, but I'm so desperate for caffeine to make it through Afternoon Take Two, I co-opted it.

"Sorry, I was obviously going on old intelligence."

"Yeah, I'm sorry I didn't call you again. We just got really busy with the party and everything, and then Jack and Charles and I shot a quick nine holes. And Charles wound up taking us all out for dinner before we left."

"Yeah, I heard you the first time," he says, looking at me like I'm raving. "Chuck was brilliant. *Brilliant*, I say," he adds, launching into some imitation of somebody. Usually I'm on his wavelength, but the jet lag must really be getting to me.

"Okay, are we done talking about our weekends now?" I say, draining the latte and tossing the cup in the trash. "How was the walk-through with the magazine?"

"Fine. It always is with Oscar there to hold their hands, and in the case of the publisher, literally."

"Wait, who is their publisher now?"

"Some woman. She's new. Think she came from *Parents* magazine or one of those million health magazines. Who can keep track of publishers these days? They're all on suicide missions. Like terrorists or Miramax employees."

"Well, barring any more personnel changes, are we good on *TV Guide*'s Emmy party then?" I say, heading for my desk, and the stack of mail, messages, and trades that piles up whenever I leave the office for two minutes.

"Well, if you don't count the gift bag, we are," he says. "And the fact that we still have to round up a decent list, and given their dismal history of events and all the competing parties, not the least of which are *Entertainment Tonight*'s and HBO's, that ain't going to be easy."

"Oh, come on, they have Joan and Melissa on their team now," I say.

"I rest my case," Steven says.

He's got a point. For every corporate sponsor that would see them as a draw for the ailing franchise, there was a publicist who wouldn't be caught dead letting their clients anywhere near them. "Okay, let's not emphasize Joan then," I say. "Get more of our people on it, and call over to PMK and see if some of their clients can be dragooned into showing up. And call all the networks again. Tell them it's going to be the *Vanity Fair* of Emmy parties — tell them specifically that Oscar's producing it — and they should plan on having their executives and stars stop by. And then, let's follow up the invites with e-mails. I want to at least be able to give the magazine a great RSVP list, and we can worry about the actual head count later."

I drop my bag and start leafing through the compost heap that is my desk. From the looks of it, I'll be here all night. "Oh, I almost forgot," I say, looking up. "What did Oscar say about his meeting with Jennifer this morning? Did they resolve the gift bag garter-ribbon-finish issues?"

"What do you think happened?" he says, heading for the door. "She rescheduled."

I push the mail to one side — deal with that later — dig my water bottle out of my bag, and log on to attack my e-mails in earnest.

I'm just going through them—there's at least 150 since last Thursday; doesn't *anyone* ever go on vacation out here?—when the receptionist clicks on the speakerphone. "Charles in New York."

Shit. I'd tried him in the car, but his assistant told me he was in a meeting.

"Hey," I say, picking up. "I tried you earlier when I got your e-mail."

"I'm actually here with Suzanne," he says on the speakerphone.

Speakerphone? I don't even get a private hey-that-was-a-really-fun-weekend call? It's what, not even ten hours since we were together, and already he's back to being Charles Evers, DWP-ED president. "*Okaay,*" I say slowly, pushing away from the computer.

"We're having a little meeting after a rather disturbing phone call I had earlier this morning."

"*Okaay,*" I say again, dropping into my autopilot mode: never play a card until you know what the game is.

"Andrew McFeeney called me this morning."

"*Andrew* called?" I say, sounding more incredulous than I want to.

"Exactly."

Okay, this is definitely strange. Not only is Charles acting like the past forty-eight hours never even happened, but Andrew McFeeney, editorial director of *C* magazine, is famous for never talking to anyone. Well, with the exception of Giorgio Armani or one of the Dolces or some other A-list designer aka advertiser. God knows, Andrew never talks to me or even most of his own staff. He's notoriously reclusive. Rumor has it there are at least half a dozen employees—*editorial* employees—who have never even seen him, let alone talked to him. He's the Howard Hughes of magazines.

In all my dealings with *C*, all their product launch cocktail parties with advertisers, their fall fashion gala, Christmas party, and their big Oscar party, I had dealt only with Karlin, the publisher, and Amanda, the VP of marketing, and their staffs. And whatever clueless New Yorkers they stocked their West Coast bureau with. Andrew McFeeney was never involved. At least not directly. He showed up at maybe one out of ten events, looking as uncomfortable and out of it as Leo in *The Aviator*. Plus twenty or thirty years. Minus the whole dirty-fingernails-and-long-hair thing. That Andrew had picked up the phone and called the agency was not a good sign; that he had called Charles, and not me, was even worse.

"*And?*" I say.

"And, to put it mildly, he's not happy with DWP's handling of their events," Charles says, sounding less than happy himself. "He's thinking of making some changes."

"Oh, he is?" I say, sounding more upset than I mean to, but between this speakerphone call, Charles's orange-alert attitude, and his apparent disregard for the weekend we just spent together, who wouldn't be getting pissed? "Well, that's news to me." Actually, it isn't news to me. Or the complaining part isn't. The magazine was always whining about everything. That's what they did, they whined but never actually worked up the energy to *change* anything. They really just liked to complain. It was their way of getting attention.

But now this call from Andrew, saying they may need to make actual changes, is different. Out of character. Besides, the last event we'd run for them—a Chanel fragrance launch party, the last C event before Patrice joined the magazine—had gone very well. I'd even gotten an e-mail from Karlin saying how well they thought it had gone.

"Frankly, their last event at the Chanel boutique, we had three-hundred-plus people and even got it on *E.T.* when Matthew McConaughey showed up on his motorcycle," I say. "There's no problem there as far as I'm aware."

"Okay, Alex, there's no need to get defensive," Suzanne says, interrupting. "This kind of churn happens all the time. We're just trying to figure out how—"

"I'm not defensive," I say. "I'm just telling you the facts. I still have the e-mail I got from Karlin saying what a great event it was and how especially happy everyone was with the coverage we got."

Now I'm seriously annoyed. True, I wish C would just cut and run. Let some other agency deal with them for a change. Still, there's the prestige of handling the hippest fashion magazine in Hollywood, and nobody really likes losing clients. But mostly, I don't like getting jerked around for the sake of getting jerked around, and Andrew, who wouldn't know how to conjure a Hollywood A-list if his life depended on it, calling Charles and hinting about "making some changes," is royal jerk-around treatment.

"And why is he calling you?" I add, seriously worked up now. "Or doesn't he know how to dial an area code?"

"Calm down," Charles says, sounding pretty uncalm himself. "Andrew called me because we've known each other for years. You know that. My father was his father's lawyer."

"Yes, I do know all this," I say.

"Well, that's why he called me and not you. Look, it's no big deal. Andrew and I are going to have lunch. I'll get his take on what's really going on, and let's see how we can save this thing."

How *we* can save this thing? Okay, stop right there. You might be my boyfriend and we just spent a great weekend together, or at least I thought it was a great weekend, but now you're acting like the school principal putting me on detention. "If you're having a meeting with him, then I'm going to be there," I say.

"Alex, there's no reason—" Suzanne says, but Charles cuts her off.

"It's not a meeting, it's a lunch. Between old friends. I'll just feel him out, and we—and *you*—can take it from there."

"I'm sorry, I think that just sends the wrong message."

"What wrong message? That we're willing to meet with him on his terms?"

"No, that we don't have a chain of command, a division of labor."

"You're blowing this way out of proportion," he says.

I swear, that's what men always say when they know they're wrong. Blame the woman for being hysterical. I take another deep breath. "Let me put it this way," I say coolly. "What would your reaction be if one of your clients, say Cirque du Soleil, that you just signed, called me up and told me they were unhappy with your work and I offered to step in and fix it?"

"Uh, 'thank you'?"

"You would not."

"Both of *yew* stop," Suzanne says, her steel magnolia accent in full roar now. "Look, we *survahve* loss of clients all the time. Every PR agency does. If Andrew wants to have lunch with Charles, let him. For one thing, they're both in New York, and more important, Andrew's enough of a head case that if this is what he's suggesting, then let's go along with it. For now."

"Which is what I've been saying," says Charles.

"I still disagree," I say, reluctant to give up. "I don't think we should let Andrew set the terms for how we do business. I don't think we should let anyone set the terms for how we do business."

"Alex, I'm with Charles on this," Suzanne says in her let's-wrap-this-up voice. "It's one reason why we have New York and L.A. offices, to ease the workload this way. But, Charles, once you find out what the deal is, then you turn it — and Andrew — over to Alex. Agreed?"

"It's what I've been suggesting all along," Charles says.

I slump back in my chair. "Well, if I'm outvoted, I'm outvoted."

"Okay, now can we move on and talk about other business?" Suzanne says.

We spend the next several minutes going over company business, the usual list of premieres, magazine covers, product launches, and events. We're still a small enough agency that we run most things by each other — as a courtesy — although after today, I'm giving that some serious reconsideration. Might be time for more independence, on all our parts. If I want a snowball's chance in hell of getting Charles and me *closer*, maybe I need to keep our work lives more separate.

"When's the Hawker wedding again?" Charles asks.

"Two weeks from Saturday. Coming out for that?" I say, trying to put the genie back in the bottle.

"Not on your life," he says, like I'm totally crazy to suggest it. "I've got two events that weekend myself."

"Well, if you change your mind," I say lamely, "I'm sure we can use the extra help, given Jennifer."

"Why, what's she doing?" he says, his voice rising again.

"Nothing, nothing," I say quickly, suddenly anxious to end this conversation. "She's not doing anything. She's lovely. It's fine. Look, call me later and we'll talk then."

We hang up just as Caitlin wanders in from lunch, working on the last of an iced tea.

"Hey, so how was your weekend?" she says, fiddling with the straw.

Oh, what's the point? "It sucked, thank you, and yours?"

———⏰———

I spend the rest of the afternoon going through everything that's piled up since I've been gone. No wonder I never take a real vacation. I'm out of the office for four days, three of which are an official holiday, and it takes me a full day just to catch up. And I haven't even started on personal stuff yet — all the bills that will be waiting for me at home and the messages on my home phone, including the lovely one my landlady left saying the painters would be coming in two weeks and I need to call and make the arrangements with them about getting in while I'm at work. Great. Just what I need. Workmen underfoot and a house full of paint fumes when it's 150 degrees outside, which it will be until fall finally hits. Which in L.A. means just around Thanksgiving.

"You want to grab a drink?" Steven says, sticking his head in my door.

"Now?" I say, looking up. "What time is it?"

"Quittin' time, baby."

I check my watch. Almost 7:00 P.M. PST, which means it's really, what, 10:00 P.M.? No, 11:00. No, 10:00. I give up, too tired to do the math. "No, thanks. I'm wiped," I say, slumping back in my chair for the thousandth time today. "Maybe later in the week. I'm just going to go home, open all the mail that's piled up *there*, get into bed, and see what TiVo has for me."

"You know, your life doesn't sound all that different from before you started going out with Charles."

"Thanks for that helpful observation," I say. "Now you really do sound like Helen."

"Actually, you never finished telling me about the weekend," he says, heading for the sofa in my office.

"You know, it was fine," I say, suddenly beyond exhausted. "Look, let's find a night this week and we'll go for a drink the way we used to — we can even go to Tom Bergin's — and I'll fill you in then."

Steven puts his hands over his heart and cocks his head. "They grow up so fast," he says, a fake catch in his voice.

I look on my desk for something to throw at him. The crystal paperweight — a miniature Hollywood sign with the initials D-W-P-E-D — I got when I became president? The stack of party invitations from L.A.'s hundred other event producers? My BlackBerry? "I'm too tired to even throw anything at you," I say.

"Okay, I'm going," he says, heading for the door. "But I'm holding you to that rain check. And you're buying."

It takes me another hour to finish everything up. One last check of e-mails. Spam. Screening invites. Nothing from Charles. Hmm. I've been so busy all afternoon, it only hits me now that he never called back after the speakerphone call with Suzanne. I check my watch. 8:00 P.M. 11:00 in New York. That's a little late, but I could still call him. Oh, screw it. *He* didn't call *me*, and he should have. After that phone call. If not to apologize, at least to explain without Suzanne listening in. Besides, I'm exhausted. I have no idea what's in my refrigerator, but whatever it is, it will have to do, because when I leave here I'm not stopping until I hit my front door.

I'm just gathering up my bag, bulging now with four days' worth of trades to read, or at least scan, when my cell phone goes. Ah, finally. The errant boyfriend calling to apologize. I burrow down into the bag for it and check the number. Oscar. Oh, God, do I have the energy for this?

"Hey," I say, clicking on as I head out the door, snapping off the lights. "I'm just leaving, literally. Nothing like putting in a full day after flying across the country."

"Great, meet me at Tokio for sushi and a debriefing."

"Oh, God, I can't take that much irony right now. That Asian chick in the Elvis costume stopped being funny the first time we went there. Besides, I have a date with my TiVo."

"Did I tell you I'm working on a prototype to turn TiVo into an anatomically correct man? I figure I'll make a fortune."

"Yes, you will, and you can tell me all about it — tomorrow."

"Come on, I need someone to listen to me complain about my day. I promise I'll make jokes about Jennifer."

"I thought Jennifer rescheduled."

"She did, but that doesn't stop me from making jokes about her."

"Yeah, well, don't you have about a million blondes on speed dial for this express purpose?" I say, reaching the elevator and hitting the DOWN button.

Oscar gives a little snort. "Yeah, but it's not like I want to talk to any of them."

"Oh, *talk*?" I say as the elevator glides open. "I thought you said you needed someone to *listen* to you."

"Okay, Nora, you want to bring little Asta and meet Nick for a martini or not?"

"'Not,' honey," I say, stepping into the elevator. "At least not tonight."

4

Till Death Do Us Part

"Am I missing something here?" I'm heading west on the 101, bound for "The Wedding of the Month" according to *InStyle*. Which really means something a lot less glamorous: driving my five-year-old Audi on the jammed Ventura Freeway, blinding sun in my eyes, cell clamped to my ear, and working up a sweat in my black Jil Sander sheath.

"You mean the exit?" Steven says. "It's Las Virgenes. You've done it a million times."

"No. I mean what meteorologically challenged fool plans an outdoor wedding in L.A. in September?"

"We do," Steven says. "Or, technically, our client did. And as I recall, none of us tried to talk them out of it."

"Well, one of us should have," I say, staring at the temperature gauge on the dash. 105. "It's so hot, I'm scared to get out of the car."

"It's a dry heat."

"That stopped being funny the first summer I lived here."

"Look, you're still in the Valley. It'll be cooler in Malibu. I mean, it's not like the wedding's in the desert."

"For the record, it's not Malibu — I don't care what the invitations said — it's Calabasas, which might as well be the desert," I say, spying the exit sign up ahead. "Besides, I'm at the Malibu exit and it's still 105. I'm taking that ranch off our site list."

"It's one of Oscar's favorites," Steven says.

"No, it's one of Colin Cowie's favorites, which only proves he's totally clueless. I don't know what Oscar was thinking. It's a ranch *house* miles from the ocean up a dirt road with a few goats and llamas behind a split-rail fence. Who seriously thinks that's a 'working ranch'?"

"Our client does, and honey, you're getting all worked up about stuff we can't change now. Call me back when you're in a better mood," Steven says and rings off.

That could take a while, given work lately. Ever since I got back from Philly, it's been one thing after another, so that Charles is the least of my worries. First it was Andrew and C magazine and the whole "we have to make changes" crisis call. Then there was the crisis with the *TV Guide* gift bag when MAC decided *not* to be a sponsor because suddenly it was a conflict with *E.W.*'s Emmy party — like they couldn't have figured that out weeks ago — and we had to beg, *beg* Revlon, who aren't even regular advertisers with the magazine, to cough up some new lip gloss, which they did, but only after a big wrangle with the publisher over free ad pages in exchange. It was getting so bad that we almost wound up using some new brownie mix from Pillsbury in the gift bag because they *are* a regular advertiser and are dying to "increase their Hollywood presence" — you could hear the screams around the office when *that* was announced as a possibility. We actually spent a week, a *week*, negotiating with Pillsbury to see if they could *bake* the brownies — we offered to take care of wrapping them in glassine bags tied with red satin ribbons imprinted with the company's logo — instead of just dumping the tacky envelope of mix in the bag.

And then there was the ongoing crisis of Jennifer's wedding. You'd think it was another of J.Lo's weddings. Jennifer's hysterics about the gift bag garter ribbon finishes over Labor Day weekend was the least of it. Ever since I got back from Philly, everything — from the wedding's theme and color scheme to the caterer to the flowers to the garters — had been approved, disapproved, reapproved, and ultimately replaced. Sometimes more than once. Miramax's Oscar party is less of a hassle; all they ever cared about was The List, and given that everyone wants to be seen at a Miramax party, it was never a problem.

Even though I managed to avoid the majority of the meetings, leaving Oscar and Steven to deal with Jennifer directly, there was one production meeting I did attend where (1) Jennifer spent an hour debating the number of walnuts that would be on the salad plate (answer: seven); (2) she spent another hour debating whether the chocolate cigars in the gift bag with the garter and the miniature version of the wedding invitation framed in silver plate and all the rest of the swag should be white, dark, or milk chocolate (answer: one of each), and is there a soy milk chocolate we could use? (answer: no, but the USDA is working on it); and (3) she spent a final hour agonizing about the amount of light filtering through the orchid petals in the centerpiece arrangements (answer: new "more transparent" flower arrangements). Even Oscar looked ready to open a vein after that one.

And it's not like this is the only thing on my calendar. Between the Emmys, the fall movie premieres, the holiday movie premieres, followed by the holiday parties, then Sundance, the Golden Globes, the Oscars, not to mention the endless product launch parties for our corporate clients, which include Kia — ever try to get an A-list celeb to turn up in a *Kia?* — my days are nothing but a blizzard of meetings, and my nights — well, I never thought

I'd say this, but honestly, if I never see another red carpet, I'll die happy.

And of course now all this pales in the face of the biggest event of the season — C magazine's holiday gala. After Andrew's call to Charles, followed by many, many rescheduled lunch dates, they finally met at Michael's two days ago. The upshot, negotiated over two hundred dollars' worth of lamb chops and mineral water: the magazine's Christmas party — the last event on their current contract with us — will be a test, *my* test, for keeping their business.

"Think of it as the usual end-of-contract haggling," Charles had said when he called to give me the news. At least he wasn't on speakerphone, even if he was still acting like I'd screwed up somehow and he was having to help me set the planets back in orbit. "Nothing you can't handle," he said. "Besides, Patrice is going to be the point person on the event — she was at the meeting too — and she's really great."

Great. After three years of killing myself for them, I now get to jump through hoops just to preserve the status quo. Personally, I just think it's a way for them to renegotiate their fee, which is already down around the "honorarium" level. One notch above the pro bono work we do for our nonprofit clients, like the Brittany Foundation, a grassroots animal rescue and adoption group. I can hear C already: "Gee, we're the second biggest fashion publisher in New York, but *we just can't pay you any more.*"

Excuse me, but when did it all get so hard? What with slashed budgets and personnel cutbacks, it's all become about doing more with less. Magazines, advertisers, studios, everyone's cutting back, and it just makes everyone even more tired and tense than they were before. And that's saying something in Hollywood.

Now I'll have to worm my way back into Andrew's good graces by his new gatekeeper, Patrice, and her boy wonder, Jay Reed. Officially, they are the magazine's new West Coast team, but talk about a learning curve. Jay is the L.A. bureau chief, one of those nervous, preppy, blond gays — "a sweater gay" as Steven puts it — a C-lifer who was promoted from a senior editing slot back in New York. Like most New Yorkers, he knows next to nothing about L.A. except what he's read in magazines. In town for less than a month, he's managed to hit all the clichés — a convertible, tennis lessons, and an apartment with a view of the Hollywood sign. Gilligan is Steven's official name for him.

Patrice has her own issues. One of those Brits of indeterminate lineage and intelligence but healthy self-regard, Patrice had joined that recent wave of expat English who found their own country lacking and emigrated to the U.S. to seek their fortunes convincing otherwise savvy magazine editors that they, born and raised in the Home Counties, had the inside track on America. Patrice, who had been passed around half a dozen magazines as an executive assistant, finally landed in Andrew McFeeney's lap, where he promptly promoted her to be the magazine's new entertainment editor. Given that she's been in America several years now and has yet to see a decent dentist, plus all the hair extensions, Steven has taken to calling her The Beast.

Still, if I'm to save the C account, I have to find a way to work with them, and starting now.

Or rather tomorrow. Right now, I have to focus on Jennifer's wedding. I check the time. Not even 3:00 P.M. The wedding doesn't start until 5:00 and will go on for hours, even if Jeffrey Hawker — famous for crashing his shiny red Harley the network gave him as a gift last year to celebrate his two hundredth episode of *Taskmaster* — is back on the wagon. I have *hours* of work ahead of me. Hours of work in a black wool dress, mules, and 105-degree heat. I redial Steven.

"By the way, where are you?" I say, heading up Las Virgenes into the dust brown Malibu hills.

"I'm here," Steven says. "At the ranch."

"You're already *there*? Why didn't you say so? How hot is it? I need to be prepared."

Steven says something I can't hear.

"What'd you say?"

"I said, I don't know."

"How can you be there and not know how hot it is?"

"Because I'm too scared to get out of the car."

By the time I lurch the Audi over the series of potholes that pass for the ranch's private drive, the temperature gauge still reads 105. Obviously nothing is going to change until the sun goes down. Which won't be for hours. I'll just have to cope with aspirin and water. Even the goats and llamas and, wait, is that a camel? — when did the ranch get a camel? — look like they're about to faint in their paddock.

As usual, I'm so early the valets haven't arrived, so I park myself next to the row of catering vans, HFS Cooking and Catering. They're Oscar's regular caterer, run by one Mr. HFS — aka Hot Fat Slim, or Hot Fat to his friends — a former minor league pitcher turned cook who Oscar found in a South Central rib joint. Apparently what Hot Fat used to do with curveballs is nothing compared to what he does with meat. Ever since Atkins became the rage, Hot Fat is the go-to caterer of choice. As I pull in next to the vans, I spot Oscar's old Jeep Grand Wagoneer, the faded red one with the wood paneling, parked down the aisle. Steven's Mercedes is nowhere in sight. Maybe he gave up and fled.

Steeling myself, I open the car door. The screech of saws and a blast of oven-hot air hits me — oh, God — and I quickly slam it shut. At this rate, it'll take about thirty seconds for my little chic Jackie O ensemble to wilt. I reach in my bag for a clip and twist my beautiful sixty-five-dollar blow-dry not including tip into a knot at the back of my head. Just to give it a fighting chance. I wish I'd thought to bring another outfit to wear until the guests arrive. Like a sundress and flip-flops. Oh well, too late now. I take a deep breath, open the door again, and step out into a puddle of dust. Great. Now I have a nice coating of dirt on my black suede sandals. Might as well go barefoot at this rate.

Shaking off the worst of the dust, I pick my way over the lawn toward the ranch house and the site of all that sawing. Actually it's two houses — a large stone main house and a smaller guesthouse, with a covered walkway in between. Technically, it's not a bad spot for an event. With the two houses there's tons of room for guests, tons of room for the tents — in this case two, one for the ceremony and another for the reception — and God knows, acres of parking. Besides, half a mile up a dirt road and with no visible neighbors, it's ideal in terms of privacy. The only access is by air, and Oscar's already got the sky filled with the giant white helium balloons tethered around the grounds to keep helicopters and airborne photographers at bay. Even the *Star* won't buy an aerial shot of a celebrity wedding if it looks like you're just trying to follow the bouncing balls.

By the time I reach the house, the saws are deafening, and I feel like I've wandered into a construction site. Two hours before the guests are to arrive, the wedding is still a work in progress. Crew guys in T-shirts and shorts are rushing to finish the tents and install the white lattice panels that will transform them into the "Little Chapel in the Dale." Or whatever fantasy Jennifer wound up wanting her wedding to be.

"Hey, is Oscar around?" I ask one of the guys as I peer inside the tent — a stifling white airless cave that looks like the set for one of those freaky dream sequences on *Six Feet Under*. There's the requisite Astroturf on the ground, and two guys are setting up rows of white folding chairs while two women, one in a flowing light blue dress and the other in lilac — they dressed in the wedding colors? — are attaching a nosegay of purple and blue flowers tied with a purple and blue ribbon to the back of each chair. With one hundred chairs, they'll be lucky to get them all decorated in time.

"He's out back with Hot Fat," the guy says, swinging a lattice panel over my head.

"Thanks," I say, ducking and backing out. It's marginally cooler outside the tent. Or maybe, because it's not so searingly bright, it *feels* cooler. I'm heading down the path toward the catering stations set up behind the stone wall that runs behind the house when my cell burbles. "Yeah," I say, clicking on.

"Hey," Steven says. "Where are you?"

"I'm *here*. Outside in this fucking heat. Where are *you*?"

"I'm in the house. With the air-conditioning. And the bride and groom and the bridesmaids and the groomsmen and the hairdresser and the stylist and the masseuse and all their assistants. Princess is even here, pretending to go over the guest list with the rest of our team."

"Cowards. And I'm out here getting heatstroke."

"Well, get in here. It's Oscar's job to worry about the tents and the food."

"Yeah, I'll be in in a second. Are the writer and photographer here yet?"

"No, but the video crew is out there somewhere scouting for shots."

"Okay, well, send Caitlin out here to ride herd on them for now. That'll keep her busy and out of our way. I'll be in in a minute, but I need to find Oscar and make sure he's got some fans or some portable A/C units coming. People are going to seriously pass out in those tents."

"We can only hope so."

I click off and am just turning back toward the caterers when I feel something cold and wet on my arm. "What the fuck?" I say, whipping around, braced for one of the llamas to have gotten loose or something. Oscar in his usual work mode — white T-shirt, white khakis, and a red bandanna wrapped around his bald head. An unlit cigar is in his mouth, and he's carrying two bottles of ice-cold Evian.

"Figured you could use this," he says, handing me one of the bottles. "You look fabulous, by the way."

"God, you startled me," I say, cracking the water and taking a long hit. "Thanks."

"Seriously," he says, nodding at the water. "You should drink one of those every hour or you'll start to get light-headed."

"Actually, I was hoping to feel light-headed. Could this be any more ridiculous?"

"Hey, you know I tried to talk her out of this place," he says, dropping his voice and steering me up the path away from the rest of his crew. "But she wanted a wedding that reminded her of home."

"Which is where again, Venus?"

He shrugs and takes a long slug of water. "Close. Arkansas."

"Yeah, well, in this heat it might as well be 'Little Wedding in Death Valley.'"

"Are you making fun of my work?" he says in mock anger.

"No, I just don't know why she bothered to hire us — and you — if she wanted to spend nearly half a million for over-the-top tacky."

"Honey, these are the mysteries I don't have time to ask myself. Like why you're still dating that stiff of a boyfriend."

"Hey, Charles is the perfect boyfriend," I say, whacking him on the arm with the water bottle. "At least he has the good sense to stay in New York this weekend. Besides, if you don't believe me, ask my parents. They love him."

"A ringing endorsement if I ever heard one."

"Hey, just because you never date anybody longer than a month — or over the age of thirty — doesn't give you the right to criticize those of us who choose to be in age-appropriate relationships."

"I'm just saying," Oscar says, finishing the water and shoving the cigar back in his mouth with a big grin.

I shake my head at him. I'm too hot to go down this road. Even if I wanted to. Which I don't. Especially not with Oscar. For one thing, he's like every guy in L.A.: refuses to date anyone who isn't blond, a twig, and barely out of her teens. It may be a power thing, or a *regional* thing, but it still sucks. For another thing, there's a huge gap between those men you can be friends with and a real boyfriend. Every woman I know can name at least three guys she once had as friends, and the minute you start to think about dating them or, worse, sleeping with them, it all goes to hell. It's just one of the laws of the universe. Like gravity. Or how your Barneys bill is never quite paid off.

So no, I'm not going to discuss my relationship with Charles with Oscar. Besides, there's enough to do just getting through the next nine hours.

"So is everything okay out here?" I say. "I'm worried about those tents. People are going to pass out."

"I'm more worried Hot Fat's going to pass out. He's got to grill one hundred boneless quail for the salad and another one hundred salmon filets for the entrée in this heat."

Okay, I've done enough parties to know that the last place you want problems is with the food and beverage. It's the one thing people remember at a wedding. That, and the gift bag. Still, Hot Fat is known for cooking through anything. Heat, cold, rain, mud slides, Santa Ana winds. He even catered a commitment ceremony out in the San Bernardino Mountains right through a 4.5 earthquake.

"Hot Fat isn't going to pass out," I say, sounding more certain than I feel. "That's the whole reason you hire him. He's like the mailman. Gets through anything."

"Actually, that's just his PR rap."

"His *PR rap*?" I say. "Hot Fat has a publicist?"

"Well, how do you think I found him?"

"I thought you ate at his restaurant in South Central."

"Please, L.A. isn't Chicago. White people don't go all the way to South Central for ribs."

"But he was written up in *L.A.* magazine," I say lamely.

"How do you think those tree-hugging NPR types found him? They don't go to South Central either. Frankly, *you* should have a publicist."

"*I* should have a publicist? I *am* a publicist."

"That doesn't matter. Your lawyer has a lawyer."

"I don't have a lawyer."

"Well, I do, and believe me, he has a lawyer — and a publicist."

"Okay, wait," I say, holding up my hands. "Let's just stick to the issue at hand. How do we keep Hot Fat happy and cooking?"

"Well, you start with the five cooling units I've got coming any minute," Oscar says, putting his arm around me and leading me back toward the tents. "The only question is if the generator has enough juice to power them all."

I tell Oscar to do whatever he needs to do to keep Hot Fat cool and cooking and head up the path toward the house, bracing myself to assume command central mode. Running a party is like running a battle. You prepare for the invasion, assign your staff their battlefields, take your positions, and just work it. When the smoke clears, you're exhausted, hungry, dying for a drink, and sick to death of wearing a headset and a transmitter the size of a brick. But everyone else should have had a fabulous time.

If it's a big red carpet event, it's all about the media. Which means it's all about the photographers. No one cares about the writers, except for *Variety*'s Bill Higgins and except if any of them get obnoxious. Your main objective is carpet control: keep the line of cclebs moving, keep the carpet filled but not too crowded, and be prepared to jump in and help out if any stars show up without their own publicists.

Then you have to make sure only the photographers you want inside the event get inside. Almost all of them will stay corralled outside the rope line. But depending on the size of the event, you can give inside access to one or two of the bigger photographers and, depending on the client and the guest list, a TV crew from E! or *E.T.* But even with the photographers you like and trust, even with the WireImage photographer you've hired to shoot your event, you still assign one of your publicists to trail them. Keep everything cool, everyone happy. Nothing ruins a party faster than too many photographers running around sticking their cameras in everyone's face. That, and too many fashion stylists trying to steal each other's clients.

But a private party is different. A star's birthday. A producer's wedding anniversary. A studio chief's pre-Oscar cocktail party. These events are about keeping the media *out*. Unless it's a charity thing, then you want the press there. "See how rich and generous our host is! And please, spread it around."

For a wedding like Jennifer's, it's about more than keeping the media out. It's about re-creating Fort Knox. These are competitive times in the tabloid biz, and *any* celeb wedding is fodder for the mill. I mean, look at all those *InStyle* wedding issues. You've never heard of half the couples, but God knows, they're each worth a four-page spread.

Holding Jennifer's wedding at the ranch, as hot as it is, does make sense in terms of security. So much easier than at a hotel, like what Michael Douglas and Catherine Zeta-Jones did. *Hello?* The Plaza? No wonder they wound up in court. Out in the middle of fifteen sun-blasted acres in Calabasas, you have a much better chance of keeping the drawbridge up. With Oscar's scarily beefy guys guarding the front gate — only those with invites and the password, "matte," which was not given out until this morning, get in — and the giant helium balloons bobbing overhead, we've pretty much got it covered. And with their exclusive media deal with *InStyle* — which means one writer, one photographer, and a three-man TV crew in exchange for a nice five-figure check to Jeffrey and Jennifer's favorite charity — the media are not an issue. Between Oscar and his staff, DWP-ED's event team, the network publicists, the studio publicists—who are mostly coming as guests, but still—my job is basically traffic flow.

When I finally hit the house, push through the front door— a massive oak thing right out of *Legends of the Fall* with a giant bronzed horseshoe for a knocker—the blast of cool air nearly brings me to my knees. I stagger in, pull off my shades, and look around. Steven was right. It is a party in here. Or was. Techno jazz is blaring over the sound system, and the living room looks like the Fred Segal sale—a jumble of clothes, some on racks, some in piles, boxes of photography equipment stacked everywhere, cables snaking across the carpet, trays of half-eaten sandwiches, and empty water bottles. Down the hall, I hear squealing. Must be the bridesmaids in hair and makeup.

"Well, unlike the Wicked Witch of the West, you made it without melting," Steven says, emerging from the dining room, which he's co-opted as the publicists' holding pen.

"I'm not so sure," I say, wiping my forehead with the back of my hand. "But the good news is, Oscar has five A/C units coming. I only hope the generator can handle it."

"Well, I'm not planning on leaving the building for another hour and a half."

"Speaking of that, how is everyone?" I say, nodding toward the dining room. "Did you tell Caitlin she's assigned to the TV crew?"

Steven rolls his eyes. "The network and studio publicists aren't here yet, and Caitlin's insisting she gets heatstroke, but she's not our problem," he says, holding out a headset.

"What *is* our problem? And what are you doing with a headset? We didn't rent them for this."

"Jennifer did. Or rather her assistant rented them. She wants us to wear them."

What? Jennifer's rented headsets? For one thing, we *never* discussed this, and for another, headsets are just so wrong for a private party. Plus, they're a total pain to wear. "Okay, we never discussed this," I say. "The security guys are wearing earpieces, but it's not that big of an event, there's no media to keep track of."

"I know, but she says it's 'a comfort factor' thing."

"Well, that's only because she's never worn one."

"I wouldn't be so certain of that. Apparently it was her trademark back in her pole-dancing days, when 'Rocket Man' was her theme song."

"Okay, I don't want to know," I say, holding up my hands. The girl is out of Little Rock what, a year at most, and she's already mastered the whole I-want-what-I-want-when-I-want-it celebrity vibe. "We are *not* wearing headsets," I say, clipping my sunglasses on the neck of my dress. "It's not necessary, it's too fucking hot, and it looks all wrong for a private party. This isn't the White House. I'll talk to her."

"Be my guest. I've already tried. Besides, there's another, more pressing problem," he says, handing me the clipboard he's holding. It's the most recent guest list.

"Okay," I say, scanning it quickly. "Who am I looking for?"

"You'll know it when you see it."

I run down the list. It's the same names we've been staring at for the past three weeks. Both families, including Jeffrey's twelve-year-old son, Max, from his first marriage. Or maybe it was his third. A million Schwartzbaums. About a dozen TV producers and directors, and of course, Les Moonves, the head of Viacom's TV division, here to kiss the hem of the network's third biggest star. Jeffrey's manager, his lawyer, his business manager, his acupuncturist, his trainer, his life coach, his AA sponsor, and his agent, Jeremy Latimer. There are also some ancient TV stars, like James Garner and Tom Selleck, and Jeffrey's costars from *Taskmaster* and his earlier series, *Howdy*, back when he was just another prematurely balding character actor and not the fixture in Hollywood he is now.

"I'm not seeing anything," I say, looking up.

"Here," Steven says, leaning over the board and pointing to the bottom of the list. "Mickey Delano, plus one."

"Mickey Delano?" I say, recognizing the name of the Hollywood producer who was as well known for his mega-grossing mind-numbing run-and-gun movies as for his off-camera appetites as a serial dater of young blond wannabes. "What's the problem?"

"Okay. First, you don't remember that little incident with Mickey and his alfresco blow job at that big agent's party? The one that got him publicly ejected and all over the tabs. I know it was before the Paris Hilton sex tape, but still, it was big news at the time."

I shove the clipboard back at Steven. "That was at least five years ago. The guy's been to a million parties since then and nothing's happened. I know he's a pig when it comes to women, but do you seriously think something's going to happen?"

"Second, the 'plus one.'"

I shake my head. "The latest arm candy? Who cares."

"Patrice Fielding."

"*What?*" Patrice has been in town less than a month as *C*'s Entertainment Doyenne, but already she, and her hair extensions, have been snapped up by Mickey?

"Okay, let's not jump to conclusions," Steven says. "She might legitimately just be a guest."

"Forget that for a minute," I say. "How did we not have the plus-one's name two weeks ago?"

"Because Mickey never gave it to us. Or he did, but then he changed it. I don't know. Ask Caitlin. You're the one who put her in charge of the RSVPs after she bitched about not doing anything except answer your phone."

"Oh, God," I say, rubbing my forehead. Up until now this wedding was just annoying. Now we officially have "a problem." A member of the media is now a guest at the wedding where no media, other than *InStyle*, are allowed.

"Okay, do we know if Jennifer knows what Patrice looks like?" I say. "I mean, if she doesn't recognize her on sight—"

"I think The Beast's teeth are pretty well known from coast to coast," he says.

Still, it isn't like she has the Q rating of Tina Brown or Anna Wintour. Besides, Patrice has only just gotten to town. Still, she's already wrangled her way to Mickey Delano. "Yeah," I say, "but only people in the media know her by sight at this point. Plus, it will be dark. Plus, Jennifer is a narcissist. Plus, Patrice may not even show. I mean, if Mickey had one date a week ago, he might have another today."

"Denial, denial, denial," Steven says, waving at me like he has a wand.

"Actually, I don't think so," I say, grabbing him by the arm and steering him away from the dining room. I've met Patrice only once since Andrew McFeeney handpicked her as his latest Hollywood emissary, but given her wavering accent and lack of specifics about her family background—just a lot of "Oh, Mummy this" and "Mummy that"—I'm guessing she's as much of a gold digger as Jennifer. A wannabe socialite trying L.A. on for size before heading back up the ladder to New York.

Besides, Jeffrey's wedding is hardly C magazine material.

"Consider it this way," I say to Steven. "She's got to be here just as Mickey's guest. C wouldn't cover Jeffrey's wedding if it was offered to them. I mean, his show's an aging *network* hit, the guy's in AA, and his bride is a former exotic dancer with implants and serious control issues. No one *wants* to be here. Everyone is basically attending to show support for Jeffrey being sober, employed, and God help him, happy. Even if Patrice turns up, this wedding is going to be as exciting as a UPN series or a group therapy meeting at Promises."

"Okay," Steven says. "But don't say I didn't warn you."

I cross Patrice off my list of things to worry about, at least for now, and head down the hall to the bathroom—that's another thing about event PR, you take a pit stop when you can — and then spend the next half hour in the dining room, shoes off, downing another water and going over everything one last time with Steven, Caitlin, and our team — Jill, Marissa, Maurine, Michelle, and Allie. I like to think of them as our student council presidents. Except for Caitlin, they are enthusiastic, organized, energetic, upbeat, and even more important, able to work together without fighting. In another world they would have become teachers or lawyers or editors or doctors. But instead, they've joined the Pied Piper's march into publicity. Looking at them here in their pastel dresses, lush hairdos, and unqualified eagerness, it's hard not to see them as some of Hamelin's best and brightest who got mistakenly wooed up into the mountains, never to be seen again.

"Okay, team, let's go over this one more time," I say, reclipping my hair and running down the event checklist.

- **5:00–6:00 P.M.** *Guests arrive. Cocktails and hors d'oeuvres served on the front lawn by waiters; music by the "Hey, Don" Quartet. Photographers — wedding, magazine's, and the TV crew — shoot formal and candid shots of the wedding party on the back lawn.*

- **6:00–6:45 P.M.** *Guests are escorted to the small tent for the ceremony. Rabbi Moskowitz and the minister from Jeffrey's church will preside. Jennifer's sister, Elaine, of* Cats *fame, will perform the solo; song TBA.*

- **6:45–7:30 P.M.** *Receiving line of Jeffrey, Jennifer, and Max only, which will be held on the pathway between the two tents.*

- **7:30 P.M.–TBA** *Guests and wedding party are served dinner in the large tent. Dancing and music again provided* *by the "Hey, Don" Quartet. Photographers and video crew will film throughout the evening.*

"Okay, any questions?" I say.

"I still don't get why we all had to be here if there's no media other than *InStyle*," Caitlin says, flopping back into her chair.

"Yours is not to wonder why," Steven says.

"Let's just say it's a comfort factor for the bride," I say. "You'll see. There'll be plenty to do."

"So we are or are we not wearing headsets?" says Allie.

"There's an office pool about that," Steven says.

"We are *not* wearing them," I say. "Trust me."

5

But First We Have to Get Through This Damn Ceremony

An hour later, the party is under way. Oscar's A/C units have arrived, Hot Fat has not passed out, and the temperature in the tents has dropped out of the triple digits, according to the crew guy running around with the portable thermometer. The bad news is, it's still about 100 degrees everywhere else, and I've lost the fight about the headsets with Jennifer.

"Alex, it's *not* a request," she'd said, standing in the bedroom where I was summoned after she emerged, sleepy-eyed but not discernibly calmer, from her "bride's massage." "I've rented them and you'll wear them," she said, her hand clutching her fluffy white robe across her even fluffier breasts, her white blond ponytail bobbing in fury. "It's a security issue, and it's what I *want*."

God, if I had a nickel for every time I've heard that expression. It's always about people's wants. But then, that's what I'm paid to do. Satisfy those wants. In the *Upstairs, Downstairs* of Hollywood, Jennifer is the lady of the manor and I'm her servant.

"Fine," I said, shrugging, cutting my losses. "It's your party, and if you want it to look like a commercial event, that's your choice."

"Well, it already looks like a funeral," she said, glaring at my dress. "I can't believe you wore black to my wedding."

I'm tempted to tell her that it's Jil Sander — since I'm required to look at least worthy of being in her company — and that black *is* the new black at weddings, but I think better of it. How can you argue with a woman whose taste tops out at white lattice and llamas?

"Would it make you feel any better if you thought of it as dark gray?" I said.

She peered at the dress again. "Fine," she said. "But don't let it happen again."

We can only hope.

Now I'm standing on the front porch in my shades and the head-set — *set it to channel 1, everybody!* — a glass of sparkling water in hand, watching the stream of guests make their way across the lawn, trying to pick out Patrice when — and if — she arrives. The "Hey, Don" Quartet is sawing away — "Lara's Theme," like that'll cool anybody off — while the fleet of waiters circle with the requisite trays of champagne and sparkling water. Most of the guests are in black tie, but a few, like Richard Lewis, who's wearing a black T-shirt under a black suit, are in typical fuck-you-*I'm*-a-star attire.

"I see Richard Lewis dressed up" crackles in my ear. Allie, who's somewhere down in the crowd with Maurine and Michelle keeping tabs on the magazine's writer. Jill, Marissa, and Caitlin are out back tag-teaming the video crew and the magazine's photographer, who are shooting setups with Jennifer and the brides-maids. I've got Steven down by the valets, ready to send up a signal should Patrice show.

"Yeah," I say into the microphone. "There's always somebody who has to give the finger to the dress code."

"Who's giving who the finger?" blares in my ear. Steven.

"No one is giving anyone the finger," I hiss. "And will you turn down your volume? You nearly blew out my eardrums." It's another reason why I hate headsets. Not only do they make you look like a telemarketer, but most of the time you wind up just playing one big game of telephone.

"Hey, Alex, can you send one of your team out here for a second?" Oscar breaks in. "I need to figure out exactly where the receiving line is going to be."

I'm about to say that I'll do it when I catch sight of Jeffrey coming through the front door firing up a cigar. It's the first time I've seen him all day, and with his Armani tux, his tan (probably spray-on, but a good one), his rakish black hair (clearly a dye job, but a good one), and cigar, he looks much younger than he does on TV.

"Marissa, can you go?" I say, cupping my hand over the mouthpiece. "I've got the groom here now."

I click off and turn toward him. "Hey, Jeffrey, you look like a man who's ready to get married."

"Alex!" he says, blowing smoke over my head and grabbing me in a bear hug that practically knocks my headset off. "Thanks for coming, and thanks for all this," he says, releasing me and nodding at the guests milling around below. "This is great. You guys have done a great job. And, God," he adds, turning back toward me, "don't you look beautiful."

You have to give him credit. Whatever train wreck he had been, however many motorcycles he had crashed and marriages he had busted up, he has a winning artlessness about him. Sad, really, he's winding up with Jennifer.

"Hey, thanks," I say, pulling my headset from my neck. "It's only just starting, but yes, Oscar has done a great job."

We stand there in the blazing late summer sun for several minutes, the murmur of the guests and the music drifting up and mixing with the smoke from his cigar. I look over at him and see a bead of sweat rolling down his cheek. He's probably even hotter than I am in that wool tux, but for some reason it makes him look nervous, even a little scared.

"Can I help you with that?" I say, reaching out with my cocktail napkin.

"Oh, thanks," he says, taking it and pawing at his cheek. "I should probably get out of this sun."

"Yeah," I say. "It's pretty brutal."

He balls up the napkin, shoves it in his pocket, and reaches to stub out his cigar. "Guess I better go down."

"Want me to go with you?" I say.

"Nah," he says, reaching over to kiss me on my cheek. "Just wish me luck. I'll see you afterward."

"Okay, I've got The Beast in sight" comes crackling over my headset. Steven with the first Patrice alert. We click over to channel 2 as we agreed. So he and I can talk without being overheard by the rest of the team.

"*Okay,*" I say, gazing down on the crowd, trying to make out Patrice picking her way across the lawn from the valet stand. "I can't see her," I say, cupping my hand over the mouthpiece. "What's she wearing?"

"White linen. To upstage the bride."

"Thoughtful," I say, shading my eyes. I finally spot her— a gawky, lanky column of wrinkled white. A column of white, which happens to tower over Mickey, who's dressed like a Mafia don in black suit, black shirt, and black tie.

"You want me to talk to her?" Steven says.

I sigh. "Well, that would have been good, but no, I'll come down. Meanwhile, stay on two." I click off, pull off my headset, and head for the stairs. I'm not anxious to confront Patrice. In my one lunch meeting with her, at the Ivy, which she insisted on because it reminded her of home with all the chintz, she was so patronizing, I'd vowed to deal with her only by phone and e-mail. Of course, now that she's the point person on the magazine's holiday gala, that's impossible. Still, I'm not anxious to cross paths with her again. Not here, where I have to play security cop and where Jennifer is already going off like a hand grenade.

Trying to remind myself that at least Jennifer is still safely tucked away in the house, I head down the stairs to the tuxedoed, shade-wearing throng milling around on the lawn. It's heading toward 6:00 P.M., but the sun is still searingly bright, and I'm guessing it's still north of 100 degrees. Coming down the stairs, I've lost sight of Patrice, but given how tall she is, she shouldn't be that hard to spot. I'm picking my way among the crowd, waving off the waiters swirling around with their silver trays, when suddenly she emerges just ahead. I'm trying to keep her in view when some beefy guy in an Armani tux nearly backs into me and I have to leap aside to avoid being crushed. As I glide by, I feel the heat coming off him. Like some huge barnyard animal. At least I'm not the only one who's dying out here.

By the time I reach her, Patrice, champagne flute in hand, is ensconced in some tight little conversational group with Mickey and two other couples. Great, now I have to shake her down in public.

"Hey, Patrice," I say, sidling up to her. "I wasn't expecting to see you here."

She turns and looks at me blankly. *Ohmigod.* She doesn't remember me. I'm just trying to decide if this is truly humiliating or actually hilarious when her eyes start to blink. "Umm?" she says, craning her blond pelt in my direction. I have the impression of a giraffe bending down to nibble some leaves.

"Alex. Alex Davidson," I say brightly.

"Alec?" she says, shaking her head. "Oh, *Alec.* Of course, how are *you?*" she says, bending even further down and giving me one of those pretend air hugs which are even faker than air kisses. "So bloody hot," she says, holding her glass to the side as she leans in my direction. "I mean, honestly, when everyone told me L.A. was 'hot,'" she says, making little quote marks with her fingers, "I had no idea they meant it so literally."

"I'm fine, fine," I say, ignoring her how-weird-is-L.A. riff. Had enough of that at our lunch, and it was old then. "So I didn't realize you were a friend of Jeffrey's," I say, trying to edge her away from the group.

"Who?" she says, giving me another blank look. Maybe it's just names she has trouble with.

"Jeffrey. Jeffrey *Hawker,*" I say.

Still nothing.

"He's the *groom.*"

"Oh," she says, startled. "Is that who this is for? I had no idea," she says, turning back toward Mickey. "I'm actually just here with Mickey, and apparently he's friends with — who is it, Jimmy? Or he works with him. Or has. Or wants to. I'm still not totally sure how it all works here in 'Hollywood,'" she says, making those little quote marks with her fingers.

Oh, God.

"'Right,'" I say, making little quote marks of my own. Obviously, I could leave it here. I should leave it there. Clearly, Patrice is just a guest, and a clueless one at that. Still, the memory of Jennifer railing at me over the headsets and my choice of wedding garb is still fresh. I don't want any more unexpected explosions if she discovers C magazine's entertainment editor is here. "So, Patrice," I plunge ahead, trying to sound offhand and not like I'm giving her the third degree, "you're here as Mickey's guest and not in your capacity at the magazine?"

Another blank look.

I try again. "I mean, you're only here as a civilian?"

"*Pats! Pats!* I want you to meet an old friend of mine" comes bellowing over my shoulder. I turn. Mickey pushing through the crowd. Great, the sex offender joins the party.

"Look," I say quickly, turning back to Patrice. "I'm assuming you're here only as a guest, because there's no media allowed. I just need to make that clear."

"What?" she says, pulling back like I've struck her. "What are you talking about? And why," she says, suddenly catching sight of the headset in my hand, "are you wearing a headset?"

"Pats," Mickey says, pulling up. "I've got some people I want you to meet." Next to Patrice, he's at least a head shorter. Well, whatever floats your boat. Mickey's only criteria are blond and prepubescent, although clearly an exception has been made on the sell-by date with *Pats.*

Patrice is still staring at me, so Mickey follows her gaze. "Hey," he says, turning to me and catching sight of the headset in my hand. "Are you security?" he asks. "You need to have a word with your valets. They're totally out of control down there, racing over all those potholes you call a parking lot. They practically *ruined* the transmission on my Porsche."

"You're security?" Patrice says dumbly.

"No, I'm not *security*," I say. "I'm *publicity.* We're doing the publicity, which is why," I say, turning back to Patrice, "I have to make sure you're here only as a guest."

"Wait a minute, wait a minute," Mickey says, holding up his hands. Hollywood producers hold the land-speed record for going from ignorance to belligerence, and Mickey is no exception. "You're shaking down my date because you think she's *covering* this wedding? What the fuck kind of publicist are you?" he says, his voice raising now so a few heads swivel in our direction.

Oh, this is going well.

"Look," I say, turning to him and dropping my voice, "there's no media here except for *InStyle*, and when we saw Patrice's name on the guest list, well, it raised a question."

"Well, consider it *unraised*," he says, leaning toward me. "She's my fucking date, end of fucking story. Besides," he adds, waving his glass at me so some champagne spills on my dress, "who would want to cover this? It's a fucking sauna out here."

Out of the corner of my eye, I see Steven making a beeline for us. My special teams unit.

"Hey, Patrice, Mickey," he says, gliding up. They both ignore him. So much for the special teams.

"Look, we're done here," Mickey says, grabbing Patrice by the hand. "Next time I see you," he says, nodding at me, "I want to hear the words 'I'm sorry' coming out of your mouth. Jeffrey's going to hear about this harassment of his guests."

He and Patrice lurch off over the grass. Well, that went well.

"At least he kept it in his pants," Steven says when they are out of earshot. "I count that as progress."

"Sometimes I really hate this job," I say, turning to him. "The way everyone treats us like we're idiots. Or worse, servants. Pond scum has a higher profile in this town."

Steven shrugs. "Look at it from Mickey's point of view — so much abuse, so little time."

"You're not helping," I say, sighing, pulling on my headset.

"Oh, forget it," Steven says, looping his arm through mine. "If Mickey made good on all his threats, he'd never have time to actually make movies. Besides, he'll be grabbing for the gift bag along with the rest of them."

Like all weddings, there are the criers. You just don't necessarily expect one to be the groom. But somehow when Jeffrey chokes up during his half of the vows—a mix of *Siddhartha*, AA, and *Men Are from Mars, Women Are from Venus*—it's actually touching. "I'm sorry," he says, and everyone bursts into applause when he manages to go on.

I'm standing at the back of the tent, poised to guide the guests out and into the receiving line while keeping one eye on Patrice and Mickey, when Oscar, dressed now in a black blazer and white tuxedo shirt, slides in behind me.

"So, I hear Mickey Delano was his usual charming self," he says, leaning forward.

I whip around.

"Relax," he says, leaning toward my ear. "Some of the waiters were laughing about him. He's such a dick."

"Yeah, I just don't need him being a dick about me," I say, trying to keep my voice low. "And threatening to go to Jeffrey and Jennifer."

"Come on, you honestly think she's thinking about anyone but herself right now?" he says, nodding at Jennifer, who is, at the moment, very theatrically wiping Jeffrey's tears and holding the handkerchief up triumphantly. Everyone breaks into applause and laughter. Oscar has a point.

"Speaking of weddings," he says, moving closer. "When are you and Charles getting married?"

Without turning around, I give him a shove with my elbow. "We're not getting married," I hiss. "At least not in the foreseeable future."

"*What!*" crackles in my earpiece. Steven, who's up in the big tent with Hot Fat's crew setting up. "They're *not* getting married? What *happened*?"

"Not *you*," I say, cupping my hand over the headset mouthpiece. "I'm talking to Oscar."

"Come on," Oscar says, leaning in so close I can feel his breath on my neck. "I thought you had a little engagement party back at your parents' over Labor Day."

"Shhh," I say, elbowing him again.

"I'm only asking because I want to plan it."

"Thanks, I'll keep you in mind," I whisper as a few heads swivel in our direction.

"And now, with the power vested in me by the state of California, I pronounce you husband and wife."

And then it's over. Or actually it's just beginning. Given that there's the receiving line, more photos, and then the reception with dinner and toasts and dancing for God knows how long, for which Jennifer will change out of her Vera Wang white satin wedding dress with the plunging neckline into a lavender Dolce gown with a plunging neckline. For the next five hours, my job is to make sure it all goes without a hitch. Which it does, more or less. The compressor doesn't break down, Hot Fat doesn't break down, and I make Steven play guard dog on Patrice and Mickey, who I'm relieved to see have been seated at the far end of the tent with a bunch of agents. Good, they can all outbelligerent each other. The waiters are just starting to serve the salad and I'm thinking the worst is over when my headset blares to life.

"Jennifer wants to know what happened to her walnuts!" crackles in my ear. Maurine, who's taking her turn at babysitting the bride.

"I don't know what happened to the nuts," I say into the headset, glancing around the jammed tables trying to get one of the salad plates in view. "Aren't they there?"

"No, it's just the quail, baby greens, and pomegranate seeds. She's very upset."

"Oscar," I say, trying to rouse him on the headset. "We have a nut problem."

The headset crackles. "Tell her it's a safety issue. They became rancid in the heat."

"Yeah, that'll calm her down," I say. "Maurine, just tell her the chef made a last-minute substitution for quality. Oscar," I say, "what happened to the walnuts?"

"It's on a need-to-know basis only," Oscar crackles again. "And you don't need to know."

"What don't I need to know?" I say, turning to face the tent wall and cupping my hand over the mouthpiece.

"This is your captain speaking. Please return to your seat and enjoy the flight. I'll be updating you later."

"Oscar!" I say, but he's clicked off. I'm tempted just to forget the whole thing and keep an eye on things here. But when the "Hey, Don" Quartet suddenly stops playing elevator music to lash into their version of Joe Cocker's "You Are So Beautiful to Me," I decide to chance a run down to the catering station.

I head out of the tent, squeezing by Jeremy Latimer, who's got his arms around two of the bridesmaids — typical — and head down the path, sidestepping the waiters ferrying the rest of the walnutless salads up to the tent. Before I even get to the catering station, I hear the voices. A low rumble of Spanish and then, more distinctly, Oscar and Hot Fat.

"What is going on?" I say as I round the small vinyl half tent that serves as the catering station. Whatever I expect to see, it's not Hot Fat brandishing kitchen tongs while Oscar and a couple of kitchen guys wrestle with three goats.

"Man, I'll work through anything — bitchy celebs, clients who have no taste, earthquakes — and you know I will, but I will *not* work through an animal infestation," Hot Fat says, waving the tongs. "They already ate my walnuts and half the bread and were heading for the salad greens. Now get them out of here!"

"Yeah, I get it, big guy. What do you think I'm trying to do?" Oscar says, pulling on the goats, which are starting to bleat in all the excitement.

"Oh, my God!" I say, stuck in my tracks. I've handled a lot of event emergencies — rain, flooding, food shortages, electrical outages, headset breakdowns, party crashers, and even closures by the fire department. But I've never handled any animal problems. "How did they get loose? We've got to get them back in the pen before anybody hears them."

"Tell me something I don't know," Oscar says, turning to me. "Why do you think I had the band start playing rock music?"

"That was you? I thought Jennifer had just gotten hold of the playlist."

"Alex," Oscar says, gripping the goats by the neck, or as much as he can, given that they aren't wearing collars. "I need you to come here and reach into my inside jacket pocket."

"Why?" I say, not moving.

"Just *do it*!"

"Okay, okay," I say, bolting toward him.

"I ain't helping you guys," Hot Fat says, stepping out of the way. "My contract don't call for no animal control. Besides, I got two thousand dollars' worth of salmon on the grill that needs to be turned."

"No, no, we'll take care of it," I say, trying to avoid the goats while fumbling with Oscar's jacket. "What am I looking for? A stun gun?"

"My *cigars*!" he says. "I have two in my inside pocket."

"What? Are you planning on smoking them out?"

"No!" he says, grabbing one of the cigars that I've managed to extricate from his pocket. "Goats love tobacco. They'll follow us back to the pen if we use the cigars as lures."

I have no idea how Oscar knows this, but given the way the goats are stepping all over us in their eagerness to get to the cigars, he must be right. Instinctively, I hold the cigar over my head. The goats start to leap toward my hand. "Oh no, they're *climbing* me!" I say, trying to back away.

"Put your hand down!" Oscar says. "Put it down and walk out of the tent and they'll follow you."

"But they'll eat the cigar if I do that!"

"Then we're going to move fast," Oscar says, snapping his cigar in two and holding out the two halves to the goats, who leave off jumping on me. "Come on," he says, grabbing me by the hand.

"Here, lady," one of the kitchen guys says, thrusting a pack of Marlboros at me.

"Okay, okay," I say, grabbing the cigarettes as we fly by, the goats galloping in our wake.

"You know, I once had a goat as a pet."

"Why am I not surprised?" I say, exhaling a cloud of smoke toward the stars beginning to peek through the evening sky. We're out by the corral leaning against the fence sharing the last Marlboro after we got the goats stowed away. I haven't had a cigarette in years, but somehow it seems appropriate after what we've just been through.

"My dad gave it to me when we were living on the base in Hawaii, right before he shipped out. I named it Peter."

"After the disciple?"

"After my dad."

"Ah," I say, passing him the cigarette. "And did you love it more than life itself?"

"I did," he says, taking a long drag. "I used to feed it my mom's cigarettes, which I realized later only made it more hyper. But I like to think it added a few years to her life."

"What happened?"

"My dad came home, and we moved back to the States. I had to give the goat away. I sometimes wonder what happened to Peter."

"What happened to your parents?"

"My mom died five years ago, but my dad is down in Florida. Fishes a bit. Works part-time at a local golf course. He likes it."

We stand there for a few minutes smoking silently in the dark, listening to the laughter and the music from the party floating in the night air. If only I could stay out here, away from Jennifer and Patrice and Mickey and just all of it. Suddenly I hear the familiar strains.

"Oh, no. Are they actually playing 'Rocket Man'?" I say, cocking my head.

"I believe they are," Oscar says, stubbing the cigarette on the railing. "Can't let Jennifer be the only one who dances to that," he says, reaching for my hand.

"We should get back. Before they miss us. Before Jennifer runs out of people to yell at. Before —"

"Yeah, we will," he says, pulling me into his shoulder, which smells of wool and smoke and tobacco, as he propels me across the grass. "We will in a minute."

6

Time Out

Pushing noon on Sunday, I'm still not dressed. I'm out of bed, have called Charles (got him on his cell during his run in Central Park, so he has to call me back), am collapsed on the sofa in an old pair of yoga pants and a tank top, with all the papers and coffee, but not officially dressed. And I have no intention of being. Maybe not ever.

God knows, the wedding was exhausting. Between the heat, the goats, Mickey and Patrice, and the endless toasts — who knew being on the wagon meant so much fake drinking? — I didn't get home until 2:30 A.M. But then it has to be like this — downtime as house arrest — if you're going to make it in the event business. Or just make it, period. By my calculations, once you pass thirty-five, your day isn't twenty-four hours, it's three time zones — morning, afternoon, and evening. Most women I know can do two out of three. Attempt to do them all, and you become a complete screaming lunatic. Which pretty much explains why everyone hates publicists and, for that matter, Dr. Freud, most women. You can't be that outer-directed 24/7 without paying for it.

I know. I tried. The first year I got promoted to president at the agency and was heading up the event division—which meant I had to create it, staff it, and rustle up nearly a dozen new corporate clients—my day was wall-to-wall. Up at 5:30, scan the Web and TV news; 7:00 A.M. yoga class. In the office from 9:00 A.M. to 7:00 P.M. Meetings, conference calls, lunch with a client. Then a business dinner, drinks, a screening or an event every night.

By the end of the year, the division was up and rolling, but I'd gained ten pounds—those yoga classes were the first to go; like I had time to listen to someone tell me to breathe—and lost nearly every friend I had. Frankly, I couldn't remember the last time I saw anybody that didn't have something to do with work. I certainly never saw Rachel, my old publicist pal who had bolted her job at Fox to become a unit publicist and was now always on the road babysitting movie sets. Maude, a hypnotherapist I'd met at the Iyengar Institute, was a victim of those canceled yoga classes. Evelyn, a freelance journalist and my moviegoing pal, had lasted the longest. Actually, she stopped seeing me when she became so freaked out about turning forty that she spent all her time dating plastic surgeons, the idea being if she didn't wind up marrying one of them, she could still get a good deal on the surgery. Now we just stay in touch via e-mail. Actually, it's better this way, because you don't waste all that time trying to schedule time together—which you only wind up canceling and rescheduling anyway.

I check my watch. Heading toward 1:00 P.M., which means one more cup of coffee, then check out the afternoon movies on cable, followed by a nap. Doing nothing has to be planned out, because God knows, if you don't plan to do nothing, you'll always find something to do. I grab the TV section and my coffee mug and head into the kitchen. Don't want to get too caffeinated. Might make the nap tough. Might be time to switch to water.

Might be time to realize I have a college degree and stop thinking in incomplete sentences. Like my brain has become one big BlackBerry incapable of complex communiqués. Resolve to read the Opinion section of both *L.A.* and *New York Times,* form some, and then watch movie. Preferably foreign with subtitles.

Of course, none of this planning-to-do-nothing plan would be necessary if I actually had a boyfriend who lived here. With me. In this house. As in the same place. But after three years of officially being with Charles but still waking up most Sundays alone, I know this kind of thinking only leads to self-pity followed by another argument on the phone. So, in the interest of world peace starting with my own tiny corner of it, I am now officially treating Sunday like my own private spa day. Minus any actual spa treatments, of course, unless I get an overwhelming urge to feel a man's hands on me — an urge that overrides my resistance to drive anywhere on a Sunday — and I drop in at Ole Henriksen's for a massage.

Heading into the kitchen, I wince at the glare from the windows. I vaguely recall the weatherman saying that if yesterday was hot, today would be even worse. As if that's even possible. I'm just trying to focus on the thermometer outside the kitchen window, which I can't quite make out because of the way the sun is hitting it — could it really be 120 degrees? — when I hear singing and piano playing.

Oh, good, Christy's up. My out-of-work, former sitcom star of a neighbor, whose deck — aka the piano studio — looks right onto my front yard. It's 100 degrees outside, but Christy, bless her little unemployed soul, is out there in some sort of kimono, her hair knotted wildly on her head, singing away like a contestant on *American Idol.* Given the kind of time Christy has hanging on her hands since her series was canceled last season, this alfresco concert could go on for a while, a serious blow to my plans for a quiet Sunday at home.

I'm just reviewing my options for the day — earplugs? head-phones? — when the phone rings. *Finally*, I say, lunging for the phone.

"So, did you survive last night?" Charles says, still sounding out of breath from his run.

"Oh, God, barely," I say, reaching for the coffee mug. "You should have been there. Actually, given how hot it was, be glad you weren't. I mean, Oscar had to send for cooling units at the last minute, just to try and get the temperature in the tents down, and then Jennifer had a fit when she realized —"

"Yeah, I checked the wires this morning. I didn't see anything except your press statement," he says. "So I assumed it went off okay."

"Yeah, it did," I say, feeling my cheeks flush, trying not to think he's checking up on me. Like some junior publicist having her homework checked by the boss. Like how I felt during his speak-erphone call to me about C magazine. "Where are you?" I say. "Still in the park?"

"Walking home, trying to cool off. Why?"

I close my eyes. Don't do it. Don't pick a fight for no reason. Except I actually do have a reason. One hundred and fifty-six of them to be exact — one for each Sunday of the past three years that we did not spend together. "Well, I was just wondering if this was Charles my boyfriend calling or Charles my fellow publicist, that's all."

"Hey, don't be like that," he says, dropping his voice. "You know I care about you."

"I know," I say, dropping my voice too. "I just —"

"I also care how the wedding went."

I sigh. Fine, you want to talk about work, let's talk about work. "It went really, really well," I say briskly. "Considering it was one of the hottest days of the year and the ranch leaves a lot to be desired in a heat wave. But Oscar was brilliant and the ceremony was actually very touching and Jennifer and Jeffrey left for Hawaii, two happy customers. As soon as I get the airdate from *InStyle* for their wedding special, I'll let you and Suzanne know."

"Hey, I was just asking," he says. "Take it easy."

I close my eyes again. Why is it that the last thing you feel like doing is taking it easy when someone tells you to take it easy?

"Oh, I *am* taking it easy," I say, reaching for the pot and pouring the last of the coffee into my mug. Coffee sludge is more like it. "Or I was until my boyfriend called asking about the wedding before he asked about me."

I hear him sigh. "You really want to do this? Want to have another argument on the phone?"

"No, I don't. I don't even want to be on the *phone* with you. I want to be in the same *room* with you. Why is that so hard for us? To be in the same place? Why are we always apart? We've been together for three years, and of that time I think we've actually spent less than three months physically together."

"Alex, come on," he says, and I can hear the annoyance in his voice. "We've been over this and over this. There are a lot of career couples who do this kind of arrangement. Besides, you know it's just not a good time to make any big changes in the agency management structure."

"Says who?" I say, scrunching the phone against my neck to reach in the refrigerator for the half-and-half. "I know *you've* been saying that ever since we started going out, but I don't recall my ever agreeing with it."

"You honestly think you can run our event division out of New York when what, ninety percent of our events are in L.A.?"

"When did this become about my moving to New York? It's far more feasible that you could spend half of each week in L.A."

"When I oversee the New York office, including *all* ten of our publicists and their clients?"

"Fuck," I say. "Then how are we ever going to move things forward? I mean, after three years, I still feel like we're just getting started."

"You keep acting like things are broken between us. Like something needs to be fixed."

I stop midsip. He honestly thinks this arrangement is working. "You honestly think this arrangement is working?"

"I think it's working fine," he says. "For now."

"And when is 'now' over? I mean, when will this never-being-in-the-same-city thing not be fine?"

"Look, I don't know," he says, sounding rushed again, or maybe it's just the sound of traffic in the background. "I just know that things change. They do. Things never stay the same. Even when you want them to."

Change. There's a concept. In my experience, change mostly happens involuntarily and usually for the worse. Your cat dies, your parents get older, your sister gets married and has a baby. Changing things for the better takes a lot of work. Usually too much. And even then it's fraught with peril. What if you change something—break up with your boyfriend, get a new job, stop going home every Christmas—and it turns out to be worse than before? It's why most people never change anything. *Oh, people change.* No, they don't. They sit around and complain about the status quo. It's why I have my endless to-do list. All the things I want to change. One of these days. When I make up my mind to do it. It's like saving money or losing weight. Charles and I spending more time together is never going to just *happen*. We'd have to decide to change things.

"So you're saying *we* won't be the ones to decide to change things, but that something—"

"Hang on a sec, I have another call," he says, clicking off.

I close my eyes. Again. My cozy little Sunday has suddenly withered into a desert stretching before me. A desert without a boyfriend but with a soundtrack. I open my eyes and check out the kitchen window. Christy is still banging away on the piano. Show tunes, I think, picking out the strains of "Rent." I stand there for a couple of minutes listening to her, trying to decide if she has any idea how sound carries in the hills, or if she's totally enjoying the fact that it does, when Charles clicks back.

"Sorry," he says, sounding breathless again. Like he was jogging or walking fast. "But that was Patrice."

"Patrice?" I say, turning from the kitchen window and heading into the living room.

"Patrice *Fielding*."

I freeze midstep. What is Patrice doing talking to Charles, and on a Sunday morning? It was weird enough she unexpectedly showed up at the wedding, but now she's calling Charles?

"Patrice called you?" I say casually. "Just now?"

"Yeah, well, we were trading calls Friday, and then she just reached me," he says, sounding equally casual. Maybe too casual. "She wanted to go over some things—she's coming to New York next week—and she mentioned she had seen you at the wedding and you seemed a little flustered by her presence."

A month ago, I didn't even know Patrice, and now I'm tripping over her everywhere I go? Even on my day off.

"For the record, I wasn't *flustered*," I say, realizing I sound totally flustered. "I was *concerned*. When the entertainment editor of a national magazine shows up at a wedding where there's no media allowed, I get *concerned*. Anyone would be. You would be."

"Look, don't get defensive."

"I'm not defensive, I was *concerned*," I say again. "I needed to clarify she was there strictly as a guest."

"She said you upset her date."

"I upset her date? Oh, give me a break, Mickey Delano *lives* to get upset. He loves putting on a show."

"Okay, never mind," Charles says, backtracking now. "She just brought it up, and I thought I'd mention it to you."

"And I've *explained* it," I say. A moment of silence hangs in the air. A beat too long. Like the tide receding on an empty beach. "Look, let's not talk about work, let's not talk about us," I say, rushing to fill it. "I seriously need to do nothing today."

"So what are you doing today?" we say simultaneously, and I realize this — asking each other about our different days — has become our default mode.

I stare out the living room window at the eucalyptus trees thrashing in the Santa Ana winds. "What I always do. Papers, movie, nap. Order something in later. Watch HBO," I say, not bothering to mention Christy and the piano. "You?"

"It's a gorgeous day here," he says. "You know, one of those first crisp fall days."

He keeps talking, a rundown of his day, his run in the park, lunch with friends, maybe an early movie, but his voice is like the muffled sound from an apartment down the hall. Maybe it's the heat, or our argument, or the fact that we're still in two different cities, two different time zones, with some 40 degrees and 2,800 miles separating us, but my mind drifts off. That's one of the things I miss most about living back east. The seasons. Especially fall, that sense of forward motion every September, that the planet is spinning forward, carrying you effortlessly forward. In L.A., nothing carries you forward except your own will.

"You know, maybe we can at least figure out how I can spend September and October working out of the New York office," I say suddenly, pressing my forehead to the window, feeling the coolness of the glass and the heat beyond it. "And then you could spend the winters in L.A. Bicoastal according to the seasons. Maybe that's a way to start."

"Umm, yeah," he says, like he's surprised or startled that I've interrupted him.

"Look," I say, pulling away from the window. "I'm just saying it's a way to explore making a change. A baby step. Plus, I miss New York in the fall, and you know the winters in L.A. are so —"

"Hold that thought, I have another call," he says, clicking off.

"As I was saying," I say pointlessly. I stand there a minute waiting for Charles to come back on when I hear my other line click. Oh, screw it. "Hello?" I say, clicking over.

"You are up."

Oscar. A day early by our usual Monday morning quarterbacking, our conference call with Steven where we go over everything about the event. Something must be up for him to call on Sunday. Oh, God. Maybe Jennifer already called him to complain about something?

"Yes, I'm up. Ambulatory. Caffeinated. Even read the Sunday papers. But what's wrong? Did Jennifer find out about Patrice being at the wedding and call freaking from Hawaii?"

"Why are you always braced for bad news? I don't even get a 'Hello, Oscar, how are you?'"

I take a swig of coffee, cold now and pure grit, wondering where this is going and if I'm in a mood to go there.

"You're right. Hello, Oscar. How are you? Now, please tell me what's up. I've got Charles on the other line."

"Oh, hey, tell him I need to talk to him first thing tomorrow about the Kia launch party next month."

"Sure, actually, hang on," I say, clicking back to Charles.

"Where did you go?" Charles says, sounding annoyed.

"I had another call," I say. "Oscar. Needs to go over some things about last night. He also wants to talk to you. Let me call you right back."

"No, look, go ahead and take it, I've got to get going anyway," he says, sounding rushed, mentioning the movie again. "We'll talk later."

Before I can protest, he's gone. I sigh, click back to Oscar. "Charles says to reach him at the office Monday. Now, tell me what's up with Jennifer."

"Look, Jennifer hasn't called. No one's called, and I'm bored. It's too hot to do anything except eat. Let's go to brunch."

"Brunch?" I say dumbly. "No one does brunch anymore."

"I'm offering to buy you a meal and you're turning me down?"

"I just saw you less than twelve hours ago. I don't want to go to brunch."

"*Lunch.* Call it lunch if that will make you feel better."

"Look, isn't there some wannabe actress over there you can take to brunch? Lunch?" I say. "Someone else you can play with? I thought you had a hot date last night after we finished at the ranch."

"No, I told you. Elsa's out of town."

"*Elsa's out of town,*" I say, laughing for what I realize is the first time today. "I can't believe you're dating someone named Elsa."

"I'm not 'dating' Elsa. You think no one does brunch anymore. Well, no one 'dates' anymore. I'm *seeing* Elsa."

"The way you're 'seeing' Amber, and what was that other one's name, Brandy?"

"Alex," he says with an exaggerated sigh. "Try and follow along. I'm seeing Elsa, but I hang out with Amber, and for the record, Brandy is over."

"Okay, forget the girls. Isn't there a game on? I know there's a game, somewhere, in some country, on some channel," I say, turning back for the kitchen. "Just hang up the phone, turn on the TV, and you'll forget all about brunch."

"Actually, there is a game on. Or there will be. So let's go to lunch and then we can watch the game."

"Okay, maybe that's your day off," I say, pouring the rest of the coffee down the drain and reaching in the refrigerator for a water. "My day off is watching a movie, taking a nap and maybe even a bath. Alone. Or it was," I say, checking out the window at Christy, still banging away.

"Look, Garbo, it's too hot for a bath. Besides, you have to eat. Come on, I'm buying. Meet me at Hugo's," he says, mentioning the legendary West Hollywood breakfast joint.

"Hugo's? You expect me to leave my nice air-conditioned house on a day like this to go to Hugo's and eat breakfast?"

"Yeah, because they have the best blueberry waffles in L.A."

"I haven't eaten waffles in years. Nobody eats waffles any—"

"Which is exactly why you're going to meet me there in half an hour."

"Know what the secret of a good waffle batter is?"

"No idea," I say, spearing another forkful. "Sugar?"

"Yeast. And letting the batter rest."

"Sounds like wine," I say, looking up.

"Sounds like a lot of things," he says, eyeing me over his coffee cup. "Leaven and time."

"You learn that from Hot Fat?" I say, reaching for my coffee cup.

"No, the Army."

I pause, my cup in midair. "You were in the Army? You mean, when your dad was in the Army?"

"I was in ROTC in college."

I put the cup down. "Okay, what are you, fifty? I thought that bald head was just a fashion statement."

"I told you. I was an Army brat," Oscar says, leaning back in his chair. "I was just following my old man. What's amazing is that I went to college. He never did."

"So you actually served where, Vietnam?"

"No, I was too late. Fort Hood. Three years. By the time I left, I was manager of the mess hall. How did you think I got into event production? You run the mess for a thousand guys in boot camp, nothing scares you."

I push my plate aside. Maybe it's all the sugar from the waffles, which were absurdly good, so three-dimensional compared to most breakfast foods, or maybe it's the fact that we're sitting directly under the air-conditioning vent, but the world seems much more palatable than it did an hour ago. "I thought you got into it by being a roadie or a grip or something," I say, reaching for my cup, which is pretty much empty. I drain it anyway.

"You want more?" Oscar says, nodding at me and then looking around for the waitress.

"No," I say, pushing it aside with the plate. "I've had more than enough. I should get going."

"What?" he says, turning back around. "Don't you want to hear my old Army stories? I can bore you to tears between innings of the Dodgers game they'll have on at Barney's Beanery in about" — he pauses to check his watch — "half an hour."

Being bored to tears by Oscar's old Army stories doesn't sound like the worst thing to do on a Sunday afternoon. Still, I'm not sure this is the smartest idea. My life is complicated enough dating a man I work with. Not sure I need to log more time with another male colleague. "It's not that," I say. "I just don't think I should go from waffles to beer."

"Don't you ever do anything that's not USDA approved?"

"You know what I'll feel like later? Like I ate too much, drank too much, and wasted way too much time."

"And that would be wrong?"

"Uh, *yeah*," I say, spotting some high ground — and moral at that — and heading for it. "Women are into self-improvement even in their downtime because there are not enough hours in the day to just *waste* them. Take today. I planned to spend my so-called downtime sleeping in, reading the papers, watching a movie, taking a nap, and taking a bath. All very restorative. Very self-improving. Even if it looks like I was doing nothing in particular."

"How is that different than watching the game over a few beers?"

"Calories, and it just *is*," I say, waving him off. "Look, why do you think shopping is women's number one leisure activity?"

"What's your source for that?"

"What's my *source*?" I say.

"I was a statistics major. We're big on data."

"You were a *statistics major*?" I say, realizing between the Army, his major, and his pet goat, I know virtually nothing about Oscar.

"Yeah, but go on," he says, nodding.

"Okay, let's go with common lore for now — women like to shop," I say. "It's all about the acquisition, about improving yourself by acquiring something, so even your so-called down-time — which doesn't exist, as I've explained — is about self-improvement. Personally, I think women would be better off if they bought stocks and real estate instead of clothes, but that's just fine-tuning the impulse. Guys, on the other hand, like to drink and hang out and eat and watch sports."

"And fuck, but you're wrong," he says, shaking his head. "Guys like to do nothing in their downtime. No agenda. Eat, watch the game. No agenda."

"The agenda is eat and watch the game," I say, choosing to ignore the fuck reference.

"No, trust me, it's about the lack of an agenda. Especially if you're with someone who has one."

"Okay, you want to go down that road?" I say, leaning forward. "The old male-female dichotomy? 'Honey, let's go pick out lawn furniture this weekend.' 'Fuck that, I'm watching the game.' Which means, depending on the power dynamics of that relationship, that no lawn furniture will be picked out *or* the woman will do it herself."

"Hey," he says, "I know plenty of couples where they would spend the day — the *day* — picking out not only lawn furniture but new paint for the bathroom, garden tools, and pricing refrigerators which they don't even *need*."

"This is why you only date twenty-eight-year-olds. Too young to pick out lawn furniture. Too young to fight back."

"Oh, they have their ways," he says, eyeing me.

I shake my head. "You're no different than Mickey Delano and the other ninety percent of the men in this town — successful powerful guys who just date down the food chain because it's so much less risky. In fact, you should use the algebra symbol — that sideways v — to describe your relationships. You're not 'dating' or 'seeing' or even 'sleeping' with someone. You're 'greater than' the woman. Guys like you are terrified to use the equal symbol."

"And you're just as scared," he says, leaning forward, his hands on the table. "You think men are the only ones with control issues? Think again."

"I don't have to think again," I say, realizing we're all but shouting, given the heads that have swiveled in our direction. I am *not* scared, and I do not have control issues. Jennifer has control issues. Patrice has control issues. I have a responsible, demanding job, weigh within five pounds of what I weighed when I graduated high school, and am seriously pondering buying a house — okay, I just thought of that, but I am. All as a single woman. "If you think I or any woman is scared," I say, leaning back in my chair, "well, how can you blame us when men have controlled women, economically, politically, even artistically, for centuries? I mean, I have history on my side."

"Yes, you do, and you also have syrup on your chin," he says, reaching across the table and wiping my chin with his fingers. "There. Now, do you really want to keep arguing about the male-female power dynamic, which is a valid topic, I'll concede, or do you want to watch a Dodgers playoff game?"

"Actually, I'm thinking of going to Saks," I say, checking my watch. I'm only half-serious, but I *could* use a new suit and a graceful — if pointed — exit after all that. Besides, it's only 2:30. I could even make it home in time for the bath, in which case my day off has turned into a twofer — shopping and relaxing.

"You'd rather go to Saks, spend all that energy trying on clothes and doing the math about whether you can/should buy another pair of two-hundred-dollar jeans or whatever you think you need than go down the block to my favorite bar in L.A. and watch the Dodgers game over a beer?"

"Well, when you put it like that," I say, realizing I may have overestimated my energy levels for a full-scale shopping assault. "But seriously, we can't just go from waffles to beer."

"I can. And you should."

I sigh, feeling myself starting to cave against my better judgment. "I'm going to feel terrible in about an hour, when all this sugar in my bloodstream starts to collapse."

"Don't women know anything?" he says, getting up and handing me my bag. "What do you think beef jerky's for?"

"So what, you were sitting there watching the game, and he just gets up and leaves?" Steven says.

"It was a little less abrupt than that," I say. Or rather I muffle, given that I have a cold washcloth draped over my face while the rest of me is submerged in the tub.

"What?"

I pull the cloth from my face. "No, he didn't just leave. Elsa or Amber, whoever he's 'seeing,' called him on his cell. Then he left."

"But before the game was over?"

"Yeah, but it was the bottom of the eighth and the Dodgers were losing, so it was hardly a big deal."

"Then why are you telling me about it?"

"Because I ate waffles and drank beer and watched a stupid baseball game when all I wanted to do was stay home and watch a movie and take a bath."

"And you blame Oscar for that?"

"I blame myself. He talked me into doing what he wanted to do and then, when he found someone else to play with, he just bolted. I feel used."

"Over waffles?" Steven snorts, and I hear the sound of crashing in the background. "Some people put years into a relationship before they figure out they've been used. I think you got off easy."

"It's the principle of the thing," I say, annoyed. "Where are you?"

"Lucky Strike. We're bowling for dollars, and I'm ahead. Come on down and try your luck."

"Thanks, I already did that today and lost," I say, slipping farther down into the tub.

"Look, it's my turn," he says, moving so the crashing sounds grow louder. "But let me leave you with this final thought."

"What, Dr. Phil?"

"Seems to me you've got enough things to work out with Charles—like why you guys can't be in the same place for more than five minutes—without throwing Oscar into the mix. Unless, of course, you're actually using Oscar to try and figure out how you really feel about Charles. I mean, in a way, it kind of makes sense. You work with Charles, you work with Oscar, so there's a kind of symmetry—"

"I'm not using Oscar to figure out what I think about Charles," I say, sitting up so fast I splash water over the side of the tub.

"If you say so."

"I do. Say so. Look, I'm just annoyed that I let my day get hijacked. That's all," I say, sinking back into the water.

Steven says something, but it's drowned out by more crashing sounds and laughter.

"Look, just go," I say. "We'll talk tomorrow."

"What? Sorry," he says, raising his voice over the noise, "but someone here thinks he can challenge the master."

"Will you *go*?" I say, practically yelling.

"You're going to regret that," I hear Steven say to waves of laughter.

I close my eyes, tempted to just click off.

"Okay, I'm back," he says. "Now, where were we?"

"Look, we'll just talk tomorrow," I say, realizing how stupid I sound. How stupid I am to get worked up about nothing.

"Look," Steven says, plowing on. "You ate waffles on a Sunday with a friend. You blew five hours and a couple thousand calories. What's the big deal? Unless you want Oscar to be more than a friend?"

"Now you do sound like Dr. Phil."

"All I'm saying is, I don't know what you're so scared of," he says. "You're in a three-year relationship with the man of your dreams. Or he was the man of your dreams. Or has the potential to be the man of your dreams. Concentrate on that. As for Oscar, God, it's not like you slept with him and then he left you for Elsa."

"Okay, okay, we can stop talking about this," I say. "I don't know why everyone keeps saying I'm scared."

"Who else says you're scared?"

"No one," I say, slipping farther into the water. "No one."

7

Bend Me, Shape Me, Any Way You Want Me

I attack Monday determined to put everything behind me. Oscar, Jennifer's wedding, the goats, Patrice and her weird call to Charles, Charles and our weird call, and God knows everything that transpired yesterday at Hugo's and Barney's Beanery. Enough of this Nick and Nora nonsense with Oscar. My life with Charles may not be perfect, but it's not going to get solved by hanging around with Oscar, who clearly has his own issues with women. With commitment. Besides, who needs a personal life? DWP. It's not just a job, it's an adventure.

Of course, the fact that the painters my landlady finally hired show up two hours late slows the implementation of my Marine Corps battle plan a bit. 8:00 A.M. the phone goes. Louise, with the news that the painters are on their way. This is never a good sign. Not with workmen and especially not with Louise, who is a die-hard lady of the canyon, one of those once stunningly beautiful women who came west to find their fortune and wound up with

Jim Morrison or Frank Zappa between their legs. Now an ex-groupie whose biggest claim to fame is actually owning a house — my rental house — in Laurel Canyon, Louise's only just become cognizant the sixties are over. Time is not her strong suit.

"Okay, but they are still planning to be here by eighty-thirty?" I say, checking my watch, coffee in hand. I've got a planning meeting scheduled at the office for 9:30 to lay the groundwork for C's Christmas party, along with the dozen or so other events we've got coming up in the next three months. It will go on for hours in any event, and if I have to push it back, it will just wind up eating the day.

"Oh, yeah," Louise says, with the kind of conviction one might expect from someone who lives in a depressing rental complex in North Hollywood and survives largely on the rent I pay her each month. "I mean, I'd drop by myself to let them in, but I've got to get out to Malibu to look at some horses and then —"

"No, no," I say quickly. The last time I left it to Louise to let workmen into the house, I came home to find everyone passed out in the living room, a bong in the middle of the floor. Like she was channeling Woody Harrelson. "No, I'll wait for them here," I say, clicking off and dialing the office. I leave a message for Caitlin that I'm running late and she needs to cancel my Monday morning conference call with Oscar and Steven to go over Jennifer's wedding, and to push the staff meeting to 10:30 just to be safe. I leave the same message for Steven, just to be safe. I ponder calling Charles, but the weirdness of our Sunday call is still fresh in my mind and I decide to wait to call him until after my staff meeting. Brief him with details of my plan for C's big gala.

I check my watch again — 8:15 — and consider my options. Not many when you're under house arrest, even with a Black-Berry and a high-speed Internet connection. Oh well. I pour another mug of coffee and head into the office, where the *Today* show's still on — muted, which is the only way I can take Matt and Katie on a daily basis — and turn the computer back on.

Two hours, three dozen e-mails, and all the trades read online later, the painters actually show. The fact that they are Louise's nephews or nephews of a friend or something, dark of hair, sunny of disposition, in their late twenties, and good-looking enough to pose for GQ only slightly ameliorates the fact that I have lost most of my morning waiting for them.

"So you're sure you're okay here on your own?" I say, my hand on the doorknob, clock ticking in my brain. I have to raise my voice over the boom box they've plunked down — like a dog spraying his territory — that's already thumping out KROQ or one of those stations I never listen to. They've been here less than thirty minutes and the house is already chaos. Canvas drop cloths everywhere. Ladders. I can only imagine the week ahead with my frat houseboy painters. Maybe I should consider moving into the Chateau.

"We're cool," Brad says — or maybe it's Steve, but anyway the lighter-haired one — poking his head out of the kitchen, one of my mugs in his hand. I notice he has already dispensed with his T-shirt and is now dressed in paint-spattered cargo pants and a set of abs every guy in town would kill for. "Have a good one," he adds, hoisting the mug in my direction.

"Yeah, okay," I say, glancing with some effort at the mug. "Well, you have my cell and office numbers if there are any problems."

I call Caitlin from the car and tell her to have everyone in the conference room at 11:00. No, 11:30, given the traffic on Sunset.

"Is this going to go into lunch now?" she asks in a tone of voice like I've just taken away her favorite dolly.

"Probably, so we'll order in."

I hear her sigh. "Fine, I'll let everyone know," she says, clicking off. I ponder calling Steven, but given the traffic, I toss the cell phone aside to concentrate on the drive. Midmorning and it's like rush hour. What is the deal? Not only is it still ragingly hot with the Santa Anas, but L.A. has turned into one big construction site.

It's either that or another location shoot for some movie. In any event, Sunset is down to two sun-glazed lanes.

It's a good forty-five minutes until I pull into the garage down on Wilshire. I grab my bag and run for the elevator before I catch myself and slow to a dogtrot. It's like that sometimes. I have to remind myself that I'm a boss, and if I'm running late, then I'm running late. No one's going to keep me after school.

"So the workmen, on a scale of one to ten?" Steven says, sliding in next to me as I race down the hall.

"Ten," I say. "If workmen are your thing."

"And they are," he says. "So will you be setting up a webcam to monitor their progress from the office?"

I shoot him a look.

"Or I can," he says. "I have a great tech guy who can set that up in no time."

I stop midstep. "You know, I miss our little chats," I say, "but we have a meeting to run in about five minutes."

"Correction, *you* have a meeting to run," he says, peeling off and heading back to his office. "I'll be in as soon as I finish my conference call with Kia."

I fly by Caitlin's desk, grabbing the fistful of messages she's holding out.

"Oscar's called twice wanting to go over the Hawker wedding," she says, following me into my office.

"Yeah, I'm sure he has," I say, tossing my bag to my desk. If I'm in no mood to talk to Charles, I'm really in no mood to talk to Oscar. Especially when we could have —*should* have —spent at least some of yesterday going over the wedding. At least we would have gotten some work done. Oh well, too late. I tell Caitlin to get everyone in the conference room, flip on my computer, and take a fast look at my e-mails. All thirty that have rolled in during the past hour. Oh, God. I scan the list quickly. The usual. Clients, sponsors. Assistants of clients and sponsors. Everyone needing something from me, and half of them marked urgent with that annoying red exclamation mark! No wonder I need five college-educated women to keep this flock of birds fed. There are also the morning e-mails from the girl gang. Rachel, still in New Zealand on a shoot. Maude, reminding me futilely, as she does every week, about yoga classes. Evelyn. No doubt some new crisis with her latest surgeon. Nothing from Charles, I see. Or Oscar for that matter. Well, he hates e-mail. Besides, no time to ponder these tea leaves.

I'm just gathering up my notes for the meeting when I hear my cell phone go. Shit. I reach into my bag and pull it out, expecting to see Oscar's number. My home phone. My home phone? It takes me a minute to realize it must be the painters. They've been working for what — I check my watch — less than an hour and a half, and already they have questions? Okay, this could really become a problem. Still, better they ask me than try to reach Louise.

"Yes," I say, clicking on.

"Whoa, you sound busy," the voice says. I take it to be Brad.

"Brad?"

"Yeah."

"Brad, is there a problem?" I say, gathering up the folder.

"Ah, no. We just need to know if you want the trim painted."

I close my eyes. Hadn't Louise gone over all this with them? They'd seemed clear about it when I left the house. Or at least they hadn't seemed unclear. "Look," I say, opening my eyes and gazing out my window at the ratty palm tree being blown to pieces in the desert winds. This is not the calming visual I need. Must get some kind of tropical beach scene for my screen saver, preferably with a light classical soundtrack. Something like my dentist has. "I thought you'd gone over this with Louise."

"Yeah, well, we did, but now that we have a chance to see it, the trim really needs painting, and we can't reach Louise."

I try to visualize the trim and whether it needs repainting. I realize I can't even recall what color it is, let alone its condition.

"Okay, just paint it," I say, opting for the shortest distance between two points. It's taken months for Louise to get these guys in. Not going to quibble over the trim. I can always just take the overruns out of my rent.

"She says paint the trim," Brad hollers, so loudly I have to hold the phone away from my ear. I feel like Cary Grant in *Mr. Bland-ings Builds His Dream House*, that scene where the contractor asks him if he wants his lintels rabbeted or unrabbeted, like anybody other than a carpenter knows what that means, but you just know whichever he chooses it's going to (1) be more expensive and (2) take much, much longer.

Caitlin appears in the doorway, her arms folded, her little face screwed into a pout.

I nod at her and turn away. "Okay, Brad, so we're good on the trim?" I say, trying to wrap this up.

"We are *so* good," he drawls, like he just got laid and is reaching for a cigarette.

"Okay, good then," I say. "So I'll —"

"Now, you want the same color?"

"As what?"

"As the old trim?"

Okay, this is way too much *Mr. Blandings*. At least for this morning. Clearly, Louise has just tubed it. I'm going to have to take over this job and run it myself. Like everything else in my life. "You know, hold off on the trim until I can look at it tonight."

"Yeah, okay, it's just that if we're going to paint the trim, we need to paint it first."

"Everyone's *waiting*!" Caitlin hisses from the door. I don't bother to turn around, just raise my hand and waggle my fingers.

"Look, I'll look at it tonight and let you know about the trim tomorrow," I say. "But for now you must have at least a full day and probably two of prepping the surface."

"'*Prepping the surface*'?" he says, sounding like he's about to laugh. "How do you know so much about painting?"

I don't, you fucking stoner, but I know enough to know a problem when I see it, and this is clearly a problem. God, Louise *would* hire a couple of potheads instead of real painters. "Look, do what you can today and we'll go over it all tomorrow," I say, trying to keep my voice upbeat, keep everyone moving.

"Yeah, okay," he says. "By the way, what's up with your neighbor?"

"My neighbor?" I say, blanking.

"Yeah, that girl next door?" he says. "She seems like she needs a lot of attention."

Oh, great, Christy's put in an appearance. "Okay, just ignore her," I say, reiterating my plan to meet with them in the morning before Brad can bring anything else to my attention. God forbid workmen should operate in the same time zone as the rest of us. They're like grade-schoolers — start at dawn, knock off in the middle of the afternoon. Before I've even started rolling my calls, they'll have finished for the day and adjourned to a bar somewhere. I swear, how does anyone with a real job get any work done on their house? It's like dealing with two different time zones.

It takes me a minute to get my head out of painting and back into work. Or about as long as the walk to the conference room. Padding down the hall with Caitlin at my heels, I can't help noticing how nicely our paint job here has held up. But then these offices are the one good thing about our brief but infamous merger with BIG three years ago — back when we were BIG-DWP PR. Or we were until Mr. Big, Doug Graydon, my old boss, got caught in Hollywood's scandal du jour, a kickback scheme involving our clients that made the business sections of all the major dailies as well as the trades. Doug quit, sold the rights to his story to one of his producer cronies, spent two years doing community service, and now lives out in Malibu, where he works as a life coach. If there's any more bullshit job than event planner, it's life coach.

But at least we got to keep Doug's swanky offices right down to the sisal carpet, halogen lights, and Aeron chairs. The day B-I-G got sandblasted off the glass front doors, replaced by E-D, was one of the biggest of my career.

I round the corner and head into the conference room, where my five student council presidents are already seated around the rosewood table. I've had this team for almost a year now, and it still takes me by surprise. *Staff.* What a concept.

"Sorry, you guys," I say, heading for a chair, deliberately choosing one that is not at the head of the table. When it comes to being a boss, I always think what Doug would have done and then do the opposite.

"No problem," says Marissa, who is the cheeriest, and neatest, of the bunch, always dressed in some designer outfit and her hair in a perfect ponytail, like the Kappa president she once was.

"Yeah, it's not like we can't use the time," Allie says, slumped in her chair, chewing on a pen. Allie's my iconoclast, always looks like she just rolled out of bed and into a leather jacket and stilettos. Actually, Allie used to be a serious partyer until she cleaned up her act and realized her talent for sniffing out the hottest scene was worth money. She's not great on details or anything written, but the girl can work a crowd like nobody's business, and her contacts are the best. If Allie says someone's going to show, they're going to show.

"Yeah, well, I apologize," I say, flipping open the folder and staring at my list. There are at least half a dozen events we need to go over, including the Kia launch for their new Spritz hybrid car, Barry Rose's annual Scrabble tournament, and the C Christmas party. C will be the biggest headache, not only because it's now become my test for keeping the account but because it's a pain for all the usual reasons C's events are a pain — the budget is nothing and they expect the moon for it. Moon being wall-to-wall A-list celebs followed by wall-to-wall coverage.

"Okay, let's take these in ascending order of difficulty," I say, opting to tackle the smaller events—the Ferragamo fall charity fashion event, the opening of the new Fred Segal hair salon, and Arianna Huffington's book party.

"Didn't we just do a book party for her?" says Jill, flipping through her notes with the kind of barely concealed impatience that reminds me of me and why she's my utility player. If something absolutely has to happen, and happen in the next five minutes, I sic Jill on it.

"Yeah, well, there's still too many Republicans, so she's written a new one," I say, turning the discussion toward a suitable venue. L'Orangerie? Too old-school. The Chateau? A cliché at this point. The downtown library? Too stiff.

"What about the Tower Bar at the Argyle?" says Maurine, our resident food and beverage liaison and the calmest of my team. With her dark hair and big eyes, she always reminds me of a graduate poetry student instead of a publicist. "It's got that great view, and since it recently opened they might even do a deal," she says.

"Sold to the highest bidder," I say. "Call them and see what they want and then take it to Arianna. Okay, Scrabble," I say, moving on, and everyone groans.

Barry Rose's annual tournament is a fixture in Hollywood. The kind of event everyone loves to hate except everyone really hates it. It's supposedly a fund-raiser for some hospital charity Barry and his wife, actually second wife, Barb, adopted, but it's mostly a way for Barb to parade around with the *Oxford English Dictionary* and throw some much needed business at their country club.

"Look, I know it's annoying, but it's a no-brainer, just the invites, the RSVP list, the gift bag—they want to do one this year—and then a few of us to work the check-in table," I say, trying to put a good face on it. "Besides, Barry's new movie looks like an Oscar contender, so people might actually turn out this year."

"Excuse me," Allie says, in mock hauteur and arching her pinkie. "But is *that* word in the *OED*?"

"Thank you, Allie," I say, nodding at her. "I needed a volunteer."

Everyone's still grumbling, so I decide to send Caitlin to get lunch. Charles always bitches that my interoffice food bills are the highest in the company, but I think it's worth it. A nice lunch, or even a basket from Clementine's bakery, keeps everyone's spirits up, and God knows we have a long, spirit-draining afternoon ahead of us.

"Call Ammo and get a bunch of Cobb salads, iced teas, and diet sodas," I say as Caitlin, all too happy to get out of the office, heads for the door, barely avoiding colliding with Steven, who's just coming in. "And get some of their chocolate chip cookies," I call after her.

"Where's Princess going so fast?" Steven says, pulling out a chair and tossing his notes to the table. "The mall?"

"To call in the lunch order," I say. "But she'll be gone for an hour, knowing her, so let's keep going."

By the time Caitlin gets back with the bulging white sacks, we're just wrapping up with Kia, with only C's Christmas party left.

"So, they're really up for this tent-down-on-Hollywood-Boulevard idea?" I say, tearing open one of the bags and dispensing the salads. "What does Oscar think?"

"He thinks it's better than going to Smashbox," Steven says, "which is about the only place where you can park a car inside, and we need room for two — the standard and deluxe models."

Allie raises her hand. "How many times do I have to say 'Avalon' to you guys? You can put an entire dealership in there, plus you get that funky old Hollywood vibe."

Steven makes a gagging sound.

"I don't think funky and old is what the client is going for," I say, aiming for diplomacy. "The car is not only a hybrid but supposedly the first 'vegan' hybrid."

"That club is *so* over, plus the promoters are assholes," Steven says. "Plus you have to use their food and beverage. Plus, plus, plus."

"I still like Smashbox," says Marissa.

"You always like Smashbox," says Jill, reaching for an iced tea.

"It's just very neat and contained and white," counters Marissa, looking wounded. "Plus their food concession is good."

"What about the courtyard of the PDC?" says Michelle. Michelle is Miss Paperwork of the team, the one who keeps track of invoices, bills, RSVP lists. Without her, we are dead, but she is not usually one for ideas.

"It's the right image," she adds. "Oscar can do his tents, but it's not like they're on a vacant lot on Hollywood Boulevard."

"That's a great idea," I say, mentally lopping the next twenty minutes off the meeting.

"It'll be more expensive," Steven warns, but I wave him off.

"Get Oscar to price it out and take it to them," I say, turning to my C notes. It's heading toward 2:00, and even Ammo's food isn't going to get us through much more of this.

"Okay, fine, but we still have to nail down host committee members," Steven says.

"Oh, shit," I say, pushing my folder aside and reaching for a cookie. I see my afternoon stretching in front of me. Better pace myself with the sugar. "Okay, for Kia, why don't we get the winners of whatever reality show will finish in October — they'll show up for anything — and Alicia Silverstone, Ed Begley Jr., and call it a day," I say, half-kidding.

"Because he's under contract to GE," Jill says.

I look at her blankly. "GE?"

"For his electric car," Steven says. "He's been with them for years. Gets an endorsement fee and the car."

"What about Jeff Goldblum?" someone suggests.

"He's a flake, plus he hits on every woman in sight," someone else says.

"Apple used him in those ads," Marissa says.

"Fuck Jeff Goldblum," says Allie. "And fuck Apple."

"What have you got against Apple?" Steven says, looking at her. "You have an iPod."

"Is anyone going to eat that?" Caitlin says, nodding at the last bit of salad.

"Come on, you guys, more names," I say, trying to keep this moving. "Think about all the vegans in town besides Alicia, and what about trying to get all the stars who already own hybrids, like Larry David?"

"No," Jill says, sounding aggravated. "All those Prius drivers have deals with Toyota. You just can't get them to endorse another hybrid."

"Wait a minute," I say, holding up my hand. "Am I totally behind here, or does every celebrity really have endorsement deals now?"

"Everyone has endorsement deals," they say in unison.

"Yeah, why drive a car, wear clothes, go on vacation, or do anything when you can get paid to do it?" Steven says. "Celebs don't like to admit it, but they take advantage of it. I mean, I'd be happy to get a hundred thousand dollars a year from Vitamin Water to tell everyone how great it is. I already drink a ton of it."

"You drink a ton of it because they're our client and it's all over the office," says Maurine matter-of-factly.

"Okay," I say, turning to Steven, "then this is a problem for Kia corporate. The host committee members should be those stars with whom they have endorsement deals, and we'll go from there."

He shrugs. "I don't think they have them nailed down yet."

"Then tell them they should," I say, trying not to sound as impatient as I feel. "We're not getting paid to do their entire marketing campaign, just their PR on this event." I check my watch. Oh, God, it's so late, and we haven't touched on the Kia gift bag and the C party, which will take forever by itself.

"Okay, we'll do the Kia host list once you get those names, and tell them to also start thinking about their gift bag, although I'm only assuming they want to do one," I say to Steven, "but now we have to move on to *C*'s Christmas party."

Everyone slumps back in their chairs. Everyone except Caitlin, who is still working on the salad.

"Why is *C* still our client?" Allie says, drumming her pen on the table. "I thought they hated us."

"They don't hate us," says Marissa. "They just don't know us," she adds, referring to Jay and Patrice.

"That's right, they just don't know us," I say, aiming for a chipper we-can-do-it tone, although God knows, I'm with Allie on this. "Now, ideas?"

We spend the next hour and a half running it down — possible dates in December; venues, probably a private home; the cosponsors lined up so far, starting with the Diamond Council, the magazine's big advertiser, and Absolut vodka, which always sponsors their parties because they sponsor practically every event in town; and finally the potential host committee members. The last category is going to be the toughest; given the magazine's neurotic sense of itself in the fashion/Hollywood pantheon — north of *InStyle* but south of *Vogue* — and given that we will have to vet everything by Jay and Patrice. The party is still three months away, but L.A. books up fast in December, and given all the nervous second-guessing the magazine goes through, there's not a minute to waste. Besides, I have to meet with Andrew and the rest of the team in New York next month, and I want to present a good proposal.

"Okay, I think that should hold us for now," I say, looking up from my notes. Everyone except for Marissa is slumped way down in their chairs.

"Does that mean we can go?" Allie says.

I look at her. "And to think I was going to make you point person on this."

"Oh, God," Allie says, pushing herself upright. "Kill me first."

"I'll do it," says Marissa. "I think it will be fun."

"Bless you, my child," I say. "And I think I speak for all of us."

Almost 6:00 and I'm back in my office gearing up for the last act of the day, rolling my calls, followed by a screening at 7:30 and then finally home by 10:00. Shit, the painters' stuff will still be there. I'll have to check all that out tonight before I meet with them in the morning. And somewhere in there I need to call Charles. Or call him back. Again. Nothing like trading calls with your boyfriend. Maybe in the car on the way to the screening.

"Caitlin, you ready?" I call out. Rolling calls is more typical of agents than publicists, and it does seem pretentious having my assistant place the call — "Hi, I have Alex Davidson calling" — but it's a habit I've gotten into, and God knows most publicists in town do it now, and if I took the time to talk to everyone as they called me during the day, I'd never get anything done.

I hear a muffled yelp that I take to be a yes. "Okay then, let's go," I say, pulling on my headset.

We go down the list; there are at least thirty calls to place, and of course only a few of them can actually take my call when I call, so then they start to double back on themselves, callers I just called now holding when they call me back. We press on like this for a good thirty minutes or so.

"I've got Patrice on line one and now Oscar on line two," Caitlin calls out.

Great. The two people I haven't called and don't particularly want to speak to are calling me. I debate telling Caitlin that I'll call back and then think better of it. Best to get this over with. "Tell Oscar to hold a second," I say, punching line one. "Patrice."

"Alec," she says in her plumy voice. "Alec, I wanted to let you know I'm in New York next week," she says, dispensing with any pleasantries, any mention of seeing each other at the wedding or her calling Charles and complaining about me.

"Ah, okay?" I say, not entirely clear why she's calling to tell me her travel plans.

"Well, I know Andrew and I are anxious to get going on the Christmas gala," she says, pronouncing it "gah-lah."

"Yes, and we are too," I say carefully. "In fact, we just had our first planning meeting on it today."

"Well, that's perfect then," she says. "Andrew and I can meet with you in New York and you can fill us in on what you have so far."

Oh, now I get it. "Ah, that would be good," I say. "But unfortunately, I can't be there that soon with everything else that's going on here this month." I may be the magazine's event publicist, but I have no plans to be in New York until the third week of October and have no intention of changing that to suit Patrice. If there's anything I've learned, it's that you set your boundaries early with clients and stick by them. It's like training a dog.

"Hmm," she says, temporarily stymied. "Well, I know Andrew does want something on it soon," she says, trying to turn her annoyance into some kind of demand.

"Yes, I know he does," I say evenly. "And I'll have it for him when I'm there that third week in October — as I planned. I hope you'll be able to join us for that."

I hear her sniff on the line. "Well, why don't we have lunch later this week, say Thursday, and you can walk me through the preliminaries now? That way I can run them by Andrew when I'm in New York next week."

Yes, that would suit you, wouldn't it? "Honestly, I'm booked this week," I say, not even bothering to look at my calendar. "And frankly, we're still pulling stuff together on this end. Anything I could tell you now would be virtually meaningless."

"'*Meaningless*'?" she says, sounding startled. "That doesn't sound very reassuring."

I am tempted to tell her that even though she's never done an event like this before, I have, but I think better of it. In my experience there are two kinds of clients — those who hire you, trust you as a professional — or as professional as it gets in the event planning business — let you do your job, and go home happy. Then there are those clients who hire you less for the event itself than for the chance to work out on you — second-guess your every decision, your every move — because they think making your life a living hell is all part of the fee. C was pretty much in this latter category before Patrice came on board; now I can see they are heading for the red zone.

"Look, why don't you plan to join Andrew and me at our October meeting? That way you can see how this comes together from the ground up," I say briskly. "Meantime, call me when you get back next week and let's get together then." Before Patrice can say anything more, I hang up and punch up Oscar.

"Sorry, I haven't had a chance to get back to you about the wedding," I say, heading right for professional collegiality and intending to stay there. "Any feedback yet?"

"Alex, Alex, Alex, why are you avoiding me?" he says in an exaggeratedly aggrieved voice.

"I'm not avoiding you. I spent most of yesterday with you," I blurt out without thinking. Shit. This is exactly where I did not want to go.

"Yeah, and then you just disappeared. Like your mother had died or something."

"I did not 'disappear,'" I say, trying to back out of this hole and managing only to dig myself in deeper. "We both *left*. The Dodgers were losing, you had somewhere to be and so did I. End of discussion."

"End of discussion? When did you get to be so *Robert's Rules of Order*?"

Out of the corner of my eye, I see Caitlin stick her head in the door. "Look, I've still got calls to return here, so let's touch base about the wedding when one of us hears from them," I say, looking up as Caitlin hands me a note saying that the screening has just been canceled, some problem with the print or something. "Besides, I've a screening to get to tonight, so let's talk later in the week and I'll fill you in on C's Christmas party. Patrice is already on my case about it, and it's not even October."

"Fine, play it that way," Oscar says, and I can't tell if he's actually annoyed or just cutting his losses. "I still say you're avoiding me. Call me when you can."

"Sounds like a plan," I say, clicking off. I'm about to punch up the next call when I realize Caitlin is still standing by my desk.

"What?" I say, looking at her.

"Nothing," she says with a small smile, turning for the door. "Nothing at all."

8

On Second Thought,
That Actually Hurts

It takes us another thirty minutes or so to finish all the calls.

"Okay, I'm leaving unless there's something else," Caitlin says, sticking her head in the door.

"No, fine, go ahead," I say, deep into returning e-mails now. Without the screening, I can really clear my desk tonight. Maybe even pick up my dry cleaning and swing by Whole Foods and get real food for a change. Actually spend an evening at home.

I'm just dispatching the last of the e-mails when one from Charles flashes on the screen, marked NYC. What? Where is he that he's e-mailing instead of calling me? Especially since we haven't spoken all day. Must be from his BlackBerry. I click it open.

In a late screening, will call u later, but spoke to PF. U need to be in New York next week. :) C

It takes me less than a second to put this together. That bitch. Patrice must have called Charles right after she and I spoke, not thirty minutes ago. I can*not* believe that she went around me to him. *Again.* And worse, that he bought her song and dance. Shit. I reach for the phone and punch up Charles's cell. Of course, I get his voice mail. I hang up without leaving a message and call his BlackBerry. Same thing. Damn it. Now what? I hate getting bad news, and I especially hate it when I have to wait to get the bad news straightened out. Still, this is going to require some finesse on my part. Obviously I can stick with my plan and *not* go to New York next week, but that means Charles will run the first meeting on the party with Andrew and Patrice while I'll wind up even more sidelined — and behind the eight ball — than I am now.

On the other hand, if I go, I have to rearrange my whole schedule, rush to put something down on paper about this blasted party before we even have it figured out. Worst of all, it means I'll have totally caved in to Patrice — and she'll know it — which is absolutely what I do not, *should* not, do. Completely sends the wrong signal and opens a whole can of worms with her thinking we jump to her every move. Shit. Shit. Shit.

I check my watch. Just about 7:00. What screening is going on at 10:00 P.M. in New York? And how can he have spoken to Patrice just a half hour ago and be incommunicado now? Wait, unless Patrice actually called him a couple hours ago, arranged the whole meeting in New York with him, and then called me and played all innocent. The more I think about it, the more that makes sense. Great. Maybe there's a reason Patrice has climbed to the top of the food chain at *C*, not that there's all that much food per se involved at a fashion magazine. Maybe she's more of a handful than I bargained for.

I stare out my window. Just after 7:00 P.M. and it's still searingly bright — and probably still 100 degrees outside — but the roar of the rush-hour traffic on Wilshire is plainly audible. Well, I can either sit here like an idiot and wait for Charles to get out of whatever screening he's in and call me so we can spend the rest of the night arguing about it, or I can leave, do my errands, go home, and we can argue there. Suddenly the idea of dry cleaning, grocery shopping, followed by arguing with Charles in the midst of my house filled with all the painters' stuff is too mind-numbing to contemplate. Besides, it's way too passive.

I turn back to the computer and type my reply.

Heading out now. Let's talk tomorrow. NYC could be tricky.

I read it over a couple of times, delete it, and retype it.

Spoke to PF earlier. NYC is fine, timing tough. Talk tomorrow, heading out to screening now.

I read it again — much better, nonconfrontational and yet assertive — and press SEND. I scroll back up my e-mails to Maude's weekly yoga update, click it open, and type my reply:

Hey, screening canceled, see you in 30!!

--------- 🕰 ---------

I'm halfway to the yoga institute in West Hollywood when I realize I have nothing to wear to class. I used to keep a bag of gym clothes in the car, back when I had a semblance of a regular workout schedule, but I quit hauling that around months ago when I realized it was just making me feel guilty. What now? The institute has a lost-and-found that always has T-shirts and shorts in it, although that's kind of gross, even if they do wash them. Wait, I have my earthquake kit in the trunk, if I can remember what I shoved in there. A bottle of water. Aspirin. Band-Aids. Tampax. A roll of TP. An energy bar, I think, unless I dug that out and ate it one night after working some long food-free event. I did stick some clothing in there, although I can't remember what exactly. Oh well, whatever it is, I'm wearing it. I only hope it wasn't my old ripped leggings that I used to use for painting.

It's almost 7:30 when I pull into the parking lot, and of course, two minutes before class, all six of the spaces are filled with the usual schizophrenic cars — glossy BMWs and SUVs belonging to the students and then rotting-on-their-hubs Toyotas, which are the teachers'. There's a lone cherry red VW Beetle holding the middle ground. I bump my Audi over the potholed alley to the lot behind the nail salon a few doors down and pull in between the Mercedes S class and the Range Rover parked there. More inner-directed yoga students.

I jump out of the car, pop the trunk, and fish out my old back-pack. I reach inside past the Band-Aid can, the aspirin bottle, the TP roll, and the flask — a flask? what was I thinking? — to the clothes wadded at the bottom. Great. My earthquake wardrobe, such as it is, is the paint leggings and an old, ripped LIFE GUARD T-shirt from the college summer I worked the pool at Helen and Jack's country club. Obviously perfect for the next 5.8 shaker. Oh well. No time to worry about it now. I shove the leggings and the T-shirt into my handbag, and the flask for good measure, slam the trunk, and make a dash for the studio.

They're already chanting when I slip in through the back door and head for the changing room. Haven't been here for almost a year, and nothing's changed. Still the same ratty carpet, the old high school lockers spray-painted blue, the scuffed wooden bench, and a few hooks and hangers. Two laminated signs are thumbtacked to the wall. Oh, these are new. One has a picture of a cell phone with a red line through it, and the other reads IN RESPECT TO YOUR FELLOW STUDENTS, NO PERFUMES, SCENTED OILS, LOTIONS, OR SCENTS OF ANY KIND ARE TO BE WORN.

Oh, please. No perfume? How about a sign banning all those

weird guys in their yoga diapers who just reek of curry and B.O.? Talk about no respect for your fellow students. I toss my bag to the bench and kick off my mules. They're still chanting down the hall, although I'm more than happy to miss the opening sing-along. Way too out there for me. It's only amusing if you keep your eyes open while everyone else's are closed and watch all the Brentwood yentas in their manicures and breast-lifts warble the Hindu "Kumbaya."

I'm just pulling on the leggings — man, these look worse than I remember, with all the paint spatters and the holes at the knees — when Maude pokes her head around the corner. "Alex, oh my God, you're here," she says, shoving her glasses up her nose. "I can't believe it."

"Hey, honey," I say, leaning forward, one leg still half in and half out of the legging, to give her a fast hug. I've known Maude more than a year and have yet to see her anywhere outside this studio. But with her short red hair and helpful student-teacher mien, fostered by years of volunteering at the institute, Maude is one of the only remotely normal people here. "Yeah, I sent you an e-mail," I say, turning back to wrestle with the leggings. "A screening got canceled, and I realized it had been too long since I'd taken Marla's level two class."

"Oh no," she says, looking stricken. "Didn't you read the e-mails I sent? Marla doesn't teach it on Mondays anymore."

"Oh well," I say, hopping to get the leggings adjusted and managing to rip the kneeholes even more. "Who is teaching it?"

"Sarah, and it's a level three now."

"Oh, *shit*." I don't scare easy, but a level III Iyengar class will flush the sheep from the goats in a hurry, especially when taught by a yoga Nazi like Sarah. Not only am I not a level III student — well, okay, I can hold my own in forward bends, but no way in back bends — but Sarah is one of the toughest teachers. Which in Iyengar terms puts her just shy of a cult leader. I had her twice when she was subbing for Marla last summer, and after two classes — the last one where she told me if I wasn't willing to push myself to do the poses *correctly*, I should pursue my practice at home — I never came back.

"Maybe I should just bag it," I say, staring at my ripped and paint-spattered leggings. "I'm already late."

"No, no, you'll be fine," Maude says, running her hands nervously through her baby-fine hair. "But hurry, because she hates latecomers."

The class has finished chanting, and everyone is scrambling for mats and straps when Maude and I slip in. Only a few heads swivel in our direction. I recognize a couple of faces — like the guy who owns that cool antiques shop on La Cienega, and the frizzy-haired woman who teaches something at UCLA, and isn't that Annette Bening in the corner? — but true to form, no one says hello or even cracks a smile.

"What are we doing today?" I whisper to Maude, trying to work out the Iyengar calendar in my head. What was it, first week of the month is standing poses, second is forward bends, and third is back bends, or is it back bends before forward bends? God knows how I ever thought yoga was relaxing, with all the rules.

"Back bends," she says, heading into the crowd.

Oh, great. I should just turn around and walk out now. While I'm still ambulatory. Last time I took a back bends class, I pulled my lower back so badly it took two weeks before I stopped limping around like a marionette. Besides, if I leave now, I still can make the dry cleaner's, Whole Foods, and be home having a drink in less than an hour. I'm seriously considering slipping out the door when I hear a voice at my back.

"Haven't seen you in a while." I turn. Sarah, with her whippet body all but quivering in her black leggings and turquoise tank top inscribed with some Hindu script. Probably says something like YOGIS DO IT ON THEIR HEADS.

"Yeah," I say, forcing a smile. "Well, I'm out of town a lot."

"Apparently," she says, eyeing my outfit. "Well, I hope you're up for a good workout tonight."

The thing about yoga is that if you have any flexibility at all, you can pretty much force yourself into a pose, at least for a second, before you fall out of it. You can fool yourself, or more important, fool those around you, that you can actually *do* the pose. Holding it is another matter. So even though it's been almost nine months since I've set foot in the Iyengar House of Torture, I manage to get through almost all the poses Sarah dishes out. Shoulder stand, headstand. I'm *so* there. Even the scary ones — camel, wheel, pushing yourself up into a back bend with your hands on blocks, which to my mind only makes it harder, not easier — I manage to get through. Maybe this wasn't as hard as I remembered it.

"I can't believe you haven't been here for so long," Maude says when we're partnering on one of the last poses, a killer seated pose with your body pressed against the wall, one leg twisted under you and the other pulled up the back that I have never done and that might be called octopus for all I know.

"Yeah, it's not too bad," I breathe, reaching around my back with my left arm to grab my left ankle and winch my calf up my back while Maude pushes on my hip and shoulder. Got it. Got it. Got it. Okay, don't have it. I fall out of the pose, thumping to the floor so a few heads turn in my direction. "Yeah," I say, struggling to sit up. "I totally forgot how fun this is."

"Okay, switch," Sarah calls out, clapping her hands like a balletomane.

"Gladly," I say, crawling to my knees and turning to help Maude twist herself into the pose.

I'm just pushing Maude's right shoulder to square up with her left hip as she grabs her ankle when Sarah bustles over. "Partners watch," she calls out to the class, pushing my hands out of the way. "Like *this*," she says as everyone swarms to watch her adjust Maude's back into what looks exactly like what I was just doing.

"I'm seeing too many of you do this," she says, moving her hands imperceptibly. Everyone nods sagely.

"Got it now?" she says, turning to me.

I nod. "Yeah, thanks," I say. "That really helps."

"She's only trying to help," Maude says when Sarah moves off.

"Please, she could have been on the staff at Abu Ghraib," I say, pushing on Maude's back again.

"You know, yoga isn't about ego," she says, breathing hard. "It's about letting go of ego."

"That must be why India is such a major player on the world scene," I say, pushing harder. "All that lack of ego."

"Okay, come out of the pose," Sarah calls out, and Maude and I collapse onto the floor. Actually, I collapse. Maude unwraps herself.

"Thanks, that felt great," she says, rolling her shoulder blades in their sockets.

I smile weakly, pawing at the small of my back. "Yeah, great."

"You okay?" she says, eyeing me.

"Oh, sure," I say, pushing to my feet. A searing pain flashes across my lower back. Oh, *fuck*. Just when I thought I might get away unscathed. Instead of going home like a normal person and *resting*, I had to be a maniac and spend my free night doing killer yoga.

Sarah calls out the next pose, and everyone rushes for blocks and straps. I check the clock on the wall. 8:45. This has to be the last pose. I look around. Everyone is sitting on the floor, tying their legs together with the straps and then lying backward on the blocks. Okay, at least we're lying down. I can probably get through this and then head home for a long drink and a hot bath, my bloodstream a soothing cocktail of alcohol and ibuprofen.

I'm just settling back on my block—oh, God, maybe this wasn't such a good idea after all—when a cell phone burbles down the hall. So much for the precious sign.

"Apparently someone forgot," Sarah says, accusingly gazing

around the room. No one says anything, and after a few more rings, the phone falls silent.

"Okay, settle into this and breathe," Sarah says, reaching for the light switch and dimming the room. In the murk, I hear everyone breathing gently, like babies in their cribs. Apparently, I'm the only one lying on a bed of nails. I reach under my back and try to adjust my block, but there is no way to get comfortable with a three-by-five block of unvarnished pine digging into your sacrum.

I shift around some more, trying to get comfortable or at least somewhere where the pain is less intense, when suddenly the woman lying next to me rolls off her block and begins plucking angrily at the strap around her thighs. Sarah rushes over to her. There is a whispered exchange before the woman grabs her block and strap and stalks off to the far side of the room. What's her problem? I'm the one with rigor mortis setting in.

I turn back and stare at the ceiling, trying to think calm thoughts, get some calming visual, but I'm too distracted by the cracks in the ceiling, which seem to be mirroring the spasms in my back. I'm just trying to figure out how many more seconds I can stay in this pose without crumpling to the floor when I feel warm breath on my cheek. I turn so quickly that I lose my balance, slip off my block.

"Did you miss the signs?" Sarah hisses, her face close to mine.

"It wasn't my phone," I say, struggling to sit up and realizing the pain in my back makes this impossible.

"Perfume!" she hisses again. "It's so polluting."

"I'm not wearing any," I say, propping myself up on my hands, my legs still strapped together. I look like either a seal or a paraplegic, but in any event, I'm fragrance-free. Well, other than some Magie Noire body lotion I smeared on my neck at 7:00 A.M., but that was more than twelve hours ago. What does that woman have, the nose of a coonhound?

"Next time, come *clean*," Sarah says, standing now, towering over me. "Or you'll be asked to leave."

She moves to the front of the room, leaving me sprawled on the floor. I feel the blood rise to my cheeks. Between the pain in my back and the public dressing-down, there is not going to be a "next time." I roll onto my side and attempt to sit up. Another shot of pain flashes across my back, but I force myself upright and begin to unpeel the strap from my legs.

"Okay, slide off your straps and blocks, and go into corpse pose where you are," Sarah says. Everyone rolls effortlessly off their blocks. They'd probably run off a cliff if she told them to. I stagger to my feet, trying not to wince. Everyone is flat on the floor, eyes closed. Sarah ignores me as I step over the bodies to put away my block and strap and then limp toward the door. As I step over Maude, she opens her eyes and shoots me a concerned what-gives? look. I shake my head and keep moving. If I stop now, I'm dead.

I limp down the hall to the changing room. The thought of pulling off my leggings and getting back into my skirt is too painful to contemplate. I reach in my bag for the bottle of water and fish around for my silver pill case. I shake out two ibuprofen like a junkie jonesing for a fix and take a swig of water. I just want to be home, in the tub with a glass of wine. I'm pondering taking a small hit from the flask, just to get a jump on things, when I hear the low hum of voices down the hall. Oh no, they're already chanting the ending song. I shove my feet into my mules, grab my bag, and hobble out the door.

I'm halfway across the parking lot, the fluorescent lights casting an eerie glow across the darkened cars, when the door to the institute flies open behind me. Students spill out in a murmur of voices, laughter, and the chirping sound of car alarms being deactivated. I start to hobble faster. What if the freaky woman with the nose of a coonhound is parked in the Mercedes next to me?

My mule catches on one of the potholes in the dark, and I stumble. *Oww.* I fish around in my bag for my keys. Okay, got them. Okay, almost there. I'm just putting the key in the car door lock when my cell goes. No time to answer. I pull open the door, toss my bag to the passenger seat, and crawl in after it, slamming the door behind me. The heat of the day still trapped in the car envelopes me. Oh, thank God. I press my back against the warm leather seat and close my eyes. I swear I will stop trying to do everything, be everywhere, vet everything, if only I can wake up tomorrow not in pain. I promise I will even be nice to Patrice.

I sit there for a few minutes, until the pain starts to ebb. Okay, I think I can face the drive home now. I reach forward to start the car — oops, there's a twinge — when the cell burbles again. Oh, Christ. I reach over — *oww!* — and fish it out of my bag. Charles.

"Hey," I say, trying not to mew.

"Hey," he says. "Where've you been? I've been BlackBerrying you for the past hour."

"Yeah, I went to yoga. The screening got canceled."

"Oh yeah? I thought you hated yoga."

I'm tempted to come clean. I do hate yoga, or at least the S & M way it's taught here. But given how weird it's been between us lately, how off our calls have been, I'm in no mood to concede anything. "No," I say, easing back in the seat. "I love it. Why do you think I hate it?"

"Because it practically crippled you last time."

"Well, I *love* it," I say. "I just don't get to do it often enough."

"Okay, great," he says. "I stand corrected. So anyway, put New York on your schedule for next week. Patrice will be in town, and we can get a jump on meeting with her and Andrew about the party."

"Yeah, I spoke to Patrice," I say, bending forward to rest my forehead on the steering wheel. "It's not ideal from my end and I told her so, but —"

"Look, you can work it out," he says, cutting me off. "I just think it's a chance to get everyone face-to-face on this, and the sooner the better."

Normally I'd put up a fight. List all the reasons why caving in to Patrice is so wrong on so many levels, how it will just send us down a road of pain. But given that I'm already well along a road of pain, I let it go.

"Yeah, okay." I sigh. "Just let me look at my calendar tomorrow before you go setting this in stone."

"Sure," he says. "Are you okay? You sound tired or something."

"No, I'm totally fine," I say, pushing my head off the steering wheel. Out of the corner of my eye, I see someone heading across the parking lot. Oh no. It's the coonhound heading right for the Mercedes. Oh, *shit*. I do not want a face-to-face with this woman, and given the look on her face, she's spoiling for a fight. A *Zen* fight. I'm tempted to hang up, start the car, and just bolt. But given the precarious state of my back, any sudden moves are out of the question. "Hang on a sec," I say to Charles. I switch the phone to my left hand, drop the emergency brake with my right, and carefully slide down across it — ow, ow, *ow!* — my head now in the passenger seat. "Yeah, okay," I say, whispering now.

"Look, where are you?" Charles says.

"In the car. I just dropped my water bottle."

"Why are you whispering?"

"I'm not," I say, raising my voice a little. Outside I hear the coonhound's car alarm chirp. In another minute she'll be gone and I can get the hell out of here before my back totally freezes up.

"You sound like you're in a cave," Charles says.

"No, I'm just reaching under the seat for the water," I say, trying to keep my voice casual. Suddenly, a light flashes outside the passenger window above me. Oh no, she's getting in the *Range Rover*, not the Mercedes. There's no way she won't see me now. With its height, she'll have a perfect sight line into the front seat of my car.

Okay, pain or no pain, there's only so much humiliation I'm willing to take. "Let me call you back," I say to Charles, clicking off and tossing the cell phone to the floor. I'm just pushing myself upright when I hear a rap on the passenger window. I look up. The coonhound, looking like the woman in Grant Wood's *American Gothic*. Minus pitchfork. I smile wanly, screw up all my strength, and reach across the car floor, grab the phone, and push myself up back into the driver's seat in one move. The pain is beyond intense. I lean back in the seat and push the button for the passenger window down.

"Yes?" I say.

"You know that sign is up for a reason," she says, not bothering to introduce herself.

"Polluting?" I say.

"What?" she says angrily.

"Polluting," I say, again louder. "It's all so"—I pause—"polluting."

"It's *distracting*," she says. "And dangerous. Some of us get migraines."

Migraines. From a whiff of perfume. I know everyone in L.A. is the star of their own movie, but this chick is in a class by herself. I'm tempted to ask her how the hell she gets through a day without coming into contact with any migraine-inducing scents. I mean, a red carpet event, the cleaning aisle of the grocery store, Saks cosmetic department—any of them would just lay her out. And I'd happily buy a ticket.

"Perhaps you should study privately," I say. "That might be safer. For everyone."

She looks as if I'd struck her. "There are such things as *rules*, you know. And *courtesy*."

Courtesy. Now there's a concept. I can't think of the last act of courtesy or, God forbid, kindness I've seen. Not in L.A. It's all about needs and wants and power and who has the ability to make who do what. No one has the time, or the inclination, to think of others.

"You know, you're right," I say, reaching for the window button and pushing it up. "Apology accepted."

9

Toddlin' Town

"You know you're making a big mistake?"

"Keep it up, big guy, and you're going to seriously make me cry. Besides, I'm about to board," I say, hustling down the jetway.

Actually *hustle* isn't exactly it, given that I've got my handbag, a bulging tote bag holding my laptop, the trades, and my raincoat, which is already spilling toward the floor in one hand, my cell in the other, trying to talk to Oscar while boarding American's 8:00 A.M. flight to JFK—which is now a 9:00 A.M. flight due to some delay somewhere—for my big lunch meeting with C magazine. I'm exhausted, up since 5:30, forced to abandon my time zone plan, and the capper, I have a lower back that after a week of hot baths, a massage, plenty of sauvignon blanc, and whatever over-the-counter painkillers I can get my hands on remains on the disabled list.

"You're saying my advice is too little, too late?" Oscar says.

"Look," I say, dropping my voice, as I pull up behind a Paris

Hilton wannabe in a plaid miniskirt, headphones, and holding a pink pet carrier idling in the line in front of me. "It's a command performance, and there's nothing you or I can do about it. My only hope is to act like my schedule opened up so I could make the meeting. *Surprise!* Here I am!"

"Yeah, well, good luck faking out Patrice with that act, although Charlie boy is under no such illusions, since he insisted you show," Oscar says, raising his voice. In the background I hear shouting and metal crashing.

"Where are you, the fights?" I say, hiking my bags higher up on my shoulder, trying not to wince at the pain. My long day is looking even longer if this line doesn't get moving.

"At the fish market with Hot Fat. We're getting salmon for that two-hundred-person dinner tonight."

"Wild or farm-raised?"

"Please, it's some fund-raiser for Schwarzenegger. They can all eat red dye number two for all I care."

"That's the spirit," I say, peering down the line in front of me. Suddenly the idea of spending the morning with Oscar and Hot Fat wading through slimy chum picking out salmon seems a lot more fun than getting on this plane and having lunch at Michael's tomorrow with the inmates at C. Whatever weirdness I felt toward Oscar after spending that Sunday with him has long since departed, overtaken by work, back pain, and pragmatism. A girl can be on the outs with only so many people at one time. Besides, given the all-hands-on-deck mode that happens at the agency every fall, when we're juggling more than a dozen events and parties, there's no time to waste being pissed at anyone. Except the clients, of course.

"Well, my offer still stands," Oscar says. "I can catch the red-eye tonight and make the lunch meeting tomorrow."

"That's sweet, but no, I don't want this meeting to look any more official than it has to," I say as the line starts to inch forward.

The wannabe and I shuffle around the curve of the jetway and come to a stop. My coat slithers toward the floor. I feel like joining it. Up ahead I spot an empty wheelchair. How pathetic would it be if I just went and collapsed in it?

"Well, think it over and I'll call you later," he says. "My offer is good until tonight."

I hang up, and am just trying to check my messages while attempting to pluck my coat from the floor when the wannabe turns and burbles in my direction.

"I'm sorry?" I say.

"This sucks," she says, scowling and sticking her pinkie in her mouth. "I mean, what do they think, like, we have all day?"

"We're cargo," I say, hoisting my bags and my coat higher on my shoulder. The wheelchair is looking better by the minute.

"What?" she says, pulling the headphones from her ears.

"I said, we're *cargo*. We could be handicapped for all they care. As long as we're not carrying a gun. Or scissors. Or nail scissors."

The wannabe looks startled. "You can carry a gun if you're handicapped? Don't they think terrorists could, like, figure that out? I mean, they could just get wheelchairs or crutches or something."

And they say global warming will be our undoing.

"Yeah, I know," I say, nodding at the wheelchair up ahead. "Like, who was in that chair a minute ago? I didn't see them, did you?"

"Oh, my *god*!" she says, swiveling to look first at the chair and then back at me.

I'm about to say something more, if only for the amusement factor, which, granted, is on the pulling-wings-from-a-fly level, when the line starts to move again and the wannabe and I surge forward.

"Boarding passes?" the flight attendant says, holding out her hand.

"I just showed it to the gate agent," I say, juggling my bags and coat. Of course, that was ten minutes ago. I could have morphed into a terrorist since then.

She smiles a bored smile, her hand still extended. I fumble in my bag — where is the damn thing? — and produce the stub. "Thank you," she says, glancing at it and waving me on. I stumble toward 8A, a packhorse heading for its stall.

By the time we break through the clouds over Manhattan, rain has begun spattering the window. I gaze down on my former hometown. In the rain, it looks gray, dismal, worn. I lived here for ten years, but after five years in L.A., five autumns of season-defying searing heat and light, I feel like I'm landing in a foreign country where I no longer speak the language.

And it's not just the weather but all the little things you don't even notice anymore. Like how having the right handbag — the Fendi baguette! the Mombasa! anything from Marc Jacobs! — is so important in New York, but in L.A., you can carry any kind of nice bag because your car — a hybrid! a Hummer! a BMWer! — is what people really notice about you. Or how it's more important to have killer abs in L.A. than anything from, say, the Chanel sample sale. How New York is about looking like you have money even if you don't but L.A. is about having money and looking like you don't.

The pilot clicks on — "Folks, we're sorry about our delay today, and we sure do want to thank you for your patience" — and everyone lurches into that stupor-to-frenzy mode, tossing blankets to the floor, shoving magazines into the seat pockets, retrieving jackets and coats from the overhead bins. I lean my head against the window, gaze out at the rain, and try to get my head into New York mode. That back-to-school feeling, the dark that comes earlier and earlier, the town houses glowing like jack-o'-lanterns in the dusk. A collective turning inward.

If I loved that so much, how did I wind up living in the desert, working at a job where I have no routine, where I'm hardly ever home or even in the same place twice unless you count all the red carpets I've worked?

Maybe if I was still in my twenties, it would seem exotic. God knows, people who don't work in Hollywood think that everyone who does has it made. Or needs their head examined. In either case, that we have no business complaining about it. I mean, even I used to think being a Hollywood publicist was one big fat road trip, all expenses paid, the prize for having survived one failed marriage and seven years in a fluorescent-lit cubicle editing magazine copy about postpartum depression, low-fat apple pies, and ten ways to make him beg for more.

But now that I'm starting to lose my balance on that teeter-totter of being in my thirties, sliding closer to my forties than my twenties, the idea of living my life on planes, on my cell, on the red carpet—on *call* 24/7—seems more like penance than like reward. A running away rather than a running toward. If only I had time to stop and figure it out.

"Folks, we should have you on the ground in just a few minutes."

I turn from the window and check my watch. Heading toward 3:00 P.M. I pull out the stem and spiral forward. For once, I don't feel sorry to lose three hours. I'm ready for evening, for rest. To stop.

"Ma'am, please put your seat back up, we're about to land."

I look up, fatigue hurtling toward annoyance. I *know* I need to bring my seat back up. But the flight attendant looks even more tired than I do in her ill-fitting, stained uniform, wisps of gray-blond hair escaping from the clip at the base of her neck. She wears a beige carpal tunnel bandage on her wrist and hand. I don't need to tell her about living life in multiple time zones.

"Thank you," I say, reaching to adjust my seat back. "Thanks."

The town car lurches out of the Midtown Tunnel, and rain lashes the windows. God, it's really coming down. Noah might appreciate this deluge, but I can hardly see.

"I'm going up Third unless you got a better idea," the driver says.

"No, that's fine," I say, leaning back in the seat. It's freezing in here, and the air smells heavily of leather and cigarette smoke. Between that, the fact that my back has started to ache again, and this lurching, splashing commute in rush-hour traffic, I feel slightly nauseated. I had planned to go directly to the office, meet Charles there for a preliminary staff meeting before the lunch tomorrow. But given the rain, the delay in my flight, and now my back, I've bagged that idea. Charles was already in the meeting when I reached the office after we landed — "I'll let him know you called," Taryn said — so now I'm just heading for his apartment. *Our* apartment when I'm in town.

Actually, it's his family's apartment. They've owned it for years. His father used it as a pied-à-terre when he was commuting up to New York from D.C., where his law firm is based and where Charles grew up. It's one of those stately two-bedrooms in a town house in the East Sixties with twelve-foot ceilings, wood floors, and a fireplace. There's lots of leather, plaid, even a baby grand. I swear Ralph Lauren decorated it, but Charles says it's been like that for years. Even when he moved in, five years ago, took over paying the maintenance in exchange for rent, he didn't change a thing. His parents still come up occasionally, his sister too, staying in the other bedroom. I used to think if Charles and I got married, it would become our apartment, although we might want to rethink some of that plaid. God knows, in this real estate market, there are plenty of women who would marry Charles just to get their hands on it. Guys too.

Now I don't think too much about that. At least not lately. Actually, given I can go weeks between visits to the city, the apartment seems more like a really great boutique hotel. There's always something in the fridge and a fully stocked bar, and a year ago his dad had the fireplace converted to gas, so it's about a five-minute journey to Edith Whartonville if you're of a mind. A tumbler of scotch, the fire blazing, standing at the bow front window, a finger parting the sage green velvet curtains to gaze down on the masses, such as they are in the East Sixties.

Actually, given how nauseated I feel at the moment, dry land, a fire, and a glass of scotch sound fucking perfect.

"What's the address again?" the driver says, pulling off Third and heading west toward the park.

"It's another block down," I say, giving him the address. We bounce across Lex, then Park. Finally we pull over. "You live here?" he says, turning around and handing me the clipboard with the company receipt for me to sign.

"No; well, yes, sort of. It belongs to a friend of mine," I say, signing it and handing it back.

"A good friend, I hope, for your sake," he says, reaching for the clipboard.

"So do I."

By the time I stagger in the front door with my luggage and bags, I'm pretty much soaked. Not much good having packed an umbrella when it's at the bottom of my suitcase. I shake the worst of the rain off, drop my coat in the entry-hall closet, and head straight for the bedroom. Actually, I head for the bathroom medicine chest. I down two ibuprofen, wipe the mascara from under my eyes, clip my hair, which is now in complete drowned-rat mode, up — just deal with that in the morning — and call Charles on my cell.

"Hey, I'm just wrapping up the meeting," he says when Taryn puts me through to the conference room.

"Yeah, sorry I missed it," I say, heading for my bag and fishing out my yoga pants and my black turtleneck sweater. After almost twelve hours in transit, I have got to lie down if my back is going to be in workable shape tomorrow. "So do you want to just meet here? I'm pretty wiped from the flight and all the rain."

"Uh, sure," he says. "Although I had reservations for us at Babbo."

Oh, God. Under normal circumstances, I'd be more than happy to dine with the Italian deity, but the thought of pulling myself together, doing something with my hair, and heading back out in the rain is more than I can bear. Especially when I need to be at my brightest tomorrow. "Can I take a rain check?" I say, kicking off my shoes. "I'm sorry."

"Yeah, sure," he says quickly. "Give me an hour to wrap up here and I'll be home."

It must be the flight or the rain or, okay, the finger of scotch, but the minute I finally get comfortable — which turns out to be flat on my back on the living room floor in front of the fire, my legs propped at a ninety-degree angle on the ottoman, Headline News on mute, I pretty much pass out. The next thing I know, I hear a key in the front door.

"I'm in here," I say, or rather croak, too tired to sit up.

"*Alex?* I didn't know you were here."

I scrabble around on the floor. Oh, God. It's Charles's mother, Catherine, dripping all over the Oriental in her Burberry raincoat.

"Oh, Mrs. Evers," I say, pushing stiffly to my knees. "Charles didn't tell me you were coming by."

"That's because he doesn't know," she says, glancing at me, the ottoman, and the glass of scotch. "Are you all right?"

"Yes, yes, I'm fine," I say, struggling to my feet, trying not to wince. "Actually, no, I pulled a muscle in my back. I was just trying to rest it after the flight." I might be able to lie to her son, but Mrs. Evers has the practiced eye of a full-time mother.

"Oh, I am sorry," she says, dropping her bags and unbuttoning her coat. "Can I get you anything? An aspirin? Or something stronger?" she adds, eyeing the scotch glass again.

"No, I've taken something. I just need to rest it, which is pretty much impossible when you're traveling across the country," I say, clicking off the TV and gathering up the glass. My little Whartonian respite is now clearly at an end. "So, Charles should be here any minute," I add. "He didn't tell me you would be here. I would have—"

"Well, I didn't know myself until just a few minutes ago," she says, heading down the hall for the other bedroom. "I flew up this morning for a board meeting, but with all this rain, flights are backed up," she calls out. "So I just decided to spend the night and go home in the morning."

"Great, well, it's nice to see you again," I call after her. Yeah, great. I like Catherine. The few times I've seen her. She's one of those spare, elegant mothers, in flats and heirloom diamonds and with a firm sense of her own exalted place within the family walls. I suppose I would be too if I was in her Ferragamos. Still, trying to live up to my own mother's expectations was enough to cure me of the need to curry favor with older women. Besides, I don't think she's ever gotten over the fact that her only son is divorced and that, no matter how long he and I have been together, I fall under the heading of "girlfriend"—dispensable, disposable, fungible—rather than "wife."

I'm just deciding what's the best course of action, retreat for Charles's bedroom or stand my ground in the living room—in all the time we've been together, I've never once spent a night in this apartment with his parents here—when I hear the front door open. Oh, thank God; Charles is home.

There's a commotion in the hallway, the sound of laughter. "Careful on the marble," I hear Charles say, "it's slippery." Then a woman's voice. What the hell? I turn.

"Hullo, Alec." Patrice in jeans, pearls, short black trench, and triumphant smile.

"So, Patrice, what part of England is your family from?" Catherine says, forking a gingered scallop from the take-out container. "We have very good friends in Kent."

Oh yes, Patrice, please tell us all about your bloody family. The four of us are in the living room, fire blazing, Chinese take-out, beer bottles scattered on the coffee table. I'm hunkered on the sofa, pillows wedged behind my back, nursing a Heineken, a container of fried rice, and a good case of what-the-hell-is-going-on? I can be as social as the next guy when it comes to clients — I mean, I'm a professional publicist, which means I can talk to anybody about anything — but two hours of chitchat with Patrice *about* Patrice — not the magazine, not the party, not anything work-related — is not what I had in mind when I asked Charles to meet me here for a quiet evening in.

"High Wycombe," Patrice purrs from her perch on the ottoman, where she's poking at her container of tofu and pea pods. "It's out toward Windsor. Very dull suburbia, I'm afraid, despite the allure of the castle."

Oh, God. I don't know how much more of this I can take. It's bad enough I had to get dragged to New York to accommodate her schedule, but now Patrice seems to be going for more than "demanding client." Much more, unless I miss my guess. Supposedly she has some rich boyfriend back in London, some banker or something, but given her appearance at Jennifer's wedding with Mickey and now the unctuous way she's cozying up to Catherine and how very, *very* comfortable she seems in this apartment, any boyfriend would seem to be irrelevant.

I look over at Charles in the wing chair, scraping the bottom of his General Ming's beef container, oblivious to the game being played under his nose. "Mother, I think the last time I saw Windsor was that trip we took when I was in high school," he says.

Hello, am I even *here*? What is it about the English? Put one in a room of otherwise jaded Americans, and it's like the queen landed. I toss my container to the coffee table and check my watch. Heading toward 9:00. "I'm going to check in with the office in L.A.," I say, pushing gingerly off the couch and heading for the bedroom.

"Oh, sure," Charles says, looking at me slightly startled. As if he suddenly remembered I was here. "Whatever you need."

I head to the bedroom, close the door, fish my cell out of my bag. I check my messages and then call the office. Caitlin's already gone for the day. Some doctor's appointment or something. I get my messages from reception and then ask them to put me through to Steven.

"I thought you might have drowned," he says when he picks up. "I'm watching the Weather Channel, and there's severe weather warnings all over New York."

"And that doesn't include the severe turbulence I'm encountering inside," I say, crawling onto the bed.

"Ooh, do tell."

I lay it out—the rain, my back, Catherine's arrival, and then how Patrice finagled her way into tagging along.

"That bitch is there now, eating Chinese food and cozying up to your boyfriend?"

"I wouldn't say 'eating,' actually. And she's doing much more cozying up to the mother than to the boyfriend."

"Oh, really," he says, and I can tell he's mulling this over. "Well, my real question is, what the fuck is Charles thinking?"

"I think he thinks he's just being nice to the client," I say, trying to decide how upset I am and with whom exactly.

"He can't be that stupid," he says. "You can read Patrice a mile away. Everyone is on to her. Except for Andrew, of course, who decided to give her a real job. Let's see, she can't book and she can't write. Great. Let's make her the entertainment editor!"

"Yeah, well, I think Charles just sees her as 'the client' and goes into his work mode, where he's just very into being the savvy publicist who has the clients in the palm of his hand."

"Careful there, girlfriend," Steven says. "You don't want to get your villains mixed up."

"I'm not," I say, suddenly reaching for my tote bag and fishing out my laptop. Google, my old pal. "I know exactly who I'm dealing with."

⏰

"What?"

"Nothing."

"Tell me."

"It's nothing."

It's after eleven, and Charles and I are in bed debriefing each other about the evening. I prefer to do my debriefing with the lights out—much easier to dissemble to loved ones when they can't read your face. Besides, between my back and his mother in the next room, any jump-your-bones sex is out.

"Seriously, just tell me."

"If you can't figure it out, I'm not going to tell you."

There's a rustle as Charles rolls over and turns on the light.

"Don't," I say, shielding my eyes. "Seriously, let's just forget it. I'm tired and in pain and we've got a long day tomorrow."

"Okay, okay," Charles says, dimming the light. "Look, I'll work on your back, but you have to tell me what's eating you."

"Oh, please, how can you not *know*?" I say, rocketing upright and immediately regretting it. "Ow, ow," I say, tipping to my side.

"Look, you're in no position to argue," he says, propping himself on his elbow and starting to massage my lower back.

"Stop talking," I say, my face all but muffled by the pillow. "The patient needs rest and quiet."

"Liar," he says, his hands working harder now.

"No, it's fine right where you are."

"I said 'liar,' not 'lower.' You're mad that I brought Patrice here."

"If you know so much, why even ask?"

He sighs and rolls onto his back. "Look, she was at the staff meeting, I said I was meeting you, and she asked if she could come along, as a way for all of us to get together before the meeting tomorrow. It sounded like a good idea at the time. Look, I didn't know you were in so much pain. I would never have done it if I'd known."

"Wait, are you apologizing?" I say, rolling to my side.

"Don't push your luck," he says, turning toward me and tracing the outline of my cheek with his fingers.

"Don't push yours," I say, grabbing his fingers and wrapping my hand around his. "I have to be able to walk tomorrow, and right now that's still debatable."

"Okay, okay," he says, propping himself back up. "Roll over and I'll keep working on your back."

"Let's see," I say, focusing on my watch. "Patrice was here almost two hours. I could ask for punitive damages, but I'll keep it to pain and suffering. Thirty minutes of massage should do it."

⏰

Which is why I hit Michael's the next day not only pain-free for the first time in days but also in a good mood. Nothing like the BF admitting the error of his ways to put a spring in your step.

I practically bound out of the taxi and into ground zero for the publishing world. Talk about your playgrounds for the rich and famous. The Royaltons may come and go, but Michael's lives on, although for a power commissary it's pretty plain by normal Manhattan standards. All that white, and those chairs that are a notch above porch furniture. But then Michael McCarty did get his start in Santa Monica before he set his sights on New York.

Besides, you're not supposed to see the restaurant. Like you're not supposed to see the setting of a ring. It's about witnessing the power brokers holding court in their booths. Like a publishing zoo. Here's Barry Diller in one corner. Graydon in another. In between come lesser mortals. Other Condé Nast bigwigs. Time Warner. Celebs du jour proving their intellectual credentials by lunching with fill-in-the-blank editor. If Page Six ever runs out of items, they can just print the lunch reservation list here.

"Whose idea was it to come here?" I say to Charles as we're threading our way between the tables. "It seems a little overkill for this kind of meeting."

"Andrew's," he says, nodding at the tables as we pass. "He always likes to meet here."

I catch sight of them up ahead, and my springing step slows to a walk. Even publicists have game faces. If any meeting merits it, this is one. After all, the account, annoying as it is, does hang in the balance. I scan the opposing team. The troika—Andrew, Patrice, and Amanda, the VP of marketing—already assembled and dressed to kill. In L.A., it's lunch at Orso's or the Grill, a meeting of the jeans-clad, with the exception of agents, with the real power exchange to occur at the valet stand. Porsche beats SUV. And so on. Here, it's at the table. Clothes are the weapons, the tail feathers by which pecking order is established. Charles is one notch below bespoke in his Hugo Boss three-button. But my Piazza black suit barely gets me in the door. It's a risk I'm willing to take.

Andrew's armor is some glossy Italian suit, so luminous it seems lit from within. Breathtaking, but out of sync with his ruddy, high-color face, the Irish genes that peek through, giving him the look of a man slightly ill at ease, out of step with his surroundings. Patrice is in no such danger. In a black turtleneck, suede skirt the color of butter, and a pair of black patent leather boots, she's totally of a piece. Right down to the ponytail, to show she doesn't care all that much.

Amanda does. And too much. She's one of those rock-hard New York women in their early fifties. Divorced, probably childless. Dark hair so short it hurts to look at it. White shirt as starched as a bedsheet. Gold bracelets that rattle like spinnaker lines. Probably hasn't been with a man in years. Women like her run New York. Kill off the Andrews, and the magazines will still grind out each month. Lose the Amandas, and you're in real trouble. If I have any business with anyone at this table, it's her.

We round a six-top of blondes chattering over iced teas, probably a division of *InStyle*, or some socialites celebrating something, and pull up. "Hey there," I hear behind me. I turn. Oh, God. Jay Reed is also here, and dressed in his gold-buttoned blazer and L.A. sunburn. He flew in for this? If I'd known it was going to be C's version of a war room, I would have brought Steven and Oscar. Let the games begin.

"Hey, Andrew," Charles says, reaching out to shake hands. "Patrice, Amanda. Jay, how's L.A. treating you?"

There's a few minutes of this. Andrew half rises out of his chair to acknowledge me, his hand fluttering up to his tie, his eyes darting left and right, before he sinks back down. I can never get over how a guy this powerful, this well clad, can look so damn scared. Or maybe I'm just confusing fear with misanthropy.

Charles and I take the two open seats. I'm next to Jay, and he's next to Patrice. Already I'm down a point not being next to Amanda. No chance for a private word. A whispered exchange. A cutting through the clutter. I have the venue, you have the sponsors. Thanks, we'll be in touch. Now it will be family style. Everyone chiming in. Vetting my proposals. Endless, pointless debate, until Andrew, and it will be Andrew, brings it to a close. Even before we start, I'm betting we get nothing settled today. I reach for the water glass and brace for pleasantries. I don't have to wait long.

"Alec, how are you feeling today?" Patrice asks, craning her head around Charles.

I tell her fine, never better, and thanks for asking, shooting Charles a look—Catherine must have said something about my palsied back last night when I was phoning Steven—but he's already talking to Amanda across the table, something about her Hamptons rental.

"Fine," I say again, taking the menu from the waiter. "You know how it is in yoga. One day you feel muscles you never knew you had, the next day, you can do handsprings."

Patrice smiles, reaching a pencil arm for her water glass. "I am so *bad*. I have to get into that American habit of working out now that I live in L.A. You'll have to tell me all the right gyms and things to join when we get back."

I smile and nod. Her new best friend.

"I joined a gym," Jay pipes, snapping a breadstick. "The Equation Gym in West Hollywood."

"I've been there," I say. "It's a great facility, if you can handle the crowd. All the 'beautiful' people."

"No kidding," Jay says, practically bouncing in his seat. "It's hard enough concentrating on my workout without all the eye candy around."

And to think they get an issue out each month.

I pretend to study the menu. Eating is the least of my concerns. It's up to me to bring this meeting to order. Timing is everything.

"So, Andrew," I say, raising my voice a little, putting my menu aside. "How's the December issue looking? I'm hearing you have Charlize for the cover?"

Andrew says something I can barely make out. But it's enough to cause Amanda to break off speaking to Charles. Her radar is on her boss now. Neither of us is fast enough.

"Charlize is an option for us," Patrice says, leaning forward.

"They're screening the movie for us on Thursday. We'll decide after that."

Andrew smiles nervously, adjusting his tie, murmurs something about sophomore slump, Oscar curse. Amanda nods. Well, it's not her call. But I am stunned. It's incredibly late to still be deciding the December cover, and worse, C has a shot at Charlize but they're holding out to see if the movie's any good? I can't believe PMK or whoever reps her now is going along with that. Not with *Vogue* and *InStyle* happy to take her off their hands. Something isn't right. Either C's committed to Charlize — with both the studio and her publicity agency assuming it's a lock — and it will be an earthquake if they bail, or Patrice is lying. Either way, it's a problem.

"Well, I was going to say, if you had the cover, we could start there in discussing the guest list," I say.

"We'll have to talk about that," Patrice says, leaning back to study her menu, her territory firmly established now. "We're rethinking the whole C cover concept."

"Not a model?" I say. You don't blow your December cover with a model. January, but not December.

"Britney," Jay says, waving his breadstick. "I've got first dibs on interviewing her."

I shoot Amanda a look. Her face is unreadable, but we both know this is insane — the timing, the indecision. Charlize is the answer. Britney is death. Over. Cold. Wrong. Wrong for the magazine and really wrong for hosting an A-list party. On the other hand, an Oscar winner with another shot at Oscar will be on the meet-and-greet campaign the minute the film opens. A big magazine party is right up her alley. More important, the studio's. With Charlize, we have the world. The list becomes one of dreams. Not that we won't have to work it. Limos, hair and makeup. Gifts. The usual graft/arm-twisting/pleading. But with the Diamond Council as the lead sponsor, that won't be too much of a problem.

Where is Lucienne anyway? Six-foot-tall bottle blonde in her late fifties, still married to her first husband, amazingly, she dispenses diamonds for the council with the touch of a career ambassador. Too bad her title is so vulgar: Celebrity Relations.

"Lucienne?" I say, arching my eyebrows at Amanda.

"London," she says. "She's back next week, and I'll meet with her then."

The waiter rolls up, and everyone bows their heads behind the menus. At least here it's just like L.A. Fish, water, fish, water, fish, water. Greens all around. Except for Jay, who orders the lamb chops. "And I'll have the fettuccine with mussels and cream sauce," says Patrice, smiling, handing the waiter her menu. "And the cream of tomato soup."

Yes, cream sauce for the bulimic. Google, the little engine that could.

Andrew says something again that I can't hear. Amanda's head turns like a radar dish. That's what I want in my next life. An interpreter. So I only have to murmur and flinch and my needs are met.

"Perhaps we can start there," she says, turning to the rest of us. "If we go with the third Thursday in December," she adds, pulling out her BlackBerry and scrolling down. "What are our venue options?"

And we're off. Or I am. Trotting out my list of places that Steven, Oscar, and I hammered out. There are the usual hotels, restaurants. A few off-the-wall spots. The center courtyard of LACMA. The Getty. Even Disney Hall is available for the right price. Maybe even the cathedral, for all I know. God knows, the church could use the money.

"I heard they hold high school proms at the Getty now," Amanda says, rattling her bracelets.

"They do," I say, "but not in December."

"I think our list of private venues is actually stronger," Charles says, coming alive now that I'm firmly in the lead. He may have been a prick to insist on my attending this confab, but his instincts in the room are fabulous. "Alex and her team have found a few virgins. Homes that have never been rented before."

Actually, I did come up with a good list. Or rather Oscar did, since that's technically his job. I've arranged them by neighborhood — Bel Air, Beverly Hills, Trousdale, Hancock Park, Sunset Plaza, and Los Feliz. Pick your style: old money, new money, funky, arty, retro, moderne, and just plain vulgar.

"What about something near the ocean?" Jay says. He would. He's lived in L.A. for two months now, and his concept of it is still a cross between Miami and Phoenix, when San Francisco can be closer to the truth. Like how every out-of-towner used to flock to the Mondrian, all those billowing white curtains and bleached floors. One endless beach house on the Sunset Strip, tucked in among the coffee bars and tattoo parlors populated by tongue-pierced club crawlers. As if. That's New Yorkers for you. Think they know L.A. No good trying to talk them out of it. They just think you're running for cover in Sodom-by-the-Sea.

Before I can shoot Jay's idea down, the waiters roll up with salads, and everyone leans back as the plates, mounded high with what looks like grass cuttings, are presented. All except for Patrice, who ordered the cream of tomato soup.

"I wish I could eat like you," Amanda says, her fork poised over the cuttings. I'm surprised. Why lob her that softball pitch? If I had to guess, Amanda is just as ripped about Patrice as I am. If my job is harder, hers is harder times twelve. But then again, with Andrew on hand, it pays to play nicely with others.

"It's just my metabolism," Patrice says, lifting a spoon to her mouth. "Mummy always said I burned it off."

Yeah, in the loo.

Andrew spears his greens, says something.

"Do you have any shots of the houses?" Amanda interprets.

"Not with me, but we have JPEGs that I can forward to you," I say, adding that, personally, I think the Trousdale house offers the best of what they need. Style, seclusion, a pool with a large deck and yard. And the neighborhood is just outside the Beverly Hills city limits, so there's much less hassle with permits, parking.

Amanda and Andrew nod. I talk on. Picking up speed, rhythm as I go. Everyone is nodding now. It's like winning at poker; the table starts to slide in my direction. Jay keeps burbling, but even Patrice quiets down. She'll be trouble later. But for now, with her boss at her side, she's a quiet little cobra. Smiling. Collaborative. Charlize and the cover was her power card, and she played it, and now she's letting me have my time.

The cuttings consumed, the plates are whisked away, replaced with larger plates with the perfect poached fish, the size of a pack of playing cards. Jay's chops arrive, the size of walnuts. Still, probably bigger than his balls. Patrice's fettuccine is a bowl of gold ribbons topped by mussel McNuggets. She smiles, inhaling. I picture a good half hour in the ladies' room back at the office, the one off the mail room, where she won't be so noticed.

I press on, making my case. It always boils down to the same four things at this stage — date and venue, theme, sponsors, and the beginnings of the list. Of these, we need to hammer out only the first two today. And after an hour, we're pretty close. The Trousdale house, pending review of the JPEGs, on the third Thursday in December. We even have the beginnings of a theme, a black-and-white party, an homage to Truman Capote's fabled gathering at the Plaza Hotel. This was Andrew's idea. And a good one. The rest of it — the other sponsors, the problems with the budget, the colors, the flowers, the candles, the furniture, and the list — will come soon enough.

"What about the gift bag?" Jay says, wiping his plate with a piece of bread.

The gift bag. The prize at the bottom of the Cracker Jack box. Someone should write a dissertation on this icon. "The Meaning of Swag: Then and Now." Thirty years ago, I made party favors for Amy's sixth birthday. Paper dolls I meticulously cut out after school for five days running. Each with two outfits. I left them blank, for the girls to color themselves. I put them in envelopes with each child's name written in my best handwriting. In the frenzy of the party, Helen forgot all about them and sent each girl home with an extra piece of cake. It drove Amy to tears when she discovered her birthday cake had been gutted for others. I never cried. Just took the dolls. Stored them in my desk, vowing to color them all myself. A whole family of dolls. Later, home during college one summer, I found them while cleaning out my desk for a yard sale. Paper fossils, still in their shells. The tiny white shapes, as uniform as gingerbread men. Valentines to a different time. Even then I couldn't bear to throw them away.

Now gift bags are an end unto themselves. It takes a shopping cart to hold all the graft, the bulging bags, the presenter boxes at awards shows, huge as trunks. I like free stuff as much as the next guy, but if there's meaning here other than marketing and greed, I've yet to find it.

"Maybe we should keep the bag simple," Jay says, smirking, pleased with himself. "Diamond studs and a copy of the magazine?"

Everyone smiles. We have work ahead of us.

10

Workmen's Comp

"You want to know what I think?"

"No."

"I think you should tell your landlady that every day the painters are still there you're going to withhold a day's rent."

"You want to know what I think?"

"No, but you're going to tell me anyway?"

"That you've never had to deal with painters."

Pushing 10:00 A.M. on Wednesday, and I'm home, on the phone with Steven. I'm home, because the week after New York, which is, more to the point, *two* weeks since Brad and Steve took over my house, I'm spending another morning waiting for them to show. Actually, I'm only waiting for Brad. Steve disappeared somewhere after the first week. Off on another job. Or moved back east. Or back in with his girlfriend. Whatever it is that happens to workmen who just wander off jobs, never to be seen again.

Now I'm down to Brad. At least he shows. About three hours after he says he's going to. Which means I've spent every morning since I've gotten back from New York working from home until Brad and his abs wander in and I am sprung.

"Of course I've dealt with painters." Steven snorts. "How could you forget Manuel?"

"Oh, right, cruising the Dunn-Edwards paint store was one of your more inspired dating schemes," I say, one eye cocked on the TV as I toggle among Matt and Katie, *GMA*, and *Good Day L.A.*, all on mute. Depending on your client base, this actually counts as work.

"At least he repainted the upstairs bath before we broke up."

"'Broke up' is such a cute euphemism," I say, turning from the TV to my computer and my BlackBerry to check my e-mails. And they wonder why publicists have ADD. "Why can't you just say 'before we got sick of screwing each other'? So much more honest."

"Because a girl has her pride."

"Well, I no longer do. I'd do anything to get this guy here," I say, clicking off the BlackBerry and checking my watch. I have less than half an hour before I'm to meet Oscar at his office. Today is our day to play tour guide for Patrice and Jay—guided walk-throughs of every one of the possible venues for C's Christmas party. Talk about a time suck.

Actually, it's a command performance, and Oscar's even more pissed about it than I am. Usually when planning events, we give clients two or three venue proposals. *At most.* JPEGed photos with square footage detailed, entrances marked, et cetera, and budget breakdowns including catering, parking, permits, security. But for whatever reasons, Andrew and the rest of the C team have insisted on proposals for all *six* houses Oscar found. And they couldn't just go with our recommendations and a fast visit to the most likely site—the Trousdale house. No, thanks to Patrice, who insisted on walk-throughs of all six houses before signing off, we have a field trip in our future. It had taken Oscar more than a week to get them all lined up, and as payback, he insisted I come along. God knows, hitting six houses from Bel Air to Los Feliz will take most of the day. And the capper is, we have our walk-through this evening with Kia at the PDC.

"Look," Steven says, "if Brad doesn't show soon, you should just bail. Serves him right."

Given my day, I'd sooner bail on Patrice. "If Brad doesn't show soon, Oscar's just going to have to deal with Patrice on his own," I say, reaching for the remote to turn up the TV. Matt's interviewing some Hilary Duff wannabe, or maybe it is Hilary Duff, about her latest movie. Gotta keep these blondies straight. If you lose track, it's almost impossible to catch up.

Matt's just asking her about her latest boyfriend when I hear voices outside. "Great, I think he's finally here," I say, clicking off the TV. Definitely a male voice somewhere. "Okay, look, I'll call you from the road, but if we miss each other, Oscar and I will meet you and the Kia guys at the PDC at five-thirty."

I grab my bag and head into the hallway. Through the frosted-glass door, I see the shadowy blur of Brad on his cell phone. Apparently the guy can call everyone but me, and after I've left him about a million messages?

"Hey, traffic bad again?" I say, yanking open the door. I could kill him, but I keep my voice happy, happy. Workmen are like bears, I've realized. Move at their own pace, eat everything not nailed down, leave trash everywhere. But mostly, you can't show fear or especially anger, or they will kill you where you stand.

"Ah, no, man," Brad says, clicking off and shoving the phone in his jeans. "I got tied up at this other job," he says, heading into the kitchen, dropping his backpack to the counter and reaching for the coffeemaker. Sure, dude, help yourself.

" 'Other job'?" I say, handing him a mug.

"Yeah, I was over at your neighbor's."

"My neighbor's?" I've been cooling my heels here for more than two hours and he's at one of my neighbors'?

"Yeah, that actress chick, Christy? She wanted me to price out painting her bedroom."

"You were at *Christy's* this morning?" In the two years I've had the pleasure of living next door to Ms. Former Sitcom Star turned *American Idol* hopeful, I've never actually *met* Christy. I've heard her talking on her cell on the deck, singing on her deck, fighting with some guy on her deck. I've even seen her nude on her deck during the wee morning hours after one of her especially exuberant parties. But never actually *met* her. Brad is here, what, all of two weeks? and now he's spending the morning over there?

"Yeah," he says, breaking into a grin. "She left me a note on the truck last night, asking me to come by this morning and look at her bedroom walls."

Oh, great. I'm late for work because of *Christy*.

"But I don't think she really wants any painting done," he says, shaking his head. "I think she just needs a lot of attention."

"You got that right," I say briskly. No point in going down this road. No time either. "Well, you're here now, and I've actually got to run this morning," I say, dumping the last of my coffee in the sink and putting the mug in the dishwasher. I turn and practically collide with Brad's T-shirted pecs as he reaches past me for the sugar.

"Sorry."

"Sorry," I say, ducking under his arm. Maybe Christy isn't the only one who needs attention.

"Yeah, well, I'll stick around tonight to make up for the time over there."

"Whatever," I say, grabbing my bag and my jacket. "Or just come early tomorrow. By the way, do you think you'll be done by the end of the week? Louise was asking me."

"Yeah, should be," he says, raising his T-shirt and scratching his abs.

Oh, God, there they are again. Maybe Oscar has the right idea. Date down the food chain. No muss, no fuss. Okay, what am I saying? I have to get out of here.

"Okay, great," I say, fleeing for the door. "End of the week is good."

By the time I make it down Laurel Canyon to Oscar's office, a converted bungalow just off Melrose, I'm a good fifteen minutes late. At least I don't see Patrice's Jaguar or Jay's Mustang when I pull in the driveway.

"Unless you have to pee, just get right in the hearse," Oscar says, coming out the front door and waving me toward the Jeep.

"Yeah, sorry," I say, grabbing my bag. "My painter showed up late again."

"You want me to run that job for you?" he says, climbing into the driver's side. "First thing I'll do is fire that guy and get you a real painter."

"Oh, Rhett, you would do that for me?" I say, aping a bad southern accent as I slide in next to him.

He shoots me a look. "I'm just offering my services as a project manager, Scarlett."

"Well, next time, I'll seriously consider it," I say, buckling my seat belt. "Speaking of that, I'm letting you run this dog and pony show today. I think Patrice just lives to disagree with me. By the way, where are they?"

"Patrice is meeting us at the first house, but she may have to take off. Something about a screening. Jay will hook up with us later."

"Oh, great, and after they insisted we set this up."

"After *I* set it up," he says, pulling out of the drive.

"After *you* set it up," I say, leaning back in the seat. Outside it's a gorgeous fall day for once. Perfect for a road trip. Away from the office. From painters. From Patrice. "What do you say we bag it and just go to Santa Barbara?" I say suddenly. "Have lunch at this great outdoor restaurant I know."

He looks over at me. His face is unreadable behind his sunglasses. "Don't tempt me," he says, pulling into traffic.

Patrice's Jaguar — leased and one of those it's-really-a-Ford-they-couldn't-give-away — is already in the drive when we pull up to the Bel Air house. It's a 1970s ranch, west of Roscomare and closer to the 405 than one might like, but it's got a great open floor plan and a fabulous view from the backyard.

"I see Her Ladyship is here," I say.

"Now, now, points will be deducted for not playing well with others," Oscar says, pulling in behind the Jag. He puts the car in park and looks over at me. "On the count of three?"

Before Oscar can even ring the bell, Patrice opens the door. She's in her usual over-the-top New York regalia — a black pencil skirt, three-inch heels, some fur thing around her neck, and a huge satchel of Day-Glo orange suede. In New York, you wouldn't look twice. In the glare of the desert sun, she looks garish, brittle, like an extra in a Gilbert and Sullivan musical.

"Hullo, Oscar, Alec," she says, reaching forward and bussing us each on our cheeks, dousing us in a wave of perfume.

"Hey," I say, sneezing.

"So, what do you think?" Oscar says, shielding his eyes to gaze at the house. Like a lot of the newer houses in the hills, it's pretty hideous from the road. Nondescript white stucco, right on the street. Still, what you're getting is the Bel Air address and the killer view out back.

"Well, to be quite honest, I'm a little shocked," she says, pumping her English accent hard. "This isn't the message we want the magazine to send."

"Really?" I say, reaching in my bag for the specs. "I know it's a little west —"

"First, is this even Bel Air?" she says, waving across the street. "I mean, it's not even gated."

"Look, L.A. is not the Hamptons West," I start to say, but Oscar cuts me off.

"Patrice, we're here because you wanted to see it," he says evenly, his face still unreadable behind his shades. "It was not our recommended site."

"Well, when you said 'Bel Air,' I was thinking of an *estate* with —" Patrice sputters.

"Fine, let's move on," Oscar says, turning toward the cars and beeping his car alarm. "The next one is just down the road."

Maybe it's Patrice's off-with-their-heads attitude. Or maybe I'm finally trying to do what everyone else seems to be doing these days — elevate passive-aggressiveness to an art form. "I'd like to see this as long as we're here," I say. They both look at me. "It might work for another party," I say, shrugging.

Oscar looks at Patrice. "Might as well," he says.

She shakes her head, muttering something about her screening later. "I'll meet you at the Beverly Hills one in, say" — she pauses to check the massive Cartier on her wrist — "fifteen?"

We both nod and watch her head down the walk, her heels clicking on the concrete. *Buh-bye.*

"Okay, one down, five to go," I say when she's out of earshot.

"Cheer up, baby," Oscar says, grabbing me by the shoulders and steering me toward the door. "We can always quit."

"*You* can quit," I say, letting him propel me across the threshold. "I can only get fired."

"Well, if she fires you, she's firing me," he says. "We're a package deal on this. I already told Chuckie boy that if they replace you, I'm walking."

"You did?" I say, startled. When did this conversation take place? And why didn't I know about it? "When was this?" I say, trying to sound more casual than I feel. Why would Charles be talking to Oscar about contingency plans? God, if Patrice is going behind my back and complaining to Charles already . . . Okay, don't go down that road. At least not today. Not when I have hours of Patrice hand-holding ahead of me.

"I don't know, it was earlier," Oscar says, heading down the hall. "Back when the whole C account was still up in the air."

"It's *still* up in the air," I say, reluctant to let this go.

"Alex," he says, turning to me and pulling his shades off for the first time. He squints in the light, and his eyes look tired. Tired but kind. "It's just a party. And I say that as a professional event planner."

"Okay, okay," I say, holding up my hands. I may have a compulsive terrier's attitude toward my career, running frantically across any and all lawns to catch whatever balls are tossed in my general direction, but even I know when it's time to stop yapping frantically. Actually, forget the terrier analogy; most women I know are like that, jumping up at a moment's notice to rush off and do things, because most of us are convinced that if we don't do them, things will *not get done.*

We round a corner to the living room. It's a sea of shag carpeting, white rough-sided paneling, sliding glass doors. Very *Jetsons* meet *The Brady Bunch.* The whole place needs a serious renovation, but the view is spectacular. And the back lawn could hold two hundred easy.

"Hey, didn't you run a *Details* party here once?" I say, opening the patio door and stepping out onto the pool deck.

"Oh yeah, we did," Oscar says, following me outside. "But they *are* shag carpeting. That whole metrosexual vibe. I think we served mini-cheeseburgers and malt beer in cans."

"That was a good party," I say, turning from the view to flip through the other house specs. Given Patrice's reaction here, our lineup does not look good. Three out of the six are ranches, and only one is gated. "I got to tell you," I say, "if she hates this house,

I don't think she's going to like any of the rest of them except maybe the Hancock Park one, but you said there were problems with that one."

"Yeah, the neighbors," he says, gazing out across the pool. "Make it tough pulling the permits for a party." He turns. "You through kicking the tires?"

"Yeah," I say, shoving the specs into my bag. "Let's go find Goldilocks."

I'm right. The rest of the day, or seeing the three remaining houses Patrice has time to see, is right out of "Goldilocks and the Three Bears." They're all *too* something. There's a tense moment after the Sunset Plaza house, one of those fabulous bachelor pads a mile up from the Strip that she declared "too masculine and in a very clichéd way," when Oscar points out that if the magazine's party budget had room for an estate, we would have procured an estate.

"It doesn't have to be an *estate*," she says, crossing her arms and frowning. "It just should be architecturally significant."

I look at Oscar. She's kidding, right? With their budget?

"Okay, what did you have in mind?" he says slowly. "Craftsman, Paul Williams, or Neutra?"

Patrice mulls this over. "Neutra's something of a cliché at this point, but I don't see the others working with the magazine's image."

"We can get a Neutra," Oscar says. "But it will be in Silverlake or Winnetka."

Patrice scowls. She doesn't have the faintest idea where these neighborhoods are. Well, L.A.'s a big city, and unlike New York, there are no boroughs to keep everything organized. Manhattan *good*, Staten Island *bad*.

"Winnetka's in the Valley, and Silverlake is over toward Dodger Stadium," I say finally.

"*Ohmigod*," she says, flinging her suede bag in exasperation. "I can't believe seventy-five thousand dollars isn't enough for a national magazine to throw a party in this city without going to the Valley or a Mexican neighborhood."

Oh, where to begin? She doesn't get that Silverlake is totally hip, has been that way for about ten years now, and she really doesn't get that her precious seventy-five thou doesn't get you in the door. In fact, that's what a studio will spend on the catering alone for a premiere. A *small* premiere. Editorial is always the cheapest date on the block. In New York, *C* may be up there with the gods in terms of style and cachet, but in Hollywood, style and cachet don't count for shit. Not without the cash to back them up.

"Look, we've got more houses to see," I say, rushing to plug this hole in the dam. Not only does Oscar look like he's about to deck her — so much for his little "it's only a party" speech — but if we start wrangling over the budget now, we'll never get out of this driveway. "Your budget is what it is," I say. "I went over this with Amanda again this week, and there's no give. All the houses we're showing you fit within that budget."

Patrice scowls more deeply and checks her watch. If I have to guess, I'd say she'll bolt, even if her screening isn't until later. Clearly she's not a girl used to hearing the word *no*. I can only imagine the next two months working with her. Every detail of this party is going to be scrutinized like it's a line item in an Arab-Israeli treaty. Flowers, invites, the list. Belvedere or Grey Goose. Evian or Fiji. Freesia or fig-scented. Hip-hop or Benny Carter. White vinyl or black leather.

A cell burbles, and we all cock our heads. Like mothers listening for their child's cry. "It's me," I say, pulling my phone from my bag and checking the number. Caitlin. "Yeah," I say, clicking on.

"Jay Reed's on the line. He says he can't find you guys."

That's because we didn't drop bread crumbs. "Put him on," I say.

"Hey," he says, sounding breathless. "I'm on Doheny, but where is Schuyler? I've been driving for ages and can't find it," he says.

I turn to Oscar and mouth "Jay's lost." Oscar shakes his head. "It's the other Doheny," I say, launching into directions. "You're on Doheny *Drive*, and it's off Doheny *Road*. Uh-uh. Yeah, I know. It *is* confusing," I say. Out of the corner of my eye, I watch Patrice turn and march toward her car.

"Oh, my God, look at all this wood. You never expect to see that in L.A., do you?"

We're on the last house — the Hancock Park one, another one-story but bigger, more private, and gated — where Jay, dressed in jeans, T-shirt, blazer, and backward baseball cap, is doing the play-by-play. Patrice has long since bolted. "What do you think this is?" he says, running his hand over the paneling in the dining room. "Cherry?"

"Uh, I think whatever it is, it's been put in by the new owners," Oscar says, scanning his BlackBerry. It's after 4:30 and Jay's pup-pyish enthusiasms notwithstanding, Oscar and I need to wrap this up. We're both exhausted, having skipped lunch, and now we have less than an hour before we're due at the Design Center for the walk-through with Kia.

We both move away from Jay and hit our cells. I call Caitlin and then Steven, who's already at the PDC with Marissa, Michelle, and Oscar's team.

"Hey," Steven says when I reach him, "I'm marking out where the cars will go with masking tape. Or do you think that's too déclassé?"

"For Kia?" I say.

"Hey, they're dropping three hundred grand on this thing," he says. "I don't want them to feel like they're being insulted."

"Isn't it the Japanese who read insults into everything?" I say, scanning my BlackBerry. "I thought Koreans were like the Irish. Much more laid-back."

"Have you *had* any Korean barbecue?" Steven says. "It's a fantastic sui generis culture. Foodwise anyway."

"Speaking of that, are we all set with the catering?"

Steven snorts. "Don't you talk to Oscar about anything except the C party?" he says. "Yes, the catering is set. Oscar's lined up three chefs out of Koreatown. One guy's doing Korean duck, another's doing Korean barbecue, and he's got Korean sashimi from Odaesan at a third station. I swear, people are going to come just for the food."

"Wait a minute," I say. "The car is vegan, so how can Oscar be serving meat?"

"And there's going to be a fourth station with tofu and edamame for the PETA freaks and vegans who actually show. So far we've only got Alicia Silverstone down as our vegan host committee member, and Oscar refuses to build his menu around a girl who won't even wear silk because she's worried about the mental health of the worms."

"Okay, okay," I say. "As long as the corporate guys are cool with the catering, then I don't care." Besides, it does sound good. Fun even. All those tree-hugger celebs wandering around, their fingers greasy with spareribs. Even the politically correct like to eat well.

"So I totally vote for this house," Jay says, bouncing in from the living room. Oscar and I look up from our cells and nod. I hear my other line click. "Look, we'll be there as soon as we can," I say to Steven and click over.

"So I just got a call from Patrice," Charles says.

"*And?*" I say, turning away from Jay. I can't believe I was just talking to Oscar about Patrice doing an end run around me to Charles and already it's happening.

"And needless to say, she's not happy."

"Oh, for the love of God," I say, stalking out of the dining room and Jay's earshot. "She couldn't even rearrange her schedule to *see* all of the houses," I say, trying to whisper. "Now, before we're even done, she's calling you to complain?"

"Look, I know it's annoying," he says, sounding like he couldn't be less annoyed. "But try to see it from her point of view."

Her point of view? Her point of view is totally out to lunch, given their budget. "Look, she's never done a party of this size before, and she's certainly never done a party in L.A.," I say. "She thinks every ranch house is a piece of shit and should cost a couple grand to rent. I mean, unless she can get Kelly Lynch to donate her Lautner house for the party, she's dreaming."

"Kelly and Mitch won't do that," Charles says, sounding shocked. "They're totally tight with Graydon."

"I *know*," I say. "I was being facetious."

"Look," he says, calmer now. "It's her first event for the magazine, and she obviously wants to impress Andrew, who is coming out for it, by the way."

"Oh, great." Just what I need. Miss Havisham up my ass.

Oscar rolls up. "We got to go," he says, pointing to his watch.

I shake my head and hold up my free hand. "Charles," I mouth. Oscar motions for me to hand him the phone. I wave him off.

"Well, you're just going to have to find a location she approves," Charles says.

"Look," I say. "Jay's here, and he likes this house — correction, *loves* the house — so I say let them fight it out. I'm calling Amanda and telling her Jay's approved this venue and we're good to go."

"No, no," Charles says. "We're not lobbing this into the end zone and praying it works. I want a recommendation for new sites based on what you saw today that addresses her objections. I am not having Andrew think we're fumbling this already."

"What?" I can't believe he's insisting on this. And using sports metaphors. "We don't have time for that," I say. "Not at this late date."

"Then you're going to have to make time."

Oh, I *am*? Even the terrier has its limits. I'm just about to cross a real line and ask Charles since when does he get to tell me, a copresident of the agency, what to do, when Oscar grabs the phone.

"Hey, man," he says. "The Hancock Park place is pretty great, I got to admit, and Jay's knocked out by it. I'm sorry Patrice couldn't be here. I'll send over a revised budget proposal in the morning. Think I can shave a couple thousand now that I've seen it again. But right now I got to steal your girlfriend. We got a bunch of Koreans to take care of."

He hangs up and hands me back the phone. "See how easy that was?"

Before I can say anything, Jay bounces in, his baseball cap now turned sideways. "So are we all down with this house or what?"

"Congratulations, dude," Oscar says, clapping him on the shoulder. "You got yourself a party site."

"This is Mr. Park, Mr. Pak, Mr. Park, and Mr. Song," Steven says, making the introductions. Or reintroductions. I met these guys months ago, when they first hired us, but given how busy we've been, Steven has pretty much handled the day-to-day on their event. We all nod, shake hands. We're at the PDC, lined up by the reflecting pool like some diplomatic delegation. Or a scene in a Bill Murray comedy.

"Very beautiful," Mr. Pak, or maybe it's Mr. Park, says, gesturing to the sky.

He's right. It is a killer sunset. One of those bone-dry evenings where the sky goes all orange and gold. Reflecting off the Blue Building, the air seems shot with a million colors.

"Yes, it is," I say. "Let's hope we have weather like this for your party."

They all nod and smile. I feel myself nodding and smiling back. I have no idea if they've understood a word of what I've said. According to Steven, they all speak good English. They should, since the company's U.S. headquarters are down in Irvine, although I think Steven said some of these guys have flown in from Seoul.

"Wind off the desert," Mr. Song says. I think it's Mr. Song. "Very common this time of year."

"Yes, yes," I say, nodding. Patrice is clueless, but the Koreans get L.A. right down to the weather patterns.

"Gentlemen, now, if I may," Oscar says, gesturing toward the Blue Building. "The tour starts with our catering facilities."

He leads the group off. For the next hour, he'll map out the physical layout of the party. Locations for the bar and food stations. The Porta-Johns. The tent he's setting up to create the mood of a Korean temple, right down to a gong and candles. Finally, he'll get to the arrival area, where Steven and I'll take over, walk them through the whole red carpet. What celebs we're expecting and how the photographers will shoot them on the carpet in front of the step-and-repeat emblazoned with the Kia logo and then more shots with the WireImage photographer we've hired, who'll be inside the party shooting the various company execs together with some of the celebrity guests. And finally, we'll show them the official exit and where we will be distributing the gift bags, which will include Kia mugs, Kia baseball caps, the latest issue of *Car & Driver*, and sets of car keys with Kia key chains — two of which will be for the cars on display at the event.

I'm just about to head for the reflecting pool, check out where Steven thinks the cars should go, when I hear my cell. Probably Patrice or Charles again. I fish my phone out of my bag and check the number. Amy. That's weird. Not only is it late in Bryn Mawr but Amy never communicates by anything other than e-mail.

"Hey," I say, clicking on. "What's up? I'm right in the middle of a walk-through."

"Sorry to interrupt, but I thought you'd want to know right away."

"Know what?"

"Mom's in the hospital."

11

Up in the Air

"Honey, you really don't need to come. Everything's fine. They just wanted to check her out."

"Dad, of course I'm coming. I'm already at the airport," I say, eyeing the line ahead of me—two families with mountains of luggage.

I'm in line at LAX on the phone with Jack waiting to check in with the skycaps for the 10:40 red-eye to Boston. Boston because, as it turns out, Helen and Jack were on the Cape when her heart began its perilous fluttering. Now she's in the Hyannis hospital—"but not intensive care," Jack has said so many times I can tell he's close to panicking—and I'm on my way there because Amy's stuck on some barrier island off Florida with Bevan and Barkley, who's attending some legal convention there, and she can't get a flight—flights—until tomorrow.

"Well, I'm just saying you don't have to come."

"Dad, I *want* to come. I want to be there even if she's fine," I say, inching my bag forward with my foot. Any fears I had about not making this flight are quickly evaporating. Not only is this line moving fast but the whole trip, getting a seat at the last minute, the limo, even the traffic, has all gone like clockwork. It's like for once I'm going with the current, not against it. Or maybe it's like Ritalin; speed calms the hyperactive, a real crisis calms me.

"When do you get to Boston, eight tomorrow morning?" Jack asks for what's the hundredth time. I know what he's doing. If he can focus on my itinerary, it's one more minute when he's not thinking about his wife lying in a hospital bed hooked up to a million pulsing wires.

"Yes, I get in at eight," I say, going over it again. "And my flight to Hyannis leaves at nine-thirty. I'll be there by ten."

He makes noises about driving to Boston to get me, but I tell him, again, that makes no sense. I'll get there faster by flying. Up ahead, the line shuffles forward.

"Okay, so I'll call you from the gate if there're any delays, otherwise I'll just call you when I land." He makes another effort to let him get me in Boston, and I can tell he just wants to keep talking. "Look, call Amy and tell her when I'm arriving and find out when she's planning to get there and how. I'm pretty sure she has to connect through Atlanta or D.C. or someplace."

"Okay, honey," Jack says, and I can tell he's glad to have a task. I hang up and drop my cell into my bag. I should call people. After Amy reached me at the PDC during the Kia walk-through, I'd just hung up, told Steven my mother had had a heart attack and that I was leaving. And I did. Didn't speak to anyone, not even Oscar, who was still showing the Koreans around the kitchen. I just walked to my car and left.

Now I should call them. Caitlin. Steven. Charles. Call them with backup plans and contingencies. A number on the Cape. An idea of my timetable. But it all seems like clutter. Noise I no longer have time to hear.

I hitch my bag up my shoulder and look down the line at the two families in front of me. My fellow travelers, my real companions. I study the woman closest to me. Obviously the mother, about my age. She looks tired but happy in that start-of-vacation way, loaded down with bags, totes, her family's information center, dispensing tissues and solace, games and instructions. Her husband, dressed in khaki shorts and a polo shirt with a business logo, his uniform announcing that he's a man on vacation but with a good corporate job waiting at home, is absorbed, too much I note, in moving their luggage forward, a one-man portage system. Their daughter, about five I guess, is also engrossed in her own private drama, hopping from foot to foot while she pushes her stroller, oblivious to everything but the adrenaline flying through her veins. Her brother, older, maybe ten, eleven, but not yet a teenager with that awkward self-consciousness, grips the hand of the gray-haired woman at his side, his grandmother, I assume. He is all eyes, watchful, wary.

We inch along, my little family and me. All of us on our way, our separate itineraries, but travelers together. Up ahead there is a commotion. The skycap, finally. We all lurch forward. Tickets, luggage are handed over, lashed with tags, hoisted onto a cart. The daughter hops faster. Honey, stop that. The son still grips his grandmother's hand. Here, can you carry that? A station wagon pulls up, and an older man gets out. The grandfather. But what's he doing with a car? Of course, he isn't going with them, only dropping them off. The grandmother, too, is staying behind. She starts to disentangle herself from her grandson—I can't see his face. Hugs and exclamations. The husband shakes hands with the grandfather. Thanks, thanks for everything. The daughter hops faster. Honey, say goodbye. Say thank you. Say goodbye. Goodbye. Goodbye.

————— ⏰ —————

"Ma'am, where are you headed this evening?"

I turn. The skycap. It's my turn with the skycap. I am supposed to hand him something, get this under way, but I can't think what it is.

"Your ticket?" he says, holding out his hand.

Yes, the ticket. That's right, my ticket. I am to give him my ticket. And I will, except I just need another minute. I turn back to the line, but they've already gone. Where are they? They couldn't have gone that fast. And then I see them. My little family, slipping through the sliding glass doors. They are hurrying now. Toward their gate. I crane my head. I can still see them if I stand on my toes.

"Ma'am?"

Yes, I know, the ticket, but I just need one more minute. They are going now, moving fast on the other side of the glass, their faces set for the trip, what's to come.

And then he turns. The son, his face, streaming with tears, searching the crowd for one last look.

It's dark now. We've hit our thirty thousand feet and have leveled off at our cruising altitude. The captain has turned off the seat belt sign, and we are free to move about the cabin. In 6C, I take another sip of wine and close my eyes. I picture them out there in the dark. Helen asleep in her hospital bed, Jack sitting next to her, pretending to watch the news on television, the sound off so as not to wake her. I picture Amy, somewhere in Florida, the blush of sunburn on her cheeks, tucking Bevan into bed in a strange hotel room, handing him his bear, her mind already going over their trip in the morning. I try to picture the others. Where they are, where they are going. Charles, pouring himself a drink, his tie loosened, home after a long day. Steven. Oscar. Brad, in my house, closing up the paint cans, lighting a cigarette the minute he's shut my front door.

And then I see him. The son. His eyes are closed now, his head curled into his mother's shoulder, as they speed across the night sky. The wet berry of his mouth slightly open as he sleeps, the salt film on his cheeks the only remnant of his grief. Will he remember this day? When he is the same age as his father is now, will he remember this day, when his world split in two? *Then* and *now. There* and *here. Leaving* and *arriving.* Will he remember? Or will he have grown into another traveler, another one of us hurtling forward, toward the future, what's to come?

———— ✿ ————

It's like a fifties movie, I think, blinking in the early, gray-tinged light. The Hyannis airport is like a fifties movie. A small, half-moon curve of a building with a wind sock tugging on its tether above. The air smells of the sea. Cold and salt-tanged, a foretaste of winter. I hunch into my jeans jacket, half-expecting to see men in fedoras and women in seamed stockings stepping off the curb into Packards. I have traveled not across country but back in time.

I reach in my bag and turn off my cell. I checked my messages in Boston, in between flights, and they were all there. Oscar, Charles, Steven. Caitlin. Concern in their voices. I could hear it. If there's anything they can do. Anything at all. But there's nothing I need from them. We are untethered from each other now.

I grip my styrofoam cup of airport coffee and turn my collar against the damp sea air. I scan the cars and realize I don't know which car Jack drove here from Philadelphia. Barely knew they were here. Now I will know every detail. Every beat, every fibrillation, every flutter.

I expected him at the baggage claim. Instead, there was a message on my cell. A test they needed to run at the hospital, and he would leave as soon as he could. Fifteen, twenty minutes, tops. A few cars pull in and disgorge their passengers. Mostly men, tieless, in khakis and anoraks, carrying monogrammed canvas totes. Architects, retirees, I guess, heading up to Boston for the day. It's that time of year. The off-season. Only year-rounders now.

And then I see him, in Helen's silver Volvo, making the turn into the airport, his face white, taut, and with his hair swept back as if it too were in a hurry. I feel a click and am unmoored no longer.

"You know, you used to hate hospitals as a kid."

"Every kid hates hospitals."

"But you were really bad. That time you broke your arm and we took you to the emergency room."

"I remember."

"Dislocated the bone. The doctor had to knock you out to set it. Used a huge needle."

"I *remember*."

Jack and I are sitting in the hospital waiting room. Styrofoam coffee, round three. If the Hyannis airport is a trip back in time, the hospital is utterly timeless. Fluorescent light, white linoleum, blond wood furniture with scratchy pink upholstery. That chemical smell in the air and the spongy squeak sound of the nurses' soft-soled shoes. The poets have it wrong. Death comes on little rubber feet.

Jack's right. I do hate hospitals. I have always loved airports and flying. The idea of leaving. *Escape*. But hospitals frighten me. Not just needles and pain—what a kid fears. But that dulled sense of extended layovers, of people held against their will, with no idea when or if their flights will depart, their lives begin again.

"More coffee?" I say, eyeing Jack's cup. My own has been drained, no memory of the taste or even its heat. Now it's just a worry bead I have picked apart, shredded to a few damp chips clutched in my hand.

"I love your mother, but I don't have any more stomach lining to give to the cause," he says, shaking his head and tossing his cup into the trash can. "You should eat something."

"So should you."

Neither one of us budges. We've been here nearly two hours, gone over what's being done and why. There's some discussion of a stent being installed. Or inserted, or whatever it is doctors do with stents and heart patients. But we won't know for a bit. After more waiting. More tests. So we wait. Jack and I. Amy won't arrive until tomorrow now. Something with flights and leaving Bevan in Philadelphia with the nanny.

"If you need to call people . . ." Jack says, nodding at my bag at my feet. "I mean, you do have a job."

"It's not important," I say, leaving the bag untouched.

And then it's like a scene in *E.R.* As if someone finally called "Action." The double doors bang open, and the doctor material-izes — scrubs, lab coat, closer to my age than Jack's, which startles me. The fact that doctors can be my age. George Clooney on TV is one thing, a real doctor my age is another.

There is information. I know there is, because I can see him, the doctor, Dr. Pratt by his name tag, talking animatedly to Jack. But for some reason, I can't hear them. Can't make it out. Like I'm underwater, or behind glass. Jack turns to me and smiles, mouths something I can't hear, but he is smiling. Good news. Or at least not bad.

We are moving now, the three of us, down a hall. An elevator. Another hall. Around a corner, past a nurses' station where a TV flickers. *Oprah*, I think. Finally, a room. Her room. The door is slightly ajar, the lights dim inside. Jack and the doctor push in. I hang back and close my eyes. Even if she is fine, if she is going home tomorrow, she is still here now. And the one thing I do not want to see, more than the illness and the frailty, the hallmarks of the passage of time, is my mother as a stranger, small, humped, unknown to me, in a strange bed.

"Hello, Alex," she says, her voice faint, her face pale. Pale but smiling. Like a mother greeting her newborn child.

"What are you doing? Mom can't eat that now."

I don't even bother looking up. Two days later, I'm in the kitchen at their condo, making Helen scrambled eggs — what she said she wanted — with Amy second-guessing my every move.

"They're Egg Beaters," I say, tilting the pan so the eggs cover the bottom. "Besides, Mom said she had a taste for eggs, and the doctor said the main thing was to get her to eat."

Amy scowls and moves to the refrigerator, opens it, and emerges with a carton of low-fat cottage cheese. "Well, I'm giving her this as well. She could use the calcium."

I don't say anything. We both know Mom hates cottage cheese. Ever since she went on the cottage cheese and grapefruit diet after she had Amy. Lost fifteen pounds and most of her mind. Eventually, she just gave up and started smoking again. "Best weight loss system God ever devised," she would say, sitting on the patio, her long, slim legs in Bermuda shorts, her perfectly mani-cured nails, painted coral for the summer, holding a Winston Light, an ashtray, and an iced tea on the white wrought-iron table. Lunch was served. Took a couple surgeon general's reports, a lot of warnings by her doctor, and a stroke from her closest friend and bridge partner, Bitsy Warner, before she saw the light. To his credit, Jack never said a word. Not until it was too late.

"I should have insisted she quit smoking years ago," he said in the car after he picked me up at the Hyannis airport, eyes locked on the unfamiliar roads. "None of this would have happened if I had made her quit smoking."

"Don't do this to yourself. No one can make Mom do any-thing," I said. "You know that more than any of us."

"Still, I should have tried. Foolish now, looking back. What you put up with. What you choose not to see."

Amy opens cupboards looking for plates. "I don't know where anything is in this new place."

"They're right there," I say, nodding at the china cupboard next to the refrigerator. "I thought you came up here with them earlier this summer."

"I did," she says, pulling down a salad plate. "But that doesn't mean I remember where everything goes."

I pull the pan off the stove and spoon the eggs onto the plate I've set up on a tray.

"You're using a tray?" Amy says, catching sight of the tray I've set with silver, linen napkin, and a Waterford glass. "She'll hate that whole sickbed thing."

I finish scraping the eggs, dump the pan into the sink, and turn to her. "Can we just stop this? For once, just stop? I don't even remember why or when this started, but really, just stop. If there ever was a time for us to quit acting like two sulky kids, it's now."

She looks at me, startled. Like she's never seen me before. "I'm just trying to help Mom," she says, her voice small.

"Well, so am I," I say, holding her gaze and then turning to the tray. "So let's take the fucking cottage cheese and go help her."

Oh, but we are sunny pushing into Mom's bedroom. "Hey," we both say, ducking in, laden with our offerings, heads bowed, voices hushed like we are entering a chapel.

"Oh, there you are," Helen says, pushing herself up in bed.

Jack, who's been reading *The Wall Street Journal* in the chair, puts it aside and steps toward us. "Can I give you girls a hand?" he says, reaching for the tray.

"Hope you still have that craving for eggs," I say.

"Egg *Beaters*," Amy says behind me.

"Right," I say, shooting her a look. "By decree of the surgeon general and Dr. Pratt, when we say 'eggs' we now mean 'Egg Beaters.'"

"Doesn't matter," Helen says, reaching for the tray. "It's just nice to have someone else doing the cooking. And not to be eating hospital food."

She picks up the fork, gazes at the plate and then up at the three of us, circled around the bed. "You have seen me eat before," she says wryly. "Unless I'm mistaken."

We all sink down, finding something, anything to do except stare at the patient. Someone should do a study on the personality changes that happen when people get sick. Astonishing, all the differing emotional responses to illness. For as long as I've known her, Helen has been compulsive. A perfectionist. Ordered down to the last pillow fluffed on the sofa, the Christmas cards in the mail the day after Thanksgiving. Never weighed more than five pounds above her high school weight except when she was pregnant. Gave up anything — knitting, tennis, serious cooking — she couldn't do better than 90 percent of the people she knew. Compared to her, I am walking chaos. Now, faced with the gravest of fallibilities, stunningly, she loosens rather than tightens her grip.

"Oh, and the cottage cheese is Amy's Proustian offering," I say, looking up from my perch on the edge of the bed, pretending to read Jack's paper.

It's been so long since I've heard Helen laugh, the sound takes me by surprise. Amy and I shoot each other looks, like dogs startled by a strange noise.

"Serves me right," Helen says, eyeing the plate. "Who knows, maybe I'll develop a taste for it again."

"So wait, Helen has a heart attack —"

"A mild heart attack, but yes, a heart attack."

"And the ice queen thaws?"

"Let's not make jokes about my mother, who's just had a heart attack."

"I'm sorry, I'm just so used to hearing the horror stories," Steven says.

"Yeah, I know, it takes some getting used to," I say, turning on my side to look out the window at the trees, the leaves starting to turn. I'm in the guest bedroom, lying on one of the twin beds talking to Steven on my cell. I've been here a week and have talked to him just once a day, which is some kind of record for us. Still, it's more than I've talked to Charles. Which is my fault. My elusiveness here in the sick ward. Or maybe it's not my fault. Maybe I'm finally seeing things clearly. For so long, I thought if Charles and I got closer, *physically* closer, things would become obvious. We'd see how our lives would finally mesh together. As a real couple. But that's the thing about crises. They throw everything into high relief. Like a blinding light that picks out the hidden cracks, fissures you never see in the normal light of day.

Or maybe it is just me. Ever since I got here, I've been so preoccupied with Helen — getting her home from the hospital, helping Jack run the house — that it's been hard to think of checking in somewhere else. This is where I am. When I reached Charles that first night, after Jack and I had spent nearly the whole day at the hospital, I was so exhausted, so worn out from the flights, from the time change, from the not knowing if she was going to live or die and then the relief of knowing, yes, she would live, that it was all I could do to just burst into tears, croak out a few words.

"Do you need me to come up?" he'd said, sounding like he was offering me a towel after I spilled something.

Yes, I wanted to scream, *yes, I fucking well want you to come up!* If I've *ever* wanted you to be here, with me, really be *with* me, and not have one eye on your BlackBerry and one ear on your cell phone, it's now. And I don't want to have to ask you for that. Not after three years together. I want you to just know that this is where you should be. With me. But apparently I do. Have to ask.

"No, oh God, no," I said, wiping my eyes. "I mean, yes, I do want you here. For moral support and, and all of it. But you only just met Helen, and I think it's better, for now at least, less stressful for everyone, that it's just me and Jack and Amy. Maybe later. If I'm here for a while. And you can get away."

Sure, he said, he understood. And who wouldn't? It's a family crisis, and whatever Charles and I have been for the past three years, it's not a family. It's not. And I know that. And I also know that that is what I want. I don't want a boyfriend. I don't want a relationship. I want us to be a family. Where you don't have to ask. It doesn't have to mean a million kids, and a mortgage, and in-laws every holiday. It doesn't even have to mean a marriage. Even if it's just a man, an apartment, a cat, and a fire in the fireplace, it's still a family.

I roll back on the bed. "So Mom's actually doing really well," I say to Steven. "Once the surgery's healed, it's really diet and a couple of cholesterol medications. But it is amazing. Even Amy and I are getting along. Well, sort of. I'm telling you, it's a Ph.D. thesis. How people change in the face of a life-threatening illness."

"A thesis? It's a reality show. 'Real Families. Real Health Scares. Real *Changes*.' Fox, Mondays at ten."

"That's a nine o'clock show if there ever was one," I say. "So what do I need to know? Caitlin doesn't tell me anything."

"That's because she doesn't know anything, except when the Fred Segal sale is. Or was."

It takes me a second for this to sink in. I've been gone only a week, but the office seems distant, remote. "Okay, so you get to bring me up to date. Kia went well? I'm sorry I had to miss that."

"Better than well. The food was fabulous, we had a huge

crowd—Larry David even showed—and we got amazing coverage. Let's just say, I'm a god in Koreatown."

"Yes, but can you say it in Korean?"

"I'm telling you, watch your back. I'm gunning for your job."

"Oh, take it, please," I say, "just do it before the C Christmas party."

"Speaking of that," he says. "When does Charles get there?"

"Speaking of that, when does Charles get here?" I say, not following him.

"Sorry," he says, "when you mentioned the magazine, I just flashed on Charles, since he's called me every day about their event since you left."

"Well, he's conscientious," I say, reaching out to finger the curtain. "Give him a break. Actually, he's not coming. Or he said he would fly up if I needed him, but since Helen's on the road to recovery and it's really better if it's just us here now, just the family—anyway, he's not."

Steven says nothing for a second, and I can tell he's trying to decide if I'm lying about that or if I really am okay with Charles not flying up.

"Anyway, let's not talk about Charles," I say, letting the curtain drop. "What's up with Oscar? Is Charles harassing him too, or is there blood on the floor?"

"Ah, blood, no, because Oscar's quietly taking care of it," Steven says. "Which between you and me means we're going with the Hancock Park site."

"Serves them all right," I say, catching sight of the alarm clock on the bedside table. Pushing 5:30, and I need to get going on dinner. I've never been much of a cook, but given that I'm better than either Amy or Jack and nature abhors a vacuum, I've become the designated hitter.

And actually, I'm kind of enjoying it. Much nicer coda to the day than working until 7:00, racing across town to some screening, and then falling into bed with whatever's in the refrigerator. For the past week, it's been a glass of wine, NPR on the radio, Jack offering to chop anything that needs chopping. So far I've made chicken twice and roast salmon and everything with mashed Yukon golds, Helen's favorite. For tonight, I got Jack to pick up a local bluefish at the fish market. All those omega-3 oils.

"Yes, it does," Steven says. "And it also goes to prove, if you let others do their jobs, things still get done."

"Is that a jab?"

"Honey, I'm just saying you're taking care of your mother. You got enough on your plate there. We can set up a stupid party without you."

"Okay, but I'm back Monday," I say.

We're just finishing up when there's a knock at the bedroom door. "Yeah, I'm coming," I yell, expecting Jack wondering about dinner. But Amy sticks her head in.

"Something came for you," she says. "Or actually, they came for Helen, but there's a card for you."

I hold up my hand and nod at her. "Did you send Helen something?" I say to Steven.

"Only my very best wishes. Why, should I have? Should I have sent a card? I should have sent a card to Helen. I'm hanging up now and sending a card to Helen. Goodbye."

He clicks off, and I push up from the bed.

"Dad said you got a bluefish for dinner," Amy says, eyeing me.

"Yeah, is that something you can eat?" I say, heading for the dresser mirror and looping my hair, which hasn't seen a blow-dryer in days, into a ponytail. This whole being civil to the sis is actually not as weird as it seems. Right up there with no makeup and not washing my hair every day. Certainly takes a lot less energy, which is a relief in itself.

"Umm, yeah, that sounds great," she says, holding the door open for me. "If there's something I can do to help. Except maybe not skin the fish."

Something I can do to help. Now there are six words I never thought I'd hear Amy say. Not in my lifetime. But then these are strange days. This whole week has been like a CBS Sunday night movie. Brittle mother gets sick and everyone's personality changes. Hurt feelings scab over. Feuds, too old to remember why they started, are dropped. Next thing you know, I'll be quitting my job, moving to the Cape, opening a diner, and marrying an old high school sweetheart with 2.5 kids just around the corner.

"Yeah," I say, following Amy out the door, "I'm sure we can find you something to do."

"So the flowers were a really nice gesture," I say. "Even if Helen had no idea who sent them."

"Well, didn't you enlighten the woman?"

"Yeah, after I got done explaining that they weren't from Charles."

"Hey, you know I didn't send them to upstage her future son-in-law," Oscar says.

I sigh, lean back in the chaise, and gaze up at the stars. "He's not her future son-in-law, and I know you didn't send them to upstage anybody."

Frankly, other than Helen's bridge club and a couple of their neighbors back in Philly, no one had sent flowers. Several people sent cards, but Oscar is the only one of my friends who did, and none of Amy's friends sent anything. Charles sent a card. Express Mail. Actually, it was a note written in fountain pen on his embossed stationery. Very Upper East Side. Very Emily Post. Helen was both touched and impressed. "What a nice man," she said, rubbing her fingers over the embossing.

"Yes, he is," I said, my voice nothing but cheerful. "And he's sorry he couldn't get up here," I add.

"Yes, he said so in his note," Helen said, dropping her head back on the pillow. "But now, tell me who this Oscar is. He seems very gallant."

Now I'm outside on the patio, trying to pick out Cassiopeia, my favorite constellation, which I can never find in L.A., debating whether to tell Oscar my mother's impression of him. It's easy to think someone's gallant if you don't know his weaknesses. His predilection for treating women like changes of clothes. "You know, my mother thinks you're very gallant," I say, throwing caution to the wind. "Plus, you hit it on the head. French tulips. I mean, what woman doesn't love them? They're like looking at a Vermeer painting. You just feel so still, so tasteful."

"Alex, I do this for a living. Believe me, I know what French tulips 'say' after all these years," he says. "Anyway, what did you tell her? That I *was* one of the most gallant men you'd ever met?"

"Actually, yes, you are gallant," I say, suddenly deciding to forgo my usual rant about Elsa et al. And actually, he hasn't mentioned her lately. Or any of his usual girls for that matter. Maybe people do change. Or maybe I just want them to. "You're also bald, love the Dodgers, and chomp cigars."

"The cigar's an act. To distract everyone from the baldness. Clearly, it's working terribly well."

I laugh and reach for the glass of wine I've brought outside. Jack and Amy are in the kitchen finishing the dishes. As the cook, I got sprung and have retreated to the patio, my jeans jacket buttoned against the night air, to check the stars. And my messages. Actually, I called Oscar first, to thank him for the flowers, and — I check my watch — that was almost an hour ago. Actually, I need to wrap this up. It's pushing 8:00, and there's some PBS documentary about Roman engineering techniques Jack wants to watch, and Helen's asked us to watch it with her in their bedroom, which we are all taking as a good sign. Besides, you can never know too much about Hadrian's Wall and anything to do with aqueducts.

"So you're back Sunday?" Oscar says.

"Yeah," I say, and realize, suddenly, how uneager I am to leave here. I know this little entr'acte can't, won't, last. Bevan and Barkley are coming up Saturday, and in a couple of weeks, when she's up for the drive, Helen and Jack will close up the house and head back to Philly, and this little Shangri-la will recede into the winter mists. "Yeah, late Sunday," I add. "I'll be in the office Monday."

"And you sound so excited about that."

"Yeah, I know," I say, pushing to my feet, the wind colder now.

"Look," he says, "why don't I pick you up at the airport? That'll ease your reentry into the real world."

"Thanks, but I'll just get a car," I say, not taking this offer seriously. Nobody picks anybody up at the airport in L.A. Except the limo drivers.

"Hey, your mom said I was gallant. Let me live up to my billing. I'm picking you up."

"Alex?" Jack, at the back door, peering out into the dark.

"Yeah, I'm just finishing up this call."

"It's starting, honey," he says. "And Amy's making hot chocolate."

"Okay, I'm coming," I say again, surprised at the sudden surge of happiness I feel at spending the evening watching TV with my family. In life's time line, I'm drifting backward, finding pleasure in all the things I once took for granted. Never even noticed. Next thing you know, I'll be in a fuzzy one-piece, sitting in a high chair banging my spoon for rice pudding.

"Did you hear all that?" I say to Oscar.

"Yeah," he says, laughing. "Fuck. Hot chocolate on a cold fall night? I'd show up. Just make sure she makes it with whole milk and an unsweetened chocolate with at least a sixty percent cocoa content. That way you get a good mouth feel and don't have to use too much sugar."

"Yeah, I'm sure that's exactly what little Amy is whipping up right now. I'm expecting Nestlé's and hot tap water."

"Well, it's the thought that counts."

"Yes, it is," I say, adding almost without thinking, "So, I'll see you Sunday."

12

Cooking Lessons

"So you're a publicist?"

"Sort of."

"In Hollywood?"

"Los Angeles."

"So do you know any stars? I mean, real stars. Like Paris Hilton. My kids love Paris Hilton."

The guy in 5A has me cornered. Usually I'm pretty good at fending them off. The talkers. Doesn't take much. Game face, headphones, pile of work. But this guy's tone-deaf to the nuances of life at thirty thousand feet. Already I know his whole story. Divorced. Two kids. Never sees them now that his wife has moved back east with her new husband, his kids' stepdad, *Craig*. Where he just was. Back east. A business trip he extended a couple days. Took his kids, Jason and Sara Beth, named for *his* mother, thank you, up to New Hampshire to see the colors. Not that they cared much about dying leaves. Six and nine. Like kids that age know from dying. Like they care about anything but their friends and what's on TV. Besides, all his ex-wife did was bitch that they were missing two days of school. Six and nine? Like kids that age can't miss a day of school.

"So how'd you get to be a publicist?" he says, pouring the last of his scotch into his glass.

"Took a wrong turn after grad school," I say, never taking my eyes from the TV monitor overhead. Some big-budget action thing that tanked. The same movie that was playing on my flight out. When did this happen? That the only movies you see on planes are the losers? Not that I'm really watching. I can't even be bothered to put the headphones on. My big mistake. The chink in my armor that let Mr. 5A in.

I mean, he might be kicking back after a business trip and a couple days with the kids to assuage his guilt over the divorce, but not me. I'm just coming back to earth after a near-death experience, and leaves had nothing to do with it. You can't spend time in a hospital — not with a parent looking pale and thin and so uncertain in that tissuey hospital gown, like she was pleading with you to get her out — and not have it affect you.

And we did. Get her out. Out and on the mend. Still, the memory of it sticks with you. No matter how many documentaries we watched, the lights dimmed, sipping our cocoa. I left her with Bevan and Barkley to distract her. Her energy finally back enough that she could enjoy her grandson, the sun pooling on the bedclothes as they played together after her nap. She'll be fine, Jack said, giving me a hug when he dropped me back at the Hyannis airport. Ten days, a lifetime, later.

"I know," I said, reaching down to fuss with my bag. Not trusting myself to look at him. "I know. The doctor said she could live another fifteen years without a problem. Not even a flutter."

Now, up in 5B, it's my pulse that's racing. Like whatever dam had been holding back all the adrenaline in my veins had finally been breached. And my heart can hardly keep up.

"You sound like you could use a change," Mr. 5A says, and I can feel his whiskeyish breath on my cheek. I know what's coming. He'll ask me where I live in L.A. and if I ever get to whatever neighborhood he calls home. Marina del Rey, I'm betting. Some condo with a view of the ocean. Where even the furniture's rented.

I turn toward him. His eyes are bleary with fatigue and alcohol. God, how are we ever to make it in this world? Connect. Find someone to love. To trust. Maybe if I had just spent the week in New York dealing with Patrice and Charles. Arguments over sites, sponsors, flowers. The interminable gift bag. MAC versus Stila. Gran Centarino versus Absolut. Lancôme versus Z. Bigatti. All the pretty, pointless party favors we kill ourselves over. Maybe if I was coming off that, I could play along. Sure, call me, I might say. Call me and we'll catch a drink. A screening. See some real stars.

But not now. "You're right," I say, turning away. "I do need a change."

"Hey, I see you up ahead. You don't look too bad after ten days playing nursemaid."

"Well, I don't see you." I'm outside the American terminal on my cell peering down the line of cars. LAX on a Sunday night is worse than NASCAR. Limos, buses, cabs. A million cars. All of them endlessly circling. "Are you driving the hearse?" I say, backing away from the SUV that's pulled up at the curb disgorging a family of Asians and their mound of luggage. Aren't they supposed to be picking people up down here? Departures are one floor above.

"Yeah, I even had her washed just for the occasion."

"I still don't see—" And then I do see. The familiar faded red. The wood paneling. And Oscar. Out of the car, grinning like my oldest friend, reaching for my bag.

"You're home," he says, standing up and studying my face, like he's searching for something. Some sign.

"Am I? I can't be sure."

He cocks his head. "I'd say the evidence is all here. Long flight. LAX. But then again, it's up to you."

"What if it's not up to me?"

He smiles, shakes his head. "Don't go all Plato on me, Alex. I'm double-parked."

I'm not, I want to say. It's just, is it really as simple as desire? I mean, there's history, baggage. There's Elsa. *Charles*. Doesn't all that count?

The flood of Asians surge by, yammering. One of them jostles me with his bag, and I stumble. "Sorry, lady," the guy says, sweeping by, toting some Houdini-size trunk.

I catch myself and realize Oscar has me by the arm. "Here," he says, handing me a small white bag. "I was going to give this to you later, but obviously the moment is now."

"What is it?" I say, eyeing the bag.

"Your 'Welcome Home' gift bag," he says. "Since you obviously need reminding that you are, in fact, home."

"You got me my own gift bag?"

"Even an event planner needs a gift bag now and then."

I take the bag and peer inside. A pint of whole milk and a tin of Scharffen Berger unsweetened cocoa. *Gallant* doesn't begin to cover it.

"At least sixty percent cocoa content?" I say, looking up, grinning like an idiot.

"At least," he says, smiling. "You want to get in the car now?"

"Yeah," I say, clutching my bag. "I want to get in the car now."

"So there's something I think you should know."

"Are you ever going to stop talking?"

"I think this is a really bad idea."

"Well, I don't, and since I'm bigger than you, older than you, and I'm the guy, you're outvoted."

"See, now, that's exactly what I'm talking about."

We're in my kitchen, surrounded by paint cans, drop cloths, and a ladder Brad thoughtfully left open in front of the refrigerator, staring at the pot of chocolate just coming to a boil on the stove. Actually, it's a pot of milk, and Oscar and I are deep in debate about when exactly to add the chocolate.

"It has to develop a skin on the surface — didn't you take home ec in high school? — so you know it's scalded," Oscar says, dipping a finger in the milk. "Needs a few more minutes," he adds, licking his finger.

"Why? I mean, what's the point in waiting?" I say, sticking my own finger in. Seems plenty warm.

"You have no faith," he says, opening drawers, cupboards. "Women are all the same. If it's going to get done, you think it should just get done *now*. What's the point of waiting — of timing? Right?"

"Why do I think you're about to use some sports metaphor to prove your point?" I say. "And what are you looking for?"

"A pot holder?"

"Don't own one," I say.

"And you roasted a bluefish on the Cape. Okay, that's the second thing I'm going to get you."

"No, I just think you don't have to finesse the details to such an obsessive degree," I say, reluctant to let this go. Maybe I'm overcompensating for the past ten days, for the stress of nursing Helen back to life, but debating the merits of hot chocolate techniques in my kitchen at 11:30 on a Sunday night seems blissfully, luxuriously normal.

"Oh, really?" he says, shutting the cupboard and turning to me.

"Really," I say, nodding. "It's all about the end result. The *end*, not the means."

"Okay, well, I'll prove you're wrong, and I won't use a single sports metaphor."

"Fine," I say, shrugging. "I still say —"

And suddenly Oscar's mouth is on mine. Oh, dear God, that was a long time in coming. I'm just starting to sink into the kiss, into his body, when he abruptly pulls back.

"See," he says, holding up his hands. "Exhibit A. The end without any means."

"Umm," I say, opening my eyes. "I'm not really following you."

"On the other hand, if I do this," he says, pulling toward me again, his body tight against mine as he pushes me past the ladder and up against the refrigerator.

"Uh-huh," I say.

"And this," he says, running his fingers down the side of my neck. "And this," he says, bringing his fingers along the edge of my collarbone and then slowly down along my breastbone.

"I'm starting to get the picture," I say, feeling my body grow warm.

"And then I do this," he says, pulling back and smiling at me, "before I do this." He pauses and then very, very gently pulls my face toward him, kissing me again.

"It's different," he says after a long minute, leaning his forehead on mine. "You have to admit, it's different."

"Yeah," I breathe. "It's different."

We stand there for a minute, arms entwined, gently breathing.

"So, you admit I'm right?" he says, pulling back, grinning again.

"Well, I might have to compare the evidence again," I say,

matching his grin. I hear a faint hiss and catch sight of the stove out of the corner of my eye. "But there's one thing you forgot."

"What's that?"

"You burned the milk."

———— ⏰ ————

My benchmark has always been if they spend the night. And he did. Not that we got much sleep. Well, not until later, after we were done going over all the empirical evidence again. And again. And a third time, just to be sure. When I finally woke in the morning—at 6:00 A.M., because of course I was still on EST, which means I had technically slept in until 9:00—the bed was empty but there was the smell of coffee in the air. Like I was being welcomed back to life.

"You made coffee," I say, heading into the kitchen, pulling my hair into a ponytail. Oscar is sitting at my kitchen table, shirt-sleeves rolled up, mug in hand, reading the *L.A. Times.* All the paint stuff is stacked neatly in a corner. The ladder closed and leaning against the wall.

"I did," he says, looking up and smiling—thank you, Jesus, because after that first night together, there's always that little moment of panic, doubt, like maybe it was all a huge mistake, a one-time-only offer—a totally genuine smile. "And I have to say it's the one decent foodstuff you have in this house."

"Well, I try," I say, heading for the coffee.

"Where're you going?" he says, reaching out, pulling me into his lap, and curling my ponytail around his hand.

"Umm," I say, playing along. "Unfortunately, the office."

"Let's go to Santa Barbara for the day. I know a great fish market. We'll have lunch, plus we can stop and get you some orchids on the way back at one of those wholesale nurseries just outside Montecito. You could use a few other life-forms in this house."

"You're only saying that because you haven't met my painter," I say, grabbing his shirt collar in my hands and shaking him slightly. "And he will be here any"—I crane around to read the clock on the stove—"any hour now."

"Seriously, let's go," he says, pulling on my ponytail again so my neck cranes toward him. "Come on," he says, bringing his mouth close, so I feel his breath.

"Don't you have a business to run?" I say, closing my eyes and leaning into him.

"I have a cell phone."

"Well, what about poor Patrice's party?"

"It's not for weeks."

"Well, what about all the other events we have on our calendars?"

"Alex. *Alex.*"

I open my eyes. I'm not in the kitchen in Oscar's lap but in bed. With Oscar leaning over me with a mug of coffee in his hand. "Hey," he says, smiling at me. "I thought the little girl was a goner there for a minute."

"Why does everyone quote *The Wizard of Oz* to people?" I say, struggling to sit up. Struggling to shake off the dream.

"Well, I don't know about the others, but personally I find it appropriate for almost any occasion involving a woman."

"Oh, that is comforting," I say, shooting him a look and reaching for the mug. I take a sip and realize it's almost empty. Oh, it was *his* coffee. Well, this is going well.

"Sorry," he says, nodding at the mug.

"Never mind," I say, handing it back and checking my watch. Or trying to. After all the excitement last night, it's AWOL. "What time is it?"

"Almost eight," he says, pausing nearly imperceptibly. "I've got to go."

"Yeah," I say, looking up at him, forcing a bleary smile.

"You know, I wish we could just go to Santa Barbara for the day or something," he says. "But I've got a business to run."

"Yeah, I've heard that."

"Look," he says, bending down and kissing the top of my head. Oh, great. The top-of-the-head kiss. Just what every girl wants after your first night together. "I've left coffee in the kitchen," he adds. "Call me later."

Call you later. Those are ambiguous words if I've ever heard them. Call you later and say *what*? "Hey, how's your day going?" Like we were still just friends? Just work pals? Or do I get to talk about how we are something else now? Now that we've slept together.

"Actually, you call me," I say, lobbing the ball back into his court and fumbling under the sheet for my watch. "I've got an incredibly busy day after being gone almost two weeks."

He looks at me a second. "You okay?"

"Sure, why wouldn't I be?"

"I don't know, you seem a little, ah, defensive. Compared to last night."

"I'm fine. You're leaving and I'm fine."

"I'm leaving because it's *Monday*. I have to go to work."

"Okay, okay, okay," I say, forgetting about the watch, pulling the bedclothes up to my neck, and scrunching down underneath. "Just go."

He looks at me a second.

"Just go," I say again. "And don't quote anything else from *The Wizard of Oz*."

"Look," he says, reaching out and pulling the sheet down from around my neck. "I know what you want. You want to know what this means. You want to know what last night means."

"No, I don't."

He looks at me.

"I don't. Okay, I do," I say, dropping the sheet and whatever dignity I have left. "I do want to know what it means. Maybe Elsa or Tammy or whatever their names are don't want to know what it means, or they don't care, but I do. Okay? I *do*. I'm thirty-six years old, my mother almost died, I've been married and divorced, and supposedly I have a boyfriend, so yes, I'm sorry, I want to know what it means. I don't have time to *not* know what it means. For all the women in the world who slept with someone and woke up the next morning and wanted to know what it meant but were too scared to ask, *I want to know what it means*."

"That's a really good speech."

"Oh, don't do that," I say, flinging his hands away. "We were, at least, we were friends. And friends deserve better than that."

"I'm serious. That's a really good speech, and I wish I had an answer for you."

"Oh, is this where the break-it-to-her-gently comes in?"

"No, it isn't," he says evenly. "It's where I give you my speech. Such as it is. Since we're 'friends.' You want to know what last night meant? I don't know. It's not up to me. And if you think it is, well, what does that say about you? That you're leaving it up to me to decide?"

"Well, you seem to have the answer for everything else."

"Okay, if you want it to mean something, then it means something."

"Well, it meant *something*," I say. "Or it wouldn't have happened."

"Look," he says, pushing up from the floor and easing himself onto the edge of the bed. "I'm not a bad guy."

I look at him. "No guy thinks he's a bad guy! Every guy thinks he's a prince."

"Alex, I'm not a bad guy. You said it yourself, we're friends. We wouldn't be friends if you really thought I was a bad guy."

"Okay, as a friend you're a great guy," I say, pushing the bed-clothes aside and sitting up, looping my hair behind my ears. "But all the evidence I can find when it comes to being more than a friend, is that you are not a great guy. I think you're exactly the way a lot of guys are."

"Yeah, and how's that?"

I don't even pause. "Self-protective. Evasive. And terrified of commitment."

He looks at me a minute, and then, like he's decided something, he pushes off the bed.

"Well, if that's what you really think."

What I think is we're playing emotional poker. Trying to suss each other out without hurting ourselves by wanting more than the other is prepared to give. "I don't want to think that," I say, looking up. "But you're the ex–statistics major. What's my evidence that you're not?"

"I don't want to hurt you."

"Then don't."

"You're asking a lot."

"I'm only asking you what you *want*."

"You want me to change."

"Do *you*?"

He looks at me. I hold his gaze.

"I'll call you," he says, turning for the door. "I'll call you and let you know."

13

Navigating by the Stars

As it turned out, I didn't call him. And he never called me.
Maybe we were both waiting for the other to call. Or maybe it
really was our version of Scarlett and Rhett's contretemps. At least
they got married before they had their big frankly-my-dear-I-
don't-give-a-damn scene. Oscar and I didn't even get twelve hours
together.

Not that I have all that much time to think about it. Okay, I
could always make time. A girl can *always* make time to think
about a guy. Especially after a night like that. But between work,
all our events, which are coming thick and fast now, and dealing
with Helen's ongoing recovery, which means I'm flying back to
Philly an average of every other week, I have plenty of reasons not
to think about him. Not to mention that I still don't know what I
think about the whole thing.

Besides, I'm still dealing with the painters. Because, of course,
Brad hasn't finished. Or he has finished. For now, but he had to

leave for some family thing and will be back in a couple weeks to finish up. I gave up trying to track his whereabouts when he just quit coming one day. I simply stacked all the paint stuff in the garage and called Louise. Threw it in her lap. She's the landlady, for God's sake. Let her find him and figure it out.

And then, of course, there's Charles. My boyfriend. Or ostensible boyfriend. If I don't know what I think about Oscar, I really don't know what I think about Charles. I know it hit me on the Cape that Charles and I are not a family and, without some seismic change, probably never will be. Still, it's a long way from that realization to actually breaking up. Okay, so the dish is cracked, but are you really prepared to toss it in the trash *right now*? Maybe I'm just being a coward. Or maybe I'm just being a pragmatist. Not so much about work, although that is no small consideration now that the holidays — and more to the point *C*'s gala — are imminent. I mean, a girl can deal with only so much at one time, right? And breaking up with Charles while we're in the throes of putting together one of the agency's biggest parties of the year doesn't seem like the smartest move one could make. For all of us.

Still, there's a bigger reason not to do it that has nothing to do with Oscar or Charles or work. It's the fact that I'm older now, and the idea of moving on, of remaking my life all over again, doesn't have as much appeal as it used to. After a while, you realize how much effort is required to create things. Careers. Relationships. Homes. They don't just happen overnight. And you think twice about trashing them.

So whatever the reason, and it's probably a little bit of all of them, I'm not taking my night with Oscar as any kind of sign that I no longer want to be with Charles. Charles and I might not be ideal, but I'm not going to break up with him, especially not over a guy I'm not even speaking to.

Emphasis on the *not speaking*. In fact, for somebody who never liked e-mail, Oscar's learned to love it in a hurry. Now it's the only way we communicate, since he and I also still have to work together. E-mailed work memos from Oscar Parties to the DWP-ED event staff. Re: the Ferragamo charity event. Re: Barry Rose's Scrabble party. Re: C's Christmas party. Re: Re: Re: Which is fine. And frankly, it's kind of amazing how much you can accomplish without ever actually speaking. And the beauty part is, no one seems to notice. Or almost no one.

"So, do you and Oscar ever actually talk anymore?" Steven said after a staff meeting about a month later, when I had briefed the team on no fewer than five upcoming events from a memo Oscar had e-mailed me. Or rather he'd e-mailed to Caitlin, who forwarded it on to me.

"Uh, yeah. Why?"

"Because it just seems like you guys used to talk every five minutes and now it's all e-mail."

"What? No, we speak. We e-mail. Everyone e-mails. It is speaking."

"No, it isn't," he said, shooting me a look.

"Look, it's fine," I said, hurrying down the hall. "We're all just busy."

"Okay, what do I not know?" Steven said, speeding up to keep pace with me.

"You don't know lots of things," I said, heading into my office. "You don't know when Amy's birthday is. Or Bevan's. You don't know that Helen is having to have her stent replaced because she's developed complications. You don't know—"

"Oh, no, she is?" he said, looking stricken. "I'm sorry. I had no idea."

"Yes, but the doctor says the new stent will be better. Anyway, there's lots you don't know."

He looked at me a second. A dog on the hunt. *"There's lots I don't know?* Okay, am I detecting some youthful indiscretion on your part with Oscar?"

"What?" I said, looking shocked, shocked. "No. Why would you even think that?"

He looked at me and crossed his arms. "They can run, but they can't hide."

Oh, okay. Besides, I can't be running from everyone. "Okay, look, I might concede that, except, in case you hadn't noticed, I'm not so fucking youthful anymore."

"Oh, please. What are you, thirty-two?"

"Thirty-six."

"Oh, please, what are you, thirty-six?"

I shot him a look. "Thanks for trying. Let's just leave it at 'indiscretion.'"

I could tell he was still dying for details. For dirt. For dish. Maybe my talk of Helen deterred him. Or knowing my real age. But in any case, he didn't. Go there.

"So, you're okay, right?"

"Actually, I don't really want to ask myself that question," I said, heading for my desk and sinking into my chair. "Between Helen and work and Charles being all over me about work and my having to deal with Oscar on every single one of our events — and why hasn't one of us looked into hiring another event producer? — I don't have time to ask myself that question. It's enough to get up every day and just deal with it all."

"Well, you know what they say?"

"Life sucks and then you die?"

"Time is on your side."

"Nobody ever said that."

"Mick Jagger said it. *Sang* it. It's practically a cultural anthem."

"Do yourself a favor. Do not hold up a man who still dates teenagers when he's sixty-two as any kind of role model to a thirty-six-year-old single woman."

Now, the week before Thanksgiving, the worst seems to be over. At least for now. Until Sundance starts the whole event roundelay all over again. The way our calendar stacked up this fall, all our biggest events, except for Barry Rose's Scrabble party this weekend and C's Christmas party the third week in December, are behind us. Only a couple of small, private holiday parties for DWP-ED clients, which are nothing.

Which means I'm down to my last two events dealing with Oscar. Still by e-mail, of course, but Steven has already lined up a couple new event producers — God knows, there's a new one unleashed in town every other minute — who look promising. Helen's new stent has taken, and she's feeling so much better that Jack is taking her on a cruise this Christmas. What she's always talked of doing. It'll be the first Christmas we haven't had the family command performance in Bryn Mawr, so Charles and I actually have plans to spend it in Hawaii.

I'm still not quite sure how this happened. Especially after the Cape and my realization that we weren't in fact a match made in heaven. But when Charles's parents decided to spend Christmas on safari — and that left both of us on our own for the first time since we'd been together — it sort of just happened.

"Since neither of us has to tend the home fires this Christmas, why don't we go somewhere great together?" Charles had said.

"Umm, sure," I said, so startled by the suggestion that I stopped midtype in sending e-mails. I decide you are not the man of my dreams and now you want to spend Christmas together? "Where'd you have in mind?"

Since it was either Aspen or Hawaii and I hadn't been on skis in years and — well, anyway, we now have reservations at the Four Seasons on the Big Island. Things seemed to be going so well that even Brad has resurfaced and is, finally, finishing the painting Louise hired him to do almost three months ago.

"Is Mercury in retrograde or out of retrograde or whatever it is?" I say when Steven stops by to give me the latest RSVP list for the Scrabble party.

"I'm sorry, do I look like Nancy Reagan? Why would I know if Mercury is in retrograde? Or Leningrad or wherever you think he is. Or isn't."

"Uh, because you regularly see a psychic?"

"I don't *see* a psychic. I'm *seeing* a psychic. They have personal lives, you know."

"Well, ask him if Mercury is in retrograde. Or out of it. I want to know why everything seems to be going so well these days."

"Define *well*. You think because most of our events are over and you're still not speaking to Oscar, it's because of the stars?"

"It's not just Oscar, it's everything," I say, picking up the guest list and scanning it. The usual roster of die-hard liberal Hollywood directors and writers, all of them guilt-tripped into attending Barry's annual word game. Or at least saying they're attending. Cut it in half and that's more likely to be our head count for Saturday night. "I mean, Helen's better. Brad's finally finishing the painting. Charles and I are going away for Christmas. Even Patrice is playing nice. For her."

In fact, she's been keeping a surprisingly low profile lately. Ever since she blew the December cover — held up a decision about Charlize while she negotiated with Britney's reps until they both got wind of it and walked — and had to go with a model at the last minute. She'd even agreed to Oscar's recommendation to hold the party at the Hancock Park house.

"Yeah, well, Rebecca of Sunnybrook Farm, before you get too carried away, how's your Saturday looking?"

I look up. "The Saturday before Thanksgiving, before I leave Tuesday for five days in Philly, which is also going to be our Christmas, so we're exchanging gifts, none of which I have bought yet, the Saturday of Barry Rose's Scrabble party, ah, it's looking totally open."

"Great, then you won't mind running the lunch meeting with Patrice and Jay and Lucienne."

"What idiot scheduled that right before Thanksgiving week?"

"Patrice. When she heard Lucienne was passing through town on her way to Cabo for Thanksgiving," Steven says. "You still think Mercury's in your corner?"

"What I think is that you're handling that meeting."

"Well, I am. Or I was, but unfortunately I have to leave for Florida Thursday night. My mother is having surgery."

"Wait a minute, you have *parents*?"

"Yeah, that's cute, and after I've been so supportive about Helen."

"Yes, I'm sorry," I say with mock contrition. Steven's mother is a classic. *Rita*. Lives in some monster condo in Palm Beach with her other child, her miniature poodle, Bulgari. Bridge and plastic surgery are her other two passions. Steven comes in a distant fourth. "I didn't think there was anything left to be done on her body."

"Laser surgery," he says with a shrug. "On her eyes. Or one of them. So she can get rid of her glasses. I told her I'm calling her Cyclops, but she insists she's going through with it."

"You're seriously going?" I say, realizing that now not only will I have to run the meeting with Patrice but I'll also have to be the point person on the Scrabble party instead of just doing a drive-by, as I'd intended. Shit. Even with Allie, Jill, and Maurine there, I'll have to spend most of the night there, which means I will no doubt have to deal with Oscar. In person.

"Look, I don't *want* to go," Steven says. "I'm not even staying for Thanksgiving since I'm cooking my annual bacchanalian feast for the boys here. But there was a cancellation, and she wants it done before the holidays. So yes, I'm going."

"Yeah, okay," I say, already rearranging the rest of my week in my head. If I'm to get everything done before I leave Tuesday, I'll have to spend Thursday night, Friday night, and all day Sunday shopping for Christmas gifts, spend Friday afternoon doing the final walk-through on the Scrabble party, and then Saturday do the lunch meeting, followed by my blow-dry and the party, where I'll just try to stay out of Oscar's way as much as possible. It won't be pretty, but assuming he's not interested in crossing paths with me either, I should be able to get away relatively unscathed. Besides, it's not like I have a choice. "But you're going to owe me," I say. "You and Mercury."

I'm not even awake on Saturday when I hear the front gate buzzer go. Oh, God. What time is it? I fish my arm out from under the covers. Just coming up on 8:30. *Thank you so much, whoever you are.* Must be the Jehovah's Witnesses I saw canvassing the neighborhood the other day. Like this is any way to win converts. Especially in Laurel Canyon. I pull the sheets over my head and sink back down. I had been planning on sleeping until 10:00. Just to give me a running start on the hours of work ahead. I'm just drifting off when I hear the buzzer go again. And again.

Damn it. I push out of bed, fumble for my old flannel robe, and head up the stairs.

"Who is it?" I say, grabbing the phone, which also connects to the front gate intercom.

"Hey, man, did I wake you?"

Brad. Oh, God, did he tell me he was coming today? The guy can barely show during the workweek, and now he's up at the crack of dawn on a Saturday?

"Uh, no, well, sort of," I say, pushing my hair out of my eyes. "Did you tell me you were coming today?"

"No, man. I mean, I got another job starting next week, and I figured if I got started early, I could finish you off today."

I gaze around the kitchen, which is back to Brad's usual mess. Drop cloths, paint cans, brushes, the open ladder. Could the guy ever clean up? "Uh, sure. If you think you can really finish today, come on in," I say, buzzing him in. I'm considering making a dash back downstairs for my yoga pants and a sweater, but there's no time. Oh well. It's not like Brad hasn't been here a million times already. Besides, according to Louise, he's started living with his girlfriend, some actress, over in Venice. I cinch my robe tighter and reach for a pencil to loop my hair into a makeshift ponytail.

"Oh, wow," he says, gazing at my robe, my hair, as he pushes through the front door, his toolbox in one hand and a tray of take-out coffees in the other. "I really did get you up."

"Don't worry about it," I say, eyeing the coffees. "Is Steve coming too?"

"Nah," he says, sliding everything on the counter, prying one of the coffees from the tray, and handing it to me. "Half-and-half, no sugar, am I right?"

"Yeah, right," I say, pulling off the lid and taking a hit. "How'd you know?"

"Well, you know Mercury is out of retrograde," he says, leaning against the counter and eyeing me over his coffee.

"Really?" I say casually. I *knew* something was up.

"Yeah, it's like one day you wake up and everything just *clicks*. Like, I don't even really know how you like your coffee, but then, at Starbucks, I just *knew*."

"Weird," I say, taking another hit. "And you just knew I would be here to drink it?"

"Nah," he says. "I was going to call, but I lost your number, and then I figured where else would you be?"

Where else would I be? Like I have nowhere else to be on a Saturday morning? "Well, I might have been at a yoga class. Or out of town."

He shrugs, takes another sip. "Yeah, but I saw you yesterday morning and you didn't say anything about leaving, and your boyfriend, what's his name, doesn't even live in L.A., does he?"

"No," I say, pushing the lid back on the coffee, trying to remember when I had ever said anything about Charles to Brad.

"He lives in New York," I add, sliding the coffee onto the counter. "But what does that have to do with my being here on a Saturday?"

"I just figured you'd be here. Unless you're sleeping with someone else," he says, pausing to take a sip. "But then, you don't seem like that kind of a woman."

Okay, wait a minute. Not only is this a little too personal, but he's been here what, all of two minutes, and he's got me talking about the one thing I've spent the last two months trying to avoid thinking about?

"Look, thanks for the coffee, but I'm going to get dressed now," I say, heading for the stairs.

"Hey, look, I didn't mean anything, really," he says, pushing off the counter. "I was only paying you a compliment. Honest."

I turn and shoot him an oh-sure look.

"Really," he says, holding up his hands. "You seem like a nice person. I just don't get why you're living here all by yourself. That's all."

God, do guys still think a woman can't live by herself and be happy? "Ah, maybe because I want to be?" I say.

"Really? That's cool."

"Yeah, it's very cool," I say, cinching my robe tighter. "Why wouldn't it be cool?"

"Well, only if you wanted someone else to be here and they weren't here."

"If I wanted someone here, they would be here," I say stoutly.

"Yeah?" he says, wiping his mouth with the back of his hand.

"Yeah, although sometimes there are complications. Jobs and careers and things. Although apparently you don't have that problem."

"I just don't think it's that complicated," he says, capping his coffee and putting it on the counter. "You want to be with someone. Then *be* with them," he says, turning back to me, a smile working at the sides of his mouth. "I mean, when I want to be with someone, I'm with them."

"Okay, I think we're talking about two different things," I say, turning toward the stairs. Oscar was one thing. Falling into bed with this guy is the *last* thing I need. I mean, what is he, twenty-three?

"Are you sure?" he says, leaning against the wall, his hand playing against his abs under his T-shirt.

Oh, God.

"Yeah, Brad," I say, not looking back. "I'm totally sure."

By the time I head back up the stairs, fully dressed, game face on, I realize I have more than an hour to kill before I have to meet Patrice and Lucienne at the Chateau. I check my watch. Not even 10:30. Normally, I would just be getting up now. But thanks to Brad, the smell of paint that's already overpowering, and now Christy, who I can hear playing the piano outside on her deck, I've got to go to Plan B. An hour at Fred Segal doing more Christmas shopping. Or grabbing a coffee and reading the paper at the café there. Anything, but I'm not staying here. Not with these two house invaders.

"You leaving?" Brad says when I hit the kitchen, head for the refrigerator and the six-pack of Arrowhead. He's on the ladder, shirt off, painting the ceiling.

"Yeah," I say, not even turning in his direction. "So if you get done before I get back, just let yourself out."

"Will do," he says, not breaking his brushstroke.

"So I guess this is it?" I turn and give the kitchen a once-over. It does look a lot better. Too bad it just took three months. And ended in a come-on.

"Yep," he says, dipping his brush in the bucket, wiping off the excess paint.

"Okay, well, thanks," I say, gripping my water.

"Sure," he says, turning to the ceiling again.

Okay, maybe I misread the whole thing. Maybe I'm overreacting. Maybe he was only trying to be nice. "Well, okay," I say, turning for the door.

"Okay."

"Okay," I say again. Pointlessly.

"Alex."

"Yeah," I say, turning back.

"If you change your mind . . ." he says, giving me a shit-eating grin.

I'm halfway up the front steps, cheeks on fire, before I realize what Christy is playing: "Time Is on My Side."

Even after killing an hour at Fred Segal's baby department trying to find something for less than two hundred dollars for Bevan, I'm the first to arrive at the Chateau. Since it's blazingly sunny but otherwise freezing out, I head for a chair in the lobby. I order another coffee and check my messages. Mom, saying that she's looking forward to seeing me Tuesday and that she and Jack will meet me at the airport. Amy, wondering if she's doing dessert or am I or should we split it because she has this new apple pie recipe she found? And Steven, saying Cyclops survived the surgery and to call him after the meeting. Actually, I'm assuming Lucienne flew in yesterday. I had Caitlin confirm the meeting with Patrice but never thought to check on Lucienne's actual arrival. Oh well, if it's just Patrice and Jay, I can wrap this up early and get in some more shopping before my blow-dry at four.

I lean back in the chair, one of those huge Victorian things the Chateau has in its lounge, and close my eyes. God, I wish I had been able to sleep in. It's only noon, but already I feel tired from being rousted by Brad. Oh well, at least that's the last I'll ever see of him. And the painting will finally be done. And. And. And. I'm just trying to decide if I could actually nod off in this chair, just for a second, when I hear Mercury screech to a halt in its orbit.

"*Oh, my God, Alec*, what are you doing inside on a day like today?"

I jerk upright. Patrice, in skintight cropped jeans, leopard print ankle boots, pink turtleneck, and purple ostrich handbag. And Oscar.

Ohmigod. What's *he* doing here?

"Hey, doll," Oscar says, bending down and giving me a kiss on my cheek. "Long time, no see."

Hey, doll? Not only is this the first I've seen him, I mean other than across a banquet hall, in a month, but he's going to play this—play us—like he's one of the Rat Pack? "Hey," I say, pushing to my feet and aiming for a tone of pure professional collegiality. "I didn't know you got dragooned into this."

"Alec, I'm getting us a table outside," Patrice says, heading for the patio. "It's just *too* gorgeous to be in here."

"'Dragooned'?" Oscar says once she's out of earshot. "I wasn't dragooned. Steven called and said he was leaving you to babysit these two. Three, if Lucienne actually shows. I just said I'd drop by if I could."

Steven? I should have figured he'd pull something like this. And just when I was starting to put the whole Oscar thing behind me. "Well, thanks," I say, running my hand through my hair and looking around for my bag, for anything other than Oscar's eyes. "I mean, it's just a meeting and I—"

"Besides, it's good to see you, Alex," he says.

I turn back. "And, and you," I stutter. "I mean, you're the one who got Patrice to agree to the Hancock Park site. You're the one with the magic touch."

"*Alec*, we're out here."

We both turn. Patrice in her shades, waving from the patio door.

"Oh, God," I say. "She's lived here what, five months now, and she still thinks L.A. is one endless summer? It's freezing outside."

"I'll get them to turn the heaters on," he says, turning to me. "Unless you just want to blow the meeting and get a room."

I'm so startled by this, it takes me a moment to recover. Even so, I can't tell if Oscar's serious or just fucking with me. Or if Mercury has sputtered back to life. "Don't do this," I say, turning to him. "Not now. Not here. Please?"

He looks at me a second and then draws his fingers down the side of my face. "Okay," he says, dropping his hand. "Okay."

"So the whole white-and-black idea should be a motif, not a *theme*," Patrice says, jabbing her straw against the lemon wedged in the bottom of her iced tea.

Hunched in the chair across from her, I uncross my arms to pull the collar of my suede jacket up and nod. We've been here forty-five minutes, and even with the heaters on, I'm so fucking freezing I'd agree to anything. Just to wrap this up.

"A concept," chirps Jay, wiping his plate of curried shrimp with a wedge of bread.

"I mean, it's meant to evoke, not mimic the Capote party," Patrice adds, pulling a piece of ice from the glass with her fingers and sticking it in her mouth. "Ah whe chlear?"

"Look, it's all in the staging," Oscar says, leaning forward over his latte. "You've seen the board. It's very subtle. The DJ I've got lined up is totally into the whole retro thing, and we can choose the furniture from Twentieth week after next," he adds, mentioning the hip Beverly Boulevard boutique. "They're being very generous since there was no room in the budget for anything custom."

Patrice flicks her hair over her shoulder and flags the waiter for another iced tea. Given her body temperature, she could probably just tap a vein.

"Is Lucienne coming?" I say, leaning forward to wrap my

hands around my mug of cappuccino. "All we really have left to work out is the gift bag and what she's willing to give which host committee members."

"She called me this morning and said she'd be here," Patrice says, checking her watch. "Although maybe I said we were meeting at one, not twelve."

Oh, great. Another hour on the Chateau's windswept steppe.

"Well, there's always the list," Patrice says, leaning back in her chair, closing her eyes, and turning her face to the sun. "We can go over that while we're waiting."

Right. The List. Already this is shaping up as our — as my — biggest problem. C always demands a really high-end but cutting-edge guest list. Very Gywnnie–Vincent Gallo, like those two would ever be in the same place. This is hard enough to conjure given that C isn't *Vanity Fair.* Or *InStyle.* Not that they seem to care. Now that Patrice is involved, it's spinning out of control. Whatever good behavior she had exhibited after losing the December cover is rapidly going by the boards as we get closer to the party date. Not only is her guest list absurd but she's already nixing most of the preliminary list that we had supplied. The same list of celebs, managers, agents, producers, and press we rely on to stoke every party.

"Yeah, okay," I sigh, reaching in my bag for the list Patrice had e-mailed me yesterday. I scan it again. A traffic accident waiting to happen. Or, actually, not happen. I mean, her guest list drawn from the December issue's editorial is totally lame. Without a cover, we can scratch one big chance to get an Oscar-hungry A-lister to turn out for the cameras in the middle of awards season. Plus, the stories in the issue are mostly from New York, London, and Paris, and the handful from L.A. are complete nonstarters. The hottest tennis coach? Like anyone younger than Tony Curtis still plays. An unknown male screenwriter who's just written his first novel? Who isn't writing a novel in L.A.? An overview on Hollywood's best psychics? I don't need a psychic to know that none of these people, with the possible exception of the screenwriter, are party worthy. Still, that hasn't stopped Patrice from putting down her dream team. Paris Hilton. Okay, maybe, if she's in town and we bribe her with a diamond collar for Tinkerbell. But Beyoncé, Kate Winslet, Orlando Bloom, Jack Nicholson, and Don Trump? Dream on.

"I think we've got a really strong lineup," Jay says, reaching for another slab of bread. "Jack and The Donald in the same room? I can't wait to see it."

"Yeah, well, don't hold your breath," I say.

Patrice's eyes snap open. "I can't believe you're being so negative. This is a fabulous list, and Andrew's approved it. What you sent us was"—she pauses and raises her hands, the sun glinting off the half dozen rings on her fingers—"was beyond ordinary. I mean, Selma Blair? China Chow? Michael Chiklis? And who exactly is Jason Weinberg?"

"Those are people who actually show up at parties," I say, trying to keep my voice even. "And Jason happens to be one of the hottest managers in town. We do a lot of work with him and his clients."

I can tell this means nothing to her. None of it does. And no one is going to talk her out of it. Oscar and I have laid the groundwork for a really fantastic party, but I swear if she doesn't back off and let me—let us—do our job, she's going to fuck it up. And it's going to be my head on the line, not hers.

"Yeah, well, that may be okay for your other parties," she says, flicking her hair, "but it's not where we want ours to be."

"Look," I say, trying a different tactic. "Think of our list as not the final list, but a starting place. Once we get the host committee members nailed down with Lucienne's help, which is why she and the Diamond Council are your—our—key sponsor, we can come up with a group of A-listers who are likely to attend. And then we can go from there."

Patrice doesn't say anything, just rattles the ice in her glass.

"Look," Oscar says, leaning forward. "It's all about building the word-of-mouth, and Alex and her team are really good at that. We wouldn't be here if she wasn't."

I shoot him a look. Okay, at least we're still colleagues. Still on the same team, professionally.

"Well, I want to go over my list one name at a time," Patrice says, slumping back in her chair. "If you have such a problem with it, I want to hear the pros and cons on each one."

I sigh, the afternoon stretching out in front of me. Endless. Endless and freezing. I will be a frozen, overcaffeinated corpse that will need to be pried off this chair and brought back to life with the ministrations of a hot blow-dryer if I'm to get through the rest of the day.

"*Hulllooo.*"

We all turn. Lucienne, in white shirt, white pants, shades, and diamond studs of Oprah dimensions, striding toward us. "God, you wouldn't believe what I just escaped," she says, bustling up and giving us all air kisses. "It was actually snowing in New York when I left. So fabulous to be out here in the tropics. All this sun."

"It's actually a Mediterranean climate," Oscar says, rising out of his chair with a smile. "Not that we'll hold that against you."

"Oh, you," Lucienne says, swatting him on the arm. "I swear, if I wasn't already married. Who are you seeing these days, anyway?" she says, sinking into a chair and waving for the waiter. "Which soon-to-be-at-a-movie-screen-near-you-blond starlet is it these days? I thought I heard you were with that new girl, what's her name?" she says, snapping her fingers. "The one who was in the latest *Scream*?"

I look over at Oscar. So much for getting a room. So much for being on the same team. And how had I missed that latest rumor? Guess he barely broke his stride after our one night together. Okay, if that's the way he's playing it. At least I know where I stand now.

"Hey, I am way, *way* down on the totem pole in this town," he says, waving her off. "Besides, I'm getting too old to be chick bait."

"Really? I didn't think that was possible in this town," I say, leaning forward. Am I mistaken, or is he trying to avoid looking at me? At any of us? Suddenly, lunch is looking a lot more interesting.

"Oh, trust me," Oscar says, shaking his head, fiddling with his coffee cup. "It's more than possible."

"Not you," hoots Lucienne. "You're legendary."

"Well, at some age it just gets pathetic," Patrice says, putting her iced-tea glass down with a thump, clearly miffed to give up the spotlight she held just a second ago. "I mean, Sean Connery is one thing, but Woody Allen is just an embarrassment."

"I loved *Annie Hall*," chirps Jay. "He and Diane Keaton were hilarious."

"Yeah," I say. "Who's his latest romantic comedy costar, Dakota Fanning?"

"I think she dropped out," Patrice says, completely missing my joke. "It's someone else."

"And I loved *Something's Gotta Give*," Jay says. "Diane's hot. For an older woman."

"Oh, it's the same dynamic offscreen," Lucienne says, reaching for a menu. "I mean, sometimes I think I'm the only woman I know in an age-appropriate relationship."

"How long have you been married?" I say, trying to remember who her husband was. Is. Some Wall Street guy, I think.

"Stan and I knew each other in college," she says. "The only reason we're still together is it's too much effort to split up. Too expensive. I mean, one of us would have to give up the Hamptons house and the other one would have to give up the co-op, and that's not going to happen. Not the way real estate is going these days. Oh, I know who it was," she says, turning to Oscar. "I heard you were seeing Mai Chong, that adorable Chinese actress who just got a role in the new Quentin Tarantino film. *Kill Bill Volume* whatever it is."

"You mean Lucy Liu?" Patrice says, sounding stunned as she turns to Oscar. "*You're* dating Lucy Liu?"

"I'm not dating Lucy Liu," he says, sounding embarrassed. "I'm not dating anyone."

"Oh, I know who you mean," Jay says. "Wasn't she on the Chinese Olympic diving team, although I don't think she actually medaled. We were thinking of doing a story on her in the magazine at one point."

Patrice jabs at her ice again. "Well, whoever she is, we'd have to see the movie first."

The waitress rolls up with another round of iced teas, all of which seem to be for Patrice.

"Okay, I'll have the grilled shrimp salad, although it looks like you folks have already eaten," Lucienne says, gazing at the table for the first time.

"Yeah, but go ahead," I say, my mind reeling. Blond twenty-year-old wannabes are one thing, but this is different.

"Is that who you're seeing?" I say, turning to Oscar. "The Chinese *Olympian*? Sounds like quite a catch. All those double somersaults and half twists."

"I hear they're double-jointed," Jay says, reaching for one of the iced teas. "I mean, they totally dominate the sport."

"Would that make you happy?" Oscar says, meeting my gaze for the first time.

"Does it make you happy?"

I look away. Across the table I catch sight of Patrice, chewing on her straw, eyeing us. For someone so clueless, she doesn't miss a trick.

"Alex, how much older is Charles than you?" Lucienne says, reaching for the bread.

"What?" I say, startled.

"Charles? How much older is he? You two are about the same age, aren't you?"

"He's forty-five," I say.

"Then you're the same age," Patrice says coolly.

"No," I say, turning to her. "He's older. Almost ten years older."

"Really?" she says like she's mulling this over. "I wouldn't have guessed that."

"You have an older boyfriend, don't you, back in England?" I say, recalling something in my Google search about her seeing some polo player. Lord Something or Other. From the photos he looked about fifty. But then, most Englishmen look about fifty.

"Hmm?" she says, cocking her head like she hasn't quite heard me.

"See, I *am* the only one in an age-appropriate relationship," Lucienne says. "I've just proved my own point."

"And I've got to go. I've got another event this evening, so I'll leave you guys to hammer out the list," Oscar says, rising to his feet and giving Lucienne a kiss on the cheek. "Great to see you. Whatever you need, call my office when you get back. Meanwhile, this crowd can fill you in. The event's looking really great."

"So I'll see you tonight," he says, turning to me.

I look up. I can hardly remember when we were actually friends.

"Yeah," I say. "Wouldn't miss it."

14

Or Maybe It's Just Something in the Water

"I could kill you. I could fucking kill you."

I'm on my cell to Steven, driving home after the lunch meeting followed by my blow-dry.

"Oh, come on, all I did was tell him I couldn't make the meeting and you were going to handle it."

"Well, he *showed up.*"

"Well, that was his own decision."

"You never suggested it?"

"No, I swear. He called me with some specs on the furniture he wanted me to give Patrice, and I told him I wasn't going to be at the meeting but you were."

"I still think you suggested it," I say, turning off Sunset onto Laurel Canyon.

"I didn't, but even if I did, he made the decision to go himself. Obviously, he wanted to see you."

"Yeah, whatever," I say, eyeing the traffic ahead of me, trying to decide if I should drive home through Mount Olympus, all those ghastly houses that look like apartment buildings, or if I have time to wind through the canyon. I check my watch. Almost 5:30. And I'm due at Barry's country club by 6:30. Better take Mount Olympus. It's going to be close as it is.

"Well, how was it, to state the obvious."

"That's a question, not a statement," I say. "And it was a nightmare. Did you know he's dating Mai Chong?"

"*Who?*"

"That Chinese actress. Excuse me, that Chinese Olympic diver turned actress. The one who's in the new Tarantino movie."

Steven says something, but the static drowns him out.

"Hang on a second," I say, heading up Apollo. "I'm going into the canyon."

Steven says something more, but the static is even worse. Damn hills. You can never get a signal in them. "I'll call you back when I get home," I say, and click off, tossing the phone to the passenger seat. I speed up Apollo and turn onto Jupiter. This neighborhood is so ridiculous. Plus all the speed bumps. I'm going to have about five minutes at home to change and reach Steven again before I have to leave.

I'm just rounding the corner of my street when I see Brad's truck still parked next to the garage. Oh, Christ. I totally forgot he was here. *Damn it.* After our little talk this morning, I have no interest in seeing him again. Besides, why hasn't he finished yet? He's been here for hours. I hit the garage door opener and pull in, the door shuddering down behind me. Clutching my bag and the mail, I hurry down the front steps. I try to let myself in with my key, but the front door is unlocked.

"Hey," I say, stepping into the kitchen. The paint cans, drop cloths, his toolbox, and the ladder are still out, although judging from the walls, the actual painting is finished. "Hello," I say, heading into the living room. "Brad?" Despite all his detritus, the first floor is completely empty. Where is he? Oh, God. I have a sudden fear that he's downstairs in my bedroom. "Hey," I say, calling down the stairwell. "Brad?"

No answer. Screwing up my courage, I head down, but the bedroom is the way I left it this morning. Empty. Okay, I give up. Where is this guy? I check my watch. 5:45. Shit. I have got to get out of here in the next fifteen minutes. I head back up and out the front door. Maybe he left a note on his truck or something. This is totally strange and a complete pain in the ass. If he doesn't show, I'm going to have to leave him locked out. Which means I'll have to pack up all his paint stuff tomorrow unless I want to live in a construction zone all weekend.

I push through the gate and check his truck. No note on the windshield. I peer in the driver's side window. It's the usual work-man's mess. Food wrappers, soda cans, tools, God knows what else. I look up and down the street. Okay, I'm going to have to call him on his cell, not that he ever answers it, and then just leave. Tell him he can get his stuff Monday.

I'm heading back down the front steps when a light from Christy's house catches my eye. I look over through the trees. She must have every light in the house blazing. Probably getting ready for another one of her all-night parties that always end with every-one on her deck. At least I won't be home to hear it until after midnight.

I'm just at the bottom of the steps when I see them. Down-stairs, in her bedroom, on her bed, which she has thoughtfully, for my viewing pleasure, shoved up against the glass French doors. With Brad, naked, his perfect abs poised over Christy, arching up below him.

Maybe I'm the one with the problem. Maybe we should all just fuck like rabbits and worry about it later. Or not, since nobody else seems to. Or maybe I've got more of my Philly upbringing in me than I thought I had. Can take the girl out of the Main Line, but can't take the Main Line out of the girl. Now there's a depressing thought. And I thought Kristin Davis had been my favorite on *Sex and the City* because I envied her hair. Turns out I'm a total prude and never knew it.

This is my frame of mind as I speed across Ventura Boulevard toward Barry's country club. Speeding because, of course, I'm completely late. After finding Brad in flagrante with Christy, it took me about two seconds to decide what to do — get his shit out of my house — and about a half an hour to move it all outside. I still had to clean up, change, and call Louise. Left her a rather cryptic message that Brad was finally finished and that I had no further need for any of his services, such as they were. I propped the front gate open a fraction, and once I was in the car heading out, with no chance of encountering him, I dialed Brad's cell. Opting for discreet but pointed, I told him when he was finished giving Christy an estimate on whatever it was she wanted done, he could pick up the rest of his things in my front yard. Oh, yeah. And give my regards to his girlfriend. Now I can only pray he actually gets all his stuff tonight and that will be the end of Brad.

I cross Vineland, head down Moorpark, turn in to the club's entrance, and pull up to the bored-looking guy in the guardhouse. "Scrabble," I say, and am waved through. I drive forward into the parking lot — pretty empty, not a good sign — and pull in to a space. In the dark, I see a few other latecomers straggling toward the door. No one seems in much of a hurry except me. I pass a huge Mercedes and catch a whiff of pot. Scrabble, stoned? That might be interesting. Oh, shit. In all the excitement, I realize I forgot to call Steven back and get the scoop on Oscar and the Chinese Olympian. Oh well, too late now. I'll just have to reach Steven in the morning.

I yank open the club's front door, catch a blast of the cool, stale air, smelling of mildew, antiseptic, and roasting turkey, and head down the hall. Same old plaid carpet and same old black-and-white framed shots lining the walls. Winners of the club's golf and tennis matches since time began. I round the corner, the turkey smell grows stronger, and catch sight of my student council presidents, or two of them at least, manning the obligatory check-in table.

"Okay, thank you and enjoy the game," Maurine says, beaming up at a pair of guests, an Oscar-winning screenwriter and his wife. Jill is next to her, going over the list of names.

"How's it going?" I say, sliding in next to them.

"Great," Maurine says. "I actually think we have fewer no-shows this year."

"It's okay," Jill says, looking up from the list. "Where've you been? A hot date?"

"No," I say. "Why? Do I look like I had a hot date?"

"You look a little frazzled, and Oscar said you might be late."

"Oscar said I might be late?" I say, startled. Why would Oscar be saying anything about my arrival time?

"The meeting with Patrice," adds Maurine. "He said it might go late."

"That was hours ago," I say, totally mystified at Oscar's sudden interest.

I bend over Jill to scan the list. She's right, only about half the guests are actually here. Still, if 75 percent of invitees actually sent contributions to the charity along with their regrets, Barry, or rather Barb, should go home happy. "Well, so far so good, although maybe we'll have a few extra gift bags given these numbers," I say, looking up. "Where are the bags, by the way?"

"Allie's got them shoved in some closet somewhere," Jill says, not looking up. "She'll move them out here to the table once the game gets going because" — she pauses and looks up — "as we know from experience, some people sneak out after the first round, and we wouldn't want them to miss getting their travel Scrabble game, soundtrack CD from Barry's new movie, and the most up-to-date brochure on the charity, would we?"

"Yeah, I know," I say. "Okay, sounds like a plan."

I'm just turning back to the list when I hear a familiar voice. "Well, good to see you finally joined us, Alex."

I look up. Barb, in tweed trousers, her long blond hair swept up into a ponytail — see, we're all just having fun tonight! — clutching the *OED*. The abridged version. Still, it's as bulky as a toaster.

"Hey," I say, leaning toward her for the requisite air hug, trying to avoid colliding with the dictionary. "Looks like a good turnout this year."

"Hmm," she says, reaching past Jill to scan the list. "Could be better. By the way, when is the *Variety* photographer getting here?"

"*Variety* photographer?" I say. In all the years we've handled the tournament, Barry's never once asked for any publicity. Like most private Hollywood parties, as the host, he wants industry buzz, a good turnout, but no overt publicity.

"Yes. The *Variety* photographer," she says, looking up at me, her eyes narrowing. "Barry and I agreed this year we needed to promote the tournament. For the good of the charity."

"Well, that was never conveyed to us," I say, racking my brain. I look over at Jill and Maurine, who are both, bless them, shaking their heads.

"Ah, yes it was," Barb says, looking from me to them and back again. "Barry told me he left that request with your office. Weeks ago."

Maybe he had. I mean, it's not unthinkable that Caitlin would have screwed that up. Written down "Call Barry re: party" and left it at that. Still, I would have called him back. I would have followed up even without Caitlin spelling it out in the message. He and I would have had an actual conversation about inviting press.

"Barb, I apologize if that was the case, but in all our conversations, Barry never once mentioned it," I say, dropping my voice as

I catch sight of a gaggle of latecomers heading down the hall. Before Barb can answer, I hear a familiar voice over my shoulder.

"Hey, Alex, next time a little advance notice would be nice."

I turn. Howard Finnegan from *Variety*. Okay, this is very strange. Even with Mercury flying around the heavens. "Hey," I say, reaching out to shake his hand. "Thanks for making it. Especially since we didn't actually have you down."

"Thank God, someone invited him," Barb hisses, reaching past me. "Howard, great to see you," she says, grabbing him by the arm. "Come on inside. I think there're several people here you'll recognize."

Barb sweeps off with her prize catch.

"Okay, what just happened?" I say, turning to the girls.

"Search me," Jill says, bent over the list again. "I'm still trying to figure out who's actually cut checks for the charity and who hasn't."

"At least Barb's happy," Maurine says with a shrug. "That's what counts."

"What the hell is Howard Finnegan doing here?"

We all turn. Allie, barreling out of the banquet hall, her legs moving fast despite her three-inch stilettos. "I mean, I thought we weren't doing press on this?" she says, pulling up.

"We don't know," I say, shaking my head. "None of us invited him, but Barb insists Barry told us they wanted press. Now, as if by magic, he's here. Maybe Barry invited him and forgot to tell us."

"Those trophy wives are all the same," Allie says, glancing over her shoulder. "They just want their pictures in the trades."

"Oh, come on, Barb's not that bad," I say. "Not compared to some of them."

"You watch. She'll be in Monday's edition, between two Oscar winners, clutching the *OED*."

"Well, as long as she's happy," I say, catching sight of Barry, with both kids in tow — what are the kids doing here? — being waylaid by Barb and Howard. "Look," I say, turning back to Allie.

"Stay with Howard and Barb. I'm going to talk to Barry and find out what's going on."

Allie and I head into the hall. A few of the guests have already taken their places at the game tables, but most of the crowd is still jammed around the bar. Snippets of conversation float by. The usual pre-award industry chatter, the upcoming holiday releases. Oscar handicapping.

"Hey, Alex, there you are."

I turn. Barry, heading my way, his daughter, Sophie, in one arm, his other clutching his son, Jonah. "Hey," he says, bending down, awkwardly, to give me a kiss on my cheek.

"Hey there, I was just looking for you," I say, reaching up to help hold Sophie upright on his shoulder.

"*Aww*," she squeals, falling backward, grabbing my head and a hunk of my hair.

"Hey, honey, now don't hurt Daddy's friends," Barry says, trying to reel her in. "You remember Alex. She's one of Daddy's best friends. And we don't hurt Daddy's friends, do we?"

"That's okay," I say, trying to disentangle my hair from Sophie's grip, which I realize is completely sticky.

"Sorry," Barry says with a grimace. "She just spilled her juice, and Anna isn't here yet."

"Anna?" I say, still working on my hair.

"Our nanny. Barb wanted to bring the kids this year. Get them used to the idea of philanthropy. But Anna's supposed to take them home now, except she's not here yet."

"*Daddy*, you said we were going to have turkey," Jonah says, pulling on Barry's arm. "When are we having turkey? I'm tired of *waiting*."

"Barry," I say, still trying to break free from Sophie's grip. "I wanted to ask you about Howard Finnegan, if you invited—"

"Hey there, Barry."

We both turn. Rob Reiner and his wife cruise by.

"Hey, great to see you," Barry says, trying to extricate a hand in order to shake Rob's.

"*Daddy*," Jonah yowls, hanging on harder. "*You said!*"

"Rob, let me catch up with you in a minute," Barry says, bending over Jonah. "I want to talk to you about a script I've got in the pipeline."

Rob smiles, moves off, and Barry turns back to me. "Hey, Alex, I hate to ask, but can you take the kids? I mean, just until Anna gets here," he says, passing Sophie over to my shoulder.

Like I have any choice.

"Sure," I say, reaching out for her.

"*Nooooooo*," Sophie screams, letting go of my hair to flail after her father.

"Honey, go with Alex," Barry says, bending down to dislodge Jonah's hand. "Go with Alex and she'll give you turkey."

"*Nooo!*" Jonah says, backing away from me.

"Daddy has to work now," Barry says, shooting me a sorry-I-owe-you grimace. "Go with Alex and she'll take care of you."

Barry melts into the crowd, leaving me saddled up with the Katzenjammer Kids.

"Come on, let's get something to eat," I chirp, looking from Sophie to Jonah. From the murderous cast of their eyes, they are two volcanoes about to explode. Better move fast if I want to avoid a scene. "Okay, we're going to the kitchen now. Let's see what they've got for you guys," I say, grabbing Jonah's hand and turning for the back of the hall. I push into the crowd, Sophie a squirming deadweight on my shoulder and Jonah, pulling on my other arm, doing his best imitation of a ship's anchor.

No one even glances in my direction as we lumber past. I've never met Anna, but she has my deepest respect and sympathy.

I round the bar. "Looks like you could use some help," one of the bartenders says, shooting me a smile. I give him a pained smile back. We servants like to stick together.

"Okay, here we are," I say, pulling up to the kitchen door. With both my hands otherwise occupied, I have no choice but to lower my head and butt open the swinging door. "*Oww!*" Jonah says when the door still manages to whack him on the arm.

"Sorry," I say, pulling us forward. Inside it's like an E.R. of food prep, a blaze of light and heat and cooking smells and some half dozen cooks yelling commands in Spanish and Spanglish. *Hoy, chica. You better move your muy poquito ass before I move it for you!* Okay, so perhaps this isn't the kid-friendly environment I was hoping for. I look around for a place to safely deposit the kids, but every counter is covered with plates, dishes, trays. Sophie starts to squirm against my shoulder, mewling like a cat trying to escape my grip. "Okay, Sophie, we're going to get you —" I say, but Jonah drowns me out. "I don't want to eat *here!*" he screams, yanking on my arm. "Where's Daddy? He's supposed to eat with me."

"*Hey!*"

I whirl around. Or as much as one can whirl when anchored by eighty pounds of squalling flesh. Hot Fat, in a red bandanna and white chef's jacket, sharpening a huge carving knife, glaring in my direction. What's *he* doing here? I thought Oscar was using the club's catering staff.

"Oh, hey," I say, nodding. "Good to see you again, Hot Fat."

"Don't give me none of that 'Good to see you, Hot Fat,'" he says. "Not when you got kids in my kitchen. I don't allow no kids in my kitchen."

Perhaps now is not the best moment to remind him that it's not, technically, his kitchen. That tonight, if anything, the kitchen belongs to the parents of these two kids.

"Okay, look, we're not staying," I say, yanking Jonah out of the path of one of the line cooks racing by with a huge tray of salads. "I just need to get —"

"You need to get them out of here," he says, advancing toward me. "Last time I saw you, I had goats all over my kitchen. Now you be dragging kids in here? Uh-uh," he says, shaking his head. "You and Hot Fat are no good together."

Could I be on a collision course with one more male today?

"Okay, look, those goats were not my fault," I sputter, point-lessly, given that, in all the excitement, Sophie has erupted into screams that are only partially drowned out by Jonah's wailing.

"As John Lithgow once said to Debra Winger, 'And you're so good with them.'"

I whip around. Oscar. In a black sport jacket and wool polo shirt. Talk about a rock and a hard place. It takes me about one second to choose the hard place.

"Yeah, I know," I say over Sophie's screams. "Barry dumped them on me because the nanny's not here yet and they're starving, and obviously" — I pause, nodding in Hot Fat's direction — "I'm about as welcome as Typhoid Mary in here."

"Well, Mary, let's start with these," Oscar says, grabbing two rolls from a basket on the counter and handing one to Jonah and another to Sophie, who immediately stops screaming and starts to gum the roll. "Thus temporarily sated," he says, turning back to me. "Take them out to the patio. I got some tables set up under the heaters, but no one's out there yet."

"Yeah, but I need to give them something more to eat."

"Yeah, I'll bring it," he says, turning me toward the door. "Go on and I'll meet you out there in a second."

Oscar holds the door open as I stagger through, dragging Jonah, who is engrossed in his roll now. "How do you know what they'll eat?" I say, turning back.

"You think you're the only one who's good with kids?" he says. "I'll figure it out. Go on. I'll be right there."

I press back through the crowd, which is beginning to drift toward the game tables. Across the room, I catch sight of Barry deep in conversation with Rob. Apparently he's forgotten about the kids and me. God only knows where the nanny is.

"Oh, Alex, thank God you've got the kids." I turn. Barb, whizzing by with Howard Finnegan still in tow. "I was just wondering where they'd gone to."

"*Mommeee*," Sophie squeals, holding out her roll.

Barb freezes in her tracks. "Is that carbs?" she says, turning back. "Are you giving them *carbs*?" She turns from me to Jonah. "Honey, did you eat carbs? You know our rule about carbs."

"Carbs, carbs, carbs," Jonah chants, waving what's left of his roll.

Barb reaches out, trying to grab the roll. "Honey, give me that."

"Noooo," he says, turning away, grabbing my leg.

"Honey, let Mommy have it," she says, bending down, trying to wrestle the roll from him, which only causes Jonah to squirm harder.

"Uh, I wouldn't if I were you," I say, taking a step backward, trying to brace myself as Jonah thrashes against me. "Besides, I think it's actually whole wheat."

"Whole wheat? It's completely *white*!" she says, glaring up at me. "I think I know refined flour when I see it."

"Honey, I think everyone's ready to start."

We both look up. Barry, waving in our direction. Barb stands, fluffs her bangs. "Okay, I'll deal with this later, but they are not to eat any more carbs. Do I make myself clear?"

Sir, yes, sir.

"Absolutely," I say, reaching down with my free hand to disentangle Jonah from my leg. Barb sails off, clutching the *OED* and Howard Finnegan, while I turn for the patio. As I push through the door, the cold night air hits us like a slap. Like breathing a glass of ice water after the heat of the room.

"I'm *cold*," Jonah wails, slowing now, pulling on my arm.

"Yeah, I know," I say, heading for one of the tables nearest the gas heater. "Look, it's warmer over here." I pull out a chair for Jonah and another for myself and practically collapse into it with Sophie still on my shoulder.

"God, I don't know about you guys, but I'm tired," I say, looking at them. Small talk with kids has never been my forte, but I have to do something to pass the time until Oscar shows up.

"You said 'God,'" Jonah says, looking up at me. "You said a swearword."

"I suppose I did, if I wasn't using it in a strictly ecumenical sense, which I wasn't," I say, with a sigh.

He eyes me suspiciously. "What?"

"Never mind," I say, turning toward the door. Where is Oscar with the food? "Alex is just babbling to herself."

"Who's Alex?" he says.

"I'm Alex," I say, reaching forward in the chair to extend my hand. "Allow me to introduce myself."

Jonah looks at my hand, then at me, and back at my hand. Gingerly, he sticks out a hand and takes mine. "Why do you have a boy's name?"

"Because I have such great rapport with boys. They decided to give me a boy's name."

He stares at me. "My name's Jonah."

"Like in the Bible."

"Like in the *fish*."

"Actually, it was a whale, which is technically a mammal."

His eyes narrow. I've got about ten more seconds to keep him distracted with this kind of adult chitchat. "But yes, like a fish," I say. "A very big fish."

Sophie wraps her arms around my neck tighter and starts to whimper. God, how do parents do this 24/7? Apparently, they don't. Or at least Barry and Barb don't. Suddenly the patio door bangs open, and Oscar bursts through, carrying a huge tray.

"Okay, here we go," he says, bustling up. "We've got turkey and mashed potatoes and green beans. And milk," he says, handing out the plates and glasses.

"*Turkey!*" Jonah says, jumping up and reaching for his plate.

"And for our favorite babysitter, we have a nice glass of sauvignon blanc," he says, handing me a glass. "And a candle for atmosphere," he adds, placing a lighted votive in the middle of the table. "Dinner is served.

"Here," he says, reaching for Sophie and sinking into another chair, where he starts to feed her. "So, this is fun, right?" he says, gazing around at us. "Like camping. Camping at the club."

"*Camping!*" Jonah says, spearing a piece of turkey.

"Thanks," I say, cradling the wineglass in my lap. "Thanks for bailing me out. Barry just dumped them on me and bolted."

"Well, being a single parent is tough," he says, giving Sophie a sip of milk.

"You know this from experience."

"My sister," he says, looking up. "She and her husband split up when her kids were about this age, and yeah, it was tough. I used to spend part of every summer with her, helping out."

"This was after Hawaii but before the Army?"

"Precisely."

I sigh and take a sip of wine. I don't get it. Or rather him. I don't get *him*. Earlier this afternoon, I had it all figured out. The guy's a complete asshole. Now I'm confused again. It's like the sum of the parts doesn't add up to the whole. On the surface, Oscar can seem like the greatest guy. Smart, funny, cynical, fabulous in bed. Runs a successful business without being a complete obsessive-compulsive about it, unlike most of the men in town. And he's even good with kids. But then there's all the rest of it. His penchant for Elsa and her prepubescent ilk. His inability to commit to any woman for longer than three weeks. His refusal even to call me after our one night together. And now — *shit, the Chinese Olympian* — now there's the Chinese Olympian.

"What's the matter?"

I look up. Oscar's staring at me over Sophie's head. For a second, I wonder, what if this was our life? If we were actually together. All of us. Well, not literally Sophie and Jonah, since they already have parents, such as they are. But a family.

"Nothing," I say, shaking my head, shaking off the idea. "It's just been a really long day."

"So Barb's happy. Her best friend won the tournament. She got her picture taken with Rob Reiner and two Oscar-winning screen-writers, not including her husband," says Jill.

Allie yawns. "And we only had twenty-five extra gift bags, which the charity was happy to take, so we can all go home happy."

It's after midnight, and I'm at one of the empty game tables with Allie and Jill — Maurine left about an hour ago — debriefing ourselves about the evening.

"Hey, did you ever find out who called Howard Finnegan?" Jill asks.

"No, I never got a chance to ask Barry," I say, shaking my head. "Allie, did you find out who invited him?"

She screws up her face. "Think I got a word with Howard with Barb guarding him all night? Frankly, who cares? He came, problem solved."

"Okay, then it goes down as one of the modern miracles," I say.

"Right up there with Lourdes and the dismissal of the Kobe Bryant rape case," Jill says, rolling her eyes.

"Ladies, is there anything we at the event staff can get you? More wine? Coffee? A ride home?"

We all look up, sleepily. Oscar, in his polo shirt, his jacket over his shoulder.

"No, I'm good," Jill says, pushing to her feet. "Oscar, another lovely Thanksgiving dinner, thank you," she says, pressing her hands together over her heart and bowing slightly as she heads past him. "See you guys Monday," she calls over her shoulder.

"See you then, and thanks," I say.

"Okay, I'm out of here," Allie says. "I'm going to early Mass tomorrow."

I look over at her.

"I'm kidding," she says, reaching out and squeezing my cheeks in her hand. "I know it's late, but I'm kidding, Alex."

"I get it," I say, or rather mew, since she's got my face squinched in her hand.

"So, no one needs anything?" Oscar says, nodding in the direction of the kitchen.

"Nah," Allie says, letting go of my face to grab her bag. "Later, dude, dudette," she says, ambling out.

"You all right?" Oscar says, turning to me.

"Hey, maybe you know the answer," I say, ignoring his question and pushing to my feet. "Do you know who called Howard Finnegan? I mean, we didn't have him down on the list, although Barb insists Barry told us they wanted press, but then suddenly he just showed up."

"Uh, yeah," Oscar says, running his hand over his head. "Actually I do."

"I figured it was Barry," I say, bending down to retrieve my bag. "A last-minute call to keep Barb happy after he screwed up and forgot to tell us."

"Actually, it was me."

I stop and look up. "What do you mean, it was you?"

"I called him."

It takes a minute for this to sink in. "You called him? Why would you call Howard? Why would you even think to call him?"

"Because I'm the best event producer in town, because I overheard Barb bitching about there being no press, because I have Howard's cell phone number in my cell phone, because, because, because. Mostly because I figured it was one less headache for you."

"And because you had no time to check with me? To see what we had arranged about the press?" I can't believe this. Whatever is — was — going on between me and Oscar has nothing to do with our jobs. He would never get involved in event publicity, just like I would never go around him and make decisions about what caterer or security company to use.

"Yeah, well, apparently you didn't arrange it, and don't worry about thanking me," he says, raising his hands.

"Hey, I *didn't* arrange for publicity, because Barry never asked me to arrange it. I can't believe you took it upon yourself to call *Variety* because you heard Barb bitching. Oscar, if Barry really didn't want press and suddenly you invited Howard, it could have been a problem."

"Well, it wasn't a problem," he says. "And frankly, it solved a big problem — for you. So like I said, don't bother thanking me."

"Notice that I'm not."

He looks at me and shakes his head. "Okay, I was just trying to help out, but you want to be a bitch, then be a bitch."

Blood surges to my cheeks. In all the time I've known him, I've never heard Oscar talk like this. Not to me. Not to anyone. Whatever I may have wondered about us out on the patio tonight with the kids is totally gone now. This is a side of Oscar I've never seen, and I don't want to see any more. I grab my bag and turn for the door. "You like doing this?" I say, pausing briefly as I pass him. "You like picking fights with the women you fuck over? Is that how you assuage your guilt?"

"Hey," he says, reaching out and grabbing my arm. "I never fucked you over. I wouldn't fuck you over."

"Well, it feels pretty terrible anyway," I say, my voice small, my mind spinning. "But I don't want to think about this anymore," I say, trying to pull my arm free. "I can't, right now."

"Then later," he says, letting go of my arm. "Think about it later."

"Yeah, later," I say, turning for the door, my eyes filling with tears. "Later."

15

Starting Over, Again

"You got everything? All the gifts, your mittens, your self-
esteem?"

"Yeah," I say, smiling and wiping my nose. I put the phone to
my other ear and turn to face out the window at the 737 glinting
on the tarmac. The one that just landed from someplace where
it's really winter — Boston, Minneapolis, Chicago maybe — the
same one that will be taking me back home. Funny, I've lived in
L.A. for five years, and I still think of Philadelphia as home. At
least at the holidays.

"So you'll have fun, seeing everyone, especially since you
won't be together at Christmas," Steven says.

"You can stop trying to make me feel better," I say, watching as
the gate agents, crisp in their navy and white uniforms, unbolt the
jetway door. "It's been three days. Even Christ rose from the dead
after three days. I can certainly get over Oscar's little meltdown
after three days."

"That's the spirit," he says. "I still can't believe he called you a bitch. That bitch."

I sigh and wipe my nose again. "Well, I probably deserved it at the moment. I was pretty angry."

"And neither one of you thought to consider that maybe you weren't really fighting about poor Howard Finnegan but something more personal, more important? I mean, do the words *misdirected anger* mean nothing to you?"

"Yeah, I know," I say, watching as the arriving passengers — first class, puffed with self-consciousness even if they're upgrades, and then the coach hordes — stream through the gate. Judging by the scarves and coats bundled under their arms like discarded skins, their pale faces turning instinctively to the sun pouring through the windows, I'm right; refugees from back east. "But it doesn't matter now," I say, turning from them, jealous of their arriving when I have my trip still ahead of me. "I just have to get through the C party, and then Oscar's finally out of my life. Out of our lives.

"So tell me what you're serving at Thanksgiving," I say, anxious to stop talking about Oscar. I already look a wreck after three days of off-and-on crying, and a five-hour flight isn't going to help things along.

"Tofu and chateaubriand. I'm going for a vegan/Atkins meal this year. What do you think?"

"I think traditionalists will be disappointed."

"Traditionalists are always disappointed in a free society. They're like Republicans or Martha Stewart, only happy when we're all going along with their plan. So what's Helen serving?"

"Turkey," I say. "But the fact that she finally feels up to cooking is what we're really celebrating."

"Absolutely. Speaking of traditionalists, Charles is where exactly, since he won't be with you?"

I check my watch. "Actually, he's on the Metroliner even as we speak, going to his parents' in D.C. He's spending Thanksgiving with his family this year too, since we won't be with them at Christmas."

Steven says something, but the airport address system blaring to life drowns him out. "What?" I say, reaching into my bag to check my boarding pass. "They're calling some flight."

"I said, when you do the wishbone with Amy, make sure you get the bigger half. It's time you had some good luck in your life."

"You're telling me this?" I say, smiling for the first time in days. "The man who didn't know from Mercury being in or out of retrograde? Yeah, I'll let you know."

"You look terrible. Was the flight awful?"

"No, just my life," I say, handing Amy the shopping bag of Christmas gifts and stooping to kiss Bevan. Here in baggage claim, it's my turn to play arriving relative.

"What do you mean, your life?" she says, shifting Bevan to her other arm to take the bag. "I thought your life was perfect."

I shoot her a look. "I'm a publicist. That's what I do, say things are perfect. Even when they're not."

"Okay, so why isn't your life perfect?" she says, reaching out to brush some strands of hair from my face. "Because Charles isn't here?"

"No, we planned to do Thanksgiving with our own families this year."

"So what's not perfect then?"

I look over at her. Amy and I haven't confided in each other since high school, but ever since Helen's heart attack, we've been in some kind of start-over truce. Like shaking an old snow globe and watching the flakes flicker down into new, different arrangements. "You remember that guy who sent Mom the flowers?"

"The French tulips? Yeah, I remember. Mom was very impressed."

"Yeah, well, it turns out he's also capable of being a complete —" I pause and shoot Bevan a look. He's two, but that's about the age kids start turning into parrots, repeating every word they hear. "*Asshole*," I mouth.

Amy rolls her eyes. "Yeah, I know he's getting to that stage."

"Who is, Oscar?"

"Who's Oscar?"

"His name is Oscar — the asshole," I mouth again, "who sent the flowers."

"No, I meant Bevan is getting to that stage where we have to watch what we say around him. I picked him up after leaving him with Dad one afternoon while he watched the Phillies, and all he kept saying on the ride home was 'Bunt, you idiot.' Which actually came out more like 'Bun, you idid.'"

"*Bun you idid*," Bevan crows, flinging his arms about Amy's neck.

"See what I mean," she says, rolling her eyes again. "Hey, isn't that your bag?"

I look over at the baggage carousel and see my black Tumi with my little identifying swatch of turquoise ribbon whizzing by. "Yeah," I say, diving into the crowd and sprinting after it.

When I get back, sweating slightly in my coat, the same black cashmere I bought the first year I moved to L.A. and have yet to wear out, Amy's on her cell, Bevan still gripping her neck, chanting loudly. Several people look in our direction, their weariness erupting into smiles. Nothing like a precocious child to bring out the holiday spirit.

"Yeah, her bag's here, so we'll look for you out front," she says, raising her voice over Bevan's. She clicks off and turns to me. "Okay, Barkley'll meet us outside with the car. As for you," she says, turning to Bevan. "That's enough about bunting for today. Besides, baseball's over. We'll have to get Grandpa to teach you something new to say."

"How about 'fourth down and inches'?" I say, grabbing my bags and turning for the exit. "That's seasonal, and there has to be an Eagles game on this weekend."

"God, remember how Dad used to make us watch the Penn State games with him when we were kids?" she says, switching Bevan to her other arm and reaching for the bag of gifts. "He said it was our obligation, because he didn't have a son."

"Yeah, and Mom went along with it because it was the only way she could get us to take a nap on Saturdays. We'd just pass out on the sofa while Dad was yelling, 'The tight end's wide open.' Like any college team has a passing game."

"Tie en wide open!" Bevan crows, looking at me.

"That sounds a little obscene coming from you, mister," I say, reaching out and rubbing his head.

"And you think 'fourth down and inches' doesn't?"

"We could always go for the basic," I say. "'One, two, three, hike!'"

"One, two, free, hike!" Bevan says, throwing his head back. *"One, two, free, hike!"*

"I've created a monster," I say, leaning into the door, letting them go ahead of me.

"Oh, please," Amy says. "He's a boy. He'll do anything for attention."

We step into the icy night air, and I gasp at the cold. It's like sex. Always takes you by surprise, no matter how hard you try to remember.

"So wait, you never told me about Oscar," she says, turning back.

"Oh, please," I say, pulling my coat tighter. "He's a boy. He'll do anything for attention."

———— ✦ ————

"So at the risk of being overly sentimental," Dad says, standing over the turkey, knife in hand, looking vaguely Norman Rockwellish in his cardigan sweater. "I'd like to say how very grateful I am — we all are — to be together this year."

"Jack," Helen says, looking up reproachfully.

"*One, two, free, hike,*" Bevan says, banging on the table.

"Dad, you're going to make Mom cry again," Amy says, sliding a piece of bread into Bevan's mouth, temporarily silencing him.

"Or me," I say, holding up my glass of wine in a mock toast. "I'll cry instead of Mom. Give her a break."

"Hey, speaking of crying, remember that Thanksgiving we all went to Los Angeles to visit you and all it did was rain?" Barkley says, turning to me.

"'Speaking of *crying*' reminds you of L.A.?" I say, looking at him.

"Yes, it did rain, but we had a lovely time anyway," Helen says, unfolding her napkin.

"You did?" I say, trying to remember that far back but recalling only the endless rain.

"As I was saying," Jack says, looking down at us.

"Okay, Dad, go ahead," Amy says, dropping her hands into her lap. "Just don't upset Mom. Remember what the doctor said, 'no undue stress.'"

"I thought he said 'low salt and no more cigarettes,'" Barkley says.

Jack looks slightly crestfallen. "Well, in that case, I've said all I needed to say."

We all groan and look up.

"Jack, I'm sorry. Please go ahead," Helen says, raising her glass. "I'm sure my nervous system can take a holiday toast."

"I'll do it," I say, standing suddenly.

"Thank you," Jack says, nodding at me and sitting down.

I stand there a minute, gazing down at them. I feel like I'm in the middle of a carousel, clutching the center pole, stepping backward, carefully, in order to stay in the same place as everyone;

everything whirls by. Another Thanksgiving. Another Christmas. Another summer. Another birthday. *Another. Another. Another.*

Is this how you define a moment's happiness? The celebration of what's here, what's happening? Or is it something closer to loss? The realization of what hasn't happened, hasn't come to pass? Like math, the positive is not the negative. Or like winter's final snowfall, you never know it's happened until long after it's gone. Is that it, then? Happiness is the death avoided? The argument that doesn't occur? The resentment, like water, that finally evaporates?

"To us," I say, raising my glass. "To us."

I don't say this last part out loud, but in my mind I do. When we are all clinking glasses and repeating "To us," and some of us are wiping our eyes and others are thinking ahead to "light or dark meat?" I say to myself, "Because even when that didn't seem like enough, it was. We were. Enough."

"So Amy says this Oscar is apparently kind of an asshole."

I freeze where I am, loading the dishwasher in the kitchen with Helen and Amy.

"Umm, I don't know that I used those exact words," I say, turning to Helen, who is rinsing glasses and stacking them on the counter. She's also a little what Grandma used to call "merry," after half of one of the bottles of pinot noir Jack served with the turkey.

"Yeah, you did," Amy says, heading for the cabinet with two of the goblets. "You said he was capable of being an asshole despite sending Mom those beautiful tulips."

"Yeah, okay," I say, turning from her to Helen. "I just don't recall ever hearing the word *asshole* spoken in this house."

"Well, that's what a heart attack gets you," Helen says, rinsing another glass and stacking it neatly. "You get to do and say things you never thought you would."

"So is he or isn't he?" Amy says, reaching for two more glasses.

I shoot them both another look. Okay, fine, so it's a brave new world. "Uh, well, that's part of the problem," I say slowly. "I don't know if he is. Or sometimes he is and sometimes he isn't."

"Interesting," Helen says, turning to me. "And please notice, I'm not saying a word about Charles."

"I'm noticing," I say, eyeing her. Maybe she had more than half a bottle. Or maybe death cheated is way underrated as a mood enhancer.

"Okay, go on," she says, turning back to the glasses. "Start from the beginning. Once upon a time, there was a man named Oscar, who did what exactly?"

"Yeah, the beginning," Amy says, "because I don't think I ever heard the beginning."

Jack pushes through the kitchen door, a half-empty glass of wine in his hand. "It's halftime, so I thought I'd check what's going on in here."

"That's what I'd like to know," I say.

"We're on KP, so give me that when you're through," Helen says, nodding at his glass. "But pull up a chair. Alex is telling us why Oscar—you remember, he sent me those beautiful flowers—is really an asshole."

If her language startles Jack, he doesn't let on. "Oscar?" he says. "What about Charles?"

"We're not asking about Charles," Helen says.

"Well, not yet," Amy adds, reaching to arrange the glasses in the cabinet.

"I liked Charles," Jack says, leaning against the counter and swirling his wine. "Maybe not as much as I liked his golf swing, but he and I were going to shoot a round this spring. I mean," he says, looking at me, "if he got invited back."

"You guys should sell tickets," I say, turning back to the dishwasher.

"Well, that depends on the story," Helen says, pulling her hands from the water and drying them on her apron. "So?" she says, nodding at me. "Start from the beginning."

In the end, after I just gave up and went through the whole thing — although, weirdly, it didn't seem so bad, so awful in the retelling, weirder actually that I was telling *them* anything about my life — they all gave me their two cents, and some of it was worth more than others. But then some of us were still drinking wine and others had switched to tea. Jack was leaning toward Charles, but that was largely out of self-interest for his golf game, although he thought Oscar's obsession with sports was promising and everyone was impressed by his aptitude with flowers and food. Given that he was straight.

"I think you way overreacted when he invited the guy from *Variety*," Amy says, blowing on her mug to cool her tea. "I mean, Oscar was only trying to help you out."

"No, I think Alex was right," Helen says. "It was a very passive-aggressive thing for him to do. Especially after he didn't call her after their one date."

I stare at her. "'*Passive-aggressive*'? Mom, what do you know about passive-aggressive?"

She looks at me a moment. "Why, I thought I wrote the book on that."

"Whoa, Mom," Amy says, almost choking on her tea. "Excellent comeback."

"Is everyone here on drugs except me?" I say, looking at them.

"I'm taking Plavix, does that count?" Helen says.

"More wine?" Jack says, nodding at my glass. I shake my head.

Helen taps her spoon against her mug. "Okay, we've heard enough. I think we should vote now."

"You're *voting*?" I say, looking at them all.

Helen ignores me. "All in favor of Alex getting together with Oscar instead of Charles say aye."

"Oh, God, I'm leaving the room," I say, getting up and heading for the sink with my glass.

A chorus of *ayes* wells up behind me.

I turn. "Seriously? I have a perfectly good boyfriend, not to mention reservations with him on the Big Island, and you still think —"

"Honey, you're talking to three married people," Helen says.

"Four," Amy interjects, "if Barkley wasn't passed out with Bevan in front of the TV."

"What has that got to do with it?"

"Well, if Barkley was here, he'd be voting too," Amy says.

"No, I mean what does the fact that you're all married have to do with anything?"

Helen looks at Jack and then at Amy. "Should I tell her?"

Jack shrugs. "Go ahead, you're her mother. You know more than any of us."

"Honey, because after God knows how many meals together, we know more than anyone does: If you have a chance to wind up with a man who knows how to cook, you go for it."

"They actually *voted*?"

"I know, it was frightening," I say, cradling my cell against my shoulder as I push my bag ahead with my foot. Sunday night on Thanksgiving weekend, the security line at the Philly airport is a battle of inches.

"More frightening that you actually told your parents about your life," Steven says. "I think I stopped talking to Rita about anything serious when I turned five."

"I don't know, it's like Helen's a different person now," I say.

"The whole conversation kind of just happened. Anyway, how'd the tofu-chateaubriand menu go over?"

"Not so fast," he says. "So what are you going to do? Are you seriously going to break up with Charles because your parents gave the thumbs-up to Oscar, a guy they've never even met?"

"Hey, he sent Helen flowers. And no, I'm not. I'm not doing anything. At least, not right away."

"Coward."

"I'm not a coward. I'm *thinking*. About everything. I mean, part of me still thinks Oscar's an asshole, but I also realize I was interested in Charles partly because I thought my parents would like him. That it would make things easier with them. I mean, after Josh, who they didn't like. Well, not that they didn't like him, just not as their son-in-law."

"Honey, the heart wants what the heart wants. Not what the Social Register wants."

"I know you're quoting Woody Allen here, but I thought it was the penis wants what the penis wants," I say, and a few heads in line swivel in my direction. "Anyway, enough about me, Dr. Phil, how was your Thanksgiving menu?"

"Didn't."

"Didn't go over?"

"Didn't make it. Caved and made a turkey."

"And you're calling me a coward?"

"Yeah, I know," he sighs. "But I realized traditional is back. Besides, it was simpler to go with my wants than everyone else's needs."

"Usually is," I say, peering down the line at the security gate. My flight leaves in thirty; this is going to be close. "So listen, in all my weeping and gnashing of teeth last week, I forgot to ask you again about Oscar and the Chinese Olympian Lucienne mentioned at lunch."

"Oh, God, Lucienne's such an idiot sometimes," he says,

laughing. "Although I'd still take a pair of free diamond studs from her."

"Yeah, well, so what's the deal? Are they an item or not?"

"Don't you read Page Six anymore?" He snorts. "'What up-and-coming Asian starlet just tapped by Hollywood's hippest director has been making the rounds with L.A.'s hottest party planner?'"

"Guess I missed that one," I say, feeling oddly calm. If the ship has sailed with the Olympian on board, then the ship has sailed. "Well, Elsa will be disappointed."

"Then she — and you — are fools."

"Thanks," I say. "And why, he who knows all life's mysteries, are we fools?"

"Because the Olympian, my dear, is a dyke."

16

With More Names to Come . . .

"I have The Insider *on one, Patrice on two, and Oscar on* three. Who do you want?" Caitlin says, poking her head around the door.

"Like you have to ask," I say, punching up one. "Hey, Cheryl, so tell me we're good, because you know we went to you first, and I say that with the deepest respect for your colleagues over at *E.T.*"

"Yeah, I know, but yes, after some in-house horse-trading, we're good."

"Thank you, Jesus," I say, flopping back in my chair and reaching for one of the Hershey's Kisses that somehow wound up on my desk. Love the holidays. Chocolate arrives out of the air.

Of all the things I had to do today, nailing down *The Insider* as our lead electronic on the C party was it. God knows, the arrival of that show has made life so much easier for publicists. Not only is it one more place to get TV coverage but you get much more air-time than with its snarkier sister show, and also they don't try to ask your talent all sorts of tabloidy questions on the carpet. They play the game. Make it clear who the client is, give you good footage of the step-and-repeat, and best of all, because it's considered part of *E.T.*, clients love it. No more freak-outs when you tell them that *E.T.*'s not covering their event because they always have to have the lead position on the carpet or whatever bee is up their ass that week, but that you do have *Access Hollywood*, *Extra*, and the entertainment reporters from the local affiliates. Now you say, "We have *The Insider*, *Access Hollywood*, *Extra*, and the entertainment reporters from the local affiliates," and everyone goes home happy.

"Yeah, well, don't celebrate too soon. I still think you guys are nuts to hold that *this* Friday," she says. "I mean, the last weekend before Christmas, everyone's already in Aspen or Hawaii — except those execs whose movies open on Christmas Day — and we won't even go to air until Monday."

"Look," I say, dropping my voice. "You don't have to tell me it's a gamble. Let's just say I was outvoted by our client."

"Too bad," she says, "because your tip sheet looks a little thin, which I know isn't your fault."

I sigh, resisting the urge to tell her our anemic list was like pulling rabbits from hats — even dangling the carrot of Lucienne's half-carat diamond studs for our host committee members. Between Patrice and Jay and the holidays and C's pathetic budget and sudden attack of morality — "no cars, no honorariums, no Sally Hershberger hairstyling" — it's been a bitch to get the two dozen names we've got, and even a couple of those are pretty much pulled right off my own personal Santa list. All I want for Christmas is Will and Jada, Demi and Ashton, Gwyneth and Jack Black to show up.

"Yeah, I know," I say, trying to sound as upbeat as possible, which isn't that hard now that I've got Cheryl and her crew lined up. "But as always, we have more names to come. You see that right down there on the last line of 'Who,' right after Brad Grey and Jerry Bruckheimer: 'With More Names to Come.' Trust me. There will be more names."

I make a few noises about our ongoing talent outreach efforts, go over the details of the red carpet arrivals, promise to go out for drinks after the holiday insanity, and hang up. I'm just trying to decide if I want to call Patrice or Oscar with the good news when Steven heads in.

"I just got our amended list back from Patrice, and she and Jay have dinged at least a dozen more names," he says, looking up. "I mean, just when I think they can't get any more clueless and self-defeating, they get more clueless and self-defeating. They don't like our list, but then look at these names they keep sending over — I think they're up to almost seven hundred for a party that's budgeted at three hundred — which now include most of the major fashion designers who are one, based in New York, and two, on vacation. I mean, we're going to wind up with forty people at this rate."

"Never mind that, we just got *The Insider*," I say, leaning back in my chair.

Steven looks up from the list. "Great, let's just hope they have someone to shoot once they get there."

"Oh, come on," I say. "This is a big get. Now all we have to worry about is the list, and we always have to worry about the list."

"I'm telling you, the woman is a witch," he says, shaking his head. "She didn't like any of our party sites. Then she decreed they weren't doing a gift bag this year. 'Too commercial.' Like that's a negative? Now, she's dinging more than half our guest list. Trust me, Patrice will find a way to bitch about it."

"How can she possibly complain about *The Insider*? We just got our lead electronic, plus we already have commitments from *Access Hollywood* and the local affiliates. Plus all the rest of the media who've been credentialed, including both trades and the *L.A. Times*. I mean, a week before Christmas, this is right up there with turning the water into wine."

"As much as I appreciate your seasonally appropriate Christ

metaphors, Patrice will find a way to piss all over this," he says, tossing the list on my desk. "She who just dinged Megan Mullally, Bill Peterson, and the entire cast of *Desperate Housewives* because they don't have, and I'm quoting here, 'the C mystique,' even though they've been on the cover of *Vanity Fair*."

"Fifty bucks," I say, reaching for the list, ignoring for the moment the impossibility of disinviting celebrities who've already been invited.

"You're on. Call her. Let's do it on speaker," he says, sinking into my office couch.

I buzz Caitlin and tell her to call Patrice.

"I just had her," Caitlin says.

"Okay," I say. "Let's get her back."

I lean back and wait for her to put the call through.

"You might start making that check out now," Steven says. "Although on second thought, I prefer cash."

"Don't be such a pessimist," I say, tossing a Hershey's Kiss at him. "Come on, get in the holiday spirit."

"You're only saying that because you haven't been on the phone to her every hour for the past week," he says, flopping back on the couch and shoving the chocolate in his mouth. "Got any more of those?" he says, nodding at my desk.

I toss him two more. "Better you than me."

"Tho as I wasth saying," he says, popping the chocolates like they were aspirin. "Every hour for the past week when I've also been on the phone to every personal assistant and manager who will still take my calls about wrangling their talent. I'm telling you, at times like this, I realize I should have given law school another shot."

"Isn't Allie helping you out? That's what she's best at, working the street."

My phone buzzes. "I've got Patrice," Caitlin says.

"Patrice," I say, punching her up on the speaker, "I've got some good news."

There's silence on her end, then her plumy voice. "Alec, hang on, I'm just getting off the line with Andrew."

I look over at Steven. He mouths, "See what I mean?" I wave him off. We sit there a few more minutes on hold.

"Okay, this is ridiculous," I say, leaning forward to disconnect the line, when Patrice's voice roars to life.

"Alec, I've been trying to reach you. We've got to talk about this list Steven keeps sending over. I mean, there are real problems here. I was just talking to Andrew about it. What are you people thinking?"

I look over at Steven and shrug.

"Hi, Patrice," he says.

"Oh, Steven," she says, not missing a beat. "Much easier to get this done in one call then."

"Look," I say, "we'll get to the list in a second. I was calling to tell you we just confirmed our lead electronic, and I think you'll be pleased. *The Insider* has agreed to cover it."

There's a slight pause. "What about *E.T.?* I thought you were getting *E.T.?*"

Steven leaps up, pumping the air with his fist. I give him the finger. He holds up five fingers and makes an O with his other hand. I give him the finger with both hands.

"Patrice, *The Insider* is going to give us much better coverage. I mean, as *E.T.*'s sister show they're —"

"I know what it is," she says archly. "And I know that Andrew is letting me handle the media end of things, so I'm telling you —" She pauses for a second. "I'll have to call you back. Andrew's on the line again."

She hangs up.

"I told you so," Steven says. "She's a witch. Beyond bitch. Now hand it over. Five big ones."

"Okay, okay," I say, "although can I just say I have issues with the word *bitch* because there is no male equivalent? I mean, *bastard* doesn't even come close."

"Forget your issues with the English language. The point is," he says, leaning forward on my desk, "that you feel a teeny, tiny amount of the pain I've been feeling thanks to her. So pay up."

"See the cashier on the way out," I say, waving him off. "I'm calling Oscar to—"

"Wait, you're calling Oscar? For the first time since your big fight? I'm staying for this."

"Out. I'm simply returning his call, and then let's have a meeting with everyone in"—I check my watch—"half an hour to go over the list, and I'll update us on our media coverage."

"Okay, but I want the transcript," he says, heading for the door.

I run my fingers through my hair, take a hit of water, and buzz Caitlin. "Call Oscar back, can you?" I say, going over a few scenarios in my mind—aloof, friendly, sad, distant but with a hint of wistfulness—and settle on strictly business. It's the first time we'll have spoken since our fight at the Scrabble party, but given that C's party is in four days, I don't really have a second to spend figuring out our relationship. Or if we even have one.

"Oscar, line one."

I reach for the phone and feel my pulse jump. Shit. I take a deep breath. "Oscar, I was just on the phone with Patrice and—"

"Yeah, I know, she was dialing you as she left the walk-through with me," he says tersely. In the background I hear hammering and sawing.

"Yeah, well, how'd it go?" I say, braced for the worst, although given his tone, I'm unsure whether his mood or Patrice's endless complaints counts as the worst.

"Let me start with the fact that she's insisting on seeing the DJ's playlist."

"What?" I say. "That's absurd."

"Well, she wants to see it. She also wants modifications to"—he pauses and I hear paper rustling—"the arrival lighting, the event lighting, the location of the generators, the florals, the sponsor's display, and placement of the bar and catering stations. She does, however, sign off on the café tables on the pool deck that I have lit, as she put it, 'like a sea of stars around a sea of water.'"

"Very poetic," I say. "But wasn't all this in the CADs she and Jay signed off on?"

"'CADs'? You mean as in computer-animated drawings that are normal standard operating procedure for every event producer? Well, no, they didn't sign off on the CADs because Patrice couldn't be bothered to look at the CADs," he says, sounding even angrier.

"Sorry, I forgot. Well, if it's any consolation, she doesn't like our —"

"But my biggest problem is, and why I called you," he says, cutting me off. "Is that she's got a list that's heading toward seven hundred, which, even given your usual RSVP–no-show ratio, is still way too high for the three-hundred-person event she's contracted for. The three-hundred-person event, which I've permitted with the fire department, the police department, and the valet, bar, and catering staff."

"Yeah, I know the list is a problem," I say, reaching for another chocolate. "But I also know that it's a complete wish list on her part. We're going to be lucky to have forty people at this rate."

"Forty is better than seven hundred."

I sigh. "Look, I'm going into a meeting now about it. Let me call you afterward. Meanwhile, just know that we got our electronic finally nailed down. In addition to *Access Hollywood*, we have *The Insider*."

There's a pause. "At least something's going the way it's supposed to."

At least he sounds less angry.

"Look, it's always bad at this stage, you know that," I say, trying to sound conciliatory. I close my eyes. Oh, go for it. "So how was your Thanksgiving, by the way?"

"Actually, it's not always this bad," he says, ignoring my olive branch. "This is *especially* bad, and after Friday, I'm out. You do another event with her, don't call me. I'm serious. Life's too short."

"Look, I'm sorry," I blurt out, and realize I am. Sorry. For all of it. For Patrice being so out of control. For the event being such a nightmare. But mostly for having thought we could move the boundaries of our friendship without losing something. If I could put it all back, go back to being friends and colleagues, I would do it in a heartbeat. Sex is easy; friendship is the killer.

"It's not your fault," he says, adding quickly, before either of us can say anything more, "Look, I have to go."

The rest of the day, the week, is a blur. But then it usually is right before a major event. Like a NASA shuttle launch. Everything is in countdown mode. After my call to Oscar, we have our staff meeting to collectively bleat and moan about The List. It's like Goldilocks. Too big, too small, at the same time.

"What exactly do they think this party is supposed to be?" Allie says, scanning Patrice's latest memo. "The Oscars meets Fashion Week? Like we're seriously going to get J.Lo and Tom Ford," she says, looking up and shaking her head.

"Maybe Tom Ford," I say. "But only if Andrew makes the call, and according to Patrice, he's declining to call anyone."

"For seventy-five grand, you'd think they might be willing to do a little more heavy lifting," Jill says.

"Try *any* heavy lifting," says Steven. "I mean, between their nonexistent budget, the no-cars no-hairstylist no-graft rule, we're screwed."

"Well, I think there's only one answer," I say, scanning the various lists — our original list, Patrice's amended lists, and our RSVPs to date.

"Wrangler?" Steven says. "I mean, I'd almost pay the ten grand myself to drop this in someone else's lap, to conjure celebs out of thin air."

"Is there any chance they'd pay for that?" Allie says, tossing Patrice's memo to the table. "I mean, I'm killing myself on my contacts, but almost everybody is already out of town."

"I'll check with Amanda," I say, "but let's not get our hopes up."

"So what are we going to do?" Maurine says, looking genuinely worried. So cute. So young. So earnest.

I shake my head. "Worry not, ladies. There's a reason diamonds are a girl's best friend."

In the end, which is to say less than twenty-four hours later, Lucienne comes through. Just like I hoped. Maybe she just gets it. I mean, her job is celebrity liaison for the whole diamond industry. Or maybe she just wants another two hours on the red carpet being photographed with Gwynnie et al., draped in her swag, especially since there's no gift bag to remind everyone who really sponsored the evening. Whatever her reasons, she stepped up to the plate. Bumped up the "gift" for the six key host committee members from studs to a new "Third Eye" diamond pendant retailing for north of ten thousand dollars.

"Oh, my God, we can totally hit the whole Kabbalah crowd with this," Allie said the morning Lucienne sent over one of the necklaces.

"Do we get to wear them too?" Jill says, fingering the necklace.

"Hardly," I say, reading Lucienne's accompanying memo. "We get diamond studs or drops — three-quarter-carat — or a solitaire pendant to wear during the party, all of which must be returned at the end of the party."

"Cinderella, Cinderella," Allie chants, trying on the necklace, which does look pretty amazing. "I'm feeling really, *really* centered with this on," she says, closing her eyes and holding her forefingers and thumbs in the Om circle.

"Even you?" Jill says, looking up. "I can't believe you don't get to keep the earrings."

I shrug. At this point, I just want to get this party over and out of our lives. Swag is the last thing I'm worried about. "Trust me, I do not need a piece of jewelry to remind me of Patrice."

"I don't know, I think I could live with her memory if I got to keep this," Allie says, stroking the necklace.

"Sweetie, I hate to turn you back into a pumpkin, but we have to get moving," I say, scanning the new list of potential host committee members. If we can get two-thirds of these names, we should squeak this one out. Whether the party is any fun or not is another matter entirely. In the end, all you need for a successful event is the perception of it. Which means the right people on the red carpet talking to the right electronic. "Okay," I say, looking up. "Everyone work with Lucienne on this list and give me a status report by the end of the day, before we send out the next tip sheet."

"Where are you going?" Allie says, unclasping the necklace.

"From the frying pan into the fire," I say, turning for the door. "To the walk-through with Patrice and Oscar."

There are actually three walk-throughs before Friday, an average of one a day, which is about right. Mostly these are Oscar's dog and pony shows — "and here's where the portable toilets go" — but given his dark mood, I'm giving him and them a wide berth until the last possible minute. I skip the Tuesday walk-through with Patrice and Jay. Ditto for the one Wednesday with Lucienne. And on Thursday, there's supposed to be a final walk-through with all of us — Patrice, Jay, Lucienne, Charles, Andrew, if he chooses to attend. Except when Charles's flight is delayed at the last minute or he's delayed for some dinner he has to attend, that walk-through gets moved.

"I'm not doing it twice because Prince Charles can't make Thursday," Oscar says. "I'm rescheduling for Friday."

"Isn't that cutting it a little close?" I say.

"Thursday's cutting it close. What's a few more hours?" he says. "I'll see you guys at noon."

Friday arrives like the eye of the storm. Cold, blazingly sunny, not a cloud in the sky. But then the actual day of an event is always strangely calmer than the days, weeks, leading up to it. You have your media or you don't. You have your talent or you don't. In our case, the media are no problem. I've already got Allie and Maurine set to spend part of the afternoon laying out the rope line and place markers where everyone goes. *The Insider* gets the lead position, followed by the other electronic, and then print. It's like a seating chart, and while not every publicity agency runs events this way, we do. Just avoids confusion and fights, and there's enough of that on the carpet without adding to it.

As for our talent, well, on paper we look good. Better than good. Lucienne's necklaces really were the tipping point—a fistful of actresses who are this year's Oscar contenders. Nothing like getting your diamond-bedecked mug on TV right before the Academy ballots go out. Still, I know you can have thirty celebs confirmed and no way of guaranteeing that any of them will actually show. It's not like an awards show or the *Vanity Fair* and Miramax Oscar parties, when you know everyone will turn up and it's only a matter of keeping people *out*. For any party lower down the totem pole, there's always that come-to-Jesus moment, when you're on the carpet, the media in place, and no one's there yet, and you're sweating bullets, just praying someone, even a C-lister, shows.

But that's still hours off when I pull up to the house just before noon. With no valets and the driveway still jammed with trucks and vans, I park on the street and make my way up the drive. I haven't been here in a few days, and Oscar's really made headway.

The cherry red carpet is unfurled down the drive, and behind it, two of his crew are installing the step-and-repeat emblazoned with Cs and the Diamond Council's logos.

"Hey, you guys," I say as I head up the carpet, my heels sinking into its cushiony recesses.

"The man's inside," one of them says, turning to me. "And by the way, he's not happy."

"Wouldn't expect it any other way," I say, giving them a cheery wave. Should only get more festive once Patrice and Charles show. I push through the front door and am greeted with the usual deafening sounds of sawing and hammering. The room is totally empty except for a huge white shag carpet, white sheers at the windows, and about three pieces of white and chrome leather furniture. For a second I flash back to Jeffrey's wedding in September. It's like thinking about first grade. How simple and easy Jennifer and her silly latticed tents seem compared to this. How simple and easy my job then seems compared to now.

"Congratulations, you're the first to arrive," Oscar says behind me. I whip around. It's the first time I've seen him since Barry's Scrabble party, and my pulse jumps.

"Here," he says, handing me a take-out coffee. "We had an extra."

"Thanks," I say, reaching for the cup. At least he's being civil, if a tad brusque. "So where are we on our punch list?" I say, deciding to play it safe and head right for the business at hand.

He eyes me over his cup, wiping one hand on his T-shirt. "'Punch list'? That's such contractor lingo," he says, smiling at me. Or is he laughing at me?

"You know what I mean," I say.

"Yeah, I do, and it's not 'our' punch list. It's mine, and other than the generators that can't be moved because there is nowhere else to move them, I am up to speed with Her Highness's requests. Of course, that was twelve hours ago, and I'm sure she has more today."

"Well, it looks amazing," I say, gazing around the room. He might be civil, but he's definitely not his old self. "It actually reminds me of something."

"Lobby of the Mondrian? Every other party you've been to in the past year?"

I turn back, startled. "That's not what I was going to say."

"I'm saying it," he says, waving dismissively at the sea of white. "It's *way* too Ian Schrager. But this is what every New Yorker thinks is L.A. Like the beach is just around every corner. I mean, why didn't they just hold this at the hotel, light some fucking fig candles, and call it a day?"

I'm about to murmur something appropriately sympathetic back when my cell goes. I check the number. Charles. "Hey," I say, clicking on, "where are you?"

"In the car on the way to the office," he says, sounding rushed. "I'm meeting Patrice there. We need to massage the list some more. Keep working the phones. Which means we'll have to do the walk-through later. Say, sixish."

"*Sixish?*" I yelp. "Wow, that's cutting it really close." This is insane. Yes, there's always a final, final walk-through right before an event starts. But given Patrice's proclivities for last-minute meddling, and the fact that she hasn't been to the site since Tuesday, a 6:00 P.M. walk-through for an 8:00 event is a disaster in the making.

"Look, there's no time to argue," he says. "Get Oscar to walk you through it now since you're there and then head back here to help. I'll see you there."

We hang up, and I turn to Oscar. "Uh, there seems to be —"

"Let me guess — they're not coming," he says, crumpling his empty coffee cup.

"Not until later," I say, my voice small. "I'm sorry."

"No skin off my nose," he says, turning for the door. "I'm here all day anyway."

He leaves me standing in the living room. My cell goes again.

Steven. "Yes, I've heard, I'm on my way back," I say before he can say anything.

"I'm quitting after Friday," he says. "I'm *fucking* quitting. She's in the conference room, hallucinating. *Russell Crowe. Cate Blanchett—*"

"Cate's on our list."

"Not anymore. Her assistant just called and said she can't make it."

"At least she called."

"I'm telling you, start thinking about my severance package."

"Okay, I'll be there as soon as I can," I say, clicking off. So much for the eye of the storm. So much for any of these prima donnas. "Hey," I call after Oscar. "I might as well see it since I'm here."

"Yeah," he yells from somewhere down the hall. "I'll send one of the guys to walk you through it. I'm going out."

<hr />

"How many of these are actually confirmed now?"

"You can see for yourself. Those are all the RSVPs."

Charles looks at the list and scowls. "I'm with Patrice, this doesn't look all that deep. I mean, with bona fide A-listers. If Cate canceled this afternoon, who's to say the others won't."

I look up from my desk. It's almost five. We've been at this list, phoning, cajoling, pleading, for hours. In the end, Patrice broke down and offered to send cars for the six key host committee members. "Look," I say. "It's going to be what it's going to be at this point. It's time to stop chasing the dragon. Besides, I have to go home and change."

He tosses the list to my desk. "All right, we'll just have to see how the chips fall."

"Yes, we will, as we do on every event," I say, reaching for my bag. "You want to come with me and leave your stuff at the house while I change?"

"Umm, I'm actually not staying over," he says, checking his watch. "I'm catching the red-eye back."

"What? I thought you were spending the weekend here. That's what we talked about. What I had planned on."

I can't believe he's going back tonight. And that he's only just telling me now. So much for the party — he'll have about an hour before he has to leave for the airport — and so much for our weekend together.

"Well, Mom decided to move the family holiday party to this Saturday, and I have to be back for it since I won't be there for Christmas," he says, coming over and putting his hands on my shoulders. "Don't be mad. I'll be back in a week. In fact, why don't you come with me tonight?"

"You know I can't do that," I say sulkily, since we both know I'll be working the party to the bitter end. "Can't you at least go in the morning?"

"Look, I only came out to walk Andrew in. So he feels like the troops have been massed. You'll be fine. As you say, it will be what it will be at this point."

I don't know which is more upsetting — his saying he only came out to walk Andrew in, his acting like the party is already a failure, or his complete disregard for including me in his plans. I know I came to a realization about our relationship while I was on the Cape dealing with Helen, but it's not like I ever discussed it with him. Given how busy we've been and our usual opposite coast living arrangements, I figured Hawaii would be the first chance we'd have to really talk. But clearly I've been fooling myself about our relationship for a long time now. It's obvious he and I have two different definitions of what a relationship is. What intimacy is. I mean, the man I'm supposed to be spending Christmas with — and in Hawaii, no less — is acting like my boss, not my boyfriend.

"All right, fine," I say, turning for the door. "You want to at least ride with me over to the party?"

"Actually, I'm going with Patrice to get Andrew and Amanda at the hotel," he says, checking his watch again. "We're meeting for a quick calm-the-nerves drink. So why don't we all meet at the house at, say, sixish?"

"Sure," I say, not even bothering to protest. "See you at six."

17

Inside Access Limited

I don't take it as a good sign that the first person I see when I pull up to the house—other than the valets gathering at the curb like a flock of birds and the waiters rushing up the drive, jackets and ties thrown over their shoulders—is the Chinese Olympian, in a tiny white satin dress, long black ponytail, and spike heels, picking her way up the red carpet. The media haven't even arrived—even Jill, Maurine, Allie, and the rest of our staff aren't here yet—but Oscar's latest is here. I swear, if she's a lesbian, I'm reconsidering my sexual orientation.

"I know what you're thinking, and I'm telling you, you're wrong."

I whip around. Steven cruises up behind me, putting his arm around my waist. "Besides, that whole Susie Kwan look is such a cliché."

I shake my head. "Nice to know our party planner brought his own date."

"She's not his date," he says, putting his mouth close to my ear. "She's an early guest. Look at it that way. She's another pretty face to put on camera. Besides, if you want to worry about something, worry about Patrice bad-mouthing us to Andrew."

"Thanks, that really cheers me up."

We head up the carpet, push through the front door into the first crisis of the night. Instead of the usual pre-party chaos, the house looks like a jewelry convention. The shag carpet is still here, along with the white leather sofas and the white sheers fluttering at the windows, and some of Oscar's staff are rushing around setting out vases of white calla lilies and white votive candles. But there are now a dozen giant Plexiglas display cases lined up around the room—all of them filled with diamonds, necklaces, rings, bracelets, draped over white coral branches—lit by blazing halogen spotlights and guarded by half a dozen security guys in shades and headsets.

"Oh, my God," I say, turning to Steven. "When did this happen? It looks like a—"

"Trade show?" he says, sounding just as stunned as I am. "Uh, when I was here Tuesday, the cases were jewelry box size and stashed down the hall in one of the other rooms."

"And that's where they were this morning," I say, trying to work out the chronology. Lucienne must have had Oscar change the cases after I'd done my walk-through at noon. With an editorial event, it's always a tug-of-war between the sponsors and the magazine. Usually the invitation, the step-and-repeat, and the gift bag pretty much take care of any product promotion. But given that Patrice had nixed the gift bag this year, Lucienne must have decided the sponsor needed more prominence at the party itself.

"Oh, God," I say. "Patrice is going to freak."

"Well, that'll teach her to tube a walk-through," Steven says, gazing around the room, which is lit as brightly as a car dealership.

"Welcome to the Diamond Council showroom."

We both turn. Oscar in a white dinner jacket and white

T-shirt, and holding an unlit cigar. He looks incredibly sexy. And very, very cynical.

"What the hell happened?" I say, grabbing his arm. "These weren't here earlier. Who put these in?"

"Why, we did. Who else would have done it?" he says, leaning over and giving me a kiss on my cheek.

Okay, *that's* interesting. If I had a second to read these tea leaves. Which I don't. "Okay, just tell me what's going on, please. Before Patrice and Andrew get here."

Before he can say anything, Lucienne sweeps up in white pants and a white chiffon shirt as stiff as her spiky blond hair. Diamonds the size of walnuts perch on her ears. "Alex, thank God you're here. We missed you at the hotel. This is what you're wearing," she says, opening a small box and pulling out a pair of diamond solitaires, big as gumballs, dangling at the ends of very fragile-looking white-gold wires.

"Oh, my God, they're beautiful," I say, temporarily distracted by the size of the stones. "But I don't think I should wear them. I mean, with all the running around I have to do tonight, I'll probably lose one."

"Shit, I'll wear them," Steven says.

"Nonsense, they're perfectly balanced," Lucienne says, reaching for my ear with one of the earrings.

"Ooooh, you are so lucky." I turn, or turn as much as I can with Lucienne gripping my ear. The Chinese Olympian. Sliding her teeny tiny arm through Oscar's. Oh, perfect.

"Oh, hey," he says, planting a big kiss on her cheek. "Everyone, this is Mai. Mai, this is everyone."

We all stand there, awkwardly smiling and nodding, while Lucienne finishes sliding the earrings through my earlobes.

"There," she says, standing back. "Now you finally look like you're representing this party the way it should be represented."

I reach up and gingerly touch the earrings. "These probably cost as much as my car," I say, trying to feel if there are any backs on the earrings but finding none. Only the long gold wires running through my ears. And a feeling that I have just been bought off.

"More. I've seen your car," Lucienne says, snapping the box shut and sliding it into her bag.

"Is there nothing in your Santa's bag for me? Or maybe something in these cases?" Steven says, turning to the Plexiglas towers.

"Yeah, Lucienne, about the display cases —" I start to say.

"Don't even think about touching these cases," she says, swatting Steven on the shoulder. "They're locked, bulletproof, and our insurance doesn't cover us if they're opened in the house."

Oh, great. I hope she's got better insurance on my earrings. "Yeah, okay, but has Patrice or Andrew seen these?" I say, reaching for her arm and steering her away from Oscar and Mai. No point in alerting little Mai there's trouble in River City.

"We do display cases every year," she says, turning to me, a smile plastered to her face. "Everyone knows they're here."

Steven shrugs. "There you go. Problem solved."

I shoot him a look. "Well, do they know they're this big and out here, in the main party space?" I say, dropping my voice. "When I was at the walk-through today, they were much smaller and down the hall in another room."

"Those were just temporary until the real cases arrived," she says, smiling at the security guards and reaching out to brush some invisible dust from one of the cases. "When these finally arrived, Oscar and I decided they needed to be displayed out here."

"*Oscar* and you decided?" I say, turning back, but he's engrossed, or pretending to be engrossed, in talking to Mai.

"Well, he and I were the only ones here. Who else would decide?"

"Well, Patrice was supposed to be here, and I think she's going to freak. I think you should be prepared to move them."

She looks at me as if I'm crazy. "Alex, my dear, who do you think is paying for this party? The diamonds are staying out here. Besides, the cases are locked to the floor. They can't be moved."

"Like I said," Steven says. "Problem solved."

I glance at the cases — she's right, they are locked to the floor — and make noises about letting her explain all this to Patrice, and Andrew, and Amanda. Let them fight it out. Besides, it's not like I don't have a million other things to deal with between now and the start of the party. Like making sure there are no other little surprises before the guests start arriving.

I turn back to Oscar and Mai. "Can I steal your boyfriend for a second?" I say, giving her a big smile.

"Oh, sure," she says, turning to Oscar and giving his arm a squeeze. "Bye, honey."

Bye, honey? Maybe she's a dyke after all. Oscar would never be involved with a "Bye, honey" type.

"Thanks," I say, giving her another big smile, grabbing him by the elbow, and heading out back for the pool deck.

"So, how do you like our party so far?" he says, a grin working at the corners of his mouth. I can't tell if he's laughing at me or Mai or just the whole ridiculous evening, but his cynical, detached mood is starting to get really old.

"Can we get serious for a minute, because we have a big explosion in our immediate future, when Patrice gets here," I say when I catch sight of the pool deck. "Oh, my God, this looks totally beautiful." Like the rest of the house, the pool deck has been completely transformed. More white leather couches have been set up on the patio, along with steel-and-glass Eileen Gray tables lit with aluminum and Lucite lamps. Suspended over the pool, a cluster of George Nelson bubble lamps glows. Between all the lights and their reflection off the water, the effect is dazzling.

"How'd you get all these lights to work out here like this?" I say, reaching out to finger one of the lamps.

"Ah, with a lot of tricky wiring," he says, grabbing my hand and pulling it back. "It took me and the electrician several hours to get it all figured out."

"Well, Patrice is right about one thing, this does look great," I say, turning around and catching sight of the glowing Plexiglas towers inside the house. "But she is going to fucking freak about those cases. I can't believe you just went along with Lucienne and bolted those to the floor after I'd seen the site."

He looks at me and shakes his head. "Look, if Her Royal Highness can't be bothered to show up at the walk-through with her own sponsor, then it's not my problem if there are mixed signals and she's unhappy."

"Okay, okay, it's just that I've got Charles all over me about this party," I say, reaching up to run a hand through my hair and managing to catch both my fingers and my hair in one of the earrings and nearly pull it loose. "Shit. I knew these were going to be a problem."

"Here, let me," he says, reaching out to untangle it. We stand there a minute as he works to free the earring. In the damp December air, I start to shiver in my black wool sheath. I realize it's the same stupid dress I wore to Jeffrey's wedding.

"God, remember Jeffrey's wedding?" I say. "It seems like ages ago."

"It was," he says, his face so close I feel his breath. "Don't tell me you miss it?"

"Compared to this? Yeah, don't you?"

"Well, that depends on —"

"Hope I'm not interrupting."

We turn. Charles in a black suit and a mood to match. "I think you're both wanted inside," he says, eyeing us. "There's a bit of a discussion, as you might imagine, about the sponsor's display."

Discussion doesn't begin to cover it. *Hysteria* is more like it. Even before Oscar and I reach the house, we can hear Patrice.

"Whot bloody fool put these here?"

I turn to Oscar. "You want to do it or shall I?"

He looks at me. For the first time since our fight, he seems like himself. "You up for it?" he says.

"Sure," I say, shrugging. "We're pretty much fucked on this event anyway. Might as well go down swinging."

"That's the spirit," he says, throwing his arm around my shoulders. We step in through the doorway. "So, what seems to be the problem?" he says, smiling broadly.

Steven is nowhere to be seen, but Andrew, Amanda, Jay, Lucienne, and Patrice are huddled around the cases. At the sound of Oscar's voice, they all turn, and I nearly burst out laughing at the expressions on their faces. Patrice, in a white satin, floor-length gown pinned with an enormous diamond brooch, looks ready to kill someone; Lucienne looks triumphant; Jay looks as clueless as the vintage white suit he's wearing; and Andrew, in black Prada, looks like he would rather be anywhere on the planet but here. Only Amanda, in a black taffeta skirt, is as expressionless as the security guards.

"This is *outrageous,*" Patrice says, moving toward us. For a second, I think she might actually hit me. Oscar would surely hit her back. "It looks like a trade show in here, not a party. Who approved these?"

"Well, have you considered the obvious?" Oscar says. "That your sponsor had them installed?"

Lucienne clears her throat. "Patrice, if you just—"

But Patrice cuts her off. "As the client of this event, I expect to be informed of all changes to the original plan—*by the event planner.*"

Oscar sighs and shakes his head. "And you would be if you actually showed up when you say you will."

"That has absolutely nothing to do with—" she starts to say.

"Actually, I approved them," I say.

Everyone turns to me. "*You* approved them?" Patrice says, staring. "How could you approve them? You're just the publicist."

"Alex, you had no authority to do that," Charles says, stepping to Patrice's side. In his black Armani suit, he looks like a groom taking his place next to his bride.

"Actually, I do have the authority," I say, turning to him. "DWP-ED is the event contractor, Oscar is our subcontractor. Which means not only do I have the authority, but since none of you actually made the walk-through, someone needed to make these decisions. So I did."

Patrice crosses her arms and scowls. "Then you can be in charge of moving them out of here. *Immediately.*"

I nod at the cases. "Actually, I think you're going to have to live with them. They're bolted to the floor. For security reasons."

"Then *fucking* unbolt them," she says, taking a step toward me.

"Actually," I say, turning to Lucienne, "and I think Lucienne will back me up on this, the insurance coverage is contingent upon them remaining bolted and locked here during the evening."

"Yes, that's right," Lucienne says, stepping forward. "And of course, having the security detail here as well."

"I don't care what either of you says. This is my party and I want —" Patrice sputters.

"Leave them. Leave them," Andrew says, his face flushed a deep red. "Just . . . leave them." He gives a halfhearted wave at the cases and then, without glancing at Patrice, nods to Amanda, and the two of them head for the back patio. Oscar moves quickly to join them.

I turn to Patrice. "You might want to see the rest of the lay-out — now that you're here."

She takes a step toward me. "If you think you can embarrass me in front of Andrew like that, think again."

"Patrice, I don't think anything other than the fact that we have about three hundred people arriving here in" — I check my watch — "about an hour. I suggest we get through the rest of the night as amicably as possible, unless you want to really ruin your party."

She glares at me and then, gathering up her gown, turns and sweeps out the front door. Charles looks at her and then at me. Neither of us says a word. I feel like I'm staring at my future. Correction. What was my future. He looks at me a minute longer, and then, shaking his head, he turns and walks out after her.

I stand there feeling my heart race. Funny how you can wind up making decisions without even realizing you're making them. Like there's some part of you that already knows the answer, even when the rest of you is still trying to figure out the question.

Lucienne turns to me. "Alex, thank you, but you absolutely didn't have to do that. I mean, I was prepared —"

"Actually, I did," I say, not bothering to mention that she could have stepped in anytime and didn't. "For my own self-respect, I did."

"Well, I hope she doesn't have you fired on my account."

"Actually, I'm counting on it," I say, turning to her. "So now that I have your deep appreciation, I have a couple of requests about the cases."

In the end, I get Lucienne to knock down the wattage on the halogen spots from surgical ward level to something resembling lounge lighting. I also get her to agree to cut the security detail in half. So when Steven rolls in asking what he missed when he was out checking the catering stations with his staff, and Allie comes flying in to say that the *Insider* crew and half the paparazzi have arrived and could we get our butts out there, we are pretty squared away.

"Nothing like a party where none of the hosts are speaking to the others," Steven says when we pull on our headsets and take our meet-and-greet positions at the head of the carpet.

"Let's just say I'm prepared to kiss this goodbye right now," I say, reaching for one of the clipboards from Maurine.

"What, you're leaving?" she says, looking up, startled.

"No, I just meant, however this shakes out, I'm going to be Zen about it."

"And you're not even wearing the Third Eye necklace," Allie says, staring at my earrings. "Although these look pretty calming."

"You want to wear them?" I say. "I think I'm just going to lose one."

Steven snorts. "Knowing Lucienne, the insurance probably covers them only if you're wearing them."

We stand there, bantering, going over the lists while I try to put Charles out of my mind, until the first of the guests start rolling in. More of Oscar's fillers, the first of our inside media, Howard Finnegan and *The Reporter*'s party writer, and some local fashion designers and their entourages. It's like watching the tide come in. Inch by inch, the beach gets covered. I check my watch. 8:15. For the next two hours, we'll be out here, working the carpet until the party reaches its tipping point somewhere around 10:00, or more likely 11:00, and the exiting begins. A trickle at first, but then faster, until the whole thing will be drained empty somewhere around 2:00 in the morning.

I click on my headset. "You guys ready?"

A chorus of *yeah*s blares in my ear. Except for Allie. "I still want to wear those earrings if you don't."

"Talk to me in an hour," I say. "Okay, so let's work it this way," I say, and carve up the duties. I keep Allie and Jill and Maurine with me on the carpet, along with Steven's three staffers to man the check-ins. I send Marissa in with the WireImage photographer. "Take the first hour with him," I tell her, "and then we'll trade off." Riding herd on your inside photographer, getting the pix you know the host will want while fending off the C-listers, is one of the more hectic parts of event publicity. And it will be even touchier with Andrew, who is notoriously camera shy.

"What do you want to do about Patrice and Lucienne?" Jill says.

I turn and check up the carpet. Neither of them is in sight, but I know as soon as the traffic picks up, when the first host committee members pull up — Queen Latifah, Chloë Sevigny, and Mischa Barton — and slide an ankle out of their limos, they'll materialize. Like flies. "They're heat-seeking missiles," I say. "They're on their own."

And it pretty much goes like that. For the next two hours I play chief traffic cop, moving the talent — and from the looks of things, about two-thirds of our list is here — this way and that, here a photographer, there a moment with the *Insider* crew. There's a tense moment when Marissa clicks on to tell me Portia de Rossi wants to be photographed with Andrew, and I know Andrew will freak. Being photographed with Uma is one thing, Portia is totally another, even if she's with Ellen De Generes now. "Do *not* set that photo up," I say into my headset, stepping out of the carpet traffic for a second. "Steven, help her out. Portia can talk to Andrew, but absolutely no photos."

I step back onto the carpet. "Hey," "Hey," "Great to see you." We're moving up the food chain now. Bigger fish. Bigger names — Tracee Ross, a fleet from Fred Segal, Magda Berliner, Jeremy Scott, Kristy Hume, all trailing their own entourage. Guys in vintage shirts and spiky hair, women in old Pucci. The younger socialites, China Chow and Jacqui Getty, the stars of *Nip/Tuck*, Eddie Furlong and a couple of the Johnson heiresses. It's like that moment in *The Wizard of Oz* when Dorothy steps out and the whole world's in garish Technicolor. After weeks of staring at black-and-white lists, the actual parade of people is a riot of color, noise.

"How's it going?" crackles in my headset. Oscar.

"Uh, great," I say, watching as coltish Mischa Barton and her cheekbones emerge from a limo, the Third Eye necklace glinting on her bony chest. "How's it look in there?"

"Packed," he says. "How are Patrice and Lucienne behaving?"

"Hang on," I say, turning and looking up the carpet. Over the crowd, I see them catch sight of Mischa. Like lasers locking on to their target. "Actually, if you want some fun, come out and see which of them gets more face time with Mischa."

"Oh, that does sound amusing. But I'm busy running out of white wine."

We click off, and I check my watch. Going on 10:00. I'll give it a few more minutes here and then head in, check the pulse of the party. Always good to know the vibe of the room, although judging by this river, it'll be fine. More than fine. I'm just starting to head in when a cry goes up behind me and Uma Thurman practically runs up the carpet. The photographers explode into a blaze of lights and screamed entreaties: "Uma, Uma!"

"Wow," I say, checking the clipboard, "was she on our list?"

"One of Patrice's last-minute invites," Steven says in my ear. "Although it pains me to have to say that."

"Well, good for her," I say, handing my clipboard to one of Steven's staffers and turning up the carpet. I make my way through the crowd to the front door and into the house. It's already so packed I can hardly move. Forget about the display cases. No one can even see them, given all the bodies. And the blinding noise. The techno-pop pulsing through the sound system and the roar of voices fueled by hormones, endorphins, Absolut, and the proximity to other beautiful strivers, the promise of sex, of money, of possibilities. It's like Red Bull straight to the brain. I push on, heading for the patio, squeeze past the bodies, practically grazing Joely Richardson—God, she's tall. I'm just catching my breath, admiring the effect of Oscar's lights reflecting off the pool and the crowd, when my headset crackles.

"Andrew wants a shot with Uma, but she's saying no," Marissa says, sounding vaguely panicked.

"Who's asked her?" I say, cupping my hand over my mouthpiece. "And where are you guys?"

"Me, and out here by the pool house."

"Steven, can you ask her?" I say, standing on my toes and peering over the crowd in the direction of the pool house at the far end of the yard. "You've met her and I haven't. It might be better coming from you."

"No problemo," he says. "The carpet's slowing now anyway. Even Patrice is heading in."

I click off, pushing into the crowd again in the direction of the pool house. I'm just heading across the grass, feeling my heels sink into the spongy dampness, when the Lucite lamps on all the tables flicker and go dark. There's a momentary silence — only the sound system keeps blaring, the theme song to *The Saint* — followed by nervous laughter. The crowd's just starting to surge back to life again when the George Nelson bubble lights snap off and the entire backyard goes dark. *Oh, shit.*

"*Oscar!*" I click on. "Oscar, what's going on?"

"Well, as you can see, the lights went fucking out."

"Tell me you can fix them, and soon," I say.

Marissa clicks on. "What's going *on?*"

Steven's not far behind her. "Trying for mood lighting so I can sweet-talk Uma?"

"Hardly," I say, plunging into the crowd. "Oscar, where are you?"

"Behind the garage. Checking the fuses."

I push through the crowd, which is starting to surge back to life. Still, with all the lights out, it's ridiculously dangerous. I push toward the direction of the garage, past the DJ, who is holding a lit cigarette lighter and obliviously flipping through his albums. I turn down the side path, round the corner of the garage, and spot Oscar, jacket off, flanked by two of his crew holding flashlights, working on the fuse box.

"Can you fix it?" I say, pulling up.

He doesn't even glance in my direction. "As soon as I know, you'll know."

I stand there for a minute, uselessly.

"Damn it," he says, dropping the fuse box door.

"What?" I say. "Can't you fix it?"

He turns to me. "Yes, but not here."

"What does that mean?"

"It means I have to crawl under all the tables and find out where it shorted out."

"What? You mean they're all connected? Like Christmas tree lights?"

"Yeah. Christmas lights that somebody trampled on."

"Oh, God, that's going to take forever," I say, picturing Andrew and Amanda out in the dark. At least the house is still lit up. And the red carpet. "Okay, I'll help you look," I say. "I mean, we have to get this fixed before somebody takes a header into the pool."

"There are *twelve* tables in case you haven't counted them," he says, looking at me like I'm nuts. "No, the guys will help me find it."

"If you let me help you, we only have to check three tables each. It will go much faster."

"Okay, you want to get dirty, be my guest."

He turns and heads up the path. I practically have to run to keep up with him. We round the corner. The backyard is a sea of undulating dark shadows. Oh, God, this is going to be harder than I thought. "Which tables should I take?" I call out, but Oscar has disappeared into the crowd.

Steven hisses in my ear. "Are you guys fixing this or do I have to light my hair on fire to see anything?"

"Yeah, as soon as we can," I say, spying a table and diving for it. "Just stay on Uma and Andrew for the time being."

"Excuse me," I say, reaching past a guy in a porkpie hat — who let him in? — talking to some anorexic blonde. I squat down, lift the tablecloth, and, balancing on my toes, try to feel under the table for the lamp cord. Shit. I find only wet grass. Great. I'm going to have to go farther underneath to find it. I hitch my dress over my knees and, trying not to totally collapse, sink onto my hands and knees and creep under the table. At least no one can see me in the dark, with the tablecloth draped over my backside like a saddle blanket.

"Oh, my God, is there someone under that table?"

"Yes," I call out. "We're trying to get the lights back on."

I reach around in the dark, my nails sinking into the dirty grass. Where are the fucking cords? Oh, here they are. I feel a long cord—actually, two cords. I feel along it for a minute and then realize I have no idea what I'm feeling for. And what to expect when I find it. Perhaps a massive, life-ending electrical shock. I can see the *Variety* headline now: "In the Line of Fire — Flak Fried in Freak Power Outage."

"Oscar," I say, clicking on. "What am I looking for?"

"That would be a break in the line."

"Yeah, I know, but what is it exactly? A plug pulled out of its socket? I mean, am I going to get electrocuted here?"

"Yes and no," he says. "All the lamps have cords that plug into the main power cord."

"And one of them knocked out of the socket takes out the whole *thing*," I say, feeling for the lamp cord. "They don't even make Christmas lights like that anymore."

"Look, you want to go work for GE when we're done, be my guest. Just let me know if you find it."

I click off and feel down the end of the lamp cord until I find it plugged into the power cord. Intact. Okay, I'm out of here. I back out from under the table and push to my feet. At least Mr. Porkpie has moved off. I head for the next table — fortunately it's empty — and drop to my knees. Shit. Forgot to hike my dress up first. Oh well, I'll just have to hope the grass stains don't show too badly. I crawl under and feel around for the cords. Okay, here they are, here they are. Okay, they're good. I crawl back out and push to my feet. Okay, third time's the charm. Where's the next table? I spy two of them in the dark. And that would be the next question: How do we know which tables have been checked? Oh well. I'll just check both.

I head for the nearest one, hike my dress, lift the tablecloth, and hit the ground. Okay, where are the cords? Okay, here's the lamp cord. I'm feeling down, down, and it ends in a plug. A plug, unplugged. Oh, my God, I got it. Okay, where's the socket? I reach around on the grass and find the power cord. "Oscar, I got it," I say, clicking on.

"You found the break?" he says.

"Yeah, prepare for liftoff," I say, feeling along the cords—I swear I'm going to get shocked—and push them together. Nothing. Still pitch-dark. Pitch-*fucking*-dark.

"*Oh, damn it.*"

"Did you do it?" Oscar says. "Did you connect them?"

"Yes, but it's not working. Why isn't it working?"

"Okay, where are you? I'm coming to you."

"Where am I? I'm under a table. It's not like they have names."

"All right, I'll find you," he says. "Stay there."

I pull my headset off, sink back on my heels, pondering whether I should crawl out or just stay here in what I realize is a perfect cat position. If I was doing yoga.

"Hey, here's an empty table," a woman's voice says.

Oh, no. "Excuse me," I call out, "we're actually working here trying to—" Then I feel a foot land on my ankle. "*Ow.*"

"What the *fuck*?" the woman says, and I can hear her stumble.

"Are you okay?" a male voice says. I hear a rustle and feel the tablecloth being lifted off my back. "What the hell are you doing under there?" he says angrily. "You nearly tripped my friend."

"We're trying to fix the lights," I say, turning and looking over my shoulder. I feel like a cow with its ass in the air, but the table's so small, there's no room for me to turn around to face him.

"Well, do it in a way that doesn't jeopardize others," he snaps. "She nearly fell."

"Hey, she's only doing her job, guy," another male voice says. "So why don't you find another table and let us deal with this one?"

I turn. In the dark, I make out Oscar, his headset around his neck, holding up the tablecloth, a grin on his face.

"Thank God," I say. "Will you get under here so I can get out."

"Actually, I kind of like you like this."

"You would," I say, starting to back up but nearly colliding with him as he crawls under.

"Okay, where's this connection?" he says, taking my hands and feeling along for the cords.

"Right here," I say, pushing them into his hands.

He works at them for a second. "Okay, hang on." A light suddenly flares, and I blink in the blaze.

"You have *matches*?"

"Yeah, the guys have the flashlights. This is all I've got." We look at each other a moment, and the light burns out.

"Oh shit," I say, starting to laugh.

"Wait, I have more," he says, laughing. "Actually, here," he says, pushing the matches into my hand. "You light them, and I'll fix the cord."

I take the matches. I strike one and hold it up while Oscar examines the cords. "There's got to be some cut in the line."

•   The match burns out. I strike one and then another. "What are you planning on fixing the break with when you find it?" I say.

"A Swiss Army knife and electrical tape."

"You have a Swiss Army knife and electrical tape but you don't have a flashlight?"

"Well, you don't have any of them and you're under here."

"I don't know about you, but I'm only here because I'm being paid to be here."

I light another match and am startled to see Oscar staring at me with a look I can't quite make out. Like he's remembering something. Or maybe he's just tired. "What?" I say.

"Nothing," he says, shaking his head and turning back to the cords. "Nothing."

I light another match and hear a flurry of Spanish above us. Oscar calls out something in Spanish, and I feel the tablecloth being lifted. I turn; a flashlight nearly blinds me. His crew. Finally. "Okay, I'm going," I say, backing out. One of the guys slides under in my place. I push to my feet. My back is killing me and my knees are soaked. Oh, God. I stand there for a minute while the two of them work under the table. Suddenly the lights blaze on. A cheer goes up and a smattering of applause. I look down. My hands are covered in dirt, and I have grass stains on my dress and my shins. I reach down and try to wipe the worst of it off, then pull my headset back on.

Steven crackles in my ear. "Took you guys long enough."

"Yeah, well, what's going on with Uma?" I say as I watch Oscar and the crew guy emerge from under the table.

"Well, now that I can *see* her, I'll be able to let you know."

"Please do," I say, pushing my hair off my face with the back of my hand.

I'm just trying to decide if I can make a break for the ladies' room to clean up when Oscar turns to me and brushes my hair back with his hand. His fingers graze my cheek, for what seems like a second too long. "Sorry about all the dirt," he says, nodding at my hands.

Steven crackles in my ear. "And feel free to join us. Now that you're done playing electrician."

"I'm on my way over," I say, gazing at Oscar.

"It's the first pool house on the left. You can't miss it."

"Uh, uh, got it," I say as Oscar slides his thumb in his mouth and then, leaning forward, takes my face in his hands and gently rubs his thumb on my cheek. "There," he says. "Good as new."

We stand there, neither of us saying anything as the party roars around us. "Look" I start to say—when my headset goes.

Allie. "Oh, my God, Charles just left," she says. "Did you know he was leaving?"

"Yeah," I say. "I knew."

"You know, I think Patrice's real problem is she's just not a giver. I mean, look at her decision about the gift bag. Like a copy of the magazine and a tin of Altoids in a bag is going to kill you?"

"Could be," I say, taking a sip of champagne and realizing it's flat. And warm. But then it's past 2:00. Steven and I are outside, slumped on one of the couches, watching as the last of the guests straggle out. I'm wearing some guy's jacket over my dress, can't remember whose. The cops have come. And gone. Andrew and Amanda left hours ago. The DJ is packing up, and Oscar's got the lights over the pool turned up to discourage any lingering. It's like watching cockroaches scramble for cover. Nobody wants to see themselves—or their dates—that clearly after six hours of partying.

"Can you turn the lights down just a tad?" I say, catching sight of Oscar on the other side of the pool helping one of the bartenders load glasses into boxes.

"Time to go home," he calls out, waving over his shoulder. A second later, the lights lower.

"Thank you," I say.

"So I do think it was hilarious Patrice spent the entire evening at the opposite end of the carpet from you," Steven says. Between his conspiratorial tone and the way he's sprawled on the couch, I can tell he's hunkering down for a long, bitchy chat. Usually this is my favorite part of the evening, debriefing ourselves, but not tonight. Between my face-off with Patrice, what I'm taking as my breakup with Charles, given that he left without saying a word, and the hours of working the carpet, not to mention the whole light fiasco, I'm wiped.

"Well, it's not like I really expected anything else from her," I say, peering at my watch. "By the way, where's my fairy godmother to take Cinderella's earrings back?"

Steven reaches for his pocket and pulls out a velvet box. "Totally forgot. Lucienne left with the diamonds, but she gave me this to give to you. She said she'll send a messenger for your earrings on Monday."

I snap open the box. Inside is a pair of studs, half-carat I'm guessing, and a note.

With my compliments . . . and thanks.

"Oh, my God," I say, staring at the earrings. Even by Lucienne's normal standards of graft, this is huge.

"Personally, I'd rather have the ones you're wearing," Steven says, leaning over to study the earrings. "But at least someone's giving you a diamond."

"Gee, thanks," I say, looking up. "And I was just starting to forget about Charles."

"Sorry," he says. "But you know I never liked him."

"You never liked him? Why didn't you say something?"

"Because you had to learn these things for yourself, Dorothy. Now repeat after me: There's no place like home." He reaches for my hand, pulling us both to our feet. "So what are you going to do about your Christmas trip to Hawaii?" he says. "Want me to go with you?"

"I don't know. I'll probably just cancel. But then maybe I'll go on my own. Might be good for me to spend some time alone. Sort things out."

We head across the lawn for the house. Inside it's a mess, with glasses, bottles everywhere. So much for the waitstaff. Oscar's crew will be here for hours. "Hey, I'm just going to tell him we're leaving," I say, turning back for the door.

"One more dance before she turns into a pumpkin?"

"You're mixing movies with fairy tales now. Say good night, Gracie."

"Good night, Gracie. Call me tomorrow."

Steven heads out the front door, and I turn back for the patio. "Where'd he go?" I ask the bartender.

"Out in the pool house, helping the other bartender pack up," he says, nodding down the yard.

I pick my way across the grass, even wetter now with dew. Even before I get to the pool house, I smell his cigar. "Hey," I say, sticking my head in the door. At the far end of the room, Oscar is leaning against the bar, cigar in hand, while the bartender, a tall blonde, sits on top of it, her bare legs crossed.

I am so, so stupid. So *fucking* stupid.

I turn and am heading for the door when Oscar catches sight of me. "Hey," he says, pushing away from the bar.

I shoot him my best professional smile. "Oh, hey, I just wanted to say I'm leaving. And thanks. Thanks again. It turned out well. In the end."

"Hang on a sec," he says to me, turning to the bartender. "Here, hold this," he says, handing her the cigar, and heads toward me. "So you're going?"

"Yeah," I say, turning for the door. "We'll talk Monday."

"You did a good thing tonight."

"You mean the lights?"

"I meant Patrice. Standing up to her. Somebody had to."

I shrug. "It probably cost us the account, but at least I won't have to deal with her again."

He looks at me. "I heard Charles left."

"Well, that makes two of us."

"I'm sorry."

"Don't be. It was a long time in coming. Where's Mai, by the way?"

"Left. To meet her girlfriend."

So Steven was right. "And you're what, the beard?"

"A friend of her parents. From Hawaii."

I look at him and then the bartender. "Well, have a nice night."

He turns, looks back at the bartender and then at me. "Look, if you want to stick around, I'm just finishing up here."

"That's okay," I say, looking at him. "I really have to go."

I turn and head out, picking my way across the lawn toward the house. For the second time tonight, I feel my heart race. For all the times you make your own decisions, there are still those times when circumstances make them for you.

"Hey, what are you doing tomorrow?" he calls out behind me.

I turn. Oscar, standing in the doorway, the light pouring out around him.

"Hugo's," he says. "I'll pick you up at noon."

I shake my head. "I have a date with my couch and the Sunday papers."

"I'll be there," he says. "Noon."

I turn, wave over my shoulder, and start for the house.

"Noon," he says again. "You watch."

18

Flight Plans

"So you got everything? Bathing suit, paperback, traveler's checks?"

"Nobody uses traveler's checks anymore. In case you hadn't noticed," I say, cradling the cell against my ear and fumbling in my bag for my boarding pass. 5A. LAX to Kona. Merry fucking Christmas.

"So, you're sure you feel okay about not going with Charles?" Steven says.

"Yeah, I think so," I say, leaning back in my seat, gazing at my fellow Hawaii-bound travelers. "I'm still not sure how it's going to be to work with him after all this, but we'll cross that bridge when we come to it."

"Hey, look at it this way. Maybe he'll actually leave you alone and let you do your job," he says. "I mean, since Andrew renewed your contract. Mr. Vote of Confidence."

"Don't remind me," I say. "I'm just praying Patrice moves on to *Vogue*, or *InStyle*, or somewhere up the food chain, since she's riding so high after the party."

Across from me, a woman and two teenage girls sink into seats. A mother and her daughters, I'm guessing. The woman has a take-out coffee, a stack of newspapers, and a slightly amused look, like being in the airport with her two children is just the kind of adventure she wants. The girls have backpacks, some sort of fruit frappes, and the careless ease of children still in their parents' care. The woman fishes out a paper, turns to the crossword.

"Adam's Rib and a pop star," she says.

"Eve," says the younger of the two.

"Oh, by the way," I say. "Helen wanted me to thank you for the lilies. She said she's never had flowers delivered to a ship's cabin before. But then she's never been in a ship's cabin before."

"I hope she didn't think they were funereal. I mean, some people take lilies the wrong way."

"She didn't," I say, watching the woman. "She said she thought your mother was a very lucky woman."

"*That* would be news to Rita," he says with a laugh. "Okay, so when's your flight? I still have a ton of shopping to do."

I check my watch. "Half an hour," I say, and feel a tap on my shoulder. I turn.

Oscar. With two take-out coffees.

"God, the Starbucks was way down the concourse," he says, handing me one and sinking into the seat next to me.

"Oscar says hi," I say to Steven, prying the lid off and taking a sip.

"Are you still talking to him?" Oscar says, reaching for the phone. I hand it to him. "Hey, I realize you two are joined at the hip, but seriously, dude, she's going to be okay. She's going on vacation."

Steven says something, and Oscar laughs. "Yeah, I'll tell her," he says. "And I'm sure she'll call you the minute we land."

He hangs up, hands me back the phone. Across the aisle the woman calls out another question. "Huxleian classic."

"*Animal Farm*," says the older girl.

"Honey, I think that was Orwell."

"*1984*," says the younger girl.

"That's Orwell too," says the older. "Oh, I know. *Brave New World*."

"Right," the woman says, penciling it in.

"You know, I haven't flown with anybody for a long time," I say, eyeing Oscar over the coffee. "It'll be weird."

"It'll be *weird*?"

"But in a good way."

"Look, Garbo," he says, sliding an arm around my shoulders. "I know this is a big step for you."

"For me?"

"Okay, for *me*. For *us*. See, this is exactly what guys don't like to do. They don't like to talk about it all the time."

"Define 'it.'"

"I don't have to. You know exactly what I mean."

"You don't even want to say the word," I say, laughing. "You can't even say the word *relationship*."

"Re-la-tion-ship," he says. "Happy now?"

"Very," I say, sitting back in my seat. "So tell me again all the places you're going to show me when we get there. Where you grew up."

"Oh, yeah," he says, turning to me. "I forgot, the first place we have to go is this little place right on the beach. An old Army buddy of my dad's bought it right before we moved back to the mainland, but we used to go down, hang out, drink beer, and watch the sunsets. He did the best grilled yellowtail. You'll love it."

"And he's still there?" I say, looking up. "After all these years?"

"Yeah," he says, shaking his head. "He's still there. You'll see. He's still there."

Acknowledgments

Thanks to the usual suspects . . . Kate and Brian, Adam and Bruce, and Janet, for her patience. Thanks to Beth Parker for her diligence and enthusiasm in spreading the word. Thanks, too, to Jill Eisenstadt, Jeffrey Best, Kelly Striewski, and especially Bryan Rabin. Without their gracious assistance, Alex wouldn't know how to throw a party, let alone satirize one. And to Michael, who keeps the Oscar-Charles dilemma entirely in the realm of fiction.

About the Author

HILARY DE VRIES is a veteran entertainment journalist who has covered Hollywood for more than a decade. In addition to being the author of *So 5 Minutes Ago*, she is a regular contributor to *The New York Times* and has written for *Vogue, Rolling Stone, The Washington Post*, W, the *Los Angeles Times*, and other publications. She lives in Los Angeles.